Baen Books by David Weber

DAVID WEBER

ON BASILISK STATION

This is a work of fiction. All the characters and events
portrayed in this book are fictional, and any resemblance
to real people or events is purely coincidental.

A Baen Books Original

Baen Publishing Enterprises
P.O. Box 1403
Riverdale NY 10471

ISBN 0-671-57772-7

Cover art by Larry Schwinger

First printing, April 1993
Third printing, August 1995
This Limited Edition, October 1998

Distributed by Simon & Schuster
1230 Avenue of the Americas
New York, NY 10020

Printed in the United States of America

To C.S. Forester,
With thanks for hours of enjoyment,
years of inspiration,
and a lifetime of admiration.

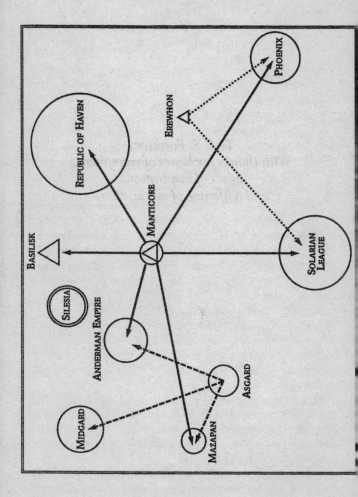

• PROLOGUE

The ticking of the conference room's antique clock was
deafening as the Hereditary President of the People's
Republic of Haven stared at his military cabinet. The secretary of the economy looked away uncomfortably, but the
secretary of war and her uniformed subordinates were
almost defiant.

"Are you serious?" President Harris demanded.

"I'm afraid so," Secretary Frankel said unhappily. He
shuffled through his memo chips and made himself meet
the president's eyes. "The last three quarters all confirm the
projection, Sid." He glowered sideways at his military col-
league. "It's the naval budget. We can't keep adding ships
this way without—"

"If we *don't* keep adding them," Elaine Dumarest broke
in sharply, "the wheels come off. We're riding a neotiger,
Mr. President. At least a third of the occupied planets still
have crackpot 'liberation' groups, and even if they didn't,
everyone on our borders is arming to the teeth. It's only a
matter of time until one of them jumps us."

"I think you're overreacting, Elaine," Ronald Bergren
put in. The Secretary for Foreign Affairs rubbed his pencil-
thin mustache and frowned at her. "Certainly they're
arming—I would be, too, in their place—but none of them
are strong enough to take us on."

"Perhaps not just now," Admiral Parnell said bleakly,
"but if we get tied down elsewhere or any large-scale revolt
breaks out, some of them are going to be tempted into trying a smash and grab. That's why we need more ships. And,
with all due respect to Mr. Frankel," the CNO added, not

sounding particularly respectful, "it isn't the Fleet budget that's breaking the bank. It's the increases in the Basic Living Stipend. We've got to tell the Dolists that any trough has a bottom and get them to stop swilling long enough to get our feet back under us. If we could just get those useless drones off our backs, even for a few years—"

"Oh, that's a wonderful idea!" Frankel snarled. "Those BLS increases are all that's keeping the mob in check! They supported the wars to support their standard of living, and if we don't—"

"That's enough!" President Harris slammed his hand down on the table and glared at them all in the shocked silence. He let the stillness linger a moment, then leaned back and sighed. "We're not going to achieve anything by calling names and pointing fingers," he said more mildly. "Let's face it—the DuQuesene Plan hasn't proved the answer we thought it would."

"I have to disagree, Mr. President," Dumarest said. "The basic plan remains sound, and it's not as if we have any other choice now. We simply failed to make sufficient allowance for the expenses involved."

"And for the revenues it would generate," Frankel added in a gloomy tone. "There's a limit to how hard we can squeeze the planetary economies, but without more income, we can't maintain our BLS expenditures *and* produce a military powerful enough to hold what we've got."

"How much time do we have?" Harris asked.

"I can't say for certain. I can paper over the cracks for a while, maybe even maintain a facade of affluence, by robbing Peter to pay Paul. But unless the spending curves change radically or we secure a major new source of revenue, we're living on borrowed time, and it's only going to get worse." He smiled without humor. "It's a pity most of the systems we've acquired weren't in much better economic shape than we were."

"And you're certain we can't reduce Fleet expenditures, Elaine?"

"Not without running very grave risks, Mr. President. Admiral Parnell is perfectly correct about how our neighbors will react if we waver." It was her turn to smile grimly. "I suppose we've taught them too well."

"Maybe we have," Parnell said, "but there's an answer to that." Eyes turned to him, and he shrugged. "Knock them off now. If we take out the remaining military powers on our frontiers, we can probably cut back to something more like a peace-keeping posture of our own."

"Jesus, Admiral!" Bergren snorted. "First you tell us we can't hold what we've got without spending ourselves into exhaustion, and now you want to kick off a whole new series of wars? Talk about the mysteries of the military mind—!"

"Hold on a minute, Ron," Harris murmured. He cocked his head at the admiral. "Could you pull it off, Amos?"

"I believe so," Parnell replied more cautiously. "The problem would be timing." He touched a button and a holo map glowed to life above the table. The swollen sphere of the People's Republic crowded its northeastern quadrant, and he gestured at a rash of amber and red star systems to the south and west. "There are no multi-system powers closer than the Anderman Empire," he pointed out. "Most of the single-system governments are strictly small change; we could blow out any one of them with a single task force, despite their armament programs. What makes them dangerous is the probability that they'll get organized as a unit if we give them time."

Harris nodded thoughtfully, but reached out and touched one of the beads of light that glowed a dangerous blood-red. "And Manticore?" he asked.

"That's the joker in the deck," Parnell agreed. "They're big enough to give us a fight, assuming they've got the guts for it."

"So why not avoid them, or at least leave them for last?" Bergren asked. "Their domestic parties are badly divided over what to do about us—couldn't we chop up the other small fry first?"

"We'd be in worse shape if we did," Frankel objected. He touched a button of his own, and two-thirds of the amber lights on Parnell's map turned a sickly gray-green. "Each of those systems is almost as far in the hole economically as we are," he pointed out. "They'll actually cost us money to take over, and the others are barely break-even propositions. The systems we really need are further south, down towards the Erewhon Junction, or over in the Silesian Confederacy to the west."

"Then why not grab them straight off?" Harris asked.

"Because Erewhon has League membership, Mr. President," Dumarest replied, "and going south might convince the League we're threatening its territory. That could be, ah, a bad idea." Heads nodded around the table. The Solarian League had the wealthiest, most powerful economy in the known galaxy, but its foreign and military policies were the product of so many compromises that they virtually did not exist, and no one in this room wanted to irritate the sleeping giant into evolving ones that did.

"So we can't go south," Dumarest went on, "but going west instead brings us right back to Manticore."

"Why?" Frankel asked. "We could take Silesia without ever coming within a hundred light-years of Manticore—just cut across above them and leave them alone."

"Oh?" Parnell challenged. "And what about the Manticore Wormhole Junction? Its Basilisk terminus would be right in our path. We'd almost have to take it just to protect our flank, and even if we didn't, the Royal Manticoran Navy would see the implications once we started expanding around their northern frontier. They'd have no choice but to try to stop us."

"We couldn't cut a deal with them?" Frankel asked Bergren, and the foreign secretary shrugged.

"The Manticoran Liberal Party can't find its ass with both hands where foreign policy is concerned, and the Progressives would probably dicker, but they aren't in control; the Centrists and Crown Loyalists are. They hate our guts, and Elizabeth III hates us even more than they do. Even if the Liberals and Progressives could turn the Government out, the Crown would never negotiate with us."

"Um." Frankel plucked at his lip, then sighed. "Too bad, because there's another point. We're in bad enough shape for foreign exchange, and three-quarters of our foreign trade moves through the Manticore Junction. If they close it against us, it'll add months to transit times . . . and costs."

"Tell me about it," Parnell said sourly. "That damned junction also gives their navy an avenue right into the middle of the Republic through the Trevor's Star terminus."

"But if we knocked them out, then *we'd* hold the Junction," Dumarest murmured. "Think what *that* would do for our economy."

Frankel looked up, eyes glowing with sudden avarice, for the junction gave the Kingdom of Manticore a gross system product seventy-eight percent that of the Sol System itself. Harris noted his expression and gave a small, ugly smile.

"All right, let's look at it. We're in trouble and we know it. We have to keep expanding. Manticore is in the way, and taking it would give our economy a hefty shot in the arm. The problem is what we do about it."

"Manticore or not," Parnell said thoughtfully, "we have to pinch out these problem spots to the southwest." He gestured at the systems Frankel had dyed gray-green. "It'd be a worthwhile preliminary to position us against Manticore, anyway. But if we can do it, the smart move would be to take out Manticore first and *then* deal with the small fry."

"Agreed," Harris nodded. "Any ideas on how we might do that?"

"Let me get with my staff, Mr. President. I'm not sure yet, but the Junction could be a two-edged sword if we handle it right. . . ." The admiral's voice trailed off, then he shook himself. "Let me get with my staff," he repeated. "Especially with Naval Intelligence. I've got an idea, but I need to work on it." He cocked his head. "I can probably have a report, one way or the other, for you in about a month. Will that be acceptable?"

"Entirely, Admiral," Harris said, and adjourned the meeting.

• CHAPTER ONE

The fluffy ball of fur in Honor Harrington's lap stirred and put forth a round, prick-eared head as the steady pulse of the shuttle's thrusters died. A delicate mouth of needle-sharp fangs yawned, and then the treecat turned its head to regard her with wide, grass-green eyes.

"Bleek?" it asked, and Honor chuckled softly.

" 'Bleek' yourself," she said, rubbing the ridge of its muzzle. The green eyes blinked, and four of the treecat's six limbs reached out to grip her wrist in feather-gentle handpaws. She chuckled again, pulling back to initiate a playful tussle, and the treecat uncoiled to its full sixty-five centimeters (discounting its tail) and buried its true-feet in her midriff with the deep, buzzing hum of its purr. The handpaws tightened their grip, but the murderous claws—a full centimeter of curved, knife-sharp ivory—were sheathed. Honor had once seen similar claws used to rip apart the face of a human foolish enough to threaten a treecat's companion, but she felt no concern. Except in self-defense (or Honor's defense) Nimitz would no more hurt a human being than turn vegetarian, and treecats never made mistakes in that respect.

She extricated herself from Nimitz's grasp and lifted the long, sinuous creature to her shoulder, a move he greeted with even more enthusiastic purrs. Nimitz was an old hand at space travel and understood shoulders were out of bounds aboard small craft under power, but he also knew treecats belonged on their companions' shoulders. That was where they'd ridden since the first 'cat adopted its first human five Terran centuries before, and Nimitz was a traditionalist.

A flat, furry jaw pressed against the top of her head as Nimitz sank his four lower sets of claws into the specially padded shoulder of her uniform tunic. Despite his long, narrow body, he was a hefty weight—almost nine kilos— even under the shuttle's single gravity, but Honor was used to it, and Nimitz had learned to move his center of balance in from the point of her shoulder. Now he clung effortlessly to his perch while she collected her briefcase from the empty seat beside her. Honor was the half-filled shuttle's senior passenger, which had given her the seat just inside the hatch. It was a practical as well as a courteous tradition, since the senior officer was always last to board and first to exit.

The shuttle quivered gently as its tractors reached out to the seventy-kilometer bulk of Her Majesty's Space Station *Hephaestus*, the Royal Manticoran Navy's premiere shipyard, and Nimitz sighed his relief into Honor's short-cropped mass of feathery, dark brown hair. She smothered another grin and rose from her bucket seat to twitch her tunic straight. The shoulder seam had dipped under Nimitz's weight, and it took her a moment to get the red-and-gold navy shoulder flash with its roaring, lionheaded, bat-winged manticore, spiked tail poised to strike, back where it belonged. Then she plucked the beret from under her left epaulet. It was the special beret, the white one she'd bought when they gave her *Hawkwing*, and she chivied Nimitz's jaw gently aside and settled it on her head. The treecat put up with her until she had it adjusted just so, then shoved his chin back into its soft warmth, and she felt her face crease in a huge grin as she turned to the hatch.

That grin was a violation of her normally severe "professional expression," but she was entitled. Indeed, she felt more than mildly virtuous for holding herself to a grin when what she really wanted to do was spin on her toes, fling her arms wide, and carol her delight to her no-doubt shocked fellow passengers. But she was almost twenty-four years old—over forty Terran standard years—and it would never,

never have done for a commander of the Royal Manticoran Navy to be so undignified, even if she *was* about to assume command of her first cruiser.

She smothered another chuckle, luxuriating in the unusual sense of complete and simple joy, and pressed a hand to the front of her tunic. The folded sheaf of archaic paper crackled at her touch—a curiously sensual, exciting sound—and she closed her eyes to savor it even as she savored the moment she'd worked so hard to reach.

Fifteen years—twenty-five T-years—since that first exciting, terrifying day on the Saganami campus. Two and a half years of Academy classes and running till she dropped. Four years working her way without patronage or court interest from ensign to lieutenant. Eleven months as sailing master aboard the frigate *Osprey*, and then her first command, a dinky little intrasystem LAC. It had massed barely ten thousand tons, with only a hull number and not even the dignity of a name, but God how she'd loved that tiny ship! Then more time as executive officer, a turn as tactical officer on a massive superdreadnought. And then—finally!—the coveted commanding officer's course after eleven grueling years. She'd thought she'd died and gone to heaven when they gave her *Hawkwing*, for the middle-aged destroyer had been her very first hyper-capable command, and the thirty-three months she'd spent in command had been pure, unalloyed joy, capped by the coveted Fleet "E" award for tactics in last year's war games. But this—!

The deck shuddered beneath her feet, and the light above the hatch blinked amber as the shuttle settled into *Hephaestus*'s docking buffers, then burned a steady green as pressure equalized in the boarding tube. The panel slid aside, and Honor stepped briskly through it.

The shipyard tech manning the hatch at the far end of the tube saw the white beret of a starship's captain and the three gold stripes of a full commander on a space-black sleeve and came to attention, but his snappy response was flawed by a tiny hesitation as he caught sight of Nimitz. He flushed and twitched his eyes away, but Honor was used to that reaction. The treecats native to her home world of Sphinx were picky about which humans they adopted. Relatively few were seen off-world, but they refused to be parted from their humans even if those humans chose space-going careers, and the Lords of Admiralty had caved in on that point almost a hundred and fifty Manticoran years before. 'Cats rated a point-eight-three on the sentience scale, slightly above Beowulf's gremlins or Old Earth's dolphins, and they were empaths. Even now, no one had the least idea how their empathic links worked, but separating one from its chosen companion caused it intense pain, and it had been established early on that those favored by a 'cat were measurably more stable than those without. Besides, Crown Princess Adrienne had been adopted by a 'cat on a state visit to Sphinx. When Queen Adrienne of Manticore expressed her displeasure twelve years later at efforts to separate officers in her navy from their companions, the Admiralty found itself with no option but to grant a special exemption from its draconian "no pets" policy.

Honor was glad of it, though she'd been afraid it would be impossible to find time to spend with Nimitz when she entered the Academy. She'd known going in that those forty-five endless months on Saganami Island were deliberately planned to leave even midshipmen without 'cats too few hours to do everything they had to do. But while Academy instructors might suck their teeth and grumble when a plebe turned up with one of the rare 'cats, they recognized natural forces for which allowances must be made when they saw one. Besides, even the most "domesticated" 'cat retained the independence (and indestructibility) of his cousins in the wild, and Nimitz had seemed perfectly aware of the pressure she faced. All he needed was a little grooming, an occasional wrestling bout, a perch on her shoulder or lap while she pored over the book chips and to sleep curled neatly up on her pillow, and he was happy. Not that he'd been above looking mournful and pitiful to extort tidbits and petting from any unfortunate who crossed his path. Even Chief MacDougal, the terror of the first-form middies, had succumbed, carrying a suitable stash of the celery stalks the otherwise carnivorous treecats craved and sneaking them to Nimitz when he thought no one was looking. And, Honor reflected wryly, running Ms. Midshipman Harrington ragged to compensate for his weakness.

Her thoughts had carried her through the arrival gate to the concourse, and she looked about until she found the color-coded guide strip to the personnel tubes. She followed it, unburdened by any baggage, for she had none. All her meager personal possessions had been freighted up this morning, whisked away by stewards at the Advanced Tactical Course facility almost before she'd had time to pack.

She frowned a bit at that thought while she punched up a tube capsule. All the scramble to get her here seemed out of character for a navy that preferred to do things in an orderly fashion. When she'd been given *Hawkwing*, she'd known two months in advance; this time, she'd been literally snatched out of the ATC graduation ceremonies and hustled off to Admiral Courvosier's office with no warning at all.

The capsule arrived, and she stepped into it, still frowning and rubbing gently at the tip of her nose. Nimitz roused to lift his chin from the top of her beret and nipped her ear with the scolding tug he saved for the unfortunately frequent moments when his companion worried. Honor clicked her teeth gently at him and reached up to scratch his chest, but she didn't stop worrying, and he sighed in exasperation.

Now why, she wondered, was she so certain Courvosier

had deliberately bustled her out of his office and off to her new assignment? The admiral was a bland-faced, cherubic little gnome of a man with a bent for creating demonic tac problems, and she'd known him for years. He'd been her Fourth Form Tactics instructor at the Academy, the one who'd recognized an inborn instinct and honed it into something she could command at will, not something that came and went. He'd spent hours working with her in private when other instructors worried about her basic math scores and, in a very real sense, had saved her career before it had actually begun, yet this time there'd been something almost evasive about him. She knew his congratulations and satisfied pride in her had been real, but she couldn't shake the impression that there'd been something else, as well. Ostensibly, the rush was all because of the need to get her to *Hephaestus* to shepherd her new ship through its refit in time for the upcoming Fleet exercise, yet HMS *Fearless* was only a single light cruiser, when all was said. It seemed unlikely her absence would critically shift the balance in maneuvers planned to exercise the entire Home Fleet!

No, something was definitely up, and she wished fervently that she'd had time for a full download before catching the shuttle. But at least all the rush had kept her from worrying herself into a swivet the way she had before taking *Hawkwing* over, and Lieutenant Commander McKeon, her new exec, had served on *Fearless* for almost two years, first as tactical officer and then as exec. He should be able to bring her up to speed on the refit Courvosier had been so oddly reluctant to discuss.

She shrugged and punched her destination into the capsule's routing panel, then set down her briefcase and resigned herself as it flashed away down the counter-grav tubeway. Despite a peak speed of well over seven hundred kilometers per hour, the capsule trip would take over fifteen minutes—assuming she was lucky enough not to hit too many stops en route.

The deck shivered gently underfoot. Few would have

detected the tiny bobble as one quadrant of *Hephaestus*'s gravity generators handed the tube off to another, but Honor noticed it. Not consciously, perhaps, but that minute quiver was part of a world which had become more real to her than the deep blue skies and chill winds of her childhood. It was like her own heartbeat, one of the tiny, uncountable stimuli that told her—instantly and completely—what was happening around her.

She watched the tube map display, shaking off thoughts of evasive admirals and other puzzles as her eyes tracked the blinking cursor of her capsule across it. Her hand rose to press the crispness of her orders once more, and she paused, almost surprised as she looked away from the map and glimpsed her reflection in the capsule's polished wall.

The face that gazed back should have looked different, reflecting the monumental change in her status, and it didn't. It was still all sharply defined planes and angles dominated by a straight, patrician nose (which, in her opinion, was the only remotely patrician thing about her) and devoid of the least trace of cosmetics. Honor had been told (once) that her face had "a severe elegance." She didn't know about that, but the idea was certainly better than the dread, "My, isn't she, um, *healthy* looking!" Not that "healthy" wasn't accurate, however depressing it might sound. She looked trim and fit in the RMN's black and gold, courtesy of her 1.35-gravity homeworld and a rigorous exercise regimen, and that, she thought, critically, was about the best she had to say about herself.

Most of the Navy's female officers had chosen to adopt the current planet-side fashion of long hair, often elaborately dressed and arranged, but Honor had decided long ago there was no point trying to make herself something she was not. Her hair-style was practical, with no pretensions to glamour. It was clipped short to accommodate vac helmets and bouts of zero-gee, and if its two-centimeter strands had a stubborn tendency to curl, it was neither blond, nor red, nor even black, just a highly practical, completely unspectacular dark brown. Her eyes were even darker, and she'd always thought their hint of an almond shape, inherited from her mother, made them look out of place in her strong-boned face, almost as if they'd been added as an afterthought. Their darkness made her pale complexion seem still paler, and her chin was too strong below her firm-lipped mouth. No, she decided once more, with a familiar shade of regret, it was a serviceable enough face, but there was no use pretending anyone would ever accuse it of radiant beauty . . . darn it.

She grinned again, feeling the bubble of delight pushing her worries aside, and her reflection grinned back. It made her look like an urchin gloating over a hidden bag of candy, and she took herself firmly to task for the remainder of the trip, concentrating on a new CO's responsibility to look cool and collected, but it was hard. She'd done well to make commander so soon even with the Fleet's steady growth in the face of the Havenite threat, for the life-extending prolong process made for long careers. The Navy was well-supplied with senior officers, despite its expansion, and she came of yeoman stock, without the high-placed relatives or friends to nudge a naval career along. She'd known and accepted from the start that those with less competence but more exalted bloodlines would race past her. Well, they had, but she'd made it at last. A cruiser command, the dream of every officer worth her salt! So what if *Fearless* was twice her own age and little larger than a modern destroyer? She was still a cruiser, and cruisers were the Manticoran Navy's eyes and ears, its escorts and its raiders, the stuff of independent commands and opportunity.

And responsibility. That thought let her banish the grin at last, because if independent command was what every good officer craved, a captain all alone in the big dark had no one to appeal to. No one to take the credit or share the blame, for she *was* all alone, the final arbiter of her ship's fate and the direct, personal representative of her queen and kingdom, and if she failed that trust no power in the galaxy could save her.

The personnel capsule ghosted to a stop, and she stepped out into the spacious gallery of the spacedock, brown eyes hungry as they swept over her new command at last. HMS *Fearless* floated in her mooring beyond the tough, thick wall of armorplast, lean and sleek even under the clutter of work platforms and access tubes, and the pendant number "CL-56" stood out against the white hull just behind her forward impeller nodes. Yard mechs swarmed over her in the dock's vacuum, supervised by vacsuited humans, but most of the work seemed to be concentrated on the broadside weapon bays.

Honor stood motionless, watching through the armorplast, feeling Nimitz rise straight and tall on her shoulder to join her perusal, and an eyebrow quirked. Admiral Courvosier had mentioned that *Fearless* was undergoing a major refit, but what was going on out there seemed a bit more major than she'd anticipated. Which, coupled with his deliberate lack of detail, suggested something very special was in the wind, though Honor still couldn't imagine what could be important enough to turn the admiral all mysterious on her. Nor did it matter very much to her as she drank up her new command—*her* new command!—with avid eyes.

She never knew exactly how long she stood there before she managed to tear her attention away at last and head for the crew tube. The two Marine sentries stood at parade rest, watching her approach, then snapped to attention as she reached them.

She handed over her ID and watched approvingly as the senior man, a corporal, scrutinized it. They knew who she was, of course, unless the grapevine had died a sudden and unexpected death. Even if they hadn't, only one member of any ship's company was permitted the coveted white beret. But neither displayed the least awareness that their new mistress after God had arrived. The corporal handed back her ID folio with a salute, and she returned it and walked past them into the access tube.

She didn't look back, but the bulkhead mirror at the tube's first bend, intended to warn of oncoming traffic coming round the corner, let her watch the sentries as the corporal keyed his wrist com to alert the command deck that the new captain was on her way.

The scarlet band of a zero-gee warning slashed the access tube deck before her, and she felt Nimitz's claws sink deeper into her shoulder pad as she stepped over it. She launched herself into the graceful swim of free-fall as she passed out of *Hephaestus's* artificial gravity, and her pulse raced with quite unbecoming speed as she eeled down the passage. Another two minutes, she told herself. Only another two minutes.

Lieutenant Commander Alistair McKeon twitched his tunic straight and smothered a flare of annoyance as he stood by the entry port. He'd been buried in the bowels of a vivisected fire control station when the message came in. There'd been no time to shower or change into a fresh uniform, and he felt the sweat staining his blouse under his hastily donned tunic, but at least Corporal Levine's message had given him enough warning to collect the side party. Formal courtesies weren't strictly required from a ship in yard hands, but McKeon would take no chance of irritating a new captain. Besides, *Fearless* had a reputation to maintain, and—

His spine straightened, and a spasm of something very like pain went through him as his new captain rounded the tube's final bend. Her white beret gleamed under the lights, and he felt his face stiffen as he saw the sleek, cream-and-gray shape riding her shoulder. He hadn't known she had a treecat, and he smothered a fresh spurt of irrational resentment at the sight.

Commander Harrington floated easily down the last few meters of tube, then spun in midair and caught the final, scarlet-hued grab bar that marked the edge of *Fearless's* internal grav field. She crossed the interface like a gymnast dismounting from the rings to land lightly before him, and McKeon's sense of personal injury grew perversely stronger as he realized how little justice the photo in her personnel jacket had done her. Her triangular face had looked stern and forbidding, almost cold, in the file imagery, especially framed in the dark fuzz of her close-cropped hair, but the pictures had lied. They hadn't captured the life and vitality, the sharp-edged attractiveness. No one would ever call Commander Harrington "pretty," he thought, but she had something far more important. Those clean-cut, strong features and huge, dark brown eyes—exotically angular and sparkling with barely restrained delight despite her formal expression—discounted such ephemeral concepts as "pretty." She was herself, unique, impossible to confuse with anyone else, and that only made it worse.

McKeon met her scrutiny with a stolid expression and fought to suppress his confused, bitter resentment. He saluted sharply, the side party came to attention, and the bosun's calls shrilled. All activity stilled around the entry port, and her hand came up in an answering salute.

"Permission to come aboard?" Her voice was a cool, clear soprano, surprisingly light in a woman her size, for she easily matched McKeon's own hundred and eighty centimeters.

"Permission granted," he replied. It was a formality, but a very real one. Until she officially assumed command, Harrington was no more than a visitor aboard *McKeon's* ship.

"Thank you," she said, and stepped aboard as he stood back to clear the hatch.

He watched her chocolate-dark eyes sweep over the entry port and side party and wondered what she was thinking. Her sculpted face made an excellent mask for her emotions (except for those glowing eyes, he thought sourly), and he hoped his own did the same. It wasn't really fair of him to resent her. A light cruiser simply wasn't a lieutenant commander's billet, but Harrington was almost five years—over eight T-years—younger than he. Not only was she a full commander, not only did the breast of her tunic bear the embroidered gold star denoting a previous hypercapable command, but she looked young enough to be his daughter. Well, no, not that young, perhaps, but she *could* have been his niece. Of course, she was second-generation prolong. He'd checked the open portion of her record closely enough to know that, and the anti-aging treatments seemed to be proving even more effective for second- and third-generation recipients. Other parts of her record— like her penchant for unorthodox tactical maneuvers, and the CGM and Monarch's Thanks she'd earned saving lives when HMS *Manticore*'s forward power room exploded— soothed his resentment a bit, but neither they nor knowing why she seemed so youthful could lessen the emotional impact of finding the slot he'd longed for so hopelessly filled by an officer who not only oozed the effortless magnetism he'd always envied in others but also looked as if she'd graduated from the Academy last year. Nor did the bright, unwavering regard the treecat bent upon him make him feel any better.

Harrington completed her inspection of the side party without comment, then turned back to him, and he smothered his resentment and turned to the next, formalized step of his responsibilities.

"May I escort you to the bridge, Ma'am?" he asked, and she nodded.

"Thank you, Commander," she murmured, and he led the way up-ship.

Honor stepped out of the bridge lift and looked around what was about to become her personal domain. The signs of a frenzied refit were evident, and puzzlement stirred afresh as she noted the chaos of tools and parts strewn across her tactical section. Nothing else even seemed disturbed. Darn it, what *hadn't* Admiral Courvosier told her about her ship?

But that was for the future. For now, she had other things to attend to, and she crossed to the captain's chair, surrounded by its nest of displays and readouts at the center of the bridge. Most of the displays were retracted into their storage positions, and she rested her hand for a moment on the panel concealing the tactical repeater display. She didn't sit down. By long tradition, that chair was barred to any captain before she'd read herself aboard, but she took her place beside it and coaxed Nimitz off her shoulder and onto its far arm, out of the intercom pickup's field. Then she set aside her briefcase, pressed a stud on the near arm, and listened to the clear, musical chime resounding through the ship.

All activity aboard *Fearless* stopped. Even the handful of visiting civilian techs slid out from under the consoles they were rewiring or crawled up out of the bowels of power rooms and shunting circuits as the all-hands signal sounded. Bulkhead intercom screens flicked to life with Honor's face, and she felt hundreds of eyes as they noted the distinctive white beret and sharpened to catch their first sight of the captain into whose keeping the Lords of Admiralty in their infinite wisdom had committed their lives.

She reached into her tunic, and paper crackled, whispering from every speaker, as she broke the seals and unfolded her orders.

"From Admiral Sir Lucien Cortez, Fifth Space Lord, Royal Manticoran Navy," she read in her crisp, cool voice, "to Commander Honor Harrington, Royal Manticoran Navy, Thirty-Fifth Day, Fourth Month, Year Two Hundred and Eighty After Landing. Madam: You are hereby directed and required to proceed aboard Her Majesty's Starship *Fearless*, CL-Five-Six, there to take upon yourself the duties and responsibilities of commanding officer in the service of the Crown. Fail not in this charge at your peril. By order of Admiral Sir Edward Janacek, First Lord of

Admiralty, Royal Manticoran Navy, for Her Majesty the Queen."

She fell silent and refolded her orders without even glancing at the pickup. For almost five T-centuries, those formal phrases had marked the transfer of command aboard the ships of the Manticoran Navy. They were brief and stilted, but by the simple act of reading them aloud she had placed her crew under her authority, bound them to obey her upon pain of death. The vast majority of them knew nothing at all about her, and she knew equally little about them, and none of that mattered. They had just become *her* crew, their very lives dependent upon how well she did her job, and an icicle of awareness sang through her as she finished folding the heavy sheet of paper and turned once more to McKeon.

"Mr. Exec," she said formally, "I assume command."

"Captain," he replied with equal formality, "you have command."

"Thank you." She glanced at the duty quartermaster, reading his nameplate from across the bridge. "Make a note in the log, please, Chief Braun," she said, and turned back to the pickup and her watching crew. "I won't take up your time with any formal speeches, people. We have too much to do and too little time to do it in as it stands. Carry on."

She touched the stud again. The intercom screens went blank, and she lowered herself into the comfortable, contoured chair—*her* chair now. Nimitz swarmed back onto her shoulder with a slightly aggrieved flip of his tail, and she gestured for McKeon to join her.

The tall, heavyset exec crossed the bridge to her while the bustle of work resumed about them. His gray eyes met hers with, she thought, perhaps just an edge of discomfort . . . or challenge. The thought surprised her, but he held out his hand in the traditional welcome to a new captain, and his deep voice was level.

"Welcome aboard, Ma'am," he said. "I'm afraid things are a bit of a mess just now, but we're pretty close to on schedule, and the dock master's promised me two more work crews starting next watch."

"Good." Honor returned his handshake, then stood and walked toward the gutted fire control section with him. "I have to admit to a certain amount of puzzlement, though, Mr. McKeon. Admiral Courvosier warned me we were due for a major refit, but he didn't mention any of this." She nodded at the open panels and unraveled circuit runs.

"I'm afraid we didn't have much choice, Ma'am. We could have handled the energy torpedoes with software changes, but the grav lance is basically an engineering system. Tying it into fire control requires direct hardware links to the main tactical system."

"Grav lance?" Honor didn't raise her voice, but McKeon heard the surprise under its cool surface, and it was his turn to raise an eyebrow.

"Yes, Ma'am." He paused. "Didn't anyone mention that to you?"

"No, they didn't." Honor's lips thinned in what might charitably have been called a smile, and she folded her hands deliberately behind her. "How much broadside armament did it cost us?" she asked after a moment.

"All four graser mounts," McKeon replied, and watched her shoulders tighten slightly.

"I see. And you mentioned energy torpedoes, I believe?"

"Yes, Ma'am. The yard's replaced—is replacing, rather—all but two broadside missile tubes with them."

"All but two?" The question was sharper this time, and McKeon hid an edge of bitter amusement. No wonder she sounded upset, if they hadn't even warned her! *He'd* certainly been upset when he found out what was planned.

"Yes, Ma'am."

"I see," she repeated, and inhaled. "Very well, Exec, what does that leave us?"

"We still have the thirty-centimeter laser mounts, two in

each broadside, plus the missile launchers. After refit, we'll have the grav lance and fourteen torpedo generators, as well, and the chase armament is unchanged: two missile tubes and the sixty-centimeter spinal laser."

He watched her closely, and she didn't—quite—wince. Which, he reflected, spoke well for her self-control. Energy torpedoes were quick-firing, destructive, very difficult for point defense to stop. . . and completely ineffectual against a target protected by a military-grade sidewall. That, obviously, was the reason for the grav lance, yet if a grav lance could (usually) burn out its target's sidewall generators, it was slow-firing and had a *very* short maximum effective range. But if Captain Harrington was aware of that, she allowed no trace of it to color her voice.

"I see," she said yet again, and gave her head a little toss. "Very well, Mr. McKeon. I'm sure I've taken you away from something more useful than talking to me. Have my things been stowed?"

"Yes, Ma'am. Your steward saw to it."

"In that case, I'll be in my quarters examining the ship's books if you need me. I'd like to invite the officers to dine with me this evening—I see no point in letting introductions interfere with their duties now." She paused, as if reaching for another thought, then looked back at him. "Before then, I'll want to tour the ship and observe the work in progress. Will it be convenient for you to accompany me at fourteen-hundred?"

"Of course, Captain."

"Thank you. I'll see you then." She nodded and left the bridge without a backward glance.

• **CHAPTER TWO**

Honor Harrington sighed, leaned back from the terminal, and pinched the bridge of her nose. No wonder Admiral Courvosier had been so vague about the refit. Her old mentor knew her entirely too well. He'd known exactly how she would have reacted if he'd told her the truth, and he wasn't about to let her blow her first cruiser command in a fit of temper.

She shook herself and rose to stretch, and Nimitz roused to look her way. He started to slither down from the padded rest her new steward had rigged at her request, but she waved him back with the soft sound which told him she had to think. He cocked his head a moment, then "bleeked" quietly at her and settled back down.

She took a quick turn about her cabin. That was one nice thing about *Fearless*; at less than ninety thousand tons, she might be small by modern standards, but the captain's quarters were downright spacious compared to *Hawkwing*'s. Still small and cramped in planet-side eyes, perhaps, but Honor hadn't applied planetary standards to her living space in years. She even had her own dining compartment, large enough to seat all of her officers for formal occasions, and that was luxury, indeed, aboard a warship.

Not that spaciousness made her feel any better about the ghastly mutilation *Hephaestus* was wreaking upon her lovely ship.

She paused to adjust the golden plaque on the bulkhead by her desk. There was a fingerprint on the polished alloy, and she felt a familiar, wry self-amusement as she leaned closer to burnish it away with her sleeve. That plaque had accompanied her from ship to ship and planet-side and back for twelve and a half years, and she would have felt lost without it. It was her good luck piece. Her totem. She rubbed a fingertip gently across the long, tapering wing of the sailplane etched into the gold, remembering the day she'd landed to discover she'd set a new Academy record—one that still stood—for combined altitude, duration, and aerobatics, and she smiled.

But the smile faded as she glanced through the open internal hatch into the dining compartment and returned to the depressing present. She sighed again. She wasn't looking forward to that dinner. For that matter, she wasn't looking forward to her tour of the ship, after what she'd found locked away in her computer. The happiness she'd felt such a short time ago had soured, and what should have been two of the more pleasurable rituals of a change of command looked far less inviting now.

She'd told McKeon she meant to study the ship's books, and so she had, but her main attention had been focused on the refit specs and the detailed instructions she'd found in the captain's secure data base. McKeon's description of the alterations was only too accurate, though he hadn't mentioned that in addition to ripping out two-thirds of *Fearless's* missile tubes, the yard was gutting her magazine space, as well. Missile stowage was always a problem, particularly for smaller starships like light cruisers and destroyers, because an impeller-drive missile simply had to be big. There were limits to how many you could cram aboard, and since they'd decided to reduce *Fearless's* tubes, they'd seen no reason not to reduce her magazines, as well. After all, it had let them cram in four additional energy torpedo launchers.

She felt her lips trying to curl into a snarl and forced them to smooth as Nimitz chittered a question at her. The treecat's vocal apparatus was woefully unsuited to forming words. That was no problem with other 'cats, since they relied so heavily on their ill-understood telempathic sense for communication, but it left many humans prone to underestimate their intelligence—badly. Honor knew better, and Nimitz was always sensitive to her moods. Indeed, she suspected he knew her better than she knew herself, and she took a moment to scratch the underside of his jaw before she resumed her pacing.

It was all quite simple, she thought. She'd fallen into the clutches of Horrible Hemphill and her crowd, and now it was up to her to make their stupidity look intelligent.

She gritted her teeth. There were two major schools of tactical thought in the RMN: the traditionalists, championed by Admiral Hamish Alexander, and Admiral of the Red Lady Sonja Hemphill's *jeune ecole.* Alexander—and, for that matter, Honor—believed the fundamental tactical truths remained true regardless of weapon systems, that it was a matter of fitting new weapons into existing conceptual frameworks with due adjustment for the capabilities they conferred. The *jeune ecole* believed weapons determined tactics and that technology, properly used, rendered historical analysis irrelevant. And, unfortunately, politics had placed Horrible Hemphill and her panacea merchants in the ascendant just now.

Honor suppressed an uncharacteristic urge to swear viciously. She didn't study politics, she didn't understand politics, and she didn't *like* politics, but even she grasped the Cromarty government's current dilemma. Confronted by the Liberals' and Progressives' inflexible opposition to big-ticket military budgets, and signs the so-called "New Men" were inclining towards temporary alliance with them, Duke Allen had been forced to draw the Conservative Association into his camp as a counterweight. It was unlikely the Conservatives would stay put—their xenophobic isolationism and protectionism were too fundamentally at odds with the Centrist and Crown Loyalist perception that open war with the People's Republic of Haven was inevitable—but for now they were needed, and they'd charged high for their allegiance. They'd wanted the military ministry, and Duke Allen had been forced to buy them off by naming Sir Edward Janacek First Lord of the Admiralty, the civilian head of Honor's own service under the minister of war.

Janacek had been an admiral in his time, and one with a reputation for toughness and determination, but a more reactionary old xenophobe would be hard to find. He was one of the group who had opposed the annexation of the Basilisk terminus of the Manticore Junction on the grounds that it would "antagonize our neighbors" (translated: it would be the first step on the road to foreign adventurism), and that was bad enough. Unpolitical Honor might be, but she knew which party she supported. The Centrists realized that the Republic of Haven's expansionism must inevitably bring it into conflict with the Kingdom, and they were preparing to do something about it. The Conservatives wanted to bury their heads in the sand until it all went away, though they were at least willing to support a powerful fleet to safeguard their precious isolation.

But the point which most affected *Fearless* just now was that Hemphill was Janacek's second cousin and that Janacek personally disliked Admiral Alexander. More, the new First Lord feared the traditionalists' insistence that aggressive expansion like Haven's would continue until it was forcibly contained. And, finally, Hemphill was one of the most senior admirals of the red. Each of the RMN's flag ranks was divided into two divisions on the basis of seniority: the junior half of each rank were admirals of the red, or Gryphon Division, while the senior half were admirals of the green, or Manticore Division. Simple longevity would eventually move any flag officer from one division to the other, but they could also be promoted over the heads of their fellows, and with her cousin as First Lord, Lady Sonja was poised to move up to the green—especially if she could justify her tactical theories. All of which, added together, had given Horrible Hemphill the clout to butcher Honor's helpless ship.

She growled and kicked a stool across the cabin. The satisfaction was purely momentary, and she flung herself back into her chair to glower at her screen.

Her command, it seemed, was her "reward" for graduating first in Admiral Courvosier's Advanced Tactics class, for *Fearless* was also Hemphill's secret weapon in the upcoming Fleet problem. That explained the security clamped over the refit (which Courvosier had made his excuse for not warning Honor), and she didn't doubt that Hemphill was chuckling and rubbing her hands in anticipation. For herself, if Honor had known what was waiting, she darn well would have blown off a couple of percentage points just to avoid it!

She rubbed her eyes again, wondering if McKeon already knew about their role in the Fleet problem. Probably not. He hadn't been upset enough, given what it was going to do to their efficiency ratings and, beyond a doubt, to *Fearless's* reputation.

The problem was that, on paper, the whole thing made sense. Gravity sidewalls were the first and primary line of defense for every warship. The impeller drive created a pair of stressed gravity bands above and below a ship—a wedge, open at both ends, though the forward edge was far deeper than the after one—capable in theory of instant acceleration to light speed. Of course, that kind of acceleration would turn any crew to gory goo; even with modern inertial compensators, the best acceleration any warship could pull under impeller was well under six hundred gravities, but it had been a tremendous step forward. And not simply in terms of propulsion; even today no known weapon could penetrate the main drive bands of a military-grade impeller wedge, which meant simply powering its impellers protected a ship against any fire from above or below.

But that had left the sides of the impeller wedge, for they, too, were open—until someone invented the gravity sidewall and extended protection to its flanks. The bow and stern aspects still couldn't be closed, even by a sidewall, and the most powerful sidewall ever generated was far weaker than a drive band. Sidewalls *could* be penetrated, particularly by missiles fitted with penetration aids, but it took a powerful energy weapon at very short range (relatively speaking) to pierce them with any effect, and that limited beams to a range of no more than four hundred thousand kilometers.

It also meant that deep-space battles had a nasty tendency to end in tactical draws, however important they might be strategically. When one fleet realized it was in trouble, it simply turned its ships up on their sides, presenting only the impenetrable aspects of its individual units' impeller wedges, while it endeavored to break off the action. The only counter was a resolute pursuit, but that, in turn, exposed the unguarded frontal arcs of the pursuers' wedges, inviting raking fire straight down their throats as they attempted to close. Cruiser actions were more often fought to the finish, but engagements between capital ships all too often had the formalism of some intricate dance in which both sides knew all the steps.

The situation had remained unaltered for over six standard centuries, aside from changes in engagement range as beam weapons improved or defensive designers came up with a new wrinkle to make missile penetration more difficult, and Hemphill and her technophiliacs found that intolerable. They believed the grav lance could break the "static situation," and they were determined to prove it.

In theory, Honor had to concede their point. In theory. Deep inside, she even wished, rather wistfully, that they might be right, for the tactician in her hated the thought of bloody, formalistic battles. The proper objective was the enemy's fleet, not simple territory. If his battle squadrons lived to fight another day, one was forced back on a strategy of attrition and blockade—and casualties, ultimately, were far higher in that sort of grinding war.

Yet the *jeune ecole* wasn't right. The grav lance was new and might, indeed, someday have the potential Hemphill claimed for it, but it certainly didn't have it yet. With only a very little luck, a direct hit could set up a harmonic fit to burn out any sidewall generator, but it was a cumbersome, slow-firing, mass-intensive weapon, and its maximum range under optimum circumstances was barely a hundred thousand kilometers.

And that, she thought gloomily, was the critical flaw. To employ the lance, a ship had to close to point-blank range against enemies who would start trying to kill it with missiles at upward of a million kilometers and chime in with energy weapons at four times the lance's own range. It might even make sense aboard a capital ship with the mass to spare for it, but only an idiot (or Horrible Hemphill) would think it made sense aboard a light cruiser! *Fearless* simply didn't have the defenses to survive hostile fire as she closed, and thanks to the grav lance, she no longer even had the offensive weapons to reply effectively! Oh, certainly, if she got into grav lance range, and if the lance did its job, the massive energy torpedo batteries Hemphill had crammed in could tear even a superdreadnought apart. But *only* if the lance did its job, since energy torpedoes were as effective as so many soft-boiled eggs against an intact sidewall.

It was insane, and it was up to Honor to make it work.

She glowered at the screen some more, then switched it off in disgust and sprawled untidily across her bunk. Nimitz stretched and ambled down from his rest to curl up on her stomach, and this time she cooed to him and stroked his fur as he laid his jaw on her breastbone to help her think.

She'd considered protesting. After all, tradition gave a captain the authority to question alterations to her command, but *Fearless* hadn't been her command when the refit was authorized, and the right to question wasn't the same as the right to refuse. Honor knew exactly how

Hemphill would react to any protest, and it was too late to undo the damage, anyway. Besides, she had her orders. However stupid they were, it was her job to make them work, and that, as they said at the Academy, was that. Even if it hadn't been, *Fearless* was *her* ship, by God! Whatever Hemphill had done to her, no one was going to crap on *Fearless's* reputation if Honor could help it.

She forced her muscles to unknot as Nimitz's purr hummed against her. She'd never been able to decide what else he did, but that mysterious extra sense of his had to be at the bottom of it, for she felt her outrage fading into determination and knew darn well it wasn't all *her* doing.

Her mind begin to pick and pry at the problem. It was probable, she decided, that she could get away with it at least once, assuming the Aggressors hadn't cracked Hemphill's security. After all, the idea was so crazy no sane person would expect it!

Suppose she arranged to join one of the screening squadrons? That was a logical enough position for a light cruiser, and the big boys would tend to ignore *Fearless* to concentrate on the opposing capital ships. That might let her slip into lance range and get off her shot. It would be little better than a suicide run, but that wouldn't bother Hemphill's cronies. They'd consider trading a light cruiser (and its crew) for an enemy dreadnought or superdreadnought more than equitable, which was one reason Honor hated their so-called tactical doctrine.

Yet even if she got away with it once and somehow managed to survive, she'd never get away with it twice—not once the Aggressors knew *Fearless* was out there and what she was armed with. They'd simply burn down every light cruiser they saw, for Hemphill had placed her sledgehammer in too thin an eggshell to survive capital ship fire. On the other hand, succeeding even once would be a major feather in Honor's cap, at least among those who recognized the impossibility of her task.

She sighed and closed her eyes, understanding herself entirely too well. She never had learned how to refuse a challenge. If there was a way to bring off Horrible Hemphill's gambit, Honor would find it, however much it galled her soul to do it.

• CHAPTER THREE

"General signal from Flag, Ma'am. 'Preparative Baker-Golf-Seven-Niner.'"

Honor nodded acknowledgment of Lieutenant Webster's report without raising her eyes from her display. She'd expected the signal from the moment Admiral D'Orville's Aggressors settled on their final approach vector, and Seven-Niner was, in a very real sense, her personal creation. Admiral Hemphill's ops officer probably wouldn't see it that way, but Captain Grimaldi, Hemphill's chief of staff, had realized what Honor was up to and supported her hints and deferential suggestions with surprising subtlety. He'd even given her a grin of approval after the final captains' briefing, which had led Honor into a fundamental re-evaluation of him, despite his position in Horrible Hemphill's camp. Not that it took a mental giant to realize that no conventional approach would let a light cruiser, whatever its armament, survive to reach attack range of a hostile battle fleet.

There were only so many options for a commander faced by a normal space action inside the hyper limit of a star. It was relatively simple to hide even a capital ship (at longer ranges, anyway) by simply shutting down her impellers and dropping off the enemy's passive scanners, but the impeller drive wasn't magic. Even at the five hundred-plus gravities a destroyer or light cruiser could manage, it took time to generate respectable vector changes, so hiding by cutting power was of strictly limited utility. After all, it did no good to hide if the enemy went charging away from you at fifty or sixty percent of light-speed, and you couldn't hide if you accelerated in pursuit.

All of which meant an admiral simply couldn't conceal her maneuvers from an opponent without risking loss of contact. And since hiding was normally pointless, that left only two real options: meet the enemy in a head-on, brute power clash, or try misdirection by showing him something that wasn't quite what he thought it was. Given Admiral Hemphill's material-oriented prejudices, it had taken all of Honor's persuasiveness to build any misdirection at all into the battle plan, for Lady Sonja believed in massing overwhelming firepower and simply smashing away until something gave, which at least had the virtue of simplicity.

Without Grimaldi's support, it was unlikely a lowly commander, even one specially selected to command Hemphill's secret weapon, could have convinced the admiral, but that was fine with Honor. Admiral D'Orville knew Hemphill as well as anyone else, and the last thing he'd expect from her was sneakiness. If the Defenders could mislead him into misinterpreting what he saw, so much the better; if they couldn't, they lost very little of importance. Only *Fearless*.

And so Honor watched the rest of the Defender task force moving towards her. In another sixteen minutes, the entire force would overrun her and keep right on going, leaving her single light cruiser alone and lonely almost in the Aggressors' path.

Admiral of the Green Sebastian D'Orville frowned over his own plot aboard the superdreadnought HMS *King Roger*, then glanced at the visual display. Visuals were useless for coordinating battles at deep-space ranges, but they were certainly spectacular. D'Orville's ships were charging ahead at almost a hundred and seventy thousand kilometers per second—just under .57 *c*—and the starfield in the forward screens was noticeably blue-shifted. But *King Roger* raced along between the inclined "roof" and "floor" of her impeller wedge, and the effect of a meter-deep band in which local gravity went from zero to over ninety-seven thousand MPS^2 grabbed photons like a lake of glue and bent the strongest energy weapon like flimsy wire. Stars seen through a stress band like that red-shifted radically and displaced their images by a considerable margin in direct vision displays, though knowing exactly how powerful the gravity field was made it fairly simple for the computers to compensate and put them back where they belonged.

But what was possible for the generating warship was impossible for its foes. Civilian impeller drives generated a single stress band in each aspect; military impeller drives generated a double band and filled the space between them with a sidewall, for good measure. Hostile sensors might be able to analyze the outermost band, but they couldn't get accurate readings on the inner ones, and that was why no one could target something on their far side.

"Admiral Hemphill's deceleration is holding steady, Sir." His chief of staff broke into D'Orville's thoughts with a fresh update from Tactical. "We should enter missile range in another twenty minutes."

"What's the latest on her detached squadron?"

"We got a good cross-cut on their transmissions about twelve minutes ago, Sir. They're way the hell and gone in-system."

Captain Lewis's completely neutral tone almost shouted his derision for their opponent, and D'Orville hid a smile of agreement. Sonja was going to look mighty bad when they got done kicking her posterior clear back to the capital, and that was exactly what was going to happen to her if she tried a stand-up fight without those detached dreadnoughts. She should have gone on running until they could join up, not challenged this soon, but at least their absence explained her course. She was well off a direct heading for the planets she was supposed to be defending for the simple reason that it was the shortest route to the ships she'd forgotten to bring to the dance, and D'Orville was sadly tempted to ignore her and go kiting straight for the objective. It would be highly satisfying to "nuke" Manticore without letting Sonja fire a single shot in its defense, but his assigned objective was to *capture* the capital planet, not just raid it. Besides, no tactician worth his gold braid would pass up the opportunity to crush two-thirds of the enemy's forces in detail. Especially in one of the rare cases in which the opposition couldn't disengage without uncovering an objective they *must* hold.

"Is our deployment complete?" he asked.

"Yes, Sir. The scouts are falling back behind the wall now."

"Good."

D'Orville glanced into the huge main tactical tank, double-checking Lewis's report in pure reflex. His capital ships had spread into the traditional "wall of battle," stacked both longitudinally and vertically into a formation one-ship wide and as tight as their impeller wedges permitted. It wasn't a very maneuverable arrangement, but it allowed the maximum possible broadside fire; and since they could no more shoot out through their impeller bands than an enemy could shoot in through them, it was the only practical way to accomplish that.

He checked the chronometer against Tactical's projections again. Seventeen minutes to extreme missile range.

The first missiles went out as the range dropped. Not a lot of them—the chances of a hit at this distance were slight, and not even capital ships could pack in an inexhaustible supply of them—but enough to keep the other side honest.

And enough to give any good Liberal or Progressive a serious case of the hives, Honor thought, watching them go. Each of those projectiles massed just under seventy-five tons and cost upward of a million Manticoran dollars, even without warheads or penaids. No one would be fool enough to use weapons that could actually get through and damage their targets, but the Fleet had steadfastly refused every political pressure to abandon live-fire exercises. Computer simulations were invaluable, and every officer and rating of whatever branch spent long, often grueling hours in the simulators, but actual firings were the only way to be sure the hardware really worked. And, expensive or not, live-fire exercises taught the missile crews things no simulation could.

But she had other things to worry about as Admiral D'Orville charged towards her, and worry she did, for Honor wasn't precisely the RMN's best mathematician. Despite aptitude tests which regularly said she *ought* to be an outstanding number-cruncher, her Academy performance scores had steadfastly refused to live up to that potential. In point of fact, she'd nearly flunked out of multi-dimensional math in her third form, and while she'd graduated in the top ten percent overall, she'd also held the embarrassing distinction of standing two-hundred-thirty-seventh (out of a class of two hundred and forty-one) in Mathematics.

Her math scores hadn't done much for her own self-confidence at the time—and they'd driven her instructors to distraction. The profs had *known* she could handle the math. The aptitude tests said so, her tac simulator scores had blown the roof off the curve—which wasn't exactly the mark of a mathematical moron—and her maneuvering scores had been just as high. Her kinesthetic sense was acute, she could solve multi-unit three-dimensional vector intercepts in her head (as long as she didn't think about what she was doing), and none of that ability had shown up in her applied mathematics *grades*. The only person it never seemed to have bothered was Admiral Courvosier—only he'd been Captain Courvosier, then—and he'd ridden her mercilessly until she came to believe in herself, whatever the grades said. Give her a real-time, real-world maneuver to worry about and she was fine, but even today she was a poor astrogator—and she could worry herself into panic attacks just thinking about math tests. Which, she knew, was the reason for her present, carefully hidden jitters; she'd had too much time to worry about today's maneuver.

Yet this was hardly a case of hyper-space navigation, she reminded herself firmly. Just four simple little dimensions, something Sir Isaac Newton could have handled, and she probably wouldn't have worried about it if it had come at her cold. When that sort of thing happened, she didn't worry—she simply responded as Admiral Courvosier had trained her to, trusting the abilities she couldn't quite seem to lay her cognitive hands upon, and her unbroken string of "Excellent" and "Superior" tactical ratings had confounded even her most dubious Academy critics.

But in this instance, she'd had plenty of time to worry about it ahead of time, and telling herself—truthfully— that only the Aggressors' closing speed made it time-critical hadn't helped tremendously. Still, Lieutenant Venizelos, her tactical officer, had run the numbers five times, and Lieutenant Commander McKeon had double-checked them. And Honor had made herself check McKeon's calculations a dozen times in the privacy of her quarters. Now she watched the chrono counting off the last, fleeting seconds and double-checked her engineering displays. Everything on the green.

"You know, Sir," Captain Lewis murmured, "there's something a little weird about this."

"Weird? How so?" D'Orville asked absently, watching the missile traces streaking towards Hemphill's wall of battle.

"Their counter-fire's mighty light," Lewis said, frowning down at his own displays, "and it's scattered pretty wide, not concentrated."

"Umpf?" D'Orville craned his neck to glance at Tactical's target projections, and it was his turn to frown. Lewis was right. Sonja was a great believer in concentration of fire—it was one of her few real tactical virtues, in D'Orville's opinion—and given her numerical disadvantage, she ought to be pouring it on, hoping for a few lucky kills to decrease the odds. Only she wasn't, and the admiral's eyebrows drew together in puzzlement.

"Are you positive about the fix on her detached units?" he asked after a moment.

"That's what I was thinking about myself, Sir. I'm certain our fix was solid, but what if the transmitting ship was all alone out there? You think she could be leading us into a trap?"

"I don't know." D'Orville rubbed his jaw and frowned harder. "It wouldn't be like her, but Grimaldi might just have put her up to something along those lines. Bit risky if he did, though. She'd have to have them free-falling on the same base vector to pull it off, and we've got the edge in force levels even if her entire force were concentrated. . . ." He wrinkled his forehead, then sighed. "Pass the word to Tactical to prepare for a radical course change just in case."

"Yes, Sir."

A single data code blinked angry scarlet amid the massive Aggressor formation in Honor's display, and she grinned. She didn't know if Admiral D'Orville's spies (unofficial and strictly against the rules, of course) had penetrated the security screen around *Fearless*, but Admiral Hemphill's spies had penetrated his own security. Not very deeply, but far enough to ID his flagship. That was one of the great potential weaknesses in any Fleet maneuver; each side had complete files on the electronic signatures of the other side's units.

The chrono sped downward, and she raised her head to glance at McKeon and Lieutenant Venizelos.

"All right, gentlemen," she said.

"Sir! We've got a new bogey, bearing—"

Captain Lewis's frantic warning was far too late, and the range was far too short to do anything about it. Admiral D'Orville had barely begun to turn towards him when a crimson light glared on *King Roger*'s main status board, and damage alarms screamed as the vastly understrength grav lance smashed into the superdreadnought's port sidewall. It was far too weak to inflict actual generator damage, but the computers noted it and obediently flashed their failure warning—just as an incredible salvo of equally understrength energy torpedoes exploded against the theoretically nonexistent sidewall.

The admiral jerked upright in his command chair while the visual display flickered and glared with the energy torpedoes' fury. Then the display went blank, and his strangled, incredulous curse echoed across the hushed flag bridge as every weapon and propulsive system shut down.

"Direct hit, Ma'am!" Venizelos screamed, and Honor permitted herself a fierce grin of triumph as the Aggressor flagship went ballistic. Other ships peeled out of formation to maintain safe separation, but *King Roger* was "dead," locked down by her own computers to simulate her total destruction at the hands of a lowly light cruiser! It was almost worth being Horrible Hemphill's handpicked hatchet woman just to see it.

But there was still the little matter of *Fearless*'s own survival.

"Bring the wedge up now!" Honor's soprano was a bit higher than usual, if far calmer than her tac officer's voice, and Engineering's response was instantaneous. Lieutenant Commander Santos had been standing by for over an hour; now she closed the final circuit and *Fearless*'s impeller wedge sprang to life.

"Helm, execute Sierra Five!"

"Sierra Five, aye," the helmsman replied, and *Fearless* rolled madly on her gyros and attitude thrusters. She flipped up on her side relative to the Aggressor wall of battle, interposing her belly impeller bands just as the first Aggressor energy weapons began to fire. Incredulous fire control officers poured laser and graser fire at the tiny target which had suddenly materialized on their displays, but they were too late. The impeller bands bent and splattered their fire harmlessly, and Honor felt a huge smile transform her strong features.

"All right, Chief Killian." She allowed herself an airy gesture at the forward visual display. "That away—full military power."

"Yes, Ma'am!" the helmsman replied with an equally huge grin, and HMS *Fearless* leapt to an instant acceleration of five hundred and three standard gravities.

Fifty years of self-discipline allowed Admiral D'Orville to stop cursing as the computers permitted his command chair's tactical display to come back up. His com systems were still locked, preventing him from doing anything about it, but at least he could see what was happening. Not that it made him feel any better. The light cruiser that had "killed" his flagship with a single broadside held its course, speeding with ever-mounting velocity on a direct reciprocal of his own fleet's vector. Its course took it through the optimum firing arc of his entire wall, but its impeller bands laughed at his capital ships' best efforts, and not even his light units had a hope in hell of catching it. They could never dump enough velocity to overhaul, and he could almost hear its captain's jubilant rasberry as he sped towards safety.

"You were right, George," he told Lewis, fighting hard to keep his voice normal. "Sonja *was* up to something."

"Yes, Sir," Lewis said quietly. He rose from his own command chair to stand at D'Orville's shoulder and watch the only operational tactical display on the bridge. "And there's the rest of it," he sighed, and D'Orville winced as his chief of staff gestured at Hemphill's main body.

The Defender wall of battle was changing its vector. It went from partial to maximum deceleration, and even as it did the entire formation shifted. Its new course cut sharply in towards the Aggressor task force's, and the range raced downward as Sonja's formation slowed. The separation was still too great for her to achieve the classic ideal and cross his "T," firing her full broadsides straight into his teeth while only his leading units' bow weapons could reply, but the obviously pre-planned maneuver, coupled with the command confusion created by *King Roger's* "destruction," was enough to let her leading units curl in around his own. The Defenders' broadsides were suddenly ripping down his wall's throat, and if the angle remained acute, it was still sufficient to send missiles racing in through the wide-open frontal arcs of his impeller wedges. Point defense was stopping a lot of them, but not enough, and bright, vicious battle damage codes appeared beside the light dots of his lead units as long-range beam fire ripped at those delicious, unprotected targets, as well.

Admiral D'Orville clenched his fists, then sighed and made himself lean back in his chair with a wintry smile. Sonja was going to be impossible to live with for months, and he could scarcely blame her. Few of his ships would be "destroyed" before the wall got itself sorted out and altered course, but enough were already crippled to even the odds . . . and who knew when her "detached units" would suddenly appear, as well?

It was all most un-Sonja-like, but it had certainly been effective, and Admiral Sebastian D'Orville made a mental note to find out exactly whose light cruiser that had been. Anyone who could bring that little maneuver off was someone to watch, and he intended to tell him so in person.

Assuming he could keep himself from strangling the sneaky bastard long enough to congratulate him.

• CHAPTER FOUR

The ship-wide elation which had followed the "destruction" of Admiral D'Orville's flagship was noticeably absent as Honor watched her steward pour coffee. The rich aroma of the beverage filled the small briefing room's silence, but the cup Steward First Class MacGuiness placed at Honor's elbow contained hot cocoa. She never had understood how something that smelled as nice as coffee could taste so foul, and she wondered yet again if perhaps Manticoran coffee trees hadn't mutated somehow in their new environment. Such things happened, but she doubted that was the answer in this case, given the appalling relish with which most RMN officers imbibed the loathsome stuff.

Not that anyone was showing much relish today.

She hid a sigh behind her expressionless face and sipped her cocoa. Things had gone far better than she'd dared hope in the major Fleet problem of the recent maneuvers, but, as if to compensate, the subsequent problems had worked out even more disastrously than she'd feared. As expected, D'Orville and his squadron commanders had realized exactly what *Fearless* had done to them, and their humiliating showing had inspired them to make certain it never happened again. More than that, it had given them a personal grudge against *Fearless* (whatever Admiral D'Orville might have had to say about his personal admiration for their maneuver), especially after Hemphill's detached dreadnoughts turned up and battered the surviving Aggressors into ignominious retreat with forty-two percent losses.

D'Orville's captains had been waiting for Honor in the follow-up exercises. Indeed, she suspected some of them had been more concerned with nailing *Fearless* than winning the exercise! In a total of fourteen "engagements," the light cruiser had been "destroyed" thirteen times, and she'd only succeeded in taking someone with her (aside from *King Roger*, of course) twice.

The moral effect on Honor's people had been brutal. Being pounded on that way would have been hard for anyone, but it was especially painful after their elation over picking off the enemy flagship, and Admiral Hemphill's signals had made it even worse. Lady Sonja had been livid at how easily her secret weapon (and, no doubt, hopes for advanced promotion) were countered once the other side knew about it, and her messages to *Fearless's* captain had descended from congratulatory to querulous to scathing . . . and downhill from there. She had to know it wasn't Honor's fault, but knowing didn't seem to make her any happier.

Nor had it made *Fearless's* crew any happier with their new skipper. Their respect for her initial success had turned into something far less admiring, and their pride in their ship (and themselves) had eroded badly. Being "killed" that many times was sufficiently depressing for anyone, but the Aggressor crews had made it far worse with their undisguised gloating in the intervals between exercises. Her crew's loss of confidence would have been bad enough under any circumstances; for a ship with a new captain, it might well prove catastrophic. Perhaps, they thought, Captain Harrington hadn't been so brilliant after all that first day. What if it had been pure luck, not skill? What if they found themselves in a *real* combat situation and she dropped them in the toilet?

Honor understood what they were thinking. In their place, she might have been thinking the same thing; and if they thought *they* were unhappy they should try it from the captain's chair for a while.

"All right, ladies and gentlemen," she said finally, setting her cup back on its saucer and turning to her assembled officers. Coffee cups imitated her cocoa, and wary eyes looked back at her.

Honor made a point of meeting jointly with all of her senior officers on a regular basis. It wasn't required, and many captains preferred to leave all such activities to their first officers, since it was the exec's job to insure the ship ran smoothly. Honor, on the other hand, preferred to receive regular reports directly. It might require a little extra effort to avoid the appearance of undercutting her exec's traditional authority, but it seemed to her that a ship's officers generally worked more efficiently with one another (and for their CO) when they had a chance to air their problems and achievements and discuss their departments' needs together with their captain. The system had served her well in *Hawkwing*, where the enthusiastic collaboration of her officers had contributed measurably to the destroyer's successes. In *Fearless*'s case, however, it wasn't working. Honor's new subordinates were more afraid she'd lash out at them for their ship's failures than interested in the opportunity to brainstorm with her.

Now she looked at their faces and felt her own failure in their wooden postures and set expressions. Lieutenant Webster, her communications officer, had the watch, but all the others were present . . . for all the good it seemed likely to do.

Lieutenant Commander McKeon faced her from the table's far end, tense and blank-faced, an enigma hiding some inner reserve that went beyond the maneuvers' disastrous outcome. Lieutenant Commander Santos, chief engineer and junior only to McKeon, sat expressionlessly at her right hand, eyes fixed on the blank screen of her memo pad as if to shut the rest of the briefing room away. Lieutenant Stromboli, the astrogator, fleshy, dark-browed, and physically powerful, sat hunched down in his chair like a child afraid to sulk. Dapper, slim Lieutenant Venizelos sat facing him, eyes unfocused, waiting with manifest resignation for the discussion to begin. Yet the resignation held an edge of bravado, almost defiance, as if the tactical officer dared her to blame him for *Fearless*'s poor showing—and feared she did.

Captain Nikos Papadapolous sat beside Stromboli, meticulously neat in the green and black of the Royal Manticoran Marines, and, unlike the others, he seemed almost comfortable yet oddly detached. But, then, the Corps was a law unto itself in many ways, for Marines were always outsiders aboard ship. They were army troops in a naval setting and aware of the distinction, and unlike her naval personnel, Papadapolous's Marines had nothing for which to reproach themselves. They went where the ship went and did what they were told; if the effete Navy types who crewed it screwed up, that was their lookout, not the Corps'.

Surgeon Commander Lois Suchon faced Papadapolous across the table, and Honor tried not to feel a special dislike for *Fearless*'s doctor. It was hard. Both of her own parents were physicians, and her father had reached Suchon's own rank before retiring, which meant Honor had a pretty fair notion of just how much help a good doctor could be. Suchon, on the other hand, was even more detached than Papadapolous. Doctors were specialists, not line officers in the chain of command, and the thin-faced, petulant Suchon seemed totally disinterested in anything beyond her sickbay and dispensary. Worse, she seemed to regard her responsibility for the crew's health as a sort of nagging inconvenience, and Honor found it very difficult to forgive any physician for that.

Her eyes swept past Suchon to the two officers flanking McKeon. Lieutenant Ariella Blanding, her supply officer, junior to every other officer present, looked as if she expected her captain to spring upon her at any moment, despite the fact that her department had performed flawlessly throughout. Blanding was a small woman, with a sweet, oval face and blond hair, but her eyes moved back and forth endlessly, like a mouse trying to watch too many cats.

Lieutenant Mercedes Brigham sat facing Blanding, as if she'd been placed deliberately to accentuate the contrast between them. Blanding was young and fair; Brigham was almost old enough to be Honor's mother, with dark, weathered-looking skin. She was *Fearless's* sailing master, a position that was being rapidly phased out of the service, but she seemed unconcerned by the fact. She'd never caught the attention to rise above lieutenant, yet her comfortable, lived-in face normally wore an air of quiet competence, though she had to know she would never advance beyond her present rank after so long in grade. And if she was as withdrawn as the others, at least she didn't seem physically afraid of her captain.

That was something, Honor thought, completing her survey and forcing herself not to bark a demand that they show some backbone. It wouldn't help, and it *would* convince them their anxieties were justified. Besides, she knew exactly where their defensiveness came from; she herself had known captains who certainly would have taken out their own frustrations on their officers. After all, *someone* had to be at fault for things to go this wrong, and their concern that Honor would do just that was so palpable she'd started leaving Nimitz in her quarters for these meetings. The treecat was far too sensitive to emotions to subject him to something like this.

"What's the status of our request to reprovision, Exec?" she asked McKeon. The executive officer glanced at Blanding, then straightened in his chair.

"We're cleared to take on supplies Monday, beginning at twelve-thirty hours, Ma'am," he said crisply. Too crisply. McKeon was holding his personal contacts with Honor to an absolute minimum, erecting a barrier she couldn't seem to break through. He was brisk, efficient, and obviously competent—and there wasn't a trace of rapport between them.

She bit her tongue against a fresh urge to snap at him. A warship's executive officer was supposed to be the essential bridge between its captain and her officers and crew, the skipper's alter ego and manager as well as her second in command. McKeon wasn't. He was too good an officer to encourage any open discussion of *Fearless*'s failings—or her captain's—among his subordinates, but silence could speak volumes. McKeon's silence was more eloquent than most, and not only was it contributing powerfully to her isolation from her officers, but that isolation was transmitting itself to the rest of her crew, as well.

"Any word on those extra missile pallets we requested?" she asked him, trying once more to break through the icy formality.

"No, Ma'am." McKeon tapped a brief notation into his memo pad. "I'll check with Fleet Logistics again."

"Thank you," Honor managed not to sigh, and abandoned the attempt. She turned to Dominica Santos, instead. "What's the status of the grav lance upgrade, Commander?" she asked in a cool, even voice that hid her near despair.

"I think we'll have the replacement convergence circuits in place for an on-line test by the end of the watch, Ma'am," Santos responded, keying her own memo pad to life. She studied the screen, never looking up at Honor. "After that, we'll have to—"

Alistair McKeon sat back and listened to Santos's report, but his attention wasn't really on it.

He watched Harrington's profile, and dull, churning resentment burned at the back of his throat like acid. The captain looked as calm and collected as she always did, spoke and listened as courteously as ever, and that only made him resent her more. He was a tactical officer himself by training. He knew precisely how impossible Harrington's task had been, yet he couldn't rid himself of a nagging suspicion that he could have done better at it than she. He certainly couldn't have done any worse, he thought spitefully, and felt himself flush guiltily.

Damn it, what was *wrong* with him? He was supposed to be a professional naval officer, not some sort of jealous schoolboy! It was his job to support his captain, to make her ideas work, not to feel a corrosive satisfaction when they didn't, and his inability to overcome his personal feelings shamed him. Which, of course, only made them worse.

Santos finished her report, and Harrington turned with equal courtesy to Lieutenant Venizelos. That should have been another of McKeon's jobs. *He* was the one who ought to be keeping the meeting moving, bringing out the points he knew should be called to the captain's attention and subtly shoring up her authority. Instead, it was one more task he avoided, and he knew, deep inside, that he was painting himself into a corner. Habit would make it impossible for him to reclaim responsibilities he left undischarged long enough, and as Harrington came to believe, with cause, that she simply could not rely upon him, she would stop giving him the chance to prove she could.

Alistair McKeon knew where that would end. One of them would have to go, and it wouldn't be the captain. Nor should it be, he told himself with scathing, inherent honesty.

He looked around the briefing room again and felt something very like panic. He could lose all this. He'd known he couldn't hope for command of *Fearless*, but his own actions—and inactions—could take even this away from him. He knew it, yet knowing wasn't enough. For the first time in his career, recognizing where his duty lay wasn't enough for him to do it. Try as he might, he couldn't break through his resentment and the dislike springing from it.

He felt a sudden, terrible temptation to confess his feelings and his failures to the captain. To beg her to find a way through them for him. Somehow, he knew, those dark brown eyes would listen without condemning, that calm soprano would reply without contempt.

And that, of course, was what made it impossible. It would be the final capitulation, the admission that Harrington *deserved* the command he had known from the start could not be his.

He ground his teeth together and stroked the cover of his memo pad in silence.

The attention signal chimed, and Honor pressed the com button.

"Communications Officer, Ma'am," the traditional Marine sentry announced crisply, and she felt an eyebrow rise.

"Enter," she invited, and the hatch hissed open to admit Lieutenant Samuel Houston Webster.

Honor gestured at the chair across her desk from her, and Nimitz sat up on his hindquarters with a welcoming "bleek" as the gangling lieutenant crossed the day cabin to take it. As always, the 'cat was a sure barometer of Honor's own feelings. She despised captains who played favorites among their officers, but if she'd been the sort to let herself do things like that, Webster would have been her choice.

Of all *Fearless*'s officers, he was the most cheerful and seemed least wary of his captain. Or, she thought wryly, perhaps he was simply less worried about being splattered by Admiral Hemphill's evident displeasure with the said captain. He was a young, overly-tall redhead who seemed to have too little meat on his bones, but he was also very, very good at his job—and a third cousin of the Duke of New Texas. Honor often felt ill at ease with subordinates from such rarefied aristocratic heights, but no one could feel that way around Webster, and she gave him a slight smile as he sat.

To her surprise, he failed to return it. In fact, his homely face (dominated by the craggy Webster chin) wore an expression of acute unhappiness as he laid a message board on the blotter.

"We've just copied a dispatch from the Admiralty, Ma'am," he said. "Orders to a new station."

Something about the way he said it—and the fact that he'd brought it in person instead of sending it by messenger or over the intercom—filled Honor with dread. She schooled her features into calm interest and picked it up, then bit her lip in dismay as she scanned the display and the brief, terse directive.

Basilisk Station. God, she knew she'd disappointed Hemphill, but the admiral must be even more upset than she'd thought!

"I see," she said calmly. She laid the electronic message board down and tipped her chair back. Nimitz leapt lightly from his perch to her shoulder, wrapping his fluffy tail protectively about her throat, and she reached up to stroke his head.

Webster said nothing. There was very little he *could* say, after all.

"Well," Honor inhaled deeply, "at least we know." She pressed her thumb to the message board scanner, formally receipting her new orders, then handed it back to Webster. "Pass it on to Commander McKeon, please. And inform him with my compliments that I would appreciate his getting together with Lieutenant Stromboli and Lieutenant Brigham to recheck and update the Basilisk charts."

"Yes, Ma'am," the communications officer said quietly. He rose, braced to attention, and turned away. The hatch slid shut behind him, and Honor closed her eyes in pain.

The Basilisk System picket wasn't a duty station—it was exile. Oblivion.

She rose to pace the cabin, cradling Nimitz in her arms, and felt him purr against her chest, but this time not even his efforts could stave off her black depression. Officers who were frightened of her, an executive officer less approachable than a Sphinx iceberg, a crew who blamed her for their ship's failures, and now this.

She bit her lip until her eyes watered, remembering how happy and proud she'd been the day she assumed command. Now that joyful anticipation had become unreal and untouchable, even in memory, and she wanted to cry.

She stopped her pacing and stood rigid, then sucked in a tremendous breath, gave Nimitz one last squeeze, and set him on her shoulder. All right. They were sweeping *Fearless*—and her captain—under the rug, running them out of town because they were an embarrassment to Admiral Hemphill. There was nothing she could do about that, except to take her medicine, however undeserved, and do the very best she could with the duties she'd been given. And, she told herself firmly, the fact that Basilisk Station had become the RMN's purgatory didn't mean it wasn't important.

She returned to her desk, trying not to think about how her crew would react when they learned of their new orders, and punched up the Basilisk entry on her data terminal. Not so much because she needed the information as in the vain hope that rereading it would make the pill less bitter.

It wasn't as if being sent to Basilisk *should* be a disgrace. The system was of great and steadily growing economic value to the Kingdom, not to mention its strategic military importance. It was also Manticore's sole extra-system territorial possession, and that alone should have made it a prestigious assignment.

The Manticore System was a G0/G2 distant binary, unique in the explored galaxy in possessing three Earth-like planets: Manticore, Honor's own Sphinx, and Gryphon. Given that much habitable real estate, there'd never been much pressure, historically, for the Kingdom to expand into other systems, and for five T-centuries it hadn't.

It probably still wouldn't have but for the converging pressures of the Manticore Wormhole Junction and the Havenite threat.

Honor swung her chair gently from side to side, listening to Nimitz's less anxious purr, and pursed her lips.

The Manticore Junction was as unique as the system itself, with no less than six additional termini. That was one more than any other junction so far charted, and the astrophysicists argued that the survey readings suggested there should be at least one more undiscovered terminus, though they had yet to work out the math and isolate it.

In no small part, the Junction explained Manticore's wealth. The best effective speed in hyper of most merchantmen was little more than twelve hundred times light-speed. At that apparent velocity, the voyage from Manticore to Old Earth would require over five months; the Beowulf terminus of the Junction, on the other hand, delivered a ship to Sigma Draconis, little more than forty light-years from Sol, in no measurable elapsed time at all.

The commercial advantages were obvious, and the Junction's far-flung termini had become magnets for trade, all of which must pass through the central junction point (and Manticoran space) to take advantage of them. Manticore's tolls were among the lowest in the galaxy, but simple logistics meant they generated enormous total revenues, and the Kingdom served as a central warehousing and commercial node for hundreds of other worlds.

Yet logistics also made the Junction a threat. If multimegaton freighters could pass through it, so could superdreadnoughts, and the economic prize it offered was sufficient to make for avaricious neighbors. Manticorans had known that for centuries, but they hadn't worried about it overmuch before the People's Republic of Haven become a threat.

But Haven had become a threat. After almost two T-centuries of deficit spending to shore up an increasingly insolvent welfare state, Haven had decided it had no choice but to turn conquistador to acquire the resources it needed to support its citizens in the style to which they had become accustomed, and the People's Navy had proven its capacity to do just that over the course of the last five decades. Haven already controlled one terminus of the Junction—Trevor's Star, conquered twelve T-years ago—and Honor had no doubt the "Republic" hungered to add the rest of them to its bag. Especially, she thought with a familiar chill, the central nexus, for without Manticore itself, the other termini were of strictly limited utility.

Which was why the Kingdom had annexed Basilisk following its discovery twenty-odd Manticoran years before. The G5 star's single habitable (if one used the term loosely) planet had complicated the decision, for it boasted a sentient native species, and the Liberals had been horrified at the notion of Manticore "conquering" an aboriginal race. The Progressives, on the other hand, had opposed the annexation because they already realized Haven would someday turn its sights on the Silesian Confederacy, which would take them straight past Basilisk. Manticoran sovereignty, they feared, would be seen as a direct threat—a "provocation"—in Havenite eyes, and their idea of foreign policy was to buy Haven off, not irritate it. As for the Conservative Association, *anything* that threatened to embroil them in galactic affairs beyond their nice, safe borders was anathema in their eyes.

All of which explained why Basilisk had become a bone of incredibly bitter contention among the major political parties. The Centrists and Crown Loyalists had carried the annexation by only the slimmest margin in the House of Lords, despite ample evidence that the Commons (including many of the Liberals' staunchest allies) strongly favored it. But to get it through the Lords at all, the Government had been forced to agree to all sorts of restrictions and limitations—including the incredibly stupid (in Honor's opinion) provision that no permanent fortifications or Fleet bases should be constructed in the system, and that even mobile units there should be kept to a minimum.

Under the circumstances, one might have expected the restriction on the number of ships which could be stationed there to call for sending only the very best, particularly since the volume of trade through the newly discovered terminus had grown by leaps and bounds. In fact, and especially since Sir Edward Janacek had become First Lord of the Admiralty, the opposite was the case.

Janacek wasn't the first, unfortunately, to denigrate Basilisk's importance, but his predecessors at least seemed to have based their feelings on something besides personal politics. The pre-Janacek theory, as far as Honor was able to determine, had been that since they were barred from putting in forces which might stand a chance of holding the system, there was no point making the effort. Thus, even many of those who supported the annexation saw the picket as little more than a trip-wire, advanced scouts whose destruction would be the signal for a response by the Home Fleet direct from Manticore. In short, some of them had argued, if any serious attack was ever mounted, there was no point sacrificing any more ships than necessary simply for the honor of the flag.

Janacek, of course, felt even more strongly than that. Since assuming control of the Admiralty, he had reduced the Basilisk picket below even the stipulated levels, for he saw it as a threat and a liability, not an asset. Left to his own devices, he would no doubt have simply ignored the system completely, and since he couldn't (quite) do that, he could at least see to it that he didn't waste any useful ships on it. And so Basilisk Station had become the punishment station of the Royal Manticoran Navy. Its dumping ground. The place it sent its worst incompetents and those who had incurred Their Lordships' displeasure.

People like Commander Honor Harrington and the crew of HMS *Fearless*.

• CHAPTER FIVE

HMS *Fearless* decelerated smoothly towards a stop as she passed the inner perimeter of the Junction defenses. The Manticore System's G0 primary and its G2 companion were dim behind her, reduced to two more stars amid millions, for the Junction lay almost seven light-hours from them.

The duty watch manned their stations alertly, and a stranger on *Fearless's* bridge might not have recognized the air of gloom which clung to them. But a stranger, Honor thought, reaching up to rub Nimitz's jaw absently, wouldn't have lived with these people for weeks now. A stranger wouldn't recognize their humiliation at being condemned to Basilisk Station, or the way they'd withdrawn ever deeper into their shells until the duties they performed were all they really had in common with their captain.

She leaned back, hiding her desire to sigh sadly behind a calm face, and watched the tactical display. *Fearless's* projected vector stretched across it, terminating right on the half light-second outbound departure threshold of the Junction. The light cruiser's green bead tracked steadily down the thin line, threading its way through the mammoth defenses, and even in her own depression, Honor felt a familiar tingle at the firepower ringing the invisible doorway between the stars.

The smallest fortress out there massed close to sixteen million tons, twice as much as a superdreadnought, and its weapons-to-mass ratio was far higher. The forts weren't hyper-capable, for they used mass a warship might have devoted to its hyper generators and Warshawski sails to pack in still more firepower, but they were far more than immobile weapon platforms. They had to be.

Each of those forts maintained a stand-by battle watch and a 360° sidewall "bubble" at all times, but no one at this end of the Junction could know anyone was coming through it until they arrived, and no one could remain eternally vigilant. Thus a sneak attack—from, say, Trevor's Star—would always have the advantage of surprise; the attacker would arrive ready for battle, already seeking out targets for his weapons, while the defenders were still reacting to his arrival in their midst.

That was why no defensive planner placed his permanent defenses closer than a half million kilometers or so to a junction. If a hostile task force emerged within energy weapon range of the defenses, those defenses would be destroyed before they could reply, but ships transiting a wormhole junction arrived with a normal-space velocity of barely a few dozen kilometers per second, far too little for a high-speed attack run. With the closest forts so far from him and too little speed for a quick run-in to energy weapon range, any attacker must rely on missiles, and even impeller-drive missiles would require almost thirty-five seconds to reach them. Thus the forts' duty watches—in theory, at least—had time to reach full readiness while the weapons accelerated towards them. In practice, Honor suspected, most of them would still be coming on-line when the missiles arrived, which was why their point defense (unlike their offensive weaponry) was designed for emergency computer override even in peacetime.

In time of war, the forts would be augmented by thickly seeded remote laser platforms—old-fashioned, bomb-pumped laser satellites—much closer in and programmed to automatically engage anything not positively identified as friendly, but such measures were never used in peacetime. Accidents could always happen, and the accidental destruction of a passenger liner whose IFF wasn't recognized could be embarrassing, to say the very least. An attacker would still have sufficient surprise advantage for his energy batteries to kill a lot of satellites before they could respond, but enough of them would survive to handle him very roughly indeed.

Nonetheless, heavy losses could be anticipated in the inner fortress ring under the best possible circumstances, so the "forts" in the outer rings had to be able to move to fill in the gaps and mass upon an attacker. Their maximum acceleration rates were low, well under a hundred gravities, but their initial positions had been very carefully planned. Their acceleration would be enough to intercept attacking forces headed in-system, and their engines were sufficiently powerful to generate impeller wedges and sidewalls to protect them.

Yet for all their numbers, firepower, and mobility, the fortresses were too weak to stop a worst-case, multiple-transit attack by an opponent as powerful as the Havenite Navy. And that, she told herself moodily as *Fearless* killed the last of her speed and slid to a halt, was the real reason Manticore had annexed Basilisk in the first place.

The central nexus was the key to any wormhole junction. Ships could transit from the central nexus to any secondary terminus and from any secondary terminus to the central nexus, but they could *not* transit directly from one secondary terminus to another. Economically, that gave Manticore a tremendous advantage, even against someone who might control two or more of the Manticore Junction's termini; militarily, the reverse was true.

There was an inviolable ceiling, varying somewhat from junction to junction, on the maximum tonnage which could transit a wormhole junction terminus simultaneously. In Manticore's case, it lay in the region of two hundred million tons, which set the upper limit on any assault wave the RMN could dispatch to any single Junction terminus. Yet each use of a given terminus-to-terminus route created a "transit window"—a temporary destabilization of that route for a period proportionate to the square of the mass making transit. A single four-million-ton freighter's transit window was a bare twenty-five seconds, but a two-hundred-million-ton assault wave would shut down its route for over seventeen *hours*, during which it could neither receive reinforcements nor retreat whence it had come. Which meant, of course, that if an attacker chose to use a large assault wave, he'd better be absolutely certain that wave was nasty enough to win.

But if the attacker controlled more than a single secondary terminus, he could send the same tonnage to the central nexus through *each* of them without worrying about transit windows, since none would use exactly the same route. Choreographing such an assault would require meticulous planning and synchronization—not an easy matter for fleets hundreds of light-years apart, however good the staff work—yet if it could be pulled off, it would allow an attack in such strength that no conceivable fortifications could stop it.

Not even Manticore's, Honor thought as *Fearless* slowed to rest relative to the Junction. Even though the Junction fortresses accounted for almost thirty percent of the RMN's budget, the security—or at least neutrality—of the Junction's other termini simply *had* to be guaranteed.

"We have readiness clearance from Junction Central, Ma'am," Lieutenant Webster announced. "Number eight for transit."

"Thank you, Com." She glanced at her maneuvering display as the scarlet numeral "8" appeared beside *Fearless's* cursor, then turned her gaze to the duty helmsman. McKeon sat silently beside Lieutenant Venizelos at Tactical, but her eyes passed over him without even acknowledging his presence. "Put us in the outbound lane, Chief Killian."

"Aye, aye, Ma'am. Coming to outbound heading." Killian fell silent for a moment, then, "In the lane, Captain."

Honor nodded her satisfaction and glanced up at the visual display just as a stupendous bulk carrier erupted from the junction. It was an incredible sight, one she never tired of, and the display's magnification brought it to arm's length. That ship had to mass over five million tons, yet it blinked into sight like some sort of insubstantial ghost, a soap bubble that solidified into megatons of alloy in the blink of an eye. Its huge, immaterial Warshawski sails were circular, azure mirrors, bright and brilliant for just an instant as radiant transit energy bled quickly into nothingness, and then it folded its wings. The invisible sails reconfigured into impeller stress bands, and the freighter slowly gathered way, accelerating out of the nexus while it cleared its final destination with Junction Central and requested insertion into the proper outbound lane to continue its voyage.

Fearless moved steadily forward with the other outbound vessels. In time of peace, she had no greater priority than any of the gargantuan merchantmen who dwarfed her to insignificance, and Honor leaned back in her chair to savor the bustle and purposeful energy of the Junction in action.

Under normal circumstances, the Junction handled inbound and outbound vessels at an average rate of one every three minutes, day in and day out, year after year. Freight carriers, survey vessels, passenger ships, innerworld colony transports, private couriers and mail packets, warships of friendly powers—the volume of traffic was incredible, and avoiding collisions in normal space required unrelenting concentration by the controllers. The entire Junction was a sphere scarcely a light-second in diameter, and while that should have been plenty of space, each terminus had its own outbound and inbound vector. Transiting to the proper destination required that those vectors be adhered to very precisely indeed (especially when not even Junction Central knew exactly who might be inbound from where at any given moment), and that meant traffic was confined to extremely limited areas of the Junction's volume.

Chief Killian held *Fearless*'s place in the outbound

queue without further orders, and Honor punched up Engineering as they neared the departure beacon. Commander Santos appeared on her small com screen.

"Commander. Stand by to reconfigure to Warshawski sail on my command."

"Aye, Ma'am. Standing by to reconfigure."

Honor nodded, watching the freighter ahead of them drift further forward, hesitate for just an instant, and then blink out of visibility. The numeral on her maneuvering display changed to "1," and she turned to Webster and quirked an eyebrow, waiting out the seconds until he nodded.

"We're cleared to transit, Ma'am," he reported.

"Very good. Transmit my thanks to Junction Central," she said, and looked back at Chief Killian. "Take us in, Helm."

"Aye, aye, Ma'am."

Fearless drifted forward at a mere twenty gravities' acceleration, aligning herself perfectly on the invisible rails of the Junction, and Honor watched her display intently. Thank God for computers. If she'd had to work out the math for this sort of thing, she'd probably have cut her own throat years ago, but computers didn't mind if the person using them was a mathematical idiot. All they needed was the right input, and, unlike certain Academy instructors she could name, they didn't wait with exaggerated patience until they got it, either.

Fearless's light code flashed bright green as the cruiser settled into exact position, and Honor nodded to Santos.

"Rig foresail for transit."

"Aye, aye, Ma'am. Rigging foresail—now."

No observer would have noted any visible change in the cruiser, but Honor's instrumentation told the tale as *Fearless*'s impeller wedge dropped abruptly to half-strength. Her forward nodes no longer generated their portion of the normal space stress bands; instead, they had reconfigured to produce a circular disk of focused gravitation that extended for over three hundred kilometers in every direction from the cruiser's hull. The Warshawski sail, useless in normal space, was the secret of hyper travel, and the Junction was simply a focused funnel of hyper space, like the eye of a hurricane frozen forever in normal space terms.

"Stand by to rig aftersail on my mark," Honor murmured as *Fearless* continued to creep forward under the power of her aft-impellers alone. A new readout flickered to life, and she watched its numerals dance steadily upward as the foresail moved deeper and deeper into the Junction. There was a safety margin of almost fifteen seconds either way, but no captain wanted to look sloppy in a maneuver like this, and—

The twinkling numbers crossed the threshold. The foresail was now drawing sufficient power from the tortured grav waves twisting eternally through the Junction to provide movement, and she nodded sharply to Santos.

"Rig aftersail now," she said crisply.

"Rigging aftersail," the engineer replied, and *Fearless* twitched as her impeller wedge disappeared entirely and a second Warshawski sail sprang to life at the far end of her hull from the first.

Honor watched Chief Killian closely, for the transition from impeller to sail was one of the trickier maneuvers a coxswain had to deal with, but the diminutive CPO didn't even blink. His hands and fingers moved with complete confidence, gentling the cruiser through the conversion with barely a quiver. She noted his competence with satisfaction, then turned her attention back to her maneuvering display as *Fearless* gathered still more forward way.

Killian held her rock-steady, and Honor blinked as the first, familiar wave of queasiness assailed her. Very few people ever really adjusted to the indescribable sensation of crossing the wall between n-space and hyper space, and it was worse in a junction transit, for the gradient was far steeper. By the same token, however, it was over sooner, she reminded herself, and concentrated on looking unbothered as the rippling nausea grew stronger.

The maneuvering display blinked again, and then, for an instant no chronometer or human sense could measure, HMS *Fearless* ceased to exist. One moment she was here, in Manticore space; the next she was there, six hundred light-minutes from the star named Basilisk, just over two hundred and ten light-years distant in Einsteinian space, and Honor swallowed in relief as her nausea vanished, disappearing with the transit energy radiating from *Fearless's* sails.

"Transit complete," Chief Killian reported.

"Thank you, Helm. That was well executed," Honor replied, but most of her attention was back on the sail interface readout, watching the numbers spiral downward even more rapidly than they had risen. "Engineering, reconfigure to impeller."

"Aye, aye, Ma'am. Reconfiguring to impeller now."

Fearless folded her sails back into her impeller wedge and moved forward more rapidly, accelerating steadily down the Basilisk outbound traffic lane, and Honor gave an inner nod of satisfaction. Shiphandling was one of the very few areas in which she never questioned her own competence, and the routine maneuver had gone as smoothly as even she could have asked for. She hoped that might be a sign for the future.

The light codes were far sparser in the tactical display than they had been in Manticore, she noted. There were no fortifications at all, only a cluster of navigation buoys and the small (relatively speaking) bulk of Basilisk Traffic Control, almost lost in the clutter of merchantmen awaiting transit.

"Com, notify Basilisk Control of our arrival and request instructions."

"Aye, aye, Ma'am," Webster replied, and Honor leaned back and laid her forearms along the command chair's armrests. They were here. They'd hit rock bottom, for no less appealing assignment could have been devised, but perhaps she could turn that into an asset. Surely they had nowhere to go but up! And for all its indignity, Basilisk Station should give them time to put the disastrous maneuvers behind and settle down into the sort of ship's company she'd envisioned from the start.

She felt Nimitz's tail steal around her throat and hoped she wasn't just whistling in the dark.

"Message from Basilisk Control, Captain."

Honor twitched herself up out of her thoughts and gestured for Webster to continue.

"We are instructed to proceed to Medusa orbit to rendezvous with the picket's senior officer aboard HMS *Warlock*, Ma'am."

"Thank you." Honor managed to keep any trace of derision out of her response, but *Fearless* had held her initial parking position two light-seconds from the terminus for almost forty minutes. In total, she'd been in Basilisk space for over fifty-three minutes, which seemed to indicate some pretty sloppy message traffic management aboard Basilisk Control. *Fearless's* routing instructions must have been transmitted to Control well before her arrival, given the current ten-hour-plus transmission lag between the terminus and Medusa, Basilisk's single habitable planet. The fact that Control had required the next best thing to an hour just to find them did not, she thought, augur well for its efficiency in other matters.

"Thank them for the information," she went on after a moment, and turned her chair to face Lieutenant Stromboli. "Do you have a course for Medusa, Lieutenant?"

"Uh, no, Ma'am." The beefy lieutenant flushed under her steady regard, then became very busy plugging figures into his console.

She waited patiently, though he should have worked up the heading for Medusa almost by reflex, as that was obviously their most probable destination. An on the bounce astrogator tried to anticipate his captain's needs without prompting, and Stromboli's flush showed his own awareness of that. He bit his lip as he concentrated on his panel, and his eyes refused to meet hers while he worked, as if he expected her to bite his head off at any moment.

She didn't. If one of her officers needed reprimanding, she would attend to it in private, just as she made it a point to deliver praise in public. Surely they ought to be figuring *that* much out by now! She bit off another sigh and refrained from tapping her toe on the deck.

"Course is zero-eight-seven by zero-one-one at four hundred gravities, with turnover in one-five-point-zero-seven hours, Ma'am," Stromboli announced finally.

"Thank you, Lieutenant," Honor said gravely, and he flushed more darkly yet. No need for a reprimand there, she decided. Stromboli was unlikely to embarrass himself that way a second time. She glanced at Killian.

"Make it so, Helm."

"Aye, aye, Ma'am. Coming to zero-eight-seven zero-one-one. Acceleration four-zero-zero gravities," Killian replied in a deadpan voice, and *Fearless* swung onto her new heading and began accelerating. The silence on her bridge was uncomfortable, like that of school children caught out on a pop quiz by a new teacher.

"Punch up *Warlock,* please, Tactical. Let's find out who our senior officer is," Honor said, more to break the uneasy quiet than for any other reason—though, now that she thought about it, Basilisk Control should have passed that information along already. More sloppiness. Maybe it was a side effect of being banished here, but she certainly intended to see that it wasn't allowed to infect her ship, as well.

She was reaching for the insulated cup of cocoa in her armrest beverage holder when Venizelos reported.

"Here it is, Ma'am. HMS *Warlock,* CA Two-Seven-Seven. Three hundred k-tons. She's a *Star Knight*-class. Captain Lord Pavel Young, commanding."

Honor's hand froze three centimeters from her cup,

then continued its progress. It was a tiny hesitation, no more than a second in length, but Commander McKeon looked up sharply, and his eyes narrowed at her expression.

It was a subtle thing, more sensed than seen, an infinitesimal tightening of her lips. The ridges of her sharply-defined cheekbones stood out for just an instant, and her nostrils flared. That was all—but the treecat on the back of her chair rose to his full height, ears flat, lip curled back to bare needle-tipped fangs, and his hand-paws tensed to show half a centimeter of curved, white claw.

"Thank you, Lieutenant." Harrington's voice was as courteous and level as ever, but there was something in it—an uneasiness, a cold bitterness at odds with his maddeningly self-possessed captain.

He watched her sip her cocoa and replace the cup neatly, and his mind raced as he tried to recall if he'd ever heard of Lord Pavel Young. Nothing came to him, and he bit the inside of his lip.

Was there something between her and Young? Something which would affect *Fearless*? Her flash of immobility, coupled with the treecat's powerful reaction, certainly seemed to suggest there was, and with any other captain, he would have found some excuse to ask her in private. Not out of morbid curiosity, but because it was his job to know about such things, to protect his ship and his commanding officer from anything that would hamper their efficiency.

Yet the barriers sealing him off from Harrington had grown too thick for that. He felt them rising into place, holding him in his chair, and then Harrington stood. She rose without haste, but he seemed to sense a jerkiness to her movement, a hidden urgency.

"Commander McKeon, you have the watch. I'll be in my quarters."

"Aye, aye, Ma'am. I have the watch," he acknowledged automatically. She nodded, dark eyes looking right through him with a curious, dangerous hardness, then scooped up her treecat and strode into the bridge lift. The door closed behind her.

McKeon rose and crossed to the command chair, settling into it and feeling the warmth her body had left behind. He made himself look away from the bland lift door and leaned back against the contoured cushions, wondering what fresh disaster was headed *Fearless*'s way.

• CHAPTER SIX

The planet Medusa gleamed like a dull ball bearing far below as *Fearless* slid into her assigned parking orbit for rendezvous with *Warlock*. It wasn't much of a planet, Honor thought, watching it on the visual display. She was well-aware her concentration on Medusa stemmed from a need to think about anything but the upcoming interview with her senior officer, but her mood had little to do with her conclusion that Medusa had to be the most boring-looking world she'd ever seen.

It was gray-green, relieved only by weather patterns and the glaring white of massive polar ice caps. Even its deep, narrow seas were a barely lighter shade of the omnipresent gray-green—a soupy sludge of plankton and larger plant forms that thrived in a brew the environmental control people would have condemned in a heartbeat back on Sphinx. Medusa's axial tilt was extreme, over forty degrees, which, coupled with its cool primary, produced a climate more brutal even than Manticore-B's Gryphon. The planetary flora was well-adapted to its severe environment, but it showed an appalling lack of variation, for Medusa was covered in moss. Thousands—millions—of varieties of moss. Short, fuzzy moss in place of grass. Higher-growing, brushy moss in place of bushes. Even, God help us all, great, big, floppy mounds of moss in place of trees. She'd heard about it, even seen holos, but this was the first time she'd seen it with her own eyes, and it wasn't the same at all.

She gave a wry grimace of distaste and turned her eyes resolutely to the sight she'd been avoiding. HMS *Warlock* floated in the same orbit, barely a hundred kilometers clear, and she swallowed a bitter-tasting envy mixed with old hatred as she gazed at her.

The *Star Knight* class were the RMN's latest heavy cruisers, three and a half times more massive than *Fearless* and with almost six times her firepower, even before *Hephaestus* and Horrible Hemphill had butchered her. The big, sleek ship hung there, taunting Honor's elderly command with its mere presence, and knowing who commanded that beautiful vessel made it far, far worse. She'd thought she'd hit bottom when they assigned her to Basilisk Station; now she knew she had.

The duty helmsman brought *Fearless* to rest relative to *Warlock*, and she drew a deep breath, wondering if any of her crew guessed why she'd left Nimitz in her quarters. Not that she intended to tell them.

"Call away my cutter, please," she requested. "Mr. Venizelos, you have the watch."

"Aye, aye, Ma'am," Venizelos replied, and watched curiously as his captain stepped into the lift and headed for the boat bay.

Honor sat silently, arms folded, as her cutter crept across the emptiness between *Fearless* and *Warlock*. She'd been tempted, in a way, to use one of her pinnaces, but she knew why—just as she knew that that particular bit of ostentation would have been one too many. So she'd taken her cutter, despite the fact that it moved far more slowly than a pinnace would have. Even the most efficient thrusters gave a much weaker acceleration than impellers, and a cutter was too small to mount an impeller drive. It was also too small for the inertial compensator needed to offset an impeller's brutal power, though its gravity generator could compensate for the lower gee-force of its thrusters. Yet despite Honor's own impatience and need to get this over, the trip was short, even at the cutter's relatively slow speed. Too short. She'd spent the last thirty-one hours dreading this moment.

Her pilot completed his final approach, and the cutter shivered as *Warlock's* tractors captured it. It rolled on its gyros, aligning itself with the heavy cruiser's internal gravity as the brilliantly-lit cavern of *Warlock's* boat bay engulfed them, then settled into the docking cradle. Alloy clanged gently as hatch collars mated, and the green pressure light glowed.

She was alone, and she allowed herself a sigh as she stood and tucked her beret under her epaulet. Then she tugged the skirt of her tunic down, squared her shoulders, and walked briskly through the opening hatch and down the tube into the twitter of bosun's calls and the salutes of the side party.

Young hadn't come down to welcome her in person, she saw. She supposed it was a calculated insult—it was the petty sort of gesture at which he excelled—but she was relieved by his absence. It gave her a chance to settle herself and get her inner defenses in place before the inevitable confrontation.

She stopped in front of the short, squared-off commander heading the side party and saluted.

"Permission to come aboard, Sir?" she asked.

"Permission granted, Commander Harrington." He returned her salute, then extended his hand. "Paul Tankersley, *Warlock's* exec." His voice was deep and resonant, his clasp firm, but there was an edge of curiosity in his sharp eyes. Honor wondered if he'd heard rumors about her and Young.

"If you'll accompany me, Commander," Tankersley went on after a brief pause, "the Captain is waiting in Briefing One."

"Lead on." She made a tiny gesture for him to precede her, and the two of them walked through the side party to the waiting lift.

There was no small talk on the way, which, Honor reflected, probably did indicate that Tankersley knew at least a little about her. After all, he could hardly begin a

conversation with, "Do you and the Captain still hate each
other's guts, Commander?" Nor could he ask for her side of
it without seeming disloyal to his own CO. Under the circumstances, a prudent silence was undoubtedly his wisest
course, and she felt her lips twitch with acid amusement as
the lift slid to a halt.

"This way, Commander," Tankersley said, and she followed him down a short passage to the briefing room hatch.
He came to a halt, pressed the admittance button, and
stood aside as the panel slid open. She thought she saw just
a touch of sympathy in his expression as she walked past
him.

Captain Lord Young was seated behind the conference
table, perusing a sheet of hardcopy. He didn't look up as she
entered, and she gritted her teeth, amazed that such a triv-
ial insult could make her so angry. She crossed to the table
and stood silently, determined to wait him out.

He was the same flashy, handsome man he'd always
been, she noted. Putting on a little weight, perhaps, but the
short beard hid his incipient double chin quite well, and his
tailoring was excellent. It always had been, even at the
Academy, where everyone was supposed to wear the same
Navy-issue uniform. But, then, the rules never had applied
to him. Pavel Young was the eldest son and heir of the Earl
of North Hollow—a point he had no intention of allowing
anyone to forget.

Honor had no idea what he'd done to get himself banished to Basilisk Station. Probably, she thought bitterly,
he'd simply been himself. Patronage could advance an
officer's career—witness the fact that Young, who'd graduated only one form before her, had made list five years ago.
Once an officer's name was on the captain's list, his eventual
flag rank was guaranteed. Unless he did something so drastic the Fleet cashiered him, he only had to live long enough
for simple seniority to see to that.

But rank, as many a Manticoran officer had discovered,
was no guarantee of employment. An incompetent usually

found himself on half-pay, still carried on the active-duty list but without a command. Half-pay was supposed to provide a reserve of experienced officers against future need by retaining those surplus to the service's current requirements; in practice, it was used to put fumble-fingered idiots too important to dismiss from the Queen's service where they could do no harm. Obviously Young hadn't gotten himself into that category—yet—but the fact that he'd been senior officer in Basilisk for almost a T-year now seemed a pretty clear hint someone at the Admiralty was less than thrilled with his performance.

Which, no doubt, was only going to make him more poisonous than ever to deal with.

He finished pretending to read his hardcopy and replaced it fastidiously on the tabletop, then raised his eyes.

"Commander." The tenor voice was smooth, draping his enmity like velvet wrapped about a dagger's blade.

"Captain," she returned in the same emotionless tone, and his mouth twitched a brief almost-smile. He did not invite her to sit.

"I'm relieved to see your ship. We've been even more shorthanded than usual since *Implacable* left."

Honor contented herself with a silent nod, and he tipped his chair back.

"As you know, Basilisk Station is chronically understrength," he went on, "and I'm afraid *Warlock* is sadly overdue for refit. In fact, this—" he tapped the hardcopy "—is a list of our most urgently required repairs." He smiled. "That's why I'm so pleased to see you, Commander. Your presence will permit me to return *Warlock* to Manticore for the yard attention she needs so badly."

He watched her face, and Honor bit the inside of her lip and fought to keep her dismay from showing. If Young was dispatching his own ship to Manticore, he undoubtedly intended to shift to *Fearless*. The mere thought of sharing her bridge with him was enough to turn her stomach, but she managed, somehow, to stand in attentive silence with no sign of her thoughts.

"Under the circumstances," he continued after a moment, "and in view of the extensive nature of our needs, I feel it would be inadvisable to ask Commander Tankersley to assume responsibility for *Warlock's* refit." He extended a data chip and smiled as she took it without touching his hand.

"Therefore, Commander Harrington, I will be accompanying *Warlock* back to Manticore to supervise her refit in person." This time her surprise was too great to hide completely. He was the station's senior officer! Did he mean he intended to abandon his responsibility for the system?! "I will, of course, return as quickly as possible. I realize my absence will be . . . inconvenient for you, and I will make every effort to keep it as brief as possible, but I estimate that the necessary maintenance and repairs will consume at least two months. More probably—" he smiled again "—three. During that time, you will be senior officer here in Basilisk. Your orders are on the chip."

He let his chair slip back upright and picked up his hard copy once more.

"That will be all, Commander. Dismissed."

Honor found herself back in the passage outside the briefing room without any clear memory of how she'd gotten there. The data chip cut into her palm with the pressure of her grip, and she made herself relax her hand one muscle at a time.

"Commander?"

She looked up, and Commander Tankersley recoiled. Her dark eyes smoked like heated steel, a slight tic quivered at the corner of her tight mouth, and for just an instant her expression touched him with fear. But she asserted control quickly and forced a smile as she saw the concern on his face. He started to say something else, but her half-raised hand stopped him, and he retreated once more into his safe neutrality.

Honor inhaled deeply, and then deliberately drew the white beret from her shoulder. She settled it precisely on her head without looking at Tankersley, but she felt the weight of his eyes. Courtesy forbade a visiting captain to wear the white beret when a guest upon another's ship, and that made the gesture a calculated insult to the man she'd just left behind.

She turned back to her guide, beret on her head, and those dark, hard eyes challenged him to react. It was a challenge Tankersley declined, content to maintain his isolation as he escorted her silently back toward the lift.

Honor was grateful for his silence, for her brain was trying to grapple with too many thoughts at once. Memories of the Academy dominated them, especially of the terrible scene in the commandant's office as Mr. Midshipman Lord Young, broken ribs and collarbone still immobilized, split lips still puffed and distended, one blackened eye swollen almost shut, was required to apologize to Ms. Midshipman Harrington for his "inappropriate language and actions" before the official reprimand for "conduct unbecoming" went into his file.

She should have told the whole story, she thought miserably, but he was the son of a powerful nobleman and she was only the daughter of a retired medical officer. And not a particularly beautiful one, either. Who would have believed the Earl of North Hollow's son had assaulted and attempted to rape a gawky, overgrown lump of a girl who wasn't even pretty? Besides, where was her proof? They'd been alone—Young had seen to that!—and she'd been so shaken she'd fled back to her dorm room instead of reporting it instantly. By the time anyone else knew a thing about it, his cronies had dragged him off to the infirmary with some story about "falling down the stairs" on his way to the gym.

And so she'd settled for the lesser charge, the incident that had happened earlier, before witnesses, when she rebuffed his smugly confident advances. Perhaps if she hadn't been so surprised, so taken aback by his sudden interest and obvious assurance that she would agree, she might have declined more gracefully. But it wasn't a problem she'd ever had before. She'd never developed the techniques for declining without affronting his overweening ego, and he hadn't taken it well. No doubt that "slight" to his pride was what had triggered later events, but his immediate response had been bad enough, and the Academy took a dim view of sexual harassment, especially when it took the form of insulting language and abusive conduct directed by a senior midshipman at a junior. Commandant Hartley had been furious enough with him over *that*, but who would have believed the truth?

Commandant Hartley would have, she thought. She'd realized that years ago, and hated herself for not telling him at the time. Looking back, she could recognize his hints, his all but overt pleas for her to tell him everything. If he hadn't suspected, he would hardly have required Young to apologize after she'd reduced him to a bloody pulp. Young had counted on neither the strength and reaction time Sphinx's gravity bestowed nor the extra tutoring in unarmed combat Chief MacDougal had been giving her, and she'd known better than to let him up after she had him down. He was only lucky he'd tried for her in the showers, when Nimitz wasn't around, for he would be far less handsome today if the treecat had been present.

No doubt it was as well Nimitz *hadn't* been there, and, she admitted, there'd been a certain savage joy in hurting him herself for what he'd tried to do. But the response had been entirely out of proportion to his official offense, and no one had ever doubted that his "fall" had been nothing of the sort. Hartley might not have had any proof, but he would never have come down on Young so harshly under the circumstances if he hadn't had a pretty shrewd notion of what had actually happened.

Yet she hadn't realized that then, and she'd told herself she'd already dealt with the matter, anyway. That she didn't want to precipitate a scandal that could only hurt the Academy. That it was a case of least said, soonest mended, since no one would have believed her anyway. Bad enough to be involved in something so humiliating and degrading without exposing herself to *that*, as well! She'd almost been able to hear the sniggers about the homely horse of a girl and her "delusions," and, after all, hadn't she let herself get a little carried away? There'd been no need to pound him into semi-consciousness. That had gone beyond simple self-defense into the realm of punishment.

So she'd let the matter rest, and in so doing she'd bought herself the worst of both worlds. Attempted rape was one of the service's crash-and-burn offenses; if Young had been convicted of that, he would never have worn an officer's uniform, noble birth or no. But he hadn't been. She hadn't gotten him out of the service, and she had made an enemy for life, for Young would never forget that she'd beaten him bloody. Nor would he ever forgive her for the humiliation of being forced to apologize to her before Commandant Hartley and his executive officer, and he had powerful friends, both in and out of the service. She'd felt their influence more than once in her career, and his malicious delight in dropping full responsibility for the entire Basilisk System on her shoulders—leaving her with a single, over-age light cruiser to do a job which should have been the task of an entire flotilla—burned on her tongue like poison. It was petty and vicious . . . and entirely in keeping with his personality.

She inhaled deeply as the lift reached the boat bay and its door opened once more. She'd regained enough of her composure to shake Tankersley's hand and make herself sound almost normal as she bade him farewell and boarded her cutter once more.

She settled back in her seat as the cutter separated from *Warlock* and headed back to *Fearless*, and her mind reached out to grapple with her crew's reaction to this latest development. No doubt they would see *Warlock*'s departure as one more sign that they'd been demoted to the least important duty the Fleet could find and abandoned, and they would soon realize just how heavy a burden Young had dropped on them. Her single ship would be required to police the entire system and all of the traffic passing through the Basilisk terminus, and there was no way they could do it. They couldn't be in enough places at once, and trying to would impose a mind- and body-numbing strain on all of them.

Which was exactly what Young had intended. He was leaving her an impossible job, content in the knowledge that her failure to discharge it would go into her record. Unlike him, Honor had yet to make list, and if she botched her first independent command, however it had fallen on her, she never would.

But she hadn't botched it yet, and she nodded to herself—a choppy, angry nod. Even knowing that Young had set her up, that he intended for her to fail and ruin herself, was better than serving under his command, she told herself. Let him take himself off to Manticore. The sooner he got out of the same star system as her, the better she'd like it! And of one thing she was certain; she couldn't do any worse at the job than *he* had.

She'd made a mistake once where he was concerned. She wouldn't let him push her into another. Whatever it took, she would discharge her own duties and meet her own responsibilities. Not just to protect her career, but because they *were* her duties and responsibilities. Because she would not let an aristocratic piece of scum like Pavel Young win.

She straightened her spine and looked down at the data chip of her orders, and her dark brown eyes were dangerous.

• CHAPTER SEVEN

The officers in the captain's briefing room just off *Fearless*'s bridge rose as Honor came through the hatch. She waved them back into their chairs and crossed to her own, her movements brisk and intense. She sat and turned to face them all, and her face was expressionless.

"Ladies and gentlemen," she began without preamble, "*Warlock* will be departing for Manticore for refit within the hour." McKeon sat straighter in surprise, but she kept her voice cool and level, almost clipped, as she went on. "Captain Young will be accompanying her, which will leave *Fearless* the only Queen's ship in the system . . . and myself as senior officer."

She allowed herself a small smile at the almost-sound of dismay that swept the compartment, but her eyes were ice. She'd tried motivating them through opportunity and pride in self and hit a stone wall. Very well. If they wouldn't respond to her invitations to meet their responsibilities for their own sense of self-worth, she would try other means.

"Needless to say, this will leave us with a great many commitments, many of them mutually contradictory. This, however, is a Queen's ship. We *will* discharge our responsibilities, or I will know the reason why. Is that clear?"

Those cold brown eyes seemed to impale each of them in turn, and McKeon moved slightly in his chair as they lingered on him. His chin rose, but he said nothing, and she nodded.

"Good. In that case, let's move on to precisely what our duties and responsibilities are, shall we?"

She punched buttons on her terminal at the head of the conference table, and a small-scale holo display of the Basilisk System bloomed above it. She manipulated more buttons, and a bright red cursor blinked to life.

"We have a single ship, ladies and gentlemen, and our problem, in the simplest terms, is that one ship can be in only one place at a time. The Fleet is responsible for supporting Basilisk Control in management of Junction through traffic, including customs inspections as required. In addition, we are responsible for inspection of all traffic with Medusa itself or with the planet's orbital facilities, for supporting the Resident Commissioner and her Native Protection Agency police, for safeguarding all extra-Medusan visitors to the planet, *and* for insuring the security of this system against all external threats. To accomplish this, we must be here—" the cursor blinked in orbital proximity to Medusa "—here—" it blinked amid the flowing beads of traffic around the junction terminus "—and, in fact, *here.*" The cursor swept a wide circuit of the system, right on the twenty-light-minute radius of a G5 star's hyper limit.

She let the red light circle the holo display's central star for several seconds, then killed the cursor and folded her hands before her on the tabletop.

"Obviously, ladies and gentlemen, a single light cruiser *can't* be in all those places at once. Nonetheless, I have my orders from Captain Young, and I *will* discharge them."

McKeon sat silent, staring at her in disbelief. She couldn't be serious! As she herself had just proven, no single ship *could* discharge them.

But she obviously meant to try, and his cheeks burned as he realized what she'd been doing in her quarters over the three hours since her return from *Warlock.* She'd been tackling her impossible assignment by herself, wrestling with it without even attempting to involve her officers in its solution, for they'd proven that she couldn't. *He'd* proven that she couldn't.

His hands gripped together under the edge of the table. The final responsibility would have been Harrington's in any case, but captains had officers—and especially *first* officers—specifically to help them in situations like this. More, McKeon had already grasped the malice behind her new orders. He'd suspected there was something between her and Young; now he knew there was. Young was running a grave risk with his own career by quitting his station, though it seemed likely he had the patronage and influence to stave off outright disaster. But if Harrington failed to discharge the responsibilities he'd dumped on her, however impossible . . .

He shivered internally and made himself concentrate on her words.

"Lieutenant Venizelos."

"Yes, Ma'am?"

"You will select thirty-five ratings and one junior officer for detached duty. *Fearless* will escort *Warlock* to the terminus. As soon as *Warlock* has departed, I will drop you, your chosen personnel, and both pinnaces. You will rendezvous with Basilisk Control and assume the duties of customs and security officer for the terminus traffic. You will be attached to Basilisk Control for that purpose until further notice. Understood?"

Venizelos gawked at her for a moment, and even McKeon blinked. It was unheard of! But it might just work, he admitted almost unwillingly. Unlike cutters, pinnaces were large enough to mount impeller drives and inertial compensators, and they were armed. Their weapons might be popguns and slingshots compared to regular warships, but they were more than sufficient to police unarmed merchantmen.

Yet Venizelos was only a lieutenant, and he would be ten hours' com time from his commanding officer. He'd be entirely on his own, and one wrong decision on his part could ruin not only his own career but Harrington's, as well, which certainly explained his white, strained expression.

The Captain sat motionless, eyes on Venizelos's face, and her mouth tightened ominously. One tapering forefinger tapped the tabletop gently, and the tactical officer shook himself visibly.

"Uh, yes, Ma'am! Understood."

"Good." Honor regarded him levelly for another moment, tasting his anxiety and uncertainty, and made herself step firmly on her compassion. She was throwing him into the deep end, but she'd been three years younger than he was now when she assumed command of LAC 113. And, she thought mordantly, if he screwed up, Pavel Young and his cronies would see to it that *she* paid the price for it, not Venizelos. Not that she intended to tell the lieutenant that.

"I will leave you detailed instructions," she told him, relenting just a bit, and he sighed in what he clearly thought was unobtrusive relief, then stiffened again as she added, "but I will expect you to exercise your own discretion and initiative as the situation requires."

He nodded again, unhappily, and she turned her hard eyes on Dominica Santos.

"Commander Santos."

"Yes, Captain?" The lieutenant commander looked much calmer than Venizelos had, possibly because she knew there was no way Honor would detail her chief engineer for detached duty.

"I want you to confer with Lieutenant Venizelos before his departure. Get with the exec, as well. Before the lieutenant leaves us, I want a complete inventory of our on-hand recon drones."

She paused, and Santos nodded as she tapped a note into her memo pad.

"Yes, Ma'am. May I ask the purpose of the inventory?"

"You may. Once you've completed it, I want you and your department to begin stripping the sensor heads from the missile bodies in order to fit them with simple station-keeping drives and astrogation packages." This time Santos looked up quickly, her composure noticeably cracked. "I imagine we can do the job by swapping the sensor heads into standard warning and navigation beacons. If not, I want a design for a system that *will* work on my desk by thirteen hundred."

She locked eyes with the engineer, and Santos flinched. She hid her dismay well, but Honor could almost feel her racing thoughts as the magnitude of her task loomed before her. Just the man-hours involved were daunting, and if she had to design from scratch . . .

"As soon as we've dropped Lieutenant Venizelos and his party," Honor continued in that same flat, cool voice, "*Fearless* will begin a globular sweep pattern ten light-minutes from Basilisk. Lieutenant Stromboli—" the astrogator started in his chair as her glance moved to him "—will work out a least-time course for us, and we will deploy our drones as stationary sensor platforms. I realize that we will almost certainly have insufficient drones for complete coverage, but we'll concentrate on the ecliptic. We can't make patrol sweeps by the book with only one ship, but we can cover the most likely approach vectors."

"You want us to fit *all* of them with station-keeping drives, Ma'am?" Santos asked after a moment.

"That's what I said, Commander."

"But—" The engineer caught Honor's glacial glance and changed what she'd been about to say. "I expect you're right about fitting the sensor heads into standard beacon kits, Ma'am, but the numbers you're talking about are going to clean out our kits in a hurry. We're going to have to scratch-build an awful lot of drives and astro packs. That's not going to be cheap, and I don't even know if we have sufficient spares aboard."

"What we don't have, we'll fabricate. What we can't fabricate, we'll requisition from Basilisk Control. What we can't requisition, we'll steal." Honor bared her teeth in a humorless smile. "Is that clear, Commander Santos?"

"Yes, Ma'am."

"A point, Captain," McKeon heard himself say, and Harrington's eyes whipped to his face. They seemed to harden a bit more, but there was wariness—and perhaps a trace of surprise—in them, as well.

"Yes, Exec?"

"I'm not certain how many probes we have in stores, Ma'am, but I am certain you're right about our inability to achieve complete coverage even if we can—I mean, even after we *have* fitted them all with station-keeping drives." He was speaking stiffly, and he knew it, but he was also contributing to the solution of a problem for the first time since Harrington had come on board. It felt . . . odd. Unnatural.

"And?" the captain prompted him.

"We also have the problem of their endurance, Ma'am. They were never intended for long-term deployment like this. But we might be able to increase their effective time on station by setting them for burst activation. They've got a passive detection range of just over twenty light-minutes against an active impeller drive. If they're on the ten-light-minute shell, they'll have a reach of over half a light-hour from the primary—call it forty minutes' flight time."

Honor nodded. The best radiation and particle shielding available still limited a ship to a maximum speed of $.8\,c$ in normal space.

"If we set them to come up for, say, thirty seconds every half-hour, they should detect any incoming vessel under power in normal space at least twenty light-minutes out. That should give us sufficient time to respond, and at the same time increase their endurance by a factor of sixty."

"An excellent suggestion, Exec." Honor smiled at him, grateful that he'd finally come out of his shell, and his facial muscles twitched as if to return it. But then they stiffened again, as if he regretted his momentary lapse, and she smothered a frown of her own.

"Lieutenant Venizelos." The tactical officer looked

positively harried as she turned back to him, and her smothered frown turned into a smothered smile at his expression.

"Yes, Ma'am?"

"Lieutenant Cardones will be taking over your responsibilities in your absence. In addition to your other duties before departure, I want you to get with him and work out the optimum drone deployment based on the availability figures I feel certain Commander Santos and Commander McKeon will have for you within the hour."

"Yes, Ma'am."

"Very well. Now, once we've detached the pinnaces and deployed our drones, I intend to place *Fearless* in Medusa orbit. It will be necessary for me to meet and confer with the Resident Commissioner as soon as possible, which will, of course, require a visit to the planet. In addition, however, the detachment of our pinnaces will force us to rely on our cutters for all inspections of space-to-surface and orbit-to-orbit trade. Since they do not have impellers, we may be required to use *Fearless* herself to move them from orbit to orbit in order to cover all targets. Moreover, the planet lies within three light-minutes of the inner edge of our drone deployment, and our onboard sensors have far more reach than the drones will. By remaining in Medusa orbit, we will be so positioned as to allow our sensors to cover the most critical spatial volume of our responsibilities and also free drones to thicken other portions of the net. I'll want at least one drone reserved to cover the planet if we leave orbit, as I intend to run periodic sweeps of the inner system, if possible, but I'm afraid we'll find ourselves too busy to make many of them. Is all this understood?"

She sat back and swept them with her eyes. Most of them nodded; none shook their heads.

"Excellent. In that case—"

"Ah, Captain?"

"Yes, Lieutenant Venizelos?"

"Something just occurred to me, Ma'am. Commander McKeon's right about the probe endurance, and even without that consideration, getting the kind of coverage you're talking about would be a real problem with the numbers we have aboard. We could get a lot better density if we asked *Warlock* to drop off any she can spare. I mean, it's not like she's going to be needing them in Manticore."

"I appreciate the suggestion," Honor said in an absolutely toneless voice, "but I'm afraid it's impractical. We'll just have to do the best we can from our own resources."

"But, Captain—"

"I said it's impractical, Lieutenant." Her voice was even flatter than before, its very lack of expression a warning, and Venizelos closed his mouth with a snap. He shot a helpless, sidelong glance at McKeon, but the exec didn't even blink. He'd already noted that Harrington planned to detach her pinnaces *after* the heavy cruiser—and Young—had departed. Now her response to Venizelos confirmed his reading of the situation. Whatever the source of the bad blood between her and Young, it was nasty enough for him to deliberately set her up for disaster . . . and for her to see it coming. And to take steps against it only after he was no longer in a position to frustrate them.

All of which sounded ominously as though HMS *Fearless*—and her officers—might just find themselves caught in the crossfire.

Honor watched her executive officer's masklike expression and guessed was going on behind it. He was right, of course—and so was Venizelos. She deeply regretted having stepped on the tactical officer so hard, especially when he'd only offered the sort of suggestion she'd practically prayed for her officers to make, but she couldn't explain the enmity between her and Young. Even if it hadn't been unthinkable for any CO to reveal such things to her subordinates, it would have sounded entirely too much like petulant whining.

"Are there any other comments or suggestions?" she asked after a moment. There were none, and she nodded.

"I will announce our new orders and responsibilities to

the ship's company at fourteen hundred. Lieutenant Venizelos, I'll want a list of the personnel you want for your party by thirteen hundred. Commander McKeon will vet them before you submit them to me, but I want final approval made before I address the crew."

"Yes, Ma'am."

"Very well, ladies and gentlemen. You have your instructions. Let's be about them."

She nodded, and they rose and hurried from the compartment. They didn't look very happy, but at least they were actively engaged with their duties for the first time in far too long. Perhaps it was a good sign.

The hatch closed behind the last of them, and she put her elbows on the table and buried her face in her palms, massaging her temples with her fingertips. God, she *hoped* it was a good sign! She'd done her best to radiate confidence, but a terrifying number of things could go wrong. Merchant skippers could be prickly about their right of passage, and Venizelos might well provoke an interstellar incident if he pressed the wrong captain too hard. Even with McKeon's suggestion, the endurance of their cobbled-up sensor platforms would be frighteningly limited. They *might* last the three months until *Warlock* returned—with luck—if Young didn't find some excuse to extend his "refit" even further. And, worst of all, all of her plans counted on nothing going seriously wrong anywhere. If something did break, she had an excellent chance of knowing about it, but she had an even better chance of being in entirely the wrong place to do anything to *stop* it.

She sighed and straightened, then lowered her hands to the table and stared long and hard at their backs.

In the final analysis, everything depended on her crew, and she hated to think about the strain she was about to impose upon them. Marines would be of limited utility to Venizelos, so the tactical officer would almost certainly ask solely for naval ratings. That meant he would be taking almost ten percent of *Fearless*'s ship's company with him, and she would have a very hard time denying him the *best* ten percent, with the most small-craft experience. Her own customs parties for orbital traffic would have to come from what was left, and she'd already noted an appalling number of merchantmen in Medusa orbit. What they could be finding to trade with the aborigines was beyond her imagination, but they were clearly trading a lot of something, and it would be her duty to check every one of those ships.

It would be tempting, she knew, to settle for a simple examination of their manifests, but that wasn't what the Fleet expected of her. Manifest checks would do for through traffic entering the system only to transit the Junction; in the case of vessels trading with Manticoran territory, however, or those transshipping cargo here, she was supposed to inspect the cargo shuttles and ships themselves for contraband. That meant long, grueling hours for her people, and each inspection party would require an officer or senior petty officer to command it.

Even if she had to make no other detachments, that was going to leave her chronically shorthanded, and she could almost see the domino effect rippling towards her. Too few people meant longer watches, less free time, and more resentment from a crew that was already hostile at a time when she needed absolute top effort from everyone on board.

She sighed again and stood, looking around the empty compartment. So be it. Her own nature and all of her training cried out for her to *lead*, but if leadership failed she would cajole, kick, bully, or terrorize. One way or the other, whatever it took, she *would* get it done.

They could hate her guts all they liked as long as they did their duty.

● CHAPTER EIGHT

Captain Michel Reynaud, Manticore Astro-Control Service, stood at Commander Arless's shoulder and watched his display with mixed emotions as HMS *Fearless* held position near Basilisk Control and the heavy cruiser *Warlock* slid into the heart of the terminus. The heavier ship's Warshawski sails glowed brilliantly for just a moment, and then she vanished, and Reynaud was scarcely sorry to see her go. Of all the half-assed, over-bred, arrogant cretins the Royal Manticoran Navy had ever assigned to watch over Reynaud's domain, Lord Pavel Young had to have been the worst. He'd never bothered to veil his contempt for the ACS in the slightest, and Reynaud and his people had reciprocated with feeling.

But for all that, Young had been a known evil, one they'd grown accustomed to working around. Now they had a new one to worry about.

The Astro-Control Service was a civil service organization, despite its uniform and naval ranks, and Reynaud was profoundly grateful for it as he gazed at the remaining cruiser's light code. He was responsible for the smooth running of the terminus' traffic, period. The rest of the Basilisk System was the Navy's concern, and the thought of what now faced that single ship's commanding officer was enough to make Reynaud shiver. Not, he thought sourly, that the stupid bastard was likely to deserve his pity. If he was, he wouldn't have been dumped here. That was a given of Basilisk Station, and the personnel of Basilisk Control regarded the dregs with which they had to contend with all the disdain they merited.

He started to turn away, but Arless's voice stopped him.

"Just a sec, Mike. We've got a couple of inbounds from that cruiser."

"What?" Reynaud swung back to the display and frowned. Two drive sources were moving towards Control's sprawling habitat. They were far too small for full-sized ships, but the fact that they were impeller signatures indicated they were larger than most small craft. And that, in turn, suggested they must be pinnaces, but why would pinnaces be heading for his command station?

"What d'you suppose *they*'re up to?" he asked.

"Damfino." Arless shrugged. He leaned back and cracked the knuckles of his long fingers.

"You mean they didn't file a flight plan?"

"You got it. They—hold on." The controller leaned forward and flipped a switch, shunting his com channels to Reynaud's earbug.

"—ontrol, this is Navy flight Foxtrot-Able-One. Request final approach instructions."

Arless started to reply, but Reynaud stopped him with a raised finger and keyed his own pickup.

"Navy Foxtrot-Able-One, this is Basilisk Control. Please state your intentions."

"Basilisk Control, we are a naval liaison mission. I have on board my recorded orders and an explanatory dispatch for your station commander."

Reynaud and Arless stared at one another, eyebrows raised. It was certainly unorthodox. Liaison mission? What *kind* of "liaison"? And why all the mystery? Why hadn't they pre-filed a flight plan? The captain shrugged.

"Very well, Navy Foxtrot-Able-One. Make your approach to—" he craned his neck to check Arless's display "—beacon Niner-Four. You'll be met by a guide. Basilisk Control clear."

He killed the circuit and gave Arless an eloquent glance.

"Now just what the hell do you think *that* was all about, Stu?"

"Beats me, boss," the controller replied, "but look at that."

He gestured at his display, and Reynaud frowned. Even as her pinnaces separated, the light cruiser had swung away from Basilisk Control to go slashing off on a vector for the system primary, and not at the eighty percent power RMN ships normally used. She was ripping along at a full five hundred gravities, and she was already fifty thousand kilometers away at a velocity of over seven hundred KPS.

The station commander scratched his bristly gray hair and sighed. Just when he'd gotten the last uniformed jackass to at least keep his ham-fisted fingers out of Control's pie, this happened. It had taken months to convince Young that his condescending attempts to rearrange Control's well-tried traffic lanes into more "efficient" routes—so poorly designed they could only increase the workloads of Reynaud's already over-worked controllers while decreasing safety margins—were neither required nor desired. Managing wormhole junction traffic was a job for well-trained, highly experienced professionals, not twits who'd been exiled for how poorly they did their own jobs. There were lots of things the Navy could have done to facilitate ACS's routine operations if the over-bred fart had been interested in doing anything that would have required any effort on *his* part. He hadn't been, but the tin-god aspect of his personality had been pronounced. As far as Reynaud had been able to tell, Young was simply incapable of watching someone else get on with his job in an orderly fashion as long as he could interfere without exerting himself. He'd rubbed Reynaud wrong from the beginning, and the chief controller had found himself going out of his way to rub right back—with a predictable loss of efficiency he couldn't quite regret, however hard he tried.

But it appeared Young's replacement was cut from different cloth. The problem was that Reynaud didn't know what sort of cloth. Judging by the speed with which he moved, the newcomer certainly seemed to have more energy than his predecessor, but that could be good or bad. If he actually intended to assist Control, it was probably good, yet long and bitter experience made it difficult for Reynaud to visualize a senior naval officer who did more good than harm.

He shrugged. Whatever *Fearless*'s CO had in mind, the cruiser's rapid departure made it clear he intended to dump this "liaison mission" on Reynaud for the long haul, and his total lack of warning as to his intentions was peculiar, to say the very least.

He frowned again, but there was a speculative light in his eyes as he watched the light cruiser lope away. Whatever else that captain was, he clearly *wasn't* another Lord Pavel Young.

"Do you have our sweep pattern plotted, Astrogation?"

"Yes, Ma'am." Lieutenant Stromboli looked up at Honor's question. His fleshy face was drawn with weariness, for Santos and McKeon had kept revising their drone availability numbers on him. Every time they'd changed their figures, he'd had to recalculate almost from scratch, but tired or no, he never—ever—again meant to tell Captain Harrington he *didn't* have the course she needed. "We have a vector change in—" he double-checked his panel "—twenty-three minutes. We should deploy the first drone eight hours and forty-two minutes after that."

"Good. Pass the course change to Maneuvering." Nimitz "bleeked" softly in her ear, and she reached up to stroke his head. The treecat always seemed to know when it was time for him to be seen and not heard, even on the bridge, but he'd started sounding far more cheerful from the moment HMS *Warlock* disappeared. Honor knew why that was, and she allowed herself a small smile before she punched up Engineering.

She got one of Santos's assistants and waited patiently while the chief engineer was summoned to the com. Santos looked awful when she finally appeared. Her dark hair was gathered in a tight braid, her face was tired, and there was a smudge of grease down her right cheek.

"We'll be beginning drone deployment in approximately nine hours, Commander. What's our status?"

"The first pattern is almost ready to deploy now, Ma'am," Santos replied wearily, "and I think we'll have the second one by the time you need it, but I'm not sure about number three."

"Problems, Commander?" Honor asked mildly, and saw Santos's eyes flash with anger. Good. If her officers got mad enough, they might start thinking for a change instead of simply feeling sorry for themselves. But the lieutenant commander bit back what she wanted to say and exhaled sharply.

"I'm concerned about fatigue, Captain." Her voice was flat. "We're already running out of beacon kits, and the kits were never intended to deploy sensor heads of this size and sensitivity. Adapting them to fit requires modifications far outside the normal repair and maintenance parameters, and that limits the utility of our servomechs. We're doing a lot of hand-wiring and grunt work down here, we only have so many sets of hands, and it's going to get worse as the kits run out."

"Understood, Commander, but timing is critical to an orderly deployment. I advise you to expedite."

Honor cut the circuit and leaned back in her command chair with a tiny smile, and Nimitz rubbed his head against the side of her neck while he purred.

"You're *what?*" Captain Reynaud demanded, and Lieutenant Andreas Venizelos wrinkled his brow in puzzlement.

"I said I'm your customs and security officer, Captain. I'm sure Captain Harrington's dispatch will explain everything."

Reynaud accepted the message chip almost numbly, and Venizelos's puzzlement deepened. He couldn't understand why the ACS man looked so confused. It wasn't as it Venizelos were using any big words.

"Let me get this straight," Reynaud said after a moment "Your Captain Harrington actually expects you and you people to be quartered here at Control? He means to leave you here to support our operations?"

"Yes, Sir, *she* does." The darkly handsome lieutenant stressed the pronoun's gender, and Reynaud nodded, but he still looked so dumbfounded Venizelos was moved to continue. "Why do you seem so surprised, Sir?"

"Surprised?" Reynaud shook himself, then smiled oddly. "Yes, I suppose 'surprised' is a pretty good word, Lieutenant. Let me just put it this way. I've been chief controller in Basilisk for almost twenty months. Before that, I was senior assistant controller for damn near two years, and in all that time, you're the first—what did you call it? security and customs officer?—anyone's bothered to assign me. In fact, you may be the first one any station commander's *ever* bothered to assign to Control."

"I'm *what?*" Venizelos blurted, then flushed as he realized how exactly his tone matched Reynaud's original emphasis. The two of them stared at one another, and then the ACS captain began to grin.

"Now that I think about it," he said, "I believe I *did* read something in my original orders about the Navy being responsible for inspections and station security. Of course, it's been so long I can't be certain." He glanced at the habitat services tech standing at his shoulder. "Jayne, do me a favor and find the lieutenant's people some quarters and get them checked out on the basic emergency procedures, would you? I've got some station regs to plow through to find out what the hell we're supposed to do with them."

"Sure thing, Mike." The tech gestured to Ensign Wolversham, Venizelos's second in command, and Reynaud turned back to Venizelos, still grinning.

"In the meantime, Lieutenant, perhaps you'd care to join me in my data search?" Venizelos nodded, and

Reynaud's grin grew broader. "And perhaps you'd care to tell me a little something about your CO, as well. But take it slow, please. I'm not as young as I used to be, and I don't know if I'm ready for the concept of a *competent* senior officer on Basilisk Station!"

Andreas Venizelos grinned back, and for the first time in weeks, it felt completely natural.

Lieutenant Commander Dominica Santos tried not to swear as Lieutenant Manning handed her the latest projection.

They'd made the captain's deadline for the first three drone drops, but she was already heading for the fourth, and Santos glared at the chronometer with something like desperation. Less than six hours before they began deployment, and they had barely sixty percent of the drones switched over. They were losing ground steadily; there were five more drops to go; her people were drunk with fatigue; and, worse yet, they'd just run out of beacon kits. From here on out, they were going to have to build the damned conversion sets before they could even put the sensor heads *into* them!

She muttered resentfully to herself, compromising between bile and naval propriety by cursing too softly for anyone else to hear. What the hell was Harrington's problem?! If she were only willing to give Engineering two or three days, they could design a conversion set the maintenance and repair servomechs could turn out by the gross. As it was, laying out the design and troubleshooting the servomech software would take longer than building the goddamned things by hand! The captain didn't have to drive them this hard—and it wasn't fair for her to take out her own frustration with Young (whatever *that* was about!) on them.

She stopped swearing and looked around a bit guiltily. It hadn't exactly been fair of them to take out *their* resentment over the Fleet maneuvers on the captain, either, she supposed. And, she admitted unwillingly, she'd been as bad as the rest of them when it came to dragging around afterward— especially after she learned about their transfer to Basilisk Station. But still . . .

She flopped back in her chair and made herself draw a deep breath. All right. Fair or unfair didn't really come into it just now. She had a problem. She could either screen the Captain and tell her she couldn't make her deadline (and that thought wasn't at *all* attractive), or she could decide that she was chief engineer aboard this bucket of bolts and figure out how to solve it.

She swiveled the chair to face her terminal and began tapping keys. Okay. They couldn't make it if they built the beacon bodies entirely from scratch, and they didn't have time to design a new one, but . . . suppose they used the targeting bus from a Mark Fifty missile? If they yanked the warhead and sidewall penaids, they could jigger the sensor heads and astro packs into the empty spots—

No, wait! If they pulled the penaids, they should be able to convert the terminal guidance units from the same missiles into astro packs! That would save components all down the line, and the guidance units would just have to go into storage if they didn't use them. The bus thrusters wouldn't have anywhere near the endurance of a standard beacon kit, but they had *power* to burn, and the platforms only had to do their job for a couple of months. They weren't going to be moving around, so they wouldn't really need tons of endurance, either, now would they? And if she used standard components, she could use her missile maintenance mechs to do two-thirds of the work in a quarter of the time without any reprogramming at all!

Now, let's see. . . . If she sectioned the bus off here to clear the passive receptor arrays, then took out *this* panel to mate the signal booster with the main ECM emitter, then she could . . .

Lieutenant Commander Santos's fingers flew over her console with gathering speed, and a whole new sensor platform took shape on her display.

* * *

"Captain Harrington?"

Honor raised her eyes from the message board in her lap. Lieutenant (Junior Grade) Rafael Cardones, Venizelos's assistant and now *Fearless's* acting Tactical Officer, stood at her elbow, his painfully young face anxious.

"Yes, Lieutenant?"

"Uh, I think we have a problem, Ma'am," Cardones said uncomfortably. Honor raised an eyebrow, and he flinched. "It's, uh, it's the drones, Ma'am."

"What about them, Lieutenant?"

"I, well, you see— That is—" The young officer stopped and visibly took a grip on himself. "I'm afraid I misprogrammed the sensor parameters, Ma'am," he admitted in a rush. "I set them up for directional, not omnidirectional, and I, well, I think I made a little mistake in their telemetry packages, too. I . . . I can't seem to access them to accept remote reprogramming, Ma'am."

"I see." Honor leaned back in her chair and propped her elbows on its armrests, steepling her fingers under her chin. The lieutenant looked like a puppy waiting to be kicked. Worse, he looked like a puppy who thought he deserved to be kicked. His humiliation was obvious, and she wanted to pat his head and tell him everything would be all right, but she stepped on the surge of compassion.

"Well, Lieutenant," she went on after a moment, "what do you suggest we do about it?"

"*Me*, Ma'am?" Cardones almost squeaked. "I don't—" He stopped and inhaled. "I suppose we'll have to pick them up and reprogram, Ma'am," he said at last.

"Not acceptable," Honor said coolly. He stared at her in consternation, and she had to bite her tongue rather firmly. A more experienced tactical officer would already have seen the solution. Recon probe sensor heads were designed to tie directly into their mother ship's tactical data net, and the tac channel was dedicated. It couldn't have been affected by any mistakes he'd made in his telemetry programming because it was hardwired to prevent that very accident. Going in through the tac channel would be difficult—more because of the time involved than because of the task's complexity—but it would allow the standard telemetry to be accessed and even completely reprogrammed from Cardones' console through the CIC update links.

Honor knew that, but she had no intention of telling him so. He should have known to approach McKeon before exposing himself to his captain's wrath—and McKeon should have supervised an officer this junior more closely in the first place. It was a point she intended to make—with both of them—in a fashion she hoped would stick.

"Well, Lieutenant?" she said at length. He blinked. "How do you intend to fix the problem?"

"I don't—" He stopped himself again and glanced away for a moment, then looked back at her. "Do . . . Would the Captain care to make a suggestion, Ma'am?"

"I would not." He wilted under her cool soprano, and she struggled to keep her compassion out of her eyes. "You're Tactical Officer aboard this ship, Mr. Cardones," she went on, her voice equally devoid of condemnation or sympathy. "The drones' programming was your responsibility. So is the correction of your problem. Deal with it, Lieutenant."

He gave her one more appealing look, then swallowed and nodded.

"Yes, Ma'am," he said in a tiny voice.

HMS *Fearless* made her final heading change and settled into the groove, decelerating for a smooth orbital insertion. Honor was back on the bridge, watching Medusa swell in the visual display and feeling the change in the atmosphere about her. The apathy of their arrival here had faded, and if it hadn't been replaced by the *esprit de corps* she might have wished for, her crew's current attitude was at least a vast improvement.

The last six days had been rough for everyone . . . and a close approximation to Hell for some. Lieutenant Commander Santos had good justification for her exhaustion. She'd practically driven her people with a whip when it became obvious Honor had no intention of slowing her drone deployment, but she'd driven herself even harder, and to her own amazement, she'd met every deadline. That last-minute design improvisation of hers had been little short of brilliant, and the drones were in place now. Dangerous holes remained, but at least Honor had a warning net covering seventy degrees either side of the ecliptic, and Santos seemed to be having some difficulty deciding whether she was more proud of her department's achievements or infuriated by her captain's demands.

Nor was she the only one caught between pride and resentment. Lieutenant Cardones, probably more to his own surprise than anyone else's, had actually managed to correct his mistakes with the drone programming. He'd been forced to go to McKeon for help with the remote reprogramming, just as Honor had hoped, and spent endless hours on the project, but he'd dealt with it. And, truth to tell, she was pleased by how well McKeon had responded. As nearly as she could tell, he hadn't raked Cardones over at all, despite what must have been a bitter recognition that he should have kept a closer eye on him in the first place, and from what she'd overheard, he'd subtly directed the youngster into finding the CIC links on his own.

By the time Webster had gotten the drone data collection net set up to her demanding satisfaction and Stromboli had computed two separate on-the-fly course corrections to double back for misdropped drones, every one of Honor's senior officers had been worn out, intensely irritated . . . and working as a team again at last. It wasn't the way she would have chosen, but if self-defense was the only way she could goad them off their posteriors, she could stand their resultant unhappiness.

She turned her head as McKeon stepped out of the bridge lift and settled down in the executive officer's chair. He was as stiff and formal as ever, but she'd gotten past his defenses a time or two in the last week—especially with Cardones. Something was eating at him, that was clear, yet she suspected he, at least, understood exactly what she was doing. And, wonder of wonders, he wasn't fighting her on it. She more than suspected that he resented the way she'd gone about goading her crew back to life, and he wasn't exactly bending over backwards to help, nor had she been able to decide why he'd disliked her so from the beginning, but his professionalism seemed to be getting the better of whatever it was. There was no spontaneity in their relationship, no interplay of ideas, and the situation remained far from ideal, but at least they both seemed willing to admit, if only to themselves, that there was a problem. That was a major advance, and she hoped they were both professional enough to rise above their apparent incompatibility.

She shrugged the thought aside and looked back at her tactical display, frowning as *Fearless* crept through the outer parking orbits and the holo dot of a single small ship glowed crimson.

It was a courier boat, little more than a pair of Warshawski sails and an inertial compensator crammed into the tiniest possible hull, but its presence made her acutely uneasy, for it had diplomatic immunity and it was registered to the People's Republic of Haven.

She chewed the inside of her lip, wondering why seeing it bothered her so. She'd known Haven had a consulate and trade legation here on Medusa, but she hadn't realized until she read Young's official download that they maintained a diplomatic courier boat permanently on station. Legally, there was no reason why they shouldn't, but logically, the only possible purpose for a full consular mission on Medusa was covert operations of some sort. A simple trade mission could have handled Haven's legitimate interests in its traffic through the Basilisk Terminus, and the

Medusan aborigines had nothing worth exporting, despite reports of "legitimate Havenite merchants" trading with them. Those reports worried Honor. The conquest-bloated Republic no longer had any privately-owned merchantmen, and it *had* to be losing money on any conceivable exchange basis with the Medusans. Which, as far as she was concerned, obviously meant they were up to something else. But what?

Intelligence gathering to keep an eye on in-system Fleet deployments and traffic through the Basilisk Terminus made some sense. Medusa was an awfully inconvenient distance from the terminus for that purpose, but it wasn't as if there were any closer planets they could use. Maintaining a presence in the system as a counter to Manticore's might also make sense, especially given the periodic parliamentary attempts the Liberals still mounted to get Manticore *out* of the system. For all she knew, the Havenite consulate might also be the headquarters for whatever espionage was being practiced within the Kingdom itself, though she would have thought Trevor's Star a better choice for that.

Whatever they were doing, she didn't like it, and she liked the presence of that courier boat even less. Consular dispatch bags had diplomatic immunity regardless of the carrier, and there were enough Havenite merchantmen in evidence to transport any dispatches the consul needed carried. The only advantage to tying up a courier boat on permanent station here was its greater speed—and the fact that the entire vessel had diplomatic immunity and so was immune to examination or search regardless of anything *else* it might be doing. To Honor's mind, that implied some deep-seated ulterior motive, but she was well aware of her own automatic suspicion of anything Haven did. It was entirely possible that the courier boat's presence was as innocent as the Republic claimed, that only her own paranoia insisted it wasn't.

Of course it was. And it was also possible Pavel Young hadn't deliberately set out to cut her throat.

She snorted as Chief Killian put *Fearless* into orbit with his customary flawless precision and signaled "Done with engines," then turned to glance at Webster.

"Com, please raise the Resident Commissioner's office. Inform Dame Estelle that I would appreciate her finding time to meet with me at her earliest convenience."

"Yes, Ma'am."

"Thank you."

She leaned back in her chair once more, listening. Reports murmured over the intercom as the impeller wedge and inertial compensator went down and the standby thrusters took over the automatic station-keeping function. Bridge ratings moved from station to station, tapping notes into memo pads, Lieutenant Brigham was buried in the cartography section with Stromboli and his senior yeoman, updating their records on the drone net, and Honor savored the routine, orderly way they went about their duties. Despite the wracking workload she'd dumped on these people, the ship was alive once more.

Now it was up to her to redirect that aliveness into a sense of teamwork which included her as their captain, not their taskmaster.

• CHAPTER NINE

Dame Estelle Matsuko, Knight of the Order of King Roger and Resident Commissioner for Planetary Affairs on the planet Medusa in the name of Her Majesty Elizabeth III, Queen of Manticore and Defender of the Realm, rose behind her desk as her office door slid open. The tall naval commander who stepped through moved with the graceful stride of muscles accustomed to a gravity a great deal higher than Medusa's .85 g, and the treecat on her shoulder looked around with interested green eyes. Dame Estelle examined the pair of them with equal but hidden curiosity even as she extended a hand in welcome.

"Commander Harrington."

"Commissioner." The commander's crisp, clipped accent was as clear an indication of her birth world as the treecat or the way she moved, and her grip was firm but carefully metered. Dame Estelle had felt the same sort of handshake from other Sphinxians—and the few who'd absent-mindedly forgotten to watch what they were doing made her grateful for the ones who remembered.

"Won't you be seated?" Dame Estelle offered as the commander released her hand, and her brain was busy making mental notations.

Harrington carried herself with assurance, and Dame Estelle revised her original age estimate upward by five years. She was a striking woman, with a pale, strongly sculpted face and large, expressive eyes almost as dark as Dame Estelle's own. Her hair was clipped shorter than most men's under the white beret, and she wore an unmistakable air of competent professionalism. A far cry,

the commissioner reflected, from the second-raters the
Navy had been dumping on her, especially since Janacek
took over the Admiralty. Yet there was a tension under
Harrington's disciplined surface. An uneasiness. At first
she'd thought it was her imagination, but a closer look at
the commander's companion had disabused her of that
notion. The treecat was curious about his surroundings,
yes, but his long, slender body was taut and wary, and
Dame Estelle had seen enough 'cats to recognize the pro-
tectiveness with which his tail wrapped about
Harrington's throat.

"I must say, Commander, that I was somewhat surprised
by Lord Young's sudden departure," Dame Estelle said,
and almost blinked at her visitor's reaction. She'd meant the
remark as simple small talk, yet its effect was profound.
Harrington didn't actually *move* a muscle, but she didn't
have to. Her eyes said it all, narrowing with a hard intensity
that was almost frightening, and the treecat was far less
restrained. He didn't—quite—hiss, but his flattened ears
and half-bared fangs made his position clear, and Dame
Estelle wondered what she'd said.

Then Harrington gave herself tiny shake. A hand
reached up to gentle the 'cat, and she nodded courteously
to the commissioner.

"I was a bit surprised myself, Commissioner." Her
soprano was cool and uninflected, a deliberate dispassion
that set Dame Estelle's mental antennae on edge. "I understand, however, that his refit requirements had become
more urgent than anyone in Manticore realized when my
own ship was dispatched here."

"I'm sure." Dame Estelle couldn't quite keep the sour
amusement out of her own voice, and Harrington cocked
her head slightly. Then she relaxed just a bit, and some of
the treecat's tension eased, as well. So. It hadn't been so
much what Dame Estelle had said as who she'd said it
about. Well, anyone who disliked Pavel Young couldn't be
all bad.

"I was also surprised—and pleased—by your willingness to visit my office, Commander," the commissioner went on. "I'm afraid we haven't had quite the close cooperation with the Navy I could have hoped for, particularly in the last three years or so."

Honor sat motionless but nodded mentally as Dame Estelle paused as if to invite a comment. "The last three years" just happened to coincide with Janacek's assumption of the First Lord's duties, and the slight, dark-skinned woman on the other side of the desk obviously wanted to discover how Honor herself viewed Basilisk's importance to the Kingdom. The right of a serving officer to criticize her superiors was limited, but her relationship with Dame Estelle could well prove critical to her own success or failure.

"I'm sorry to hear that, Dame Estelle," she said, choosing her words with care, "and I hope we can improve the situation. That's one reason for my visit. It's a courtesy call, of course, but my original orders to Basilisk assumed that Lord Young would be remaining as senior officer, and I'm afraid my background brief on current conditions here was pretty general. I'd hoped you could enlighten me further and tell me about any specific requirements you may have."

Dame Estelle inhaled deeply and sat back in her chair in obvious relief—tinged, Honor noted, with more than a trace of surprise. That surprise both gratified and embarrassed her. She couldn't resist a sense of justification at the commissioner's reaction to her explanation, yet what she'd asked for was the minimum possible requirement if she was to meet her responsibilities, and the implication that the Navy had failed so signally in its duties as to engender Matsuko's surprise shamed her.

"I am very pleased to hear you say that, Commander," Dame Estelle said after a moment. She tilted her chair back and crossed her legs, folding her hands on her raised knee, and her voice was far less cautious. "I'll be delighted to tell you anything I can, but suppose you begin by telling me what you already know? That way I can fill in the holes without boring you."

Honor nodded and coaxed Nimitz down into her lap. The tension had flowed out of his wiry body, a clear sign he approved of Matsuko, and he curled in a contented circle and purred as she stroked him.

"I think I'm pretty well up to speed on the Junction operations, Ma'am, and I realize those aren't really your province, anyway. I'm much more concerned about my support and security duties here on Medusa. My data seem to be a bit out of date, judging from the number of freighters in orbit. I hadn't understood that there was so much trade with the planetary surface?"

"No, that's a fairly recent development." Dame Estelle frowned thoughtfully. "You know about the enclaves?"

"In a general sense. They're basically trading stations, aren't they?"

"Yes and no. Under the terms of the Act of Annexation, the Kingdom claimed the star system as a whole and established a protectorate over the Medusans but specifically renounced sovereignty over their planet. In effect, this entire planet is one huge reservation for the natives, with the exception of specific sites designated for off-worlder enclaves. That's not the normal procedure for establishing territoriality, but we were more concerned with the Junction terminus than planetary real estate, and the act attempted to make that distinction completely explicit. In fact, it obligates the Kingdom to grant the Medusans complete autonomy 'at the earliest practicable moment' just to make our lack of imperial ambitions crystal clear."

Dame Estelle's expression made her opinion of the Act of Annexation plain.

"As a direct result of the nobility of our motives," she continued, "the legal position might be considered something of a gray area. One or two nations—like Haven—argue that a protectorate without sovereignty is legally meaningless. Under that interpretation of interstellar law—which, I'm sorry to say, can be argued on the basis of some fairly strong precedents—Medusa is unclaimed territory, and I have no authority at all to issue instructions to off-worlders on its surface. That's the official position of the Havenite consul, by the way. Her Majesty's Government takes a different view, and as they say, possession is nine-tenths of the law, but the provisions of the Act of Annexation specifically delimit my powers.

"Under the terms of my commission, I have the authority to take any action necessary 'to prevent the exploitation of the indigenous race,' but I do *not* have the authority to tell other nations that they may or may not establish enclaves here. I've asked for it, and I think the Government would like to give it to me, but they haven't been able to get the necessary amendments through Parliament. So I can restrict other people's enclave *locations*, regulate their trade with the Medusans, and generally play policeman after they get here, but I can't deny them access."

Honor nodded. The Liberals had been so busy making certain Manticore couldn't exploit the "hapless natives" that they'd left the door wide open for less principled people to walk right through.

"All right." Dame Estelle swung her chair gently from side to side and frowned at the ceiling. "Initially, there were very few enclaves here on Medusa. As you no doubt know, the Medusans are somewhere in the equivalent of the late Bronze Age, and aside from some genuinely beautiful artifacts, they have very little of value in terms of interstellar trade. As a result, there was little pressure to open planetary markets, and the Native Protection Agency had the situation pretty well in hand.

"During my own tenure, however, that situation has changed, not so much because of trade with the Medusans as because of the growing volume of traffic through the terminus here. I suppose it was inevitable that an orbital warehousing and distribution network should spring up, particularly since cargoes can be transshipped here without paying the higher duties and wages incurred in Manticore. There are, of course, other incentives," she added dryly, and Honor's lips twitched unwillingly.

"At any rate, quite a few merchant houses started establishing local planet-side offices to manage their part of the network as it grew. That's where most of the enclaves came from, and most of what they need has to be shipped in from offworld, so a lot of the local space-to-surface activity is a matter of servicing those needs.

"At the same time, merchants being merchants, there's been growing pressure to establish trade with the Medusans as a sideline to help defray their operating expenses. It's mostly very small scale—precious stones, native art, *tillik* moss for the spice trade, an occasional *bekhnor* hide or ivory shipment, that sort of thing—but the Medusans' needs are so limited that trade goods can be extremely cheap. The Medusans are only just learning how to forge decent iron and wretched steel, so you can imagine how they value duralloy knives or axeheads, and modern textiles are equally prized. In fact, the poor devils are being robbed blind by most of the factors; they have no concept of how little the goods they're trading for cost the importers. Nor do they realize how easily they could become utterly dependent on those goods and the traders who supply them. We've tried to limit the dependency syndrome by slapping fairly tough ceilings on the levels of technology we'll let anyone introduce, but both the Medusans and the off-worlders resent our interference."

She paused, and Honor nodded again.

"The really frustrating part of it," Dame Estelle went on more forcefully, "is that *Manticoran* merchants are specifically restricted by Act of Parliament from trading anything more advanced than muscle-powered technology to the natives lest we make them dependent upon us. Mind you, I think there's some wisdom to that, but it means our own people are at least as irked with us as some of the other off-worlders, possibly even more so, since our proximity would give them a major competitive edge. That makes it hard for us to get an accurate reading on the entire process. Not even Manticorans go out of their way to cooperate with us, so the NPA and I are virtually outsiders on a planet nominally under our protection. Worse, I'm pretty sure the 'native trade' is being used as a cover for covert exchanges of illegal goods between off-worlders—including Manticorans—but I can't stop it, I can't prove it, and I can't even seem to get the powers that be back home to *care* about it!"

She paused and unclenched the hands which had tightened on her knee, then gave a wry chuckle.

"Sorry, Commander. I think I just punched one of my own buttons."

"Don't apologize, Commissioner. It sounds like you're even more hamstrung than I thought you were."

"Oh, it's not really as bad as I sometimes feel it is," Dame Estelle said judiciously. "The physical restriction of the enclaves to a single central location here in the Delta, coupled with my authority to control the use of off-world transport outside them, limits the physical reach of the trade networks. It doesn't stop off-worlder-to-off-worlder smuggling, if in fact there is any, and it can't completely stop the flow of off-world goods to the Medusans, but it slows it and means that most of them trickle through native merchants before they reach more distant destinations. And, truth to tell, concerned as I am about the impact on the Medusans, I'm even more concerned—as the Crown's local representative—by what else may be going on under the surface."

"Oh?" Honor sat straighter, and Nimitz raised his head as she stopped stroking his ears.

"I've reported my suspicions—well, 'feelings' might be a more honest word for them—that there's more involved here than native trade, or even smuggling, to Countess Marisa, but no one back home seems particularly concerned." Matsuko gave her a sharp glance, but Honor kept her face carefully expressionless. Countess Marisa of New Kiev was Minister for Medusan Affairs; she was also the leader of the Liberal Party.

Dame Estelle snorted softly, as if Honor's very lack of expression confirmed her own opinion of her superior, then sighed.

"I suppose I could be paranoid, Commander, but I just can't avoid the conclusion that . . . certain parties are much more concerned with their trading rights than the dollar value of the trade itself—legal and illegal alike—could possibly justify."

"Would those 'certain parties' happen to include the Republic of Haven?" Honor asked quietly, and the commissioner nodded.

"Exactly. Their consulate has an awfully large staff, in my opinion, and I *don't* think they need that many 'trade attaches.' Granted, a lot of their traffic passes through the terminus—the western third of the Republic is closer to Basilisk than it is to Trevor's Star, after all—but they keep pushing for more freedom to trade with the Medusans, as well. In fact, their consulate is officially accredited to one of the local Medusan city-states, not to Her Majesty's Government. Both the Government and Haven know that's a legal fiction under the circumstances, and I've been able to sit on them reasonably successfully so far, but it seems to me that what they're really after is more contact with the natives, a more active role in shaping the Medusans' relations with off-worlders generally."

"As a counter presence to our own?"

"Exactly!" Matsuko repeated even more enthusiastically. She produced her first genuine smile of the meeting and nodded firmly. "I *think* they're hoping the anti-annexationists back home may get their way after all. If that happens, Haven would be well-placed to move in and assert its own sovereignty, especially if they were already involved in native affairs. Lord knows they don't need any more motive than controlling the terminus, but they like to have 'moral justifications' for their propaganda machine to report to their own population and the Solarian League. That's why they're so stubborn about maintaining the official position that the terms of the Act of Annexation amount to a unilateral renunciation on our part of any legal claim in the first place. If we do pull out, they want the planet to fall into their laps like a ripe plumapple."

"And you think that's all it is?" Honor pressed.

"I . . . don't know," the commissioner said slowly. "I can't see any other advantage for them, but I can't quite shake the notion that there's something else going on. My people and I are keeping as close an eye on their consulate and factors as we can, and there certainly hasn't been anything concrete I could report to Countess Marisa, but there's— call it an attitude on their part I don't like." She shook herself, and her smile turned wry. "Of course, I don't like *them*, either, and that may be coloring my perceptions."

Honor nodded slowly, leaning back in her own chair and pursing her lips in thought. Dame Estelle did not strike her as a woman who leapt to conclusions, whatever her prejudices might be.

"At any rate," Matsuko said more briskly, "that's the basic off-worlder situation here on Medusa. As far as the natives themselves are concerned, my NPA people are spread too thin and too overworked to provide the kind of coverage I'd prefer, but our relations with the Medusans have been remarkably good ever since our arrival—far better than seems to be usual when such disparate cultures come into contact. Some of the clan chiefs want the restrictions on higher-tech imports lifted, which is causing some strain, but by and large we're in pretty good shape, especially with the city-states here in the Delta. We do have a few problems in more remote areas of the Outback, but the thing that I find most worrisome just now is that we've been picking up hints of an upsurge in the Medusans' use of *mekoha* over the last year or so."

Honor raised an eyebrow, and Dame Estelle shrugged.

"*Mekoha* is an indigenous drug. It's difficult to refine, by local standards, and I *don't* like the effect it has on its users, but it's nothing new. I suppose it bothers me because one of the first signs of a self-destructing aboriginal culture always seems to be an increase in the use of drugs and intoxicants, and I'd hate to see the Medusans go that route. My predecessor, Baron Hightower, and I have adopted the position that the original Medusan culture is inevitably doomed by our mere presence and the technological temptation we offer, but I'd like to think we can replace it with a fusion of their original values with more advanced technology—do it without their losing themselves, if you will. That's why both Baron Hightower and I have devoted our efforts to controlling the *rate* of change as much as we can. I'm afraid it's also why I rather resent the amount of effort I have to divert from that goal to keeping an eye on off-worlders, but that's part and parcel of the basic effort to keep from destroying the Medusans' cultural integrity."

"So your major requirement from me will be to assist in managing the comings and goings between the enclaves and orbital traffic?"

"I'd say that was pretty much correct," Dame Estelle agreed. "I'd like to be able to call on your Marine complement in the case of any emergency down here, but, as I say, we seem to be pretty well covered so far. If you could take over the inspection of ship-to-surface shuttles and general traffic control, it would free up a lot of my NPA personnel."

"You mean Young didn't even—?" Honor shut her mouth with a click before she said something even more revealing, and the commissioner coughed into her hand to hide a laugh.

"Very well, Commissioner, I think we can handle that. Give me a day or two to work out the details, and I'll have a pair of cutters on permanent standby for shuttle inspection. If you can spare me whoever you've had managing the situation from your end, I'd like a chance to pick their brains before we set it up."

"Done," Dame Estelle said promptly.

"I'd also like to set up some sort of permanent liaison officer," Honor went on thoughtfully. "I had to detach almost ten percent of my naval personnel to provide customs parties and security personnel for Basilisk Control—" she ignored the commissioner's raised eyebrows "—and that leaves me more understrength than I'd like. I imagine it's going to get worse when we start controlling and inspecting shuttle traffic, too. Do you have someone you could assign to me to coordinate with your office?"

"I not only can provide you a liaison officer, Commander, but I will be *delighted* to do so. And I think I have just the man for you. Major Barney Isvarian is my senior NPA field man, but he was a Marine sergeant before he retired and moved over to my side of the street. I wouldn't want him off-planet on any long-term basis, but I could certainly lend him to you for a few days. He's a good man and an old Medusa hand, and he's been involved in our own shuttle inspection efforts. How does that sound?"

"It sounds just fine, Commissioner," Honor said with a smile. She rose, extending her hand once more while Nimitz flowed back up to her shoulder. "Thank you. And thank you for the background, as well. I won't tie up any more of your time, but please feel free to screen me if there's anything I can do for you or if there's anything you feel should be called to my attention."

"I certainly will, Commander." Dame Estelle stood to grasp her hand once more, and her eyes were warm. "And thank *you*." She didn't specify exactly what she was thanking her for, and Honor suppressed a wry snort of amusement.

The commissioner walked around her desk to escort her to the door and paused for another handshake before she left. The door slid shut, and Dame Estelle returned to her chair with a bemused expression. She sat and pressed a button on her communications panel.

"George, get hold of Barney Isvarian, would you? I've got a new job for him."

"Right," her executive assistant said laconically, then paused. "How'd it go, boss?" he asked after a moment.

"It went well, George. In fact, I think it went *very* well," Dame Estelle said, and released the button with a smile.

• CHAPTER TEN

"—no help at all. So since the Navy wasn't available, we've just done the best we could on our own, Commander." Major Barney Isvarian, Medusan Native Protection Agency, was a short, sturdy man. He sat almost painfully erect in the comfortable chair, his Marine background showing in his discomfort at sitting in the presence of a warship's captain, but there was no apology in his face or voice.

"I understand, Major." Honor gestured for steward MacGuiness to replenish Isvarian's coffee cup and sipped her own cocoa, using the mug to cover a sideways glance at Alistair McKeon. The executive officer had said very little while Isvarian listed all the things the Navy hadn't done for Medusa, but she sensed the discomfort lurking behind his stiffly formal facade and wondered if he felt as ashamed as she did.

"All right." She set her mug aside and nodded. "As I understand what you and Dame Estelle are saying, Major Isvarian, your greatest immediate need is for help with inspection of orbital transfers and space-to-ground traffic. Is that correct?"

"Yes, Ma'am." Isvarian shrugged. "As I say, we do our best, but most of us don't really know what to look for . . . or where to find it, if it's hidden. A fair number of us have previous military experience, but it's not the right kind."

Honor nodded again. The NPA's officers and troopers were mainly ex-Army, ex-Marine, or regular police. It wasn't the sort of job which would attract retired Navy personnel, and had the Fleet been doing its job, their skills would have been of little value to the NPA, anyway.

"We know damned well—pardon, Ma'am—that they're getting stuff past us, but we don't know enough about cargo shuttles to find it, and it's even worse aboard ship."

"Understood. I think we'll be able to take care of that part of it, but we're shorthanded. If I can scare up inspection parties for you, do you think the NPA could help us out with flight crews for our cutters?"

"We can do better than that, Ma'am," Isvarian said. "Dame Estelle managed to, ah, find three Fleet pinnaces about a year back, and we've got two boarding shuttles on our official equipment list. I'm pretty sure we can put all five of them at your disposal, with enough NPA types to fill in any holes in their complements."

"Now, that, Major, is good news," Honor said warmly, wondering just how Dame Estelle's people had managed to "find" Fleet small craft. Especially armed ones. But she wasn't about to question such unanticipated good fortune. She'd been afraid *Fearless* herself would be tied down ferrying her slow, shorter-legged cutters back and forth between parking orbits.

She rubbed the tip of her nose with a forefinger for a moment, thinking hard, then nodded to herself.

"I think we can come up with pilots, boarding officers, and inspection parties for all of them, Major. What we'll need from you will be com officers, flight engineers, and ground-side maintenance personnel. Can do?"

"Can do, Ma'am!" Isvarian grinned as he threw the Royal Manticoran Marine Corps' motto back at her.

"Good. Then I think that only leaves the matter of general traffic control. How have you been handling that?"

"Not very well, Ma'am. We've got a flight center down in the commissioner's compound, but it was really intended for atmospheric control only. Even there, the designers never anticipated the sheer number of off-worlders we've got wandering around these days. We're short on controllers and radar, and diverting what we've got to space control's left an awful lot of Outback airspace completely uncovered."

"I see." Honor glanced at McKeon. "Exec? Suppose we reconfigure a dozen or so survey sats and tie their weather radar into the air traffic control net?"

"We could." This time it was McKeon's turn to rub his nose and frown. "We're making a mighty big dent in our equipment list, Ma'am," he warned.

"I know, but I don't see an option . . . and it's there to be used, Exec."

McKeon nodded, eyes slitted in thought, and Honor wondered if he even realized he'd said "we're" instead of "you're."

"Then I think we can do it, but their radar sets aren't going to get as good a paint off of an aircraft as standard ground radar would, and they're not set up for air traffic-quality doppler. They're intended more for radar mapping and weather observation, not real look-down capability, and air masses don't move that fast." He frowned some more. "If you'll give me a day or two with Santos and Cardones, I think between us we can come up with a fix to refine their target differentiation, and we should be able to work in a decent doppler and ranging capability, too, especially if we set them up in pairs. It'll be rough, but it should work."

"Good," Honor said. The survey satellites were standard issue and rarely used, since regular warships seldom pulled survey duty. They were also short-ranged and simple-minded, but they should suffice for this. Of course, McKeon was right about the carnage she was wreaking with her equipment list. Just her sensor network had cost the RMN somewhere in the vicinity of two hundred million dollars, even assuming most of the probe heads were recoverable, and she'd personally signed for every penny of it. But there was no other way to get the job done, and if the Admiralty objected to the cost, they should have assigned either more ships or narrower mission parameters.

Besides, the survey sats would "only" up the price tag by another half-million or so apiece.

"In that case," she went on to Isvarian, "I'd like to leave air-breathing traffic in NPA hands and set up a space traffic control center staffed by our people." She toyed with her cocoa cup for a moment while she considered. "Better make it a ground station, I think, in case something comes up out-system and we get called away. In fact, we might install it right next door to your air traffic people so they can coordinate better. What do you think, Exec?"

"I think we're going to be lucky if we're still at half-strength when the dust settles," McKeon replied, using the calculator mode of his memo pad to check figures. "By the time we crew those pinnaces and shuttles, we'll have another forty of our people on detached duty, Ma'am. We can probably use Marines to eke out the ratings in the inspection crews, but when you add enough Fleet people to man a control center on top of that—" He shrugged.

"Agreed, but I think it's necessary," Honor said quietly. She kept her gaze on McKeon's face, but her eyes cut sideways at Isvarian for a moment, reminding the exec of their audience, and McKeon nodded. It wasn't a happy nod, nor a very graceful one, but it was a nod.

"We've still got that recon head we reserved to cover Medusa in our absence," she continued after a moment. "Limited endurance won't be much of a problem if we can get at it for regular service, so we can go ahead and deploy it in high orbit to cover the far side of the planet and use our onboard instrumentation to feed the ground center from this side. If we have to pull out, the air-search radar we save with the survey sats can revert to covering space traffic in our sector."

"Who were you planning to put in command groundside, Ma'am?" McKeon asked.

"Um." Honor drummed on the tabletop for a moment, pleased to see him engaged with the problem but wishing he'd made the next step in reassuming his responsibilities and suggested someone. He'd known most of her officers months—in some cases, years—longer than she had. But she decided to concentrate on what he *was* doing after their unpromising beginning and furrowed her forehead in thought.

"I think either Webster or Stromboli," she said finally. She felt McKeon start to protest, then stop himself as he ran through the possible candidates in his own mind. "I'd really rather use Webster," she went on, half to herself and half to him. "He's younger, but I think he's more aggressive and confident. Unfortunately, we need someone with a background in astrogation and traffic control, and that means Stromboli."

"What about Ensign Tremaine?" McKeon countered. Tremaine was *Fearless's* boat bay control officer and something of a prodigy in the management of his assets, but Honor shook her head.

"Not for the controller's slot. And we need someone senior enough to assume overall command of the detachment, ground-side and upstairs, if *Fearless* has to pull out. I'd prefer to kill two birds with one stone and make that our control officer. Besides, I think we'll need Tremaine to manage the actual inspection flights."

"That'll bump Panowski to acting astrogator," McKeon mused, tapping a fingertip on his memo pad. Then he surprised both Honor and himself with a grin. "Actually, I think that might be good for him, Ma'am. He's got a tendency to coast unless someone keeps after him, and Max has been too easy on him."

"In that case, let's definitely make it Stromboli," Honor said, "with Tremaine as his exec. We'll need a few good POs to command the small craft, and I'd like them to have some experience in customs work, if possible. Do we have anyone who does?"

McKeon turned to one of the conference table's full-sized terminals and tapped the query into it. Then he shook his head.

"Sorry, Ma'am. Chief Killian did a stint as the regular helmsman for an SD's boarding officer two commissions ago, but that's as close as we've got."

"And I am *not* going to give up Chief Killian." Honor frowned, then smiled. "I think I may have another idea, though." She depressed an intercom key.

"Officer of the watch," Lieutenant Stromboli's voice replied.

"This is the Captain, Lieutenant. Please ask the bosun to come to my briefing room."

"Aye, aye, Ma'am."

Honor released the button and leaned back, hiding her enjoyment behind a serene expression as Isvarian and McKeon looked first at her and then at one another. She hummed softly to herself, letting them wonder, until the hatch hissed open.

Senior Chief Boatswain's Mate Sally MacBride stepped through it and braced to attention. MacBride's left sleeve bore five gold hash marks, each representing three Manticoran years—over five T-years—of service, and she was just about due for a sixth. She was a sturdy, level-eyed woman, and the senior non-commissioned officer aboard *Fearless*.

"The Captain sent for me?"

"Yes, thank you, Bosun." Honor nodded for MacBride to stand easy. "I need some people with rather specialized talents, and I thought you might be able to help me out."

"Whatever the Captain requires, Ma'am." MacBride was a native of Gryphon, as were a surprisingly high percentage of the RMN's noncoms, given the planet's relatively sparse population. Manticore-B's single habitable planet was the least hospitable and last settled of the Manticore System's three Earth-like worlds, and native Manticorans and Sphinxians argued that Gryphons only joined the Navy to escape Gryphon's weather. For their own part, the Queen's Gryphon-born subjects seemed to feel a sort of divine mission to keep the sissies of Manticore-A in shape. The divergence of opinion led to occasional off-duty "discussions" that could make them a bit difficult to live with, but Honor was glad she had MacBride. The bosun was the indispensable link between the bridge officers and enlisted people aboard any warship, and MacBride had all the tough, professional confidence of her years of service.

"I'm not going to ask you to betray any secrets, Bosun," Honor said, "but what I'm looking for are people who—from their own experience, let us say—would be intimately familiar with the best way to hide contraband aboard a shuttle or a starship." MacBride's left eyebrow rose fractionally; otherwise there was no change in her expression at all. "I need them to form the core of the customs inspection party I'll be detailing to Medusa, so in addition to their, um, expertise, I need people with initiative and discretion. Can you find them for me?"

"How many people was the Captain thinking of?"

"Oh, let's say fifteen," Honor said, ignoring the atypical amusement glinting in McKeon's gray eyes. "We'll be running three pinnaces and two shuttles, and I'd like to have one in each watch aboard each of them."

"I see." MacBride thought for a moment, then nodded. "Yes, Ma'am. I can find them. Will the Captain require anything else?"

"No, Bosun. Let the Exec have a list by the end of watch."

"Aye, aye, Ma'am." MacBride braced back to attention, turned smartly, and disappeared through the hatch. It closed behind her.

"Excuse me, Captain," Major Isvarian said in a very careful voice, "but did I just hear you ask the bosun to find you fifteen *smugglers* to man our customs flights?"

"Of course not, Major. This is a Queen's ship. What would we be doing with smugglers on board? On the other hand, I'm certain that, over the years, certain of my personnel have observed other personnel who have attempted to conceal proscribed materials aboard ship. Sad to say, some may even have known individuals who engaged in black market activities aboard naval vessels. I simply asked the bosun to find me some of those observers."

"I see," Isvarian murmured. He took a large sip of coffee and put his cup back down. "I see, indeed."

"Captain?"

Honor looked up as Surgeon Commander Suchon stuck her head through the open briefing room hatch. *Fearless's* doctor looked even more sour than usual, and she carried a data chip in her right hand. She held the chip as if it were a small, dead animal, and Honor felt a stronger surge of distaste for her as she recognized it.

"Yes, Doctor?"

"May I speak with you a minute?" Suchon asked. Whined, really, Honor thought.

"Come in, Doctor." Honor tried not to sigh and pressed the button by her terminal, closing the hatch behind Suchon as the commander crossed to the table and sat— without an invitation. That last action irritated Honor out of all proportion to the provocation, and she sat on her temper rather firmly.

Suchon sat silently, face screwed up in obvious indecision over how to proceed. Honor waited for a moment, then arched her eyebrows.

"What is it, Doctor?" she inquired.

"It's— Well, it's about these orders, Captain." Suchon raised her hand to display the data chip, and Honor nodded.

"What about them?"

"Captain, I don't think it's a good idea to— I mean, you've detached Lieutenant Montoya and all four of my best sick berth attendants to the customs parties, and I need them here in *Fearless*. I can't guarantee my ability to meet my medical responsibilities to the ship without them."

Suchon leaned back in her chair as she completed her sentence. There was a certain smugness in her expression, the look of someone who has just delivered an ultimatum to a superior officer, and Honor regarded her levelly for several seconds.

"I'm afraid you're just going to have to get along without them, Doctor," she said at last, and Suchon sat back upright with a jerk.

"But I can't! If I have to detach them, the sickbay workload will be impossible, and Montoya is my sole physician assistant!"

"I'm aware of that." Honor made herself maintain a level tone, but there was very little liking in her brown eyes. "I'm also aware that it's the Navy's responsibility to provide medical personnel to check the health and immunization records of any individuals visiting Medusa's surface. Every other department aboard this ship is contributing to those customs parties, Doctor. I'm afraid Medical will just have to carry its share of the burden, as well."

"But I can't do it, I tell you!" Suchon more than half-snapped. "Perhaps you don't quite understand the responsibilities Medical faces, Ma'am. We're not like oth—"

"That will be enough, Doctor." Honor's voice had not risen, but it carried such cold, quiet venom that Suchon jerked back in her chair in shock. Icy brown eyes surveyed her with deadly dispassion, and her dark face paled.

"What you mean, Doctor," Honor went on after a moment in that same cold voice, "is that if I detach your attendants—and especially Montoya, who's been carrying two-thirds of your load ever since I came aboard—*you* will be required to get up out of your comfortable chair and attend to your duties yourself."

Suchon's face darkened as flushed anger replaced the paleness of shock. She opened her mouth, but Honor stopped her with a raised hand and a thin smile.

"Before you explain to me that I don't understand the arcana of your profession, Commander," she said softly, "I should, perhaps, mention to you that both of my parents are physicians." Suchon paled once more. "In fact, my father was a surgeon commander himself before his retirement. Doctor Alfred Harrington—perhaps you've heard of him?"

Her smile grew even thinner as Suchon recognized the name. Alfred Harrington had been Assistant Chief of Neurosurgery at Basingford Medical Center, the Fleet's main hospital on Manticore, before his retirement.

"As a result, Doctor, I think you'll find I have quite an adequate grasp of precisely what your duties to this ship entail. And, I might add, since the topic has come up, that I'm not at all satisfied with the way you've discharged those duties since I assumed command." Her smile vanished, and Suchon swallowed.

"If, however, the five individuals you've mentioned are, indeed, indispensable to *Fearless*'s Medical Department," Honor went on after a short, pregnant pause, "I'm certain I can make other arrangements to keep them aboard. Of course, in that eventuality it will be necessary to find some single individual with sufficient medical experience to replace all five of them to assign to the customs detachment. Someone like you, Doctor Suchon."

She held the surgeon commander's eyes with a cold, level stare, and it was Suchon who looked away.

"Was there anything else, Doctor?" Honor asked softly. The physician gave a choppy headshake, and Honor nodded.

"Dismissed, then, Doctor." She returned her attention to her terminal, and Commander Suchon rose and walked silently from the compartment.

Lieutenant Andreas Venizelos stood with his memo board under his arm and smiled politely at the red-faced Havenite merchant skipper.

"—so you can take yourself, *and* your mangy 'customs party,' and go straight to hell!" The Havenite finished his diatribe and stood glaring at the slim officer before him.

"I'm afraid that won't be possible, Captain Merker," the lieutenant replied with punctilious courtesy. "According to Basilisk Control, you transshipped cargo at—" he consulted his memo board "—Orbital Warehouse Baker-Tango-One-Four. As I'm certain you're aware, Sir, that constitutes a materials transfer in Manticoran space. As such, under Paragraph Ten, Subsection Three, of the Commercial Regulations as amended by Parliament in 278 A.L., the senior customs officer is required to inspect your cargo before passing you for transit to the Junction's central nexus. Accordingly, I'm afraid I must insist on carrying out my duties before I can clear you for transit. I am, of course, extremely sorry for any inconvenience this may cause."

Captain Merker had turned an alarming shade of puce and sputtered incoherently. Venizelos simply cocked his head and waited with undiminished courtesy while he got his vocal apparatus unjammed.

"Goddamn it! I've been making this run for five T-years," the captain finally roared, "and this is the first time some tight-assed little faggot in a pretty uniform's boarded *my* ship and ordered *me* to heave to for inspection! I'll see you damned first, by God!"

"Perhaps, Sir," Venizelos said, allowing his smile to fade, "but if you choose to refuse inspection, you will be denied transit rights."

"And how the fuck do you think you're going to stop me, pretty boy?" Merker sneered.

"By firing into your ship if you attempt to transit," Venizelos said, and there was no give at all in his ice-cold voice.

The merchant skipper stopped in mid-sneer and gave the slightly-built lieutenant an incredulous stare.

"That would be an act of war!"

"On the contrary, Sir, it would be a simple exercise of the municipal police power in Manticoran space in strict accordance with recognized interstellar law."

"You wouldn't dare," Merker said in a more conversational tone. "You're bluffing."

"I am an officer of the Royal Manticoran Navy, Sir—" Venizelos felt an undeniable rush of adrenalin and pleasure as he faced the burly captain squarely "—and the Royal Manticoran Navy does not 'bluff.' "

He held the Havenite officer's eye steadily, and the captain's choler cooled visibly. He dropped his eyes to scowl at the deck for just a moment, then shrugged angrily. "Oh, suit yourself!"

"Uh, Captain Merker?" The freighter's purser, who had stood silent throughout the exchange, looked undeniably anxious.

"Well, what is it?" Merker growled.

"Well, Sir, it's just that I think— That is, I'm afraid there may be a few, um, errors in our manifest." Sweat dotted the purser's forehead as his harassed captain turned his scowl on him. "I'm, ah, certain they were, er, simple oversights," he continued. "I can— I mean, my staff and I can clear them up and be ready for inspection in, um, two or three hours? Sir?"

He stared at his captain appealingly, and Merker's face began to congest with fury once more. Venizelos observed its color with interest and cleared his throat.

"Ah, excuse me, Captain Merker?" The captain whirled on him with clenched fists, and the lieutenant shrugged apologetically. "I can certainly understand how these little accidents happen, Sir, and I'm entirely willing to allow your purser time to straighten out his records. Unfortunately, that will mean that your ship will lose its place in the outbound queue, and I'm afraid we probably won't be able to get back around to you until sometime tomorrow morning."

"*Tomorrow morning!*" Merker exploded. "You mean I have to cool my heels in this misbegotten rat hole of a—!" He chopped himself off and gave the hapless purser a deadly glare, then turned back to Venizelos with a snarl.

"All right! If I have to, I have to, but my embassy on Manticore is going to hear about this, Lieutenant!"

"Of course, Sir." Venizelos clicked to attention, nodded pleasantly, and marched smartly back down the tube to his pinnace. The hatch slid shut, the tube disengaged, and his pilot hit the thrusters to carry them beyond their impeller wedge's safety perimeter before lighting off the main drive.

Venizelos deposited his memo board on his pull-out desk, flopped back into his chair, and whistled a popular ditty as the pinnace turned towards the next ship on his list, a big, battered Silesian freighter. His second pinnace hovered respectfully off the Havenite ship's flank like a pointed reminder until Merker lit off his own drive and headed back beyond the departure threshold.

"Jesus, Andreas!" Hayne Duvalier, Captain Reynaud's liaison to Venizelos's customs party, stared at him in patent disbelief. "You wouldn't really have fired into him. . . would you?"

"Yep," Venizelos said.

"But—"

"I'm only doing my job, Hayne."

"I know, but for Chrissake, Andreas! We haven't enforced the com regs out here in— Hell, I don't think they've *ever* been enforced! ACS never had the manpower for it."

"I know." Venizelos turned his chair to face him. "In fact, since I got here, I've started to realize that a lot of things that should have been done never have. I'm not faulting Captain Reynaud and your people, either. It's not your job—it's ours, and we haven't been doing it. Well, we're doing it now."

"Somehow I sort of doubt your captain's going to thank you for all the ruckus it's going to raise," Duvalier said dubiously.

"Maybe not, but she gave me my orders, and one thing I can tell you about Commander Harrington, Hayne—

when she gives an order, she expects it to be obeyed. Period."

"Sounds like a real hardass to me," Duvalier grumbled.

"Oh, she is," Venizelos said with a smile. "In fact, I'm just starting to realize how hard a hardass she is. And you know something, Hayne? I like it."

• CHAPTER ELEVEN

Lieutenant Max Stromboli straightened with a bone-deep sigh and racked his tools neatly. Other members of his minute staff were busy elsewhere, mounting the transmission dishes on the tower roof, but there were too few of them for him to stand back and leave it all to the techs. Besides, he still installed a pretty mean circuit board himself, he thought, regarding the console with proprietary pride.

Not that pride was the first thing he'd felt on arriving on Medusa's surface. He'd just started to feel himself slipping back into the groove aboard *Fearless* after the shock of being banished to Basilisk Station, when he'd found himself banished yet again. This time clear out of the ship!

He dropped into the cushioned bucket seat and brought his panel on line, punching into the new space control data net fed by *Fearless*'s sensors and the deployed recon probe, and smiled as the transplanted holo display came alive. It looked perfect, but he set up a complete systems test just in case and leaned back while the computers ran it.

The Captain, he reflected, didn't do things by halves—and she didn't have much patience with anyone who did. Like a certain Lieutenant (Senior Grade) Maxwell Artois Stromboli who'd been dragging his ass and feeling sorry for himself ever since the Fleet exercise, he admitted. Max Stromboli didn't consider himself the most brilliant officer the planet of Manticore had ever produced, but he knew he was better than he'd let himself become. He'd been slacking off like a sulky kid, and when Captain Harrington asked him for that course to Medusa he didn't have—

He shuddered in memory. God, he'd expected her to bite off his head and shi—spit down his neck! And, he knew, he would have deserved it. But she hadn't. She'd only sat there, waiting patiently, and he'd felt about a centimeter high while he figured the course, mostly because she *wasn't* jumping his shit in front of the entire bridge watch.

And this job wasn't the slap in the face he'd first thought, either. He admitted that, too. Medusa's atmosphere might smell like the downwind side of a chemical refinery with buggered filtration, and the natives might look like some sort of circus freaks, but his assignment was more important than he'd thought. He'd realized that the moment he saw the jury-rigged lash-up with which the NPA had been trying to watch the high orbitals. They'd greeted him and his people with all the fervor of a relieved garrison, and they'd had only good things to say about the Captain, but the very way they said them made him uncomfortably aware of how badly—and for how long—the Fleet had let them down.

He sighed and swiveled his chair to check the first test printouts. They looked good, and he let the hardcopy spill into the printer tray and looked out the window.

Lord, what a piss-poor excuse for a planet! His newly installed control center was on the upper floor of one of the government compound's corner towers, and he had an appallingly good view of klicks and klicks of gray-green, mottled moss. It stretched down to the bank of something the natives called a river. The greasy-looking, turgid flow, heavy with silt, was one of hundreds of channels cutting through the swampy delta, and the walls of a Stilty city rose beyond it.

He lifted a pair of electronic binoculars from a console and peered through them at the distant curtain wall fronting the river. The binocs brought it to arm's length, and he marveled at the size of its stones. That rock had been quarried far upstream and ferried down, and the smallest single hunk of it must be a meter on a side. That was damned impressive engineering for a muscle-powered civilization, even in this gravity. And especially for something as stalky and ungainly looking as a Stilty.

He zeroed in on one of the natives, still unable to believe, deep down inside, that they could have built that massive wall. As on Sphinx, what passed for mammals on Medusa (there were no birds) were hexapedal, but the similarity ended there. Sphinxian beasties tended to the sturdy and blocky, aside from arboreals like the treecats, because of their native gravity. Medusans were tall and slender and trilaterally symmetrical, to boot. The natives were undeniably warm-blooded and bore living young, but they reminded Stromboli far more of a holo he'd seen of an Old Earth insect called a praying mantis than of anything *he* would have called a mammal. Except, of course, that no Solarian bug ever had its limbs arranged equidistantly about its body that way.

The dominant life form had freed its upper limbs for manipulation just as Man had, by standing upright on its rearmost limbs, but the legs were impossibly long and slender by human standards. Of course, that tripod arrangement did give them extraordinary stability once they locked all six knee joints, but those knees were another thing that bothered Stromboli. Neither they nor the hip joints above them bent; they *swiveled*, and watching a Stilty walk made the lieutenant's stomach vaguely uneasy. God only knew what they looked like when they *ran!*

The computer burped softly to announce the end of the systems check, and Stromboli laid his glasses aside and turned back to his panel. It was a miserable excuse for a planet, but its orbit traffic was all his, and he felt an unexpected eagerness to be about it.

The mammoth counter-grav cargo shuttle looked like an insect as it nuzzled alongside its Manticoran-registry mother ship. The customs pinnace tubed to it looked more like a microbe, and two of the shuttle crew stood stiffly, flanking the shuttle end of the access tube like surly sentries. Ensign Scotty Tremaine was not quite thirteen Manticoran years old, on his first deployment after graduation, but something about the way they stood there wasn't right. He knew it wasn't, and they'd looked mighty unhappy when he first came aboard, so he turned to watch PO Harkness with casual interest.

PO Harkness was, Tremaine suspected, A Character. He'd had a peek at Harkness's personnel jacket before they left the ship (the Academy instructors had always insisted an officer should do that before taking command of a detachment), and he wished he'd had more time to peruse its fascinating reading. Harkness had been in the RMN for over twenty years, almost thirty-five T-years, and he'd been up for chief twelve times by Tremaine's count. He'd actually made it, once. But PO Harkness had a weakness—two of them, in fact. He was constitutionally incapable of passing a Marine tunic in an off-duty bar without endeavoring to thump the living daylights out of its wearer, and he labored under the belief that it was his humanitarian duty to provide his shipmates with all the little things the ship's store didn't normally carry.

He was also one of the best missile techs in the service, which perhaps explained why he was still *in* the service.

But what interested Tremaine just now was what Bosun MacBride had told him before he left the ship. Tremaine liked the bosun. Even if she did regard him as a none-too-bright puppy, she seemed to feel that someday, with proper training by the bosuns whose bounden duty it was to wipe ensign's noses and bottoms and generally keep them from tripping over their own two feet, he might, possibly, make a worthwhile officer. In the meantime, her infinitely respectful suggestions usually managed to stop him just when he was about to put his foot in it.

"The ensign might want to give PO Harkness his head, Sir," MacBride had said quietly. "If anyone in the detachment can recognize a crook cargo setup, it's him. And—"

she'd given him one of her deadpan smiles "—I've . . . discussed the importance of his assignment with him."

So now Tremaine shifted position slightly, moving aside
to lean his elbow on a freight conveyer where he could
watch Harkness and still keep the corner of his eye on the
crewmen.

Harkness was prowling around the neatly stacked
counter-grav cargo pallets with a copy of the manifest,
checking canister labels. The weight of a magnetic tape
reader bulged the thigh pocket of his coveralls, but the flap
was still sealed. Now he slowed his label checks and bent a
bit closer to a pallet, and Tremaine noted the way one of the
crewmen by the tube tensed.

"Mr. Tremaine?" Harkness called without turning.

"Yes, PO?"

"I think you might find this interesting, Sir." It was amaz-
ing what a fatherly voice could come out of those battered,
prize-fighter features. Harkness sounded like a teacher
about to demonstrate a classroom experiment for a favored
pupil, and Tremaine crossed the cargo bay to stand beside
him.

"What is it, PO?"

"This, Sir." A blunt finger with scarred knuckles indicated the shiny silver customs tape running around the
canister and, in particular, the Royal Customs Service seal
with its small starship surmounted by the crowned Manticore and flanking, rampant Sphinx and Gryphon of the
Kingdom's arms. It looked perfect to Tremaine.

"What about it?"

"Well, Sir," Harkness said ruminatively, "I can't be certain, but—" The broad fingertip flipped the seal, and
Tremaine blinked as it popped right off the tape it was supposed to be an integral part of. He bent closer and saw the
clear plastic tape bridging the gap where the original seal
had been sliced away.

"You know, Sir," Harkness went on in that same,
thoughtful voice, "I'll bet those poor bloody—pardon,

Sir—" he didn't sound especially apologetic, but Tremaine let it pass; he had other things on his mind "—NPA sods have been doing their best without the right equipment for so long these fellows just got sloppy." He shook his head, a craftsman mourning slovenly workmanship. "Never would have gotten by a regular customs man."

"I . . . see." Tremaine glanced over his shoulder at the now acutely unhappy crewmen. One of them was sidling sideways towards the shuttle flight deck, and Tremaine nodded to Private Kohl. The Marine shifted position slightly and unsnapped his stunner holster. The moving crewman froze.

"What do you suppose is in there, PO?" the ensign asked brightly, beginning to enjoy himself.

"Well, Sir, according to this manifest, this here—" Harkness thumped the canister "—is a shipment of duralloy animal-drawn plows for delivery to the Hauptman Cartel factor on Medusa."

"Let's open it up and take a look," Tremaine said.

"Aye, aye, Sir." Harkness's broad grin showed teeth far too even and regular to be natural as he drew a forceblade from one capacious pocket. He flicked the switch, waking the tooth-twisting warning whine Manticoran law required of all such tools, and ran the invisible blade around the doctored Customs tape. Silver plastic slivered, and the soft "Shuuush" of equalizing pressure sounded as he sprang the canister.

He lifted the lid—then paused, frozen in mid-movement.

"Well, well, well, *well*," he murmured, adding an absent-minded "Sir" as he remembered the ensign beside him. He shoved the lid fully up until it locked. "Mighty strange looking plowshares, I'd say, Mr. Tremaine."

"So would I," Tremaine said after a moment, leaning forward to stroke a hand over the lustrous, tawny-gold fur. The canister was two meters long by one wide and one deep, and it seemed to be completely full. "Is that what I think it is, PO?"

"If you think it's Gryphon kodiak max pelts it is, Sir." Harkness shook his head, and Tremaine could almost hear the credit terminal ringing behind his eyes. "Must be two, three hundred thousand dollars worth of them," the PO mused. "In this one canister," he added as an afterthought.

"And right off the controlled species list." Tremaine's voice was so grim the petty officer straightened and looked at him in surprise. The youngster beside him didn't look young at all as he stared down into the canister and then turned to glare at the wilting crewmen. "You think they were going to transship them down on the surface, PO?"

"There or in the warehouse. Can't rightly see anything else they might have done with 'em, Sir. Sure thing the Stilties wouldn't need 'em."

"My thought, exactly." The ensign nodded to himself, then glanced around the dim cargo bay. "PO Harkness, I think you'd better check all the other customs seals." The petty officer nodded, and Tremaine smiled thinly at the sweating shuttle crew. "In the meantime, these gentlemen and I will go pay a little visit on their captain. I want to arrange a visit to his main holds, as well, I think."

"Aye, aye, Sir." The burly petty officer braced to attention, a gesture of respect he rarely wasted on ensigns who didn't yank him up short for omitting it, and jerked his head to summon the rest of his two-man team as Tremaine, Private Kohl, and two *very* unhappy crewmen left the bay.

Honor shook her head as she finished Ensign Tremaine's recorded message. Then she flicked the terminal off, making a careful mental note of the way the ensign had credited PO Harkness, not himself, with the initial discovery. That was unusual in so junior an officer, but it confirmed her original impression of the youngster.

She'd expected that when she assigned him to the Medusa detachment. What she hadn't expected was for him to confirm Dame Estelle's smuggling hypothesis quite this soon. Nor, she admitted, had she expected to find a

Manticoran vessel embroiled in it—and one on charter to the Hauptman Cartel, at that.

She turned her chair to glance across her desk at McKeon. The exec looked as if he'd just bitten into something sour, and Nimitz raised his chin from his cushioned rest to gaze thoughtfully at him.

"I don't know if Tremaine is more pleased with himself or worried over what to do next," she said, and McKeon twitched his taut shoulders. "I imagine there'll be some interesting repercussions back on Manticore."

"Yes, Ma'am." McKeon's lips worked for a moment, then he raised his eyes to meet hers. "You know Hauptman is going to deny they had anything to do with it."

"Forty-three million in illegal peltries? Of course they will—just as *Mondragon*'s captain insists the space fairies must have brought them," Honor said ironically. "I wonder what else Tremaine is going to turn up when he tears into the ship's main holds?"

"Trouble, Captain." McKeon spoke softly and seemed to be struggling with some inner conflict, and she raised her eyebrows. The exec shifted uneasily in his chair, then sighed, and some of his stiff formality seemed to fall away. "Whatever else Tremaine finds, Hauptman is going to insist they didn't have anything to do with it, and you can bet they've got the paper to 'prove' they didn't. The best we're going to manage is to nail *Mondragon*'s master and, probably, her purser."

"It's a start, Exec. And the paper may not be as cut and dried as you think."

"Look, Ma'am, I know we don't always—" The lieutenant commander broke off and bit his lip. "What I mean is, you're going to make the cartel very unhappy with you, and they've got the friends in high places to make their unhappiness felt. You've caught a shipment of illegal furs, but is it worth it? Really worth it?" Honor's eyes hardened dangerously, and he went on quickly. "I don't mean it wasn't illegal—God knows it was!—and I can see what you're trying to do. But the day we leave Basilisk Station, things are going to go right back to the way they were. This is probably a fleabite to them, something their cash flow won't even notice, but they're going to remember you."

"I sincerely hope they will, Commander," Honor said icily, and McKeon stared at her, his eyes worried. For the first time in far too long he was worried about his captain because she *was* his captain, but there was no give in that dark, armor-plated glare.

"But you're going to jeopardize your entire career over something that won't even make a difference!" he protested. "Captain, this sort of thing is—"

"Is what we're supposed to stop." Her voice cut across his like a dagger, and he winced as he saw something like hurt under the anger in her eyes. Hurt and something else. Contempt, perhaps, and that cut deep, too deep. He closed his mouth, and her nostrils flared.

"Commander McKeon," she said in that same, cold voice, "*my* duty is not affected by what others may or may not do to discharge their own. Nor do I care which criminals may engage in a criminal activity on my watch. We will support Ensign Tremaine to the maximum. In addition, I want an extra effort devoted to all other vessels—*all* other vessels, Commander—chartered by the Hauptman Cartel. Is that understood?"

"Understood, Ma'am," he said unhappily. "I only—"

"I appreciate your concern, Exec," she said sharply, "but *Fearless* will discharge her responsibilities. All of her responsibilities."

"Yes, Ma'am."

"Thank you. Dismissed, Commander."

He rose and left her cabin, confused and worried, and the burden of a strange, deeply personal shame went with him.

• CHAPTER TWELVE

The Admiralty yeoman opened the office door and
bowed the tall, dark-haired admiral through it, then closed
it behind him. Admiral of the Green Lord Hamish Alexander crossed to the huge windows and looked out over the
dazzling spires and pastel towers of the city of Landing,
capital of the Star Kingdom of Manticore.

The dark blue water of Jason Bay, for all intents and purposes an inland sea hundreds of kilometers in length,
stretched to the southern horizon, sparkling under the light
of Manticore-A, and, despite the office's air-conditioning,
he could feel that sun's radiant heat on his face through the
windows' insulated plastic. The outside temperature was
welcome, if almost uncomfortably hot, for he'd just come
from his family's home in the Duchy of High Sligo, and it
was winter in Manticore's northern hemisphere. But Landing lay less than fifteen hundred kilometers above the
equator, and brilliant greenery tossed in the brisk breeze
off the sail-dotted bay.

He turned away from the window, folding his hands
behind him, and surveyed the office of the First Space
Lord. The room was paneled in light-toned native woods,
not the extravagance it would have been on one of the
inner-worlds, and there was a fireplace in one corner. It was
functional, not merely ornamental, and that, Alexander
thought, *was* an extravagance. The Admiralty Building was
over a Manticoran century-and-a-half old and little more
than a hundred stories tall, a modest little structure for a
counter-gravity civilization, but that fireplace's chimney
bored up through thirty-odd stories of air shafts and

ventilation ducting. He could only marvel at the stubborn insistence of whoever had designed the building, especially in a climate which required air-conditioning far more often than heating.

He chuckled and checked his watch. The First Space Lord was running late—not unusual for a man with his schedule—and Alexander took a leisurely turn about the familiar office, studying the models of starships and old-fashioned oil and acrylic portraits, reacquainting himself with old friends and noting the newer additions.

He was admiring the detail of a meter-long replica of HMS *Manticore*, the pride of the Fleet, when the door opened behind him. He turned, and his rugged face lit with a smile as Fleet Admiral Sir James Bowie Webster walked through it. The First Space Lord had the Webster chin, and he grinned and clasped Alexander's hand in both of his to shake it firmly.

"Hamish! You're looking good, I see. Sorry to roust you out so close to Emily's birthday, but I needed a word."

"So I gathered," Alexander said dryly as Webster released his hand and sprawled untidily into his chair. Alexander ignored his offer of another chair and parked himself on one corner of the desk that looked big enough for a shuttle pad.

"How *is* Emily? And your father?" Webster asked, his smile fading a bit, and Alexander shrugged.

"As well as can be expected, both of them. Dr. Gagarian has a new therapy he wants Emily to try, and Father isn't taking the winter very well, but—"

He shrugged again, like a man testing an old wound and finding its familiar pain unchanged, and Webster nodded silently. Alexander's father, the Twelfth Earl of White Haven, was almost sixty-four years old—over a hundred and ten T-years—and his had been the last pre-prolong generation. He could not have many winters left, and Lady Emily Alexander was one of Manticore's greatest tragedies, one Webster—like everyone who knew her personally and thousands who had never met her at all—felt as his own. Once acknowledged as the Kingdom's premiere holo-drama performer, she remained one of its most beloved and respected writers and producers, but she had been forced from the HD stage by the aircar collision that had left her a total invalid. Her damaged nerves had persistently refused both grafts and regeneration, and not even modern medical science could rebuild destroyed motor control centers.

Webster suppressed an expression of useless sympathy he knew would only make Alexander uncomfortable and shook himself, looking more closely at the officer before him. Hamish Alexander was forty-seven—just over eighty standard years old—himself, though he looked less than a third his father's age, but there were fresh worry lines around his eyes and a few new strands of white at his temples.

"And your brother?"

"The Honorable Willie?" Hamish brightened instantly, eyes gleaming with sudden laughter. "Our noble Lord of the Exchequer is in *fine* form! Had quite a few words to say to me—rude ones, too—about the last Naval Estimates, I might add."

"He thinks they're too high?"

"No, he just thinks he's going to have the devil of a time getting them approved by Parliament. Still, I imagine he's getting used to that by now."

"I hope so, because next year's are probably going to be worse," Webster sighed.

"I imagine. But somehow I don't think you wanted to see me to hear what Willie has to say about the budget, Jim. What's up?"

"Actually, in a way, I *did* want to sound Willie out—through you—about something that's come up. Or, no, not Willie, so much, as the Government in general."

"Now that," Alexander said, "sounds ominous."

"Maybe not ominous, but certainly difficult." Webster

ran a hand through his hair in an atypically harassed gesture. "It's Basilisk Station, Hamish."

"Oho," Alexander murmured. He swung one leg, staring down at the toe of his mirror-polished boot. Basilisk had always been a political hot potato, and given the current First Lord's views on the system, it was hardly surprising that Webster should make a discreet—and unofficial—attempt to sound out the Government without involving his civilian superior.

"Oho," Webster agreed sourly. "You know what's going on there?"

"I've heard there was a little excitement." Alexander shrugged. "Nothing specific, aside from a few wild rumors."

"In this case, they may not have been all that wild." Alexander raised his eyebrows at Webster's tone, and the First Space Lord grimaced. He reached into his desk and extracted a sizable heap of message chips.

"What I have here, Hamish," he said, "is fourteen official protests from the Havenite ambassador, six from the Havenite consul in Basilisk, *sixteen* from various Manticoran and out-kingdom merchant cartels, and sworn statements from nine Havenite merchant captains alleging harassment and illegal searches of their vessels. There are also," he added almost dispassionately, "five similar statements from non-Havenite skippers and three complaints that 'unjustified threats of deadly force' have been made by Navy personnel."

Alexander's eyebrows had climbed almost into his hairline as the catalog rolled out. Now he blinked. "It seems things *have* gotten exciting," he murmured.

"Oh, yes, indeed they have."

"Well, what are all these protests and statements about?"

"They concern one Commander Honor Harrington."

"What?" Alexander chuckled. "You mean the one who potted Sebastian with a single broadside?"

"That's the one," Webster agreed with an unwilling grin

of his own. Then he sobered. "At the moment, Commander Harrington is Acting Senior Officer on Basilisk Station."

"She's *what?* What in God's name is an officer who can pull off something like that doing on Basilisk Station?!"

"It wasn't my idea," Webster protested. "It came down from on high, one might say, after Sonja's brainchild proved something of a brat in the later Fleet problems."

"Oh, so she decided to sweep her mistake under the carpet, whatever it cost the officer who actually made it work once for her?" Alexander's disdain was clear, and Webster shrugged.

"I know you don't like Sonja, Hamish. For that matter, I'm not too crazy about her myself, but I really don't think it was her idea this time. I think it was Janacek. You know how that reactionary old—" Webster caught himself. "I mean, you know he watches after the family interests."

"Um." Alexander nodded, and Webster shrugged again.

"Anyway, he made his desires known, and I was too busy horse-trading with him on the new engineering wing for Saganami Island to say no."

"All right, but what's a commander doing as SO? That ought to be at least a captain."

"Agreed." Webster tipped his chair back. "What do you know about Pavel Young?"

"Who?" Alexander blinked at the apparent *non sequitur*. "You mean North Hollow's son?"

"That's the one."

"Not much—and the little I do know, I don't like. Why?"

"Because Captain Lord Pavel Young is *supposed* to be the senior officer in Basilisk. Unfortunately, his ship required 'urgent refit,' and he felt the repairs involved were too complicated to leave in the hands of his executive officer. So he brought her home himself—leaving Harrington and a single light cruiser on the station."

Alexander stared at him in disbelief, and Webster flushed under his astonished gaze.

"Jim, I've known you for a lot of years," Alexander said at length. "So suppose you tell me why you haven't relieved him?"

"Because of politics," Webster sighed. "You should know that. That's one reason I want your impressions of how the Government is likely to react to all this. Christ, Hamish! I've got the damned Havenites screaming for blood, half a dozen cartels—headed by Hauptman's—are madder than hell, Countess Marisa is getting ready to fight the Naval Estimates tooth and nail, the goddamned 'New Men' are sitting right in her hip pocket, and you *know* what a big gun, politically speaking, North Hollow is! It's been all I can do to keep Young shuffled off onto the sidelines. Do you really think the Duke is going to thank me if I piss off the Conservative Association at a time like this by relieving the spoiled-darling son of High Ridge's second-in-command?"

"No, probably not," Alexander admitted after a moment, but the admission left a sour taste in his mouth. The majority of Manticore's aristocrats honored a tradition of public service fueled by a strong sense of noblesse oblige; those who did not were among the most self-centered and intolerant in the known universe, and Baron Michael of High Ridge's Conservative Association was their home. The Association was openly committed to "restoring the historical balance of power intended by our Founders" between the nobility and the uppity commoners—a "balance," Alexander knew perfectly well, which had never existed except in their own wishful thinking.

He chewed on his thoughts for a moment, then frowned. "What's Young like?"

"He's an arrogant, over-sexed, incompetent, bigoted snot," Webster replied so promptly his visitor's lips twitched involuntarily. "A real chip off the North Hollow block."

"That I can believe, if he shuffled his responsibilities off on a junior and hightailed it back to civilization."

"It's uglier than that, Hamish. Much uglier." Alexander

crooked a fresh eyebrow, and Webster waved his hands in frustration. "Unless I miss my guess, he deliberately set Harrington up for a fall by leaving her behind."

"Why do you think that?"

"There was bad blood between them when they were both at the Academy. I don't know all the details—Hartley was commandant then, and you know how hard it is to worm things out of him—but Young caught an official reprimand for conduct unbecoming. He goes through women like a kodiak max through Beowulf buffalo, just like his father and both brothers, and apparently he didn't want to take no for an answer. I gather it got physical."

"You mean he—?!" Alexander half-rose from the desk, his expression thunderous, but Webster interrupted him with a grin.

"I'd guess he tried, but Harrington's from Sphinx." Alexander's eyes began to gleam, and Webster nodded. "*And* she was number two on the unarmed combat demonstration team in her senior form. From what I can gather, he may have started it, but she most definitely finished it." His grin faded. "Which is why he stuck her with Basilisk Station, and I'm damned worried that he may finally have gotten her."

"How so? What're all the protests about?"

"It seems that no one told Commander Harrington that Basilisk Station is where we send our fuck-ups and deadbeats. She may only have one ship, but she's actually enforcing the commerce regs against Junction traffic. Not only that, but in the last three weeks she's deployed a few hundred million dollars worth of recon probes to cover the entire inner system, established a Navy-run space traffic control around Medusa, *and* taken over the customs function from the NPA. In fact, she's raised enough general hell that Admiral Warner tells me Young has actually stopped enjoying his self-assigned leave and started trying to expedite his repairs so he can get back there and stop her. I think he's afraid he's created a monster that may drag him down, too, patronage or no. Unfortunately, Warner's boys and girls on *Hephaestus* have Young's ship opened up like a used ration can at the moment. I'm not sure, but I have the distinct impression Warner is actually dragging his heels on the refit just to enjoy watching Young squirm, and he can't leave his ship behind without effectively admitting what he tried to pull, so there's not much he can do."

"Good God," Alexander said mildly. "Do you mean to tell me we finally have an SO on Basilisk Station who's doing her job? How remarkable!"

"Yes, she's doing her job, and damned well, as far as I can tell, but that's what all of these—" Webster waved the memo chips "—are about. She's got detachments all over the system, and whoever she left to handle the terminus inspections seems to be a real hard case. He's ramming the regs down *everybody's* throat, chapter and verse, and I *don't* think he'd be doing that without Harrington's specific backing. Of course it's got the Havenites screaming, but he's enforcing them against our own shipping, as well. That alone would be enough to tick off every merchant house in the Kingdom after the free run they've always had there, but even that's not the worst of it. You remember the rumors about smuggling through Medusa?" Alexander nodded, and Webster grinned sourly. "Well, Harrington's orbital inspection parties have seized well over nine hundred *million* dollars worth of contraband—so far—and sent it in for judgment and condemnation. And in the process, she caught the Hauptman Cartel trying to smuggle kodiak maximus pelts out through Medusa and called them on it. She's seized a four-and-a-half-million-ton freighter under charter to Hauptman—the *Mondragon*—and sent her in under a prize crew, for God's sake!"

"Oh, *my!*" Alexander pressed a hand to his ribs, trying in vain to stifle his laughter as he pictured the carnage the unknown Harrington must be strewing in her wake.

"You may think it's funny," Webster growled, "but I've had Klaus Hauptman himself in here, swearing up one side and down the other that his people are as innocent as the driven snow, that it was all *Mondragon's* master's doing, and that Harrington is harassing his other, legitimate shipments. He wants her head, and the Havenites are sharpening the axe for him with all these 'protests' of theirs! What's happening to their Junction shipping is bad enough, as far as they're concerned, but you know their official position on our claim to Medusa. Their consul is practically chewing the rug about her 'patently illegal searches of legitimate merchant vessels in the course of their lawful trading activities with an independent planet.' It's got all the makings of a first-class diplomatic incident, and it's not getting any better."

"Screw the Havenites," Alexander snapped, forgetting to laugh. "And screw Hauptman, too! It sounds to me like she's doing exactly what we're *supposed* to have been doing for years, Jim!"

"Oh? And do you think Sir Edward Janacek will share your view?"

"No, but that's no reason to come down on Harrington for doing her job. Damn it, from what you're saying, Young tried his damnedest to put a knife in her back! Do you want to stick it in for him?"

"You know I don't!" Webster ran his hands through his hair again. "Hell, Hamish, my grand-nephew is on *Fearless*. If I relieve Harrington, I'll be sending him exactly the wrong message about the discharge of an officer's responsibilities. For that matter, every officer in the Fleet will draw the same conclusion!"

"Exactly."

"Goddamn it," Webster sighed. "I'm First Space Lord. I'm not supposed to have to decide what to do with a damned *commander*."

Alexander frowned and returned to the contemplation of his boot toe, and Webster tipped his chair further back. He knew that expression.

"Look, Jim," Alexander finally said, "I know I'm junior to

you, but it seems to me we owe this Harrington a vote of thanks, not a rap in the teeth. For the first time, we've got an officer on Basilisk Station who's willing to kick some ass to get her job done. I like that. I like it a hell of a lot better than what we've been getting there, and so do you. All right, so she's making some waves and ticking some people off. Fine. Let her. Even Janacek can't change the Fleet mission in Basilisk—thank God, or he'd have had us out of there completely by now. But if we're going to tell her what to do, we can't yank the rug out from under her the minute she starts doing it." He paused.

"You've told me a lot about who's complaining about her, but what do the people in Basilisk have to say?"

"Michel Reynaud and the ACS crowd are delighted," Webster admitted. "I've got two or three glowing reports from Reynaud on this Lieutenant Venizelos she assigned to him. Mind you, Venizelos must be some kind of madman if even half of what the Havenites have to say is true, but Reynaud likes him. As for Estelle Matsuko, she seems convinced Harrington could walk across Jason Bay without getting her shoes wet. She's been so disgusted with the previous SOs, she's even stopped complaining about them; now I've got letters of thanks for our 'excellent cooperation'!"

"Well, that should tell you something, shouldn't it?"

"So you think I should just stay out of it," Webster said. It wasn't a question.

"Damn right I do. Basilisk's been a disgrace since the day we went in. It's long past time someone made a point of that. It may cause a rethink on the entire issue."

"Is this the time for it?" Webster sounded anxious, and Alexander shrugged.

"If you want, I'll sound Willie out on it and get back to you, but I think Cromarty would say yes. We've danced around the issue because of the 'political situation' for years, and the problem's only gotten worse. I don't doubt the Conservatives will bitch and moan, and so will the

Liberals, but they can't have it both ways. The Conservatives can't have their nice, safe isolation if we don't hang onto that terminus with both hands, and the Liberals can't protect the Medusans from off-world contamination if we don't police the space-to-planet traffic. For the first time, we've got an officer on Basilisk Station with the guts to make that point for them, and if they try to do anything about it, the Commons will stop them cold. I say go for it, and I think Willie will say the same."

"I hope you're right," Webster said. He stood and swept the chips back into his desk drawer, then clapped Alexander on the shoulder. "I really do hope you're right, Hamish, because whether you are politically or not, you and I both know you are from the service's viewpoint."

He looked at the wall chronometer and grinned.

"I see it's about lunch time. Care to join me in the flag officer's dining room? I think two or three good stiff ones should just about take the taste of politics out of my mouth."

• CHAPTER THIRTEEN

"Coming up on final mark. Stand by to fire." Lieutenant
(JG) Rafael Cardones's voice was soft, his eyes intent, as he
watched his targeting display with narrow eyes. His right
hand crept out, forefinger resting lightly on the big, square
button at the center of his weapons console while his senior
rating's hand hovered over the backup panel.

"Firing . . . *now*."

Cardones's finger stabbed downward, and his display
blinked bright as the master fire key went flat. A second
passed, and then the screen lit again, this time with an estimate of fire on target.

He leaned back and wiped sweat from his forehead,
shoulders tight and aching with the tension of the last forty-
five minutes' tactical exercise. He was almost afraid to
check the results, but he steeled his nerve and made himself look—then blinked in surprise. Eighty-three percent
for the energy weapons, by God! And almost as good for
the missiles—three hits out of five fired!

"Nicely done, Mr. Cardones," a soprano voice said, and
he twisted round in his chair to find the Captain standing
at his shoulder. He still wasn't quite used to how quietly
she moved, and he hadn't had the least idea she was there.
Yet she was, and her brown eyes were thoughtful as she
tapped a key at his senior tracking rating's station. The
complex, corkscrewing vectors of Cardones's painstaking
approach replayed themselves at high speed, and the
Captain nodded.

"Very nice, indeed, Guns," she said, and Cardones managed, barely, not to preen with pride. It was the first time

the Captain had awarded him the accolade of that ancient informality, and that was worth every minute of concentration—and every grinding hour of practice which had led up to it. It was certainly a far cry from the miserable day he'd had to admit he'd botched the sensor drone deployment programs.

"However," the captain went on, running Tracking's record back, "what about this maneuver?" She froze the display, tapping a finger on the screen, and her treecat cocked his head as if to study the tangled lines of light, then looked at Cardones curiously.

"Ma'am?" Cardones asked cautiously.

"At this point, you pulled a three hundred-gee levelplane heading change to oh-three-five," she said. He relaxed just a bit. There was no bite in her voice; instead, she sounded like one of his Academy instructors. "It got you around to the heading you wanted, but look here." Her finger moved to the range and bearing readouts at the top of the display. "See where his main battery was pointed?"

Cardones looked, then swallowed and blushed pink.

"Right into the front of my wedge, Ma'am," he admitted.

"Agreed. You should have skew-turned and changed planes to bring your belly bands up to cover yourself, shouldn't you?"

"Yes, Ma'am," he said, feeling some of his elation fade. But the Captain touched his shoulder and smiled.

"Don't feel too bad. Instead, tell me why the computer didn't nail you?"

"Ma'am?" Cardones looked back at the display and frowned. "I don't know, Ma'am. The beam window was wide enough."

"Maybe, maybe not." The Captain tapped the readouts again. "The human factor, Lieutenant. Always remember the human factor. The tac computer's programmed to assign a response time to your supposedly flesh-and-blood opponent, and this time—*this* time, Guns—you were lucky. The range was long enough your opponent had less than three seconds to see the opening, recognize it, and take it, and the computer decided he hadn't reacted quickly enough to get the shot off. I expect it was right, too, but don't count on that when it's for real. Right?"

"Right, Skipper!" Cardones replied, grinning once more, and Honor patted his shoulder gently before she returned to her command chair.

She didn't mention that she'd been running the same problem from the other side through her command chair displays, using Cardones's maneuvers in real time, and that she *had* gotten her shot off. The youngster had made tremendous strides in the last few weeks, and he deserved his enjoyment. Besides, she wasn't at all sure she would have seen it and responded so quickly had it been a genuine action, and she had no intention of raining on his parade over a might-have-been.

She seated herself and let Nimitz slither down into his favorite spot in her lap while she scanned her bridge. Lieutenant Panowski was running his own exercise at Astrogation, and from the looks being exchanged between Lieutenant Brigham and Panowski's senior yeoman, it wasn't going very well. She hid a smile. McKeon had been right about the assistant astrogator's tendency to coast, and he'd looked almost betrayed when Honor announced that, shorthanded or not, in parking orbit or no, *Fearless* would continue her regularly scheduled drills without break. It was difficult for her to be as hard on Panowski as he probably deserved because of her awareness of her own weaknesses as a mathematician. She was a lousy astrogator and she knew it, but McKeon, ably assisted by Brigham, was taking up the slack for her nicely.

She let her eyes drift back to the main maneuvering display, pondering the ships in orbit around Medusa. *Fearless* had been on station for almost a full Manticoran month now, and there were far fewer than there had been when she arrived five weeks before; a direct result, she suspected, of Ensign Tremaine's campaign against illegal traffic.

Medusa was no longer a good place to transship prohibited goods, and the word was getting around. She hadn't realized what a holy terror Tremaine was going to be—he seemed to be developing some sort of ESP where smugglers were concerned—and Stromboli's eagle eye on ship-to-ship traffic had guided the ensign to three midspace pounces that had netted close to half a billion more dollars of contraband. She'd seen to it they both got "well dones" for their success, and Lieutenant Venizelos had come in for quite a few of his own for his efforts at the terminus. Judging by the violence and volume of the protests they were generating, they and their people were putting an extremely painful crimp into someone's profits, and she'd made sure they knew she knew it.

And, as she'd hoped, the recognition *Fearless*'s company was earning, not just from her but from Dame Estelle, the NPA, and the ACS, as well, was turning the corner. She no longer had to bully and harass her crew into doing their jobs. The notion that they, unlike anyone else who had ever been assigned to Basilisk Station, were making a difference was pulling them together. They were overworked, dogtired, and only too well aware that they were scoring their successes in spite of the system rather than because of it, and that only made them prouder of themselves.

They deserved their pride. Indeed, *she* was proud of them, and their sense of accomplishment was starting to earn her their regard. The prize money they'd earned for their seizures didn't hurt any either, of course. The traditional award of a half percent of the value of all contraband seized might not sound like a lot, but they'd sent in over a billion and a half dollars worth of it. If all of it was finally condemned by the Admiralty Court, as Honor confidently anticipated it would be, that was more than seven and a half million dollars for the ship's company to split—and that assumed *Mondragon*'s owners would simply be fined. If their ship was confiscated, as it well might be, its assessed value would be added to the pot. The captain's share was six percent of the total, which gave Honor herself a tidy little half million so far (she'd discovered that even she could do *that* math easily enough), which was almost eight years' salary for an RMN commander, but her noncoms and enlisted personnel got seventy percent to split among them. That meant even the least senior of them would receive almost twelve thousand dollars, and by long tradition and despite periodic assaults by the Exchequer, prize money was untaxable.

Needless to say, Ensign Tremaine and Lieutenant Venizelos had become *very* popular with their crewmates, but they'd all earned every penny of their bonus, and she knew they valued their self-pride even more highly. Indeed, the prize money was more valuable to them as a vindication of their efforts, a proof of their effectiveness, than for what it could buy, and it showed. Lieutenant Commander Santos had been the first to call her "Skipper," the possessive honorific none had been willing to extend after the disastrous Fleet exercises, but more and more of her officers were beginning to use it now.

More of them, yes, she thought with a sudden, inner frown, but not all. Lois Suchon still carried a palpable aura of resentment about with her, and Honor had come to the conclusion that she always would. The surgeon was simply one of those fortunately rare individuals who were naturally incapable of pulling their weight as a member of a team.

And then there was McKeon. He was doing his job. She couldn't fault the time he'd taken with Cardones, or the long hours he'd put in coaching and ass-kicking Panowski, or the skill with which he juggled their tight-stretched human resources to keep all bases covered. Yet for all that, the barriers remained. She could see what a tower of strength he might have been. Indeed, the fact that he was accomplishing so much without ever letting her close to him only underscored his abilities. But he couldn't seem to take that final step into *partnership* with her, and she suspected from his tight expression that it frustrated him almost as much as it did her. It was as if he needed to make the transition and couldn't, and she wished she understood what the problem was. One thing was certain, it went deeper than the malaise which had gripped the rest of her crew when they were first sent here, and—

A soft chime intruded into her thoughts, and she turned her head as Webster acknowledged the incoming signal. The lieutenant said something, then nodded and turned his chair to face her.

"I have a transmission for you from the surface, Ma'am. From the resident commissioner's office."

"Transfer it to my screen," Honor said, but the com officer shook his head.

"Dame Estelle asks to speak to you privately, Ma'am."

Honor felt an eyebrow rise and smoothed it back down, then lifted Nimitz to the back of her chair and rose.

"I'll take it in my briefing room, Samuel."

"Yes, Ma'am."

Honor nodded and walked through the hatch, closing it behind her. She sank into the captain's chair at the head of the conference table and keyed an acceptance signal into the data terminal, then smiled as Dame Estelle appeared on the built-in com screen.

"Hello, Commander," the Commissioner said.

"This is a pleasant surprise, Dame Estelle. What can I do for you?"

"I'm afraid I really called to cry on your shoulder, Honor," Matsuko said wryly.

"That's what the Navy's here for, Ma'am," Honor replied, and the commissioner snorted. Honor let it pass, but she hadn't missed the fact that Dame Estelle didn't seem to regard her as really belonging to the RMN. It was part and parcel of the way the commissioner addressed her by her first name, as if to distance her from the *real* Fleet officers (i.e., deadbeat incompetents) she'd had to deal with so often.

"Yes, well," Matsuko said after a moment, "the truth is, I'm beginning to think I may have a bigger problem down here than I thought I did."

"How so?"

"Since you sent Lieutenant Stromboli and his people down to take over space control, my air traffic people have been freed up to deal with more local concerns. They've plugged a lot of the holes in our Outback aerial coverage with the extra manpower and your survey sats—not all; there are still a few left—and they've picked up a small number of unidentified flights in restricted areas."

"Oh?" Honor sat straighter in her chair and frowned. "What sorts of flights?"

"We can't tell." The commissioner sounded disgusted. "Their transponders don't respond when we query them, which, coupled with the fact that they certainly didn't file flight plans for their destinations, seems like pretty clear proof they're up to something we wouldn't like. We've tried interceptions, but the NPA's counter-grav is designed more for reliability and endurance than speed, and they run right away from us. If you hadn't made such a hole in our space-to-ground traffic, I'd guess they were rendezvousing smugglers."

"I suppose they still could be," Honor mused. "We've only been working on them for a month now. They could still be handing off stuff they'd already gotten down."

"I thought about that, but even if it was already down, they'd still have to get it back up past you to do them any good. Besides, they're too far out in the bush for that to seem very likely."

"Um." Honor rubbed the tip of her nose and frowned. The NPA's vehicles, for the most part, worked fairly close in to the enclaves, she reflected. "Could they be meeting to transship that far out just to stay beyond your interception range?"

"I doubt it. Oh, it has that effect, but they seem to operate in singletons, as far as we can tell, and they'd have to be working with very low-mass consignments, unless they have a base with their own cargo-handling equipment tucked away somewhere. And even if their cargoes were small and light enough to hand load, they're losing our radar, outbound and inbound, in the Madcat Mountains or over in the Mossybacks. If all they were doing was meeting other air traffic, why come out of the mountains where we can see them at all? They could rendezvous in one of the valleys out there, and we'd never spot them without a direct overflight. Besides, I'm beginning to have some very unhappy suspicions about what they might be up to."

"Such as, Ma'am?"

"You remember your first visit, when I mentioned *mekoha* to you?" Honor nodded, and Dame Estelle shrugged. "Well, as I said then, *mekoha's* highly sophisticated for the Medusans' technology. They're surprisingly good bathtub alchemists, but this is a pretty complex—and potent—alkaloid analogue with a kicker something like an endorphin. It's *not* an endorphin, or at least, we don't think it is, but we're only beginning to really understand Medusan biochemistry, so we could be wrong. Anyway—" she made a moue and shook her head "—what matters is that manufacturing it is a lengthy, complicated, and dangerous process for the local alchemists, especially in the final drying and grinding stages when they have to worry about breathing free dust. That means any heavy, systematic use of it has been restricted, by and large, to the wealthier natives simply on the basis of cost."

She paused, watching Honor until she nodded in understanding.

"All right. The other thing to remember about *mekoha* is that it has some really *nasty* side effects. It's extremely addictive, and the lethal dose varies widely from individual to individual, particularly with the poor quality control the alchemists can manage, so a *mekoha*-smoker usually ends up doing himself in with it eventually. It provides a short-term sense of euphoria and exhilaration and mild—at least, usually mild—hallucinations, but in the long term it produces severe respiratory and motor control damage, gradual loss of neural function, and a marked decrease in both attention span and measurable IQ. All of that is bad enough, but if the drug is sufficiently pure, it produces a strength reaction like an adrenalin-high and virtually shuts down the pain receptors, and the immediate euphoria can slide into a sort of induced psychosis with absolutely no warning, probably because of the hallucinogenic properties. Medusans don't normally indulge very much in violence. Oh, they're as fractious as any other bunch of aborigines you'd care to name, and some of the nomads are natural-born raiders by inclination, but the sort of random or hysterical mob violence you see in disfunctional societies isn't part of their matrix. Unless there's *mekoha* around. Mix in *mekoha*, and all bets are off."

"Have we tried restricting or controlling it?"

"Yes and no. It's already illegal in most of the Delta city-states—not all, but most—and restricted in the others. On the other hand, the cities are where most of the *mekoha* used outside the Delta has traditionally been made, and even the Delta councils are wary of crossing the *mekoha* traders. It brings in a lot of money, and the drug merchants are none too choosy about the means they'll adopt to protect their trade. Besides, the stuff has a firm niche in several of the Medusan religions."

"Oh, Lord!" Honor sighed, and Dame Estelle grimaced.

"Right. The NPA can't interfere with religious practices, both because we're specifically forbidden to by our charter and because, much as I hate to admit it, trying to do that would be the one sure way to destroy all the goodwill we've managed to build up. Some of the Delta priests—and more of the shamans in the Outback—are convinced that off-worlders are an evil and corrupting influence, anyway. If we try to take their holy drug away from them, we'll just be validating their feelings, so we've been forced back into education efforts, which aren't the most effective way to reach Bronze Age minds, and behind-the-scenes pressure on the manufacturers."

Honor nodded again as Dame Estelle fell silent once more, but her thoughts raced. She doubted the commissioner would have embarked on her lecture on Medusan pharmacology unless it was related to the unidentified air traffic, but that—

"Dame Estelle, are you suggesting that someone from off-world is supplying this *mekoha* to the Medusans?"

Matsuko nodded grimly. "That's exactly what I'm suggesting, Honor. We've known usage was going up even in the areas we police regularly. Since you've freed up the people I had stuck inspecting the orbital and ship-to-surface traffic, I've been able to push our routine patrols further into the Outback, and it looks like use levels are even higher there. More than that, we've gotten some samples of *mekoha* from the Mossybacks region, and it's not the same as the stuff produced in the Delta. The proportions are slightly different, and it's got a lower impurity content. Which, my people tell me, means this new version probably has more kick, too."

"And you think it's being manufactured off-world," Honor said flatly.

"That's what I'm afraid of. We can't prove it, but, as I say, it brings a high price, by Medusan standards. And however hard it is for the locals to produce, any half-competent off-world lab could churn it out in job lots if it had access to the raw *mek* moss it comes from."

"But first they'd have to get the moss off Medusa," Honor thought aloud. "And after they processed the drug, they'd have to get it back onto the planet again."

"Neither of which would have been an insurmountable problem before you and *Fearless* turned up," Matsuko put in. Honor shook her head.

"I don't know about that . . . and it still sounds too complicated to be very profitable, unless the selling price is even higher than you seem to be saying. How much of this—*mek* moss, you said?—does it take to produce, say, a gram of the refined drug?"

"A lot. Just a second." Matsuko tapped keys on her data console, then nodded. "It takes about forty kilos of green moss to produce one kilo of raw *mekoha* paste, and about ten kilos of paste to produce one kilo of the final product. Call it a four hundred-to-one ratio."

"And the most common dosage levels?"

"Lord, I don't know," Matsuko sighed. "Maybe thirty grams for a new user, but that tends to go up as the habit grows. Of course, given this new stuff's greater purity, initial dosage levels may be lower, but I expect the Medusans simply maintain their normal levels and enjoy a stronger high."

"So for every dose they sell, they'd have to transport— what?" Honor did the math in her head, then frowned at Matsuko. "Over thirteen kilos of moss or more than one-point-three kilos of paste off-world? Does that sound right?" Dame Estelle whipped through the same calculation. When she nodded, Honor shook her head again. "That sounds like too much bulk to be very practical, Dame Estelle. Besides, if there were any significant long-term traffic in it, there should still have been enough in the pipeline for us to have seen some sign of it in our earliest customs inspections even if Major Isvarian's people *had* missed it. If not the drug itself, surely the moss or paste would be hard to hide, and Ensign Tremaine's been keeping as close an eye on outbound as inbound shuttles, I assure you."

"So you don't think there's any off-world involvement?"

"I didn't say that. What I said is that it seems to me that the raw materials would be too bulky for their interstellar transport to stay hidden. Barney Isvarian and his teams may not have been trained customs agents, but I feel sure they would have noticed that much moss going off-world and brought it to your attention. But—" Honor's dark eyes narrowed "—that doesn't mean someone couldn't have shipped in the lab equipment to produce it locally. That would have required only a one-way penetration of Isvarian's customs patrols—or ours, for that matter—and from what you're saying, the mass ceiling wouldn't have been all that high."

"No," Dame Estelle said thoughtfully. "No, you're right about that. And in that case, our air traffic wouldn't be distributing *mekoha* that's been shipped in; it'd be local production, and the way you've choked off the smuggling wouldn't slow it down a bit."

"That's what I'm afraid of," Honor replied. "I'm not trying to shift responsibility for this, Dame Estelle, but it sounds to me as if the drug itself isn't coming from off-world at all."

"In which case, it's an NPA responsibility," Matsuko agreed. She breathed in deeply, then exhaled a slow, hissing breath. "I wish you were wrong, but I don't think you are."

"Perhaps. And perhaps it is an NPA responsibility. But it's *my* responsibility to assist the NPA in any way I can." Honor rubbed the tip of her nose again. "What sort of power requirement would a *mekoha* lab have?"

"I don't know." Matsuko frowned in thought. "I suppose it would depend on its production levels, but the process is fairly involved. I'd imagine the total energy cost is pretty high. It can't be *too* high, since the Medusans make do with water-power, sweat, and sunlight evaporation in the final drying steps, but they also produce it in very small lots in proportionately small 'labs.' I doubt our off-worlders—assuming we're right about what's going on—rely on that kind of technology, especially if they're producing the volumes my people suspect are in use. Why?"

"Check with Barney Isvarian," Honor suggested. "If your people can come up with some sort of parameters for the power involved, he can monitor the central grid and see if anyone's using a suspicious amount of juice. I know a lot of the enclaves have their own generators or orbital power collectors, but that would at least let you do some tentative elimination of suspects and narrow your target area."

"That's a good idea," Dame Estelle agreed, tapping notes into her terminal.

"Um. And while you're at it, see if your techs can give you an estimate for reasonable legitimate power use for the enclaves that *aren't* on your central grid. We can't do much with the ones with internal generators, but I can put some unobtrusive meters on the orbital collectors."

"Even if you find a high demand, it won't be proof," Matsuko pointed out, and Honor nodded.

"Not proof, no. But, as I say, we can probably eliminate some of the innocents, at least, and it may give us a lead." She nodded thoughtfully. "In the meantime, I'll have Ensign Tremaine make some orbital passes looking for power sources *outside* the enclaves." She grinned suddenly. "I wouldn't want him getting bored now that he and his people have the smugglers cut down to size, now would I?"

"You're a terrible person, Commander Harrington," Dame Estelle said with an answering grin.

"Dame Estelle, you have no *idea* how terrible," Honor agreed cheerfully. Then she sobered a bit. "It's not much, but it's the best I can offer. If you think of any other way we can help you out, please let me know and I'll do what I can."

"Thank you," the commissioner said gratefully. "And it's a nice change to—" She broke off with a shrug and a faint smile, and Honor nodded once again.

"You're welcome, Ma'am," she said, and switched off her com.

• CHAPTER FOURTEEN

Denver Summervale raised his head from the data terminal with a cold frown as his office door opened, and the woman who'd opened it swallowed unobtrusively. Summervale was a hard, dangerous man, with a record of dead bodies to prove it, and he disliked interruptions, but she stood her ground. It wasn't as if she had a choice. Besides, he'd been working on the books, and most of that scowl probably stemmed more from his hatred for paperwork than her sudden appearance.

"What?" he demanded in an arctic, aristocratic accent.

"There's a call for you," she said. His scowl deepened, and she hastened to add, "It's from the boss."

Summervale's face smoothed quickly into a masklike calm, and he rose with a curt nod. The woman stepped back out of the doorway, and he brushed past her with an oddly courteous apology.

She watched him vanish down the hall, moving toward the com room with his customary cat-footed grace, and felt the familiar shiver he left in his wake. There was something coldly reptilian about him, part and parcel of his upper-class accent and the sort of instinctive courtesy he showed to all about him. He was like an heirloom sword, graceful and poised, but honed and lethal as chilled steel. She'd known more than her share of dangerous, lawless men, but none quite like him, and he frightened her. She hated to admit that, even to herself, yet it was true.

The com room door closed behind him, and she turned away with another shiver, adjusting her dust mask as she opened the door to the lab and returned to her own responsibilities.

Summervale took one look at the face on his com screen, then nodded curtly to the duty operator. The man departed without a word, and Summervale seated himself in the chair he'd abandoned. Long habit drew his eyes to the panel, double-checking the scrambler circuits, before he looked up at the man on the screen.

"What?" he asked without preamble.

"We may have a problem," his caller said carefully. The man's Sphinxian accent was pronounced—possibly too pronounced, Summervale thought yet again. It had an almost theatrical quality, as if it were a mask for something else, but that was fine with Summervale. Its owner paid well for his services; if he wanted to maintain an extra level of security, that was his business.

"What problem?"

"The NPA's spotted the new *mekoha*," his caller replied, and Summervale's mouth tightened.

"How?"

"We're not certain—our informant couldn't tell us—but I'd guess it's a side effect of Harrington's operations. She's freed up a lot of NPA manpower, and they're extending their patrols."

Summervale's eyes flashed at the name 'Harrington,' and his tight mouth twisted. He'd never met the commander, but he didn't have to meet her to hate her. She represented too many things out of his own past, and he felt the familiar heat tingle in his nerves. Yet he was a professional. He recognized the danger of visceral reactions, however pleasant they might be.

"How much do they know?" he asked.

"Again, we're not certain, but they've been running analyses of the stuff they've brought in. The odds are pretty good they'll figure out it's not Stilty-produced. In fact, they may have already. One of my other sources tells me

Harrington's pulled one of her pinnaces off the customs assignment."

"To run orbital sweeps," Summervale said flatly.

"Probably," his caller agreed.

"Not probably—certainly. I told you it was risky to make the stuff so pure."

"The Stilties prefer it that way."

"Damn the Stilties." Summervale spoke almost mildly, but his eyes were hard. "You're paying the freight, so the decision's yours, but when one of these bucks gets hopped on a pipeful of our stuff, he turns into a nuke about to go critical."

"No skin off our nose," his employer said cynically.

"Maybe. But I'll lay odds that's what attracted the NPA's attention. And the same elements that give it the kick will prove it wasn't made by any Stilty alchemist. Which means it was either shipped in or made somewhere on-planet. Like here." The man on the screen began to say something else, but Summervale raised a hand. Again, it was an oddly courteous gesture. "Never mind. Done is done, and it's your operation. What do you want me to do at this end?"

"Watch your security, especially the air traffic. If they're making overflights, we can't afford to attract their attention."

"I can hold down the cargo flights. I can even reduce foot traffic around the complex," Summervale pointed out. "What I *can't* do is hide from Fleet sensors. Our power relay will stick out like a sore thumb, and once it draws their attention, we'll leak enough background energy for them to zero us despite the wall shields. You know that."

He chose not to add that he'd argued against a beamed power relay from the beginning. The extra cost in time and labor to run a buried feeder cable would have been negligible beside the investment his employers had already made, and it would have made the entire operation vastly more secure. But he'd been overruled at the outset. And while he had no intention of allowing his caller to saddle him with full responsibility for concealment at this point, there was no point rubbing the man's nose in it.

"We know that," the man on the screen said. "We never expected to have to face Fleet sensors"—Summervale knew that was as close to an apology as he was likely to get—"but now that we do, we don't expect you to work miracles. On the other hand, I doubt you'll have to. Remember, we have people on the inside. Maybe not high enough to tap into Matsuko's office or communications, but high enough to let us know if the NPA starts assembling anything big enough to come after you. We'll try to get inside Harrington's information channels and keep an eye on her recon reports, but even if we can't, we should be able to give you a minimum of six or seven hours' warning before anything local heads your way."

Summervale nodded slowly, mind racing as he considered alternatives. Six hours would be more than enough to get his people away, but anything less than a full day would be too little to get even a tithe of the equipment out. And that didn't even consider the meticulous records his employer had insisted he keep. He couldn't fault the man for wanting to track every gram of *mekoha* the lab produced—nothing could be better calculated to arouse Estelle Matsuko's fury than finding off-worlders peddling dream smoke to the Stilties, and if one of his people had set up as a dealer on his own time the odds of detection would have gone up astronomically—but maintaining complete hardcopy backups was stupid. The increase in vulnerability far outweighed the advantages, but there, again, he had been overruled.

He shrugged internally. That was his employer's lookout, and he'd made damned sure his own name never appeared anywhere in them.

"How do I handle the hardware?" he asked after a moment.

"If there's time, take it with you. If there's not—" His caller shrugged. "It's only hardware. We can replace it."

"Understood." Summervale drummed on the edge of the console for a moment, then shrugged, physically this time. "Anything else?"

"Not right now. I'll get back to you if something else breaks."

"Understood," Summervale repeated, and killed the circuit.

He sat before the silent screen for several minutes, thinking, then rose to pace the small com room. There were things about this entire operation that never had added up to his satisfaction, and his employer's apparent lack of concern over the loss of his entire lab complex was one more puzzle. Oh, the facilities weren't that expensive—*mekoha* production wasn't particularly difficult or complicated—but putting them in without detection had been a major operation. If they lost them, they also lost their production base, at least until a new one could be assembled, and installing a new lab would expose them to detection all over again.

Or would it?

He paused in his pacing, and an eyebrow curved in speculation. Suppose they already had a backup facility in place? That was certainly possible, particularly in light of some of his other unanswered questions. Like why the Organization had gone to such lengths to sell drugs, especially something like *mekoha*, to a bunch of primitive abos in the first place. He couldn't quite convince himself that Medusa hid some unknown, priceless treasure the Stilties were trading for the stuff, and any Medusan commodity he could think of could have been purchased for far less investment (and risk) with legitimate trade goods. Of course, he wasn't privy to the distribution end of the pipeline. He and his people distributed some of their production to the local chieftains and shamans in return for a network of Stilty scouts and sentinels, but the vast bulk of it was shipped out for disposal elsewhere.

And if they were going to sell drugs, why choose

mekoha? There were half a dozen other Stilty drugs and intoxicants the Organization might have chosen. Not ones that would produce the same price, perhaps, but ones that could have been manufactured even more cheaply. And ones which were far less likely to bring the NPA down on their heads, as well. *Mekoha's* violent side effects were certain to infuriate Matsuko, and not just because she felt a genuine mission to protect the Stilties from off-world exploitation. Only a lunatic would be unconcerned over the massive distribution of something that could turn the most peaceful native into a raging maniac.

But, as he'd told the man on the screen, that was the Organization's concern, not his. Besides, his lip curled unpleasantly, anything that upset the Resident Commissioner, the NPA, *and* the Royal Manticoran Navy was eminently worthwhile in its own right.

He resumed his pacing, and his eyes were dark and ugly with memories. There had been a time when Captain the Honorable Denver Summervale, Royal Manticoran Marine Corps, would have been on the other side of this problem. But today he was in his element, on the side he should have been on from the beginning, for the Marines had decided they'd made a mistake the day they accepted his oath of allegiance. One they had corrected in the formal drama of a full-dress court martial.

A dangerous snarl bared his teeth, and his pace quickened as he recalled the moment. The spectators' humming silence, with the point of his dress sword turned towards him on the table before the glittering senior officers while the president of the court read the formal verdict. The roll of drums as he was marched out in mess dress uniform to face his regiment, an officer of the Queen in gorgeous black and green, standing with emotionless face while the most junior enlisted man in his own battalion ripped the buttons and decorations from his tunic to the slow, bitter tapping of the drum. The expression on his colonel's face as his epaulets and insignia were taken from him to be ground under a booted heel. The flat, metallic crack as the blade of his archaic dress sword snapped in the colonel's gloved hands.

Oh, yes, he remembered. And, despite his hatred, he knew they'd been right. They were the sheep, but Denver Summervale was a wolf, and he'd made his way even then in the way a wolf knew best—with his teeth.

He dropped back into the chair before the com terminal, grinning dangerously at the blank screen. His father had been there, too, he recalled. His pious, noble father, clinging to the fringes of the Summervale glory despite his poverty. What had the high and mighty family ever given them, that they should ape its manners and honor its name? *Their* branch had none of the wealth, none of the power, that clung to the direct line of the Dukes of Cromarty!

Summervale's hands clenched in his lap, and he closed his eyes. His own flesh and blood sat in the prime minister's chair. Even then, the precious Duke of Cromarty had been Lord of the Exchequer, second in seniority in Her Majesty's Government, and had he raised a hand to help his distant cousin? Not he! Not that noble, proper, sanctimonious *bastard*.

But that, too, was all right. He made his hands relax, savoring the thought of the gossip and sidelong glances his disgrace must have brought upon the noble Duke and treasuring the look on his father's face as his sword snapped. All his life, his father had preached to him of duty and responsibility, of the glorious role his family had played in the history of the Kingdom. But duty and responsibility hadn't paid his debts. Family history hadn't won *him* the respect and fear it won the "true" line.

No, those things he had earned himself, earned on the "field of honor" while he laughed at their pretensions.

He opened his eyes once more, staring at his reflection in the com screen, remembering the dawn quiet and the weight of a pistol. Remembering the seconds and the master of the list's stern expression as he stared across thirty meters of smooth grass at a pale-faced opponent. It had been . . . Bullard? No. That first time had been Scott, and he shivered as his palm felt again the shock of recoil and Scott's white shirt blossomed crimson and he fell.

He shook himself. It had been a business transaction, nothing more, he told himself, and knew he lied. Oh, it *had* been business, and the money his secret sponsor had slipped him had cleared his debts . . . for a time. Until the next time. But the sensual thrill of knowing, even as Scott crumpled, that his bullet had blown his target's aristocratic heart apart—*that* had been his true reward. And the reason it had been so easy to accept the next assignment, and the next.

Yet in the end, the very people he hated with all his soul had won. "Professional duelist," they'd called him, when all the time they'd meant "paid killer." And they'd been right. He admitted that here in the quiet, empty room. But he'd killed too many of them, even when his sponsors would have been willing to settle for a wound. The blood taste had been too sweet, the aura of fear too heady, and finally the Corps had had enough.

He'd killed a "brother officer"—as if the uniform a dead man wore should matter! He wasn't the first serving officer to do so, but there were too many bodies in his past, too many families that owed too many debts. They couldn't try him for murder, for duels were legal. He'd faced his opponent's fire, and they couldn't prove he'd accepted money for it. But they'd all known the truth, and they *could* bring up his entire record: his gambling, his women, the adulterous affairs he'd used to lure targets onto the field, the arrogance he'd let color his relations with senior officers as the terror of his reputation grew. And that had been enough to find him "unfit to wear the Queen's uniform" and led to that bright, hot morning and the slow, degrading tap of the drums.

And it had led *here*, as well. Here where the money was good, but even here the money was only part of it. Only the means to an end that let him sneer at their self-proclaimed nobility of purpose and avenge himself upon them again and again, even if they never knew it.

His nostrils flared, and he pushed himself up out of the chair.

All right. He'd been warned that the operation was in jeopardy, and its security was his responsibility. So be it. There were too many records, too much evidence, in this facility, and as his employer had said, the lab was only hardware.

There were ways to evacuate, and there were ways to evacuate, he thought with a slow, hungry smile. If he had to leave the equipment behind, then he could at least abandon it in a way that would give him personal satisfaction.

He opened the com room door and walked briskly down the hall. He had arrangements to make.

• CHAPTER FIFTEEN

The well-dressed man looked vaguely out of place in the luxurious office's comfortably cushioned chair and his civilian clothing, despite his expensive tailoring. His face was dark and lean, the sort of face which has been trained to say only what its owner wants it to say, and his eyes were hard as he accepted the chilled glass and sipped. Ice rattled like brittle music as he lowered the glass, and his host sank into a facing chair and tried not to look anxious.

"I was sorry to hear about your . . . unanticipated problems, Mr. Canning." The visitor's voice was deep and well-modulated, almost gentle, but his host shifted uncomfortably. "I trust," the visitor went on, "that they aren't of such a nature as to interfere with our timetable?"

Wallace Canning, the People's Republic of Haven's consul on the planet Medusa, felt sweat bead his forehead. His guest might be in civilian clothes, but every time Canning looked at him he saw the uniform he ought to have been wearing—the green and gray uniform of a rear admiral in the People's Navy with the hourglass and sword of Naval Intelligence.

"I can't say for certain," he said at length, picking his words with caution. "Everything is too up in the air and unsettled. Until we know what this Harrington is going to do next, the best we can do is guess and double-check our potential vulnerabilities."

"I see." The business-suited admiral leaned back in his chair, swirling his drink in his hand and listening to its icy tinkle, and pursed his lips. Canning tried not to twitch under his level regard.

"It seems to me," the admiral resumed after a moment, "that there's been some sloppy execution at this end, Mr. Consul. We were assured the situation was under control. Indeed, I expected this to be a routine visit to receive your final readiness report, and now I hear that you can only 'guess' about what the opposition is going to do next." He shook his head. "Any covert operation has a built-in risk factor, but we've put too much time into this one, and Operation Odysseus is too important for guesswork or field operations that can be completely overturned by a single new factor."

"It can't be helped, and it's no one person's fault, either here or in the field," Canning said, choosing to assume the role of a man defending his subordinates and not himself. "And the 'single factor' you refer to was a complete wild card no one saw coming, here or on Haven. We *couldn't* see it coming, Adm—Sir, because there was absolutely no way to predict that we'd get someone like this lunatic assigned to Basilisk Station after all these years."

"I am aware of that. In fact, Mr. Canning, I was the one who chose the original timing for Odysseus's activation when Pavel Young was assigned here."

"Yes. Well, things were moving exactly according to plan until *she* turned up. Since then—" Canning broke off and shrugged, raising one hand, palm uppermost.

"I understand the change in circumstances, Mr. Canning." The admiral spoke with the patience of one addressing a very small child, his eyes deceptively mild, and the consul writhed internally but knew better than to protest.

"Moreover, unlike you, I have a dossier on Commander Harrington," the admiral continued. "I'm sorry to say it isn't as extensive as I'd like. As you may know, NavInt seldom builds an in-depth package on anyone who hasn't yet made list, unless they come from a particularly prominent family. All we have on her are the standard clippings and her public record, but even those are enough to indicate that she's an entirely different proposition from an over-bred cretin like Young. And, all in all, I would be forced to agree that Harrington is scarcely the sort of officer one might reasonably have expected that oaf Janacek to assign to his own private little hellhole out here."

Canning relaxed a tiny bit, only to tense anew as his guest smiled thinly.

"Nonetheless, Mr. Canning, I can't escape the conclusion that you've taken your security too lightly. From the very beginning, you seem to have relied not on your own precautions but almost solely on the RMN's inefficiency. Granted," he waved a hand gently, "that inefficiency was part of our original planning, but you shouldn't have *relied* on its continuation. Certainly it should have been evident that your arrangements required a drastic reevaluation as soon as Harrington started shaking things up."

"I—" Canning stood and crossed abruptly to the liquor cabinet. He poured himself a martini with hands that trembled slightly, took a swallow, then turned back to the admiral.

"I *have* taken some precautions, Sir, whatever you may think. Admittedly, they were long-term, routine measures, and I'll concede I was slow to realize what was happening and adjust to Harrington's presence, as well. But I've been here over six local years, and this is the first Manticoran officer who's even bothered to check manifests against canister numbers in all that time."

"If that were all she were doing, Mr. Canning, or even if she were just arresting smugglers, I would be far less concerned," his guest said with deadly precision. "But that isn't all she's doing, is it? She's actively supporting Matsuko and the NPA. The local manpower she's released from customs and space control duties alone would constitute a major threat to operational security. When you add the overflights she's ordered to what your informants are reporting—" He shook his head sadly, and Canning took another long swallow of his drink.

"We're not exactly completely naked, Sir," he said. "I know it's only a matter of time before her recon flights hit pay dirt, but as I've said, and despite any overconfidence on my part, we do have a multi-level cover in place against exactly that eventuality. And despite her activities in space, she hasn't even come close to bothering Captain Coglin. As for the rest of her actions," he added a bit more defensively, "I've done everything I can to get her recalled. I've lodged over twenty individual protests, now, and I'm using my contacts with other off-world merchant factors to generate more of them. The Manticoran Admiralty has to be feeling the heat, particularly in light of the political ramifications."

"I know about the protests, Mr. Canning. But while you're no doubt correct about the pressure they're placing on their admiralty, have you considered the fact they've no doubt also given her superiors ample confirmation that she's doing something we don't like?"

Canning flushed, and the first slow flickers of anger burned through his anxiety. All very well for the admiral to waltz in here after the fact and criticize, but what else did he expect Canning to do? Damn it, protests were the only offensive weapons he had! And, he thought resentfully, if he *hadn't* lodged them, the admiral would be chopping his ears off for *that!*

"Well, so much for spilt milk." The admiral sighed, setting his glass on a small table and rising. "Why don't you tell me what's gone right, instead?"

He crossed to Canning's desk and bent over the unrolled map spread across the blotter. The paper chart was far less detailed and much more difficult to manipulate than a holo map would have been, but it had never entered the consulate's electronic data base, either. And, unlike an individual holo map reader, it could be rolled up and shoved into a vault with a thermal-destruct security system. Those were considerations that made any incidental inconvenience unimportant.

Now the admiral frowned down at the map, tracing terrain features with a fingertip. Unlike the majority of his naval contemporaries, he was as comfortable with planetary maps as ʋith star charts, for his particular nameless branch of NavInt was more concerned with Trojan Horses than open warfare. Now he tapped the map and looked up at Canning.

"The lab here on the plateau. It has a direct up-link to our orbital collector?"

"No, Sir." Canning crossed to the desk and managed his first smile of the interview. "It relays through ground stations here and here—" he indicated two mountain peaks in the Outback "—and the initial ground station doesn't link to our collector at all." He met the admiral's inquiring gaze, and his smile turned into something like a grin. "We've been tapping into Dame Estelle's own backup collector."

"You mean you're drawing your power from the *Manticoran* grid?"

"No, Sir. It never enters the grid. This is their secondary collector, for use only if the main goes down for maintenance or repairs. Aside from their regular demand tests, we're the only station on it. Even if they find our tap, it won't tell them who set it up, and trying to figure out how it got there should point their attention in some very . . . interesting directions."

"I see." The admiral nodded with the first, faint signs of approval. "But, of course, if they *do* find it, they'll also find the ground station it feeds, won't they?"

"Yes, Sir, they will, but that's where the cover plan I mentioned comes in. Colonel Westerfeldt has operational responsibility for the field activities, and he's done an excellent job of hiding our tracks and planting red herrings. In fact, we *want* them to find the ground stations—and the lab—if they look hard enough."

The admiral raised his eyebrows, and Canning felt himself smile almost naturally as he continued.

"We've set up a fallback lab that uses its own hydro generators, and if they do find this one, it won't tell them much—unless they pick up some of our personnel, of course. But even if they do, none of the equipment was made in the Republic. In fact, most of it was built by . . . a certain Manticoran merchant cartel, shall we say?" He paused, and this time it was the admiral's turn to smile faintly in understanding. "More importantly, the local security man and the techs operating it are also Manticoran, and they have no idea they're working for us. They believe they're working for a domestic criminal syndicate. We've had to bring in some of our own people to operate the backup lab if it comes to that, but even there, almost all the equipment was manufactured in Manticore. Finally, we've had our Manticoran fall guys maintaining a meticulous set of books for their fictitious employers. If the NPA hits the lab, they'll find records the people working in the lab fully believe to be genuine and which point directly away from us."

"I see," the admiral repeated. His finger drew idle patterns on the map, and his smile faded as he frowned down at it. Then he tapped a spot far south of the vast plateau. "And the main site?"

"Completely secure, Sir," Canning said confidently. "Every bit of it's underground, and there's never been any direct contact between it and either of our lab facilities, even by air. Every shipment's routed through this staging area—" his own finger tapped a spot well to the west "—and shipped in from there on the ground using Stilty caravaneers. In addition, Colonel Westerfeldt's on-site personnel were all very carefully chosen for deniability, even if the NPA should stumble right over them. Unlike our backup lab techs, all of them are Manticorans with long criminal records, and none of them knows exactly whom the colonel is working for."

"Indeed." The admiral cocked his head, then allowed a fresh smile, much stronger than the first, to cross his own face. "I may, perhaps, have been overly pessimistic, Mr. Canning. You seem to have built in more security than I'd anticipated."

"It wasn't all my doing," Canning replied. "As I say, Colonel Westerfeldt's our field man here, and your own people, picked an excellent cover for Coglin's presence. And, of course, Ambassador Gowan has actually coordinated most of the operation from Manticore." He hid an inner smirk as the admiral nodded. Gowan was a very big fish, a retired Dolist manager with powerful friends back home on Haven. It never hurt to spread the credit (and any potential blame) over broader shoulders than one's own, and even NavInt would hesitate to antagonize Gowan.

"So," the admiral said after a moment, crossing back to his chair to reclaim his drink. He sipped thoughtfully, staring out the office windows into the night and the floodlit brightness of the consulate's grounds. "Your ground-side security is in better shape than I'd feared, but that still leaves the orbital side wide open, and that's where this Harrington can hurt us worst."

"Yes and no, Sir." Canning moved up to stand at the admiral's shoulder and gaze out into the grounds. "It's too late for her to intercept any of the really critical shipments. Everything we need is already down and in place, except for the *mekoha* we're still manufacturing, and I canceled the last two off-world shipments on my own initiative when I realized what was happening. I'd really prefer to have them down here, but we can live without them, and having them spotted in transit would be far too revealing. As for Coglin, he should be completely secure as long as he just sits tight aboard ship. If there's no contact with the surface, Harrington will have neither cause nor justification for interfering with him at all."

"Good." The admiral sounded markedly less hostile, and Canning let himself relax a bit further. But then the admiral pursed his lips again. "Still, even if everything else goes perfectly, *Fearless*'s mere presence in Medusa orbit could derail the entire operation when it kicks off. I don't like how tightly Harrington is integrating her own operations with the NPA. She's got the better part of a company of Manticoran Marines up there, with enough combat equipment to make a real difference."

"With all due respect, Sir, I think that's unlikely. They'd have to know what was coming and lay contingency plans ahead of time to affect the actual operation in any material way. Oh, I don't deny they can probably limit the damage, but I don't see any possible way that they could limit it enough to make a real difference. As long as they can't stop it entirely, we still have our opening, and not even a full company of Marines already in place in the enclaves can do that."

"Perhaps." The admiral rocked on his toes for a moment, rubbing the rim of his glass with a fingertip. "And perhaps not. What do your sources in Manticore have to say about Young?"

"He's got his ship at *Hephaestus*, and our network's a lot weaker on the military side, but all the indications are that he realizes he's screwed up. I'd guess—but it's only a guess, of course—that he's making every effort to get back here before Harrington makes him look any worse."

"It would be difficult," the admiral observed with a cynical smile, "for *anyone* to make Pavel Young look worse than he is."

He rocked in silent thought for a few more seconds, then nodded to himself.

"Find out how long he's going to be there, Mr. Canning. I have no doubt his first action on returning here will be to send Harrington as far away from Medusa as the limits of Basilisk Station permit, and I'd far rather have *him* in Medusa orbit when the penny drops. If he'll be back in less than—oh, another Manticoran month or so—I want the operation delayed until he returns."

"That may be difficult," Canning said cautiously. "We've got almost everything in place, and our shaman is primed.

I'm not positive he can hold them in check that long. The actual H-hour has always been rather indeterminate, you know. Then, too, there's probably a limit to how long Coglin can sit up there without someone like Harrington getting suspicious."

"Perhaps. But, as I say, I don't want Harrington close to the planet when it kicks off. If at all possible, I want her several hours away, far enough for us to get the running start we need. As for Coglin, I think his cover will hold a while longer, and I can arrange to hold our other assets on station for up to three or four Manticoran months if I have to."

"I'll see what I can do, Sir." Canning still sounded doubtful, and the admiral smiled.

"I'm sure you will, Mr. Canning. And, in the meantime, I'll see what we can do to . . . redirect Commander Harrington's energies."

"I've pretty much exhausted the diplomatic options, Sir," Canning pointed out.

"No, Mr. Consul. You've exhausted *Haven's* diplomatic options." The admiral turned to face him with a much broader smile, and Canning's eyebrows rose.

"I'm not sure I see what you're driving at, Sir."

"Oh, come now! Haven't you just been telling me how hard you've worked to provide the Manticorans with a culprit closer to home? Well, what use is a cat's-paw if you don't use it?"

"You mean—?"

"Of course, Mr. Canning." The admiral actually chuckled. "I'm quite certain Harrington has irritated the Manticoran merchant cartels as badly as she has us. From what you've reported about her operations, she's already cost them a bundle, and that doesn't even consider the humiliation she's no doubt inflicted by catching them with their hands dirty. I suspect most of them are just as eager as we are to see her teeth pulled, wouldn't you agree?"

"Yes," Canning agreed with a slow smile. "Yes, I imagine they are. But by the same token, Sir, doesn't it seem likely they've already put all the pressure they can on the Government and Admiralty?"

"Perhaps. But I was thinking about something a little more direct than that," the admiral said unpleasantly, "and I've been studying our dossier on Commander Harrington since I learned of the situation here. As I say, it's not as complete as I might wish, but it does offer some potentially useful information. For example, did you know that her father and mother are both doctors?" Canning shook his head. "Well, they are. In fact, they're both senior partners in Duvalier Medical Associates on Sphinx. It's an excellent outfit, with a high reputation in neural and genetic surgery . . . and it just happens that seventy percent of Duvalier Medical's public stock is held by Christy and Sons, which, in turn, is a wholly owned subsidiary of the Hauptman Cartel." The admiral smiled almost dreamily. "I always knew keeping an eye on Hauptman would be useful some day, even before this operation came up."

"But does Hauptman even realize it, Sir?"

"Perhaps not yet, but I'm sure we can call it to their attention—discreetly, of course. But, then, we've already called several items to Hauptman's attention, haven't we?"

"Yes, Sir, we have," Canning agreed. He furrowed his brow as he considered ways and means. "My regularly scheduled courier to Ambassador Gowan leaves tomorrow morning," he said thoughtfully.

"An excellent suggestion, Mr. Canning." The admiral nodded and raised his glass in a toast. "To Commander Harrington, may she have other things to concern herself with very shortly," he murmured.

• CHAPTER SIXTEEN

Scotty Tremaine hit the powered adjustment button and
stretched hugely as the purring motor moved the copilot's
seat back from the pinnace's console. He rotated his shoulder joints, grimacing as he worked the stiffness from them,
then rose.

"I'll be back in a few minutes, Ruth," he told his pilot.

"No sweat, Mr. Tremaine." Coxswain Third Class Ruth
Kleinmeuller grinned. "I don't guess the planet's going anywhere till you get back, Sir."

"Probably not," he agreed, and opened the cockpit
hatch. He made his way down the cramped passage (pinnaces were little larger than pre-space jumbo jets) to the
flight engineer's cubicle and poked his head in.

"How's it going?"

"Nothing, Sir." The rating manning the sensor equipment wrinkled her nose at him. "As far as this outfit's
concerned, we're flying over lots and lots of nothing."

"I see." Tremaine smothered a smile at her tone. Her
reply was respectful and reasonably cheerful, but he heard
the disgust under its surface. His people had been less than
pleased to be detached to customs work at the outset, but
that had changed over the past few hectic weeks. They'd
learned to take a positive glee in making a major bust, and
what it was doing to their bank accounts back home didn't
hurt. Now they actively resented any diversion from the
steadily thinner pickings of the orbital traffic.

"Y'know, Sir," a voice said from behind him, "without
more pinnaces, this is going to take a long time."

Tremaine turned to face PO Harkness.

"Yes, PO, I do know," he said mildly. "But unless you happen to have a half-dozen more of them tucked away in your locker, I don't see anyone else we can assign to it. Do you?"

"No, Sir," Harkness said. The ensign, he reflected, had come a long way since that first contraband discovery. Harkness liked Tremaine—he was neither an arrogant snot, like too many ensigns who were afraid of betraying their inexperience, nor the sort to avoid responsibility—but he'd been testing the youngster. There were many ways to find out just what an officer had inside, and there were depths to young Mr. Tremaine the casual observer might not suspect.

"I was just thinking, Sir," the petty officer went on after a moment.

"About what, PO?"

"Well, Sir, it occurred to me that we're diverting one pinnace full-time from customs work, right?" Tremaine nodded. "With the close passes we have to make, this is going to take days then," Harkness went on, "but what about all the other boats?" Tremaine cocked his head and made a little "go on" gesture with his fingers. "The thing I was thinking, Sir, is that each of those other boats is making at least six space-to-ground passes every day—down and back every time they change off crews—and that got me started wondering. Couldn't we maybe reroute their landings and liftoffs? I mean, they've got the same sensors we've got, don't they?"

"Hmmmm." Tremaine rubbed his chin. "That's true enough. We could lay off flight paths to cover this entire hemisphere, couldn't we? And that would free *us* up to cover the other side of the planet." He nodded slowly, eyes narrowing in thought, and Harkness nodded back.

"This, PO," the ensign said judiciously, "bears thinking on. Thanks."

"You're welcome, Sir," Harkness said, and Tremaine headed back to the cockpit and the pinnace's com.

* * *

Lieutenant Commander Santos stepped into the briefing room and paused behind the captain's chair. Honor was busy perusing the latest data on planetary power usage and didn't hear her come in, but she looked up at the sound of a sudden, juicy crunch.

Nimitz's buzzing purr confirmed her suspicions, and she shot a humorous glare at Santos as she saw the celery stalk clutched in the treecat's right hand-paw. Nimitz's carnivore fangs weren't designed for vegetable matter, despite his tree-dweller origins. Treecats were the top of Sphinx's arboreal food chain, preying on the smaller vegetarians and omnivores who inhabited their domain, and his needle-sharp teeth shredded the celery into stringy green strands—*wet*, stringy green strands—as he chewed.

Santos gave her a half-apologetic glance as she watched the 'cat make a blissful mess, and Honor shook her head.

"You know that stuff's bad for him, Dominica," she chided.

"But he likes it so much, Skipper," Santos excused herself.

"I know he does, but he can't metabolize it—not fully, anyway. He's got the wrong enzymes for terrestrial cellulose. It just fills him up, and then he picks at his supper."

Nimitz paused in his chewing. His vocal apparatus might be utterly unsuited to anything resembling human speech, but he understood a surprisingly large vocabulary, and he'd heard this particular speech from his person too often over the years. Now he gave her a disdainful glance, flirted his tail, and rose on his rear feet to rub his head against Santos's arm, making *his* views on the subject abundantly clear. The engineer was his favorite among *Fearless*'s officers—probably, Honor reflected darkly, because she always had a stash of celery somewhere about her person these days—and Santos grinned down at him.

"Well," Honor sighed finally, "I guess I should be used to

it. The little devil always finds *someone* to pander to his vices."

"He is kind of cute, isn't he?" Santos agreed. She gave the 'cat an affectionate chin rub, then sank into an empty chair at the table, and Honor smiled. She was, she reflected, a terrible sucker where people with a kindness for treecats were concerned.

"You wanted to see me about something?" Santos asked after a moment.

"Yes." Honor tapped her data display with a stylus. "I've been looking at Barney's figures on probable power usage. They seem awfully vague to me."

"Well, it's not an easy thing to quantify, Skipper." Santos ran her fingers through her hair and frowned thoughtfully. "He doesn't have very solid data on what they've got to use their power *on*, so his people have had to make a lot of WAGs." Honor raised an eyebrow, and Santos grinned. "That's a technical term we engineers use. It means 'Wild-Assed Guess,' " she explained. "They can feed in some hard figures from outside observation—things like exterior lighting, com traffic, and heat exchangers—but without complete specs on an enclave's interior hardware, they're shooting in the dark. Just knowing whether or not a given set of people remember to turn the lights off when they leave the room could throw any estimate off by a pretty wide margin."

"Um." Honor rubbed the tip of her nose and leaned back in her chair, listening to Nimitz crunch and slurp away at his celery. "How are we coming on the collector taps?" she asked suddenly.

"We've got three—no, four—to go," Santos replied. "Sorry it's taking so long, but with just the cutters—"

Honor waved a hand, cutting her off, and smiled.

"Don't apologize. You're doing well, especially since we're trying to keep anyone from noticing what we're up to." She rocked her chair slightly, still gazing at the data on her terminal, then shrugged.

"All right, let's see if we can come at this a different way, Dominica," she murmured, and pressed her intercom key.

"Officer of the watch," Lieutenant Webster's voice replied.

"Com, this is the Captain. Is the exec on the bridge?"

"No, Ma'am. I think he's down in Missile Two. Tactical's been having some problems with the magazine feed."

"I see. Well, buzz him, would you? If he's free, I'd like to see him in my briefing room. And ask Lieutenant Cardones to come in, too, please."

"Yes, Ma'am." The intercom was silent for a few moments, then spoke again. "They're on their way, Ma'am."

"Thank you, Samuel." Honor keyed off and looked at Santos. "If Barney can't give us hard numbers, maybe we can make his WAGs work for us, instead."

"How?"

"Well, it occurs to me that—"

Honor broke off as the briefing room hatch opened to admit Cardones. The lieutenant nodded just a bit shyly to Santos, then looked at Honor.

"You wanted me, Ma'am?"

"Yes. Have a seat, Guns. I've got a problem I need you and the exec to help me solve."

"Problem, Ma'am?" Cardones sounded a trifle wary, and Honor smiled.

"Nothing to do with your department. It's just—"

She paused again as the hatch opened once more. McKeon wore coveralls over his uniform, and there was grease on them. That was one thing Honor unreservedly approved of in her prickly executive officer; he was never above getting his own hands dirty.

"You sent for me, Captain?" he asked, far more formally than Cardones. Honor nodded, feeling her own face stiffen with a chill of answering formality, and pointed at the chair opposite Santos.

"I did," she said. McKeon sat. "How's the missile feed problem?" she asked, trying—again—to draw him out.

"Nothing major, Captain. I think it's pretty much solved," he replied crisply, and she hid a sigh. Behind her, Nimitz stopped crunching his celery for a moment, then resumed with more restrained gusto.

"Well," she said, "as I was telling Rafe, we have a problem. We're trying to spot unusual power flows, and we don't have a reliable base usage to pick them out of." McKeon nodded, gray eyes thoughtful but cool in his expressionless face.

"What I want you and Rafe to do," Honor went on, "is take all the input from the solar collector taps and compare it to Major Isvarian's rough estimates. What I'm looking for is a total usage figure over several days' time for each enclave, one we can relate to his estimate on a proportional basis."

She paused, and Cardones glanced at the first officer, as if waiting for him to ask a question. When McKeon only nodded, he cleared his own throat.

"Excuse me, Ma'am, but what good will that do us?"

"Maybe not a lot, Rafe, but I want to see how close Barney came in his original estimate. If he's close, or if he's off by the same proportion in each case, then we'll have both an indication of his numbers' reliability and some idea of what a given enclave's power needs *should* look like. If he's close in most cases but off by a large factor in one or two instances, we'll have an indication that the ones outside his estimate bear closer examination."

Cardones nodded. McKeon simply sat silently, waiting.

"In addition," Honor went on, "I want the changes in power demand tracked on an hourly basis. Get a feel for the pattern. In particular, I want to know if any of them use large amounts of power during local down periods—especially late at night, for instance. Compare the fluctuations in power usage between all the enclaves on a time basis. If demand drops by a lower percentage in one or two of them, I want to know about it. From what Major Isvarian and his NPA types tell me, a *mekoha* lab wouldn't be able to shut down in mid-process, so if someone's power levels remain high when all their neighbors' drop, we may have an indication that we're closing in on the lab."

Cardones nodded again, eyes bright with interest. Unlike, Honor noted, McKeon's.

"I'll get right on it, Ma'am," the exec said after a moment. "Will there be anything else, Captain?"

"No," Honor said quietly, and McKeon rose with a quick nod. He beckoned to Cardones, and the two of them filed out. Honor watched the hatch close behind them and sighed.

"Skipper?" It was Santos, her voice soft, and Honor flushed. She'd forgotten the engineer's presence, and she castigated herself silently for betraying her concern over McKeon in front of one of her other officers. She made herself turn to Santos, hiding her chagrin.

"Yes, Dominica?"

"I—" The engineer paused, looking down at her hands on the edge of the table, then squared her shoulders. "About the commander, Ma'am," she said. "I don't—"

"Lieutenant Commander McKeon isn't your concern," Honor said quietly.

"I know that, Ma'am, but—" Santos drew a deep breath, disregarding her captain's clear hint to drop the subject. "Skipper, I know you're concerned about him. For that matter," it was her face's turn to darken, "I know you were concerned about *all* of us. We . . . weren't exactly on the top of our form when we got here, were we?"

"Have I complained?" Honor asked, and met Santos's eyes levelly when the engineer looked up.

"No, Ma'am. But, then, you wouldn't, would you?" Santos's voice was as level as Honor's eyes, and Honor made a tiny, uncomfortable gesture with her hand. Nimitz swarmed down into her lap, still clutching the stub of his celery stalk, and lifted the front third of his body onto the table to look back and forth between the two women.

"The thing is, Skipper, I've known Alistair McKeon for a

long time," Santos went on quietly. "He's a friend—and I'm your next senior officer."

Honor sighed and leaned back. She ought to shut Santos up, she thought. If there was one thing she hated, it was discussing an officer behind his back, especially with one of his juniors. But she was very nearly at the end of her rope where McKeon was concerned. She'd tried everything she could think of to reach him—to make him the true second-in-command she needed, not simply an efficient, perpetually unengaged automaton—and failed. And there was no malice or spite in Santos's voice, only concern. Besides, Dominica was right; she *was* Honor's next most senior officer, third in *Fearless*'s chain of command, with not just the right but the duty to speak up if she saw a problem.

The engineer's expression relaxed a bit at her captain's reaction, and she reached out to stroke Nimitz's ears, keeping her eyes on her fingers.

"Alistair is a good officer, usually, Skipper," she said. "More than that, he's a good man. But if you'll pardon my saying so, it's pretty obvious the two of you just aren't on the same wavelength, and I don't think it's because you haven't tried. I've never seen him like this, and I'm worried about him."

Honor watched Santos thoughtfully. There was no self-serving edge in the engineer's voice, only concern. This was no attempt to curry favor with her commander or cut her immediate superior's throat when he was absent and unable to defend himself.

"And?" she said, unable—and unwilling—to criticize McKeon by agreeing with Santos's statement and voicing her own concern.

"I just—" Santos paused, staring down at the fingers caressing the treecat. "I just want you to know that whatever's wrong is hurting him, too, Skipper," she said finally. "He tries not to show it, but I think he thinks he's letting you down—letting the *ship* down. And he is, in a way. I don't know why, but he's just not *involved* the way he was under Captain Rath, and he loves every scrape and dent of this old ship." She raised her head and looked around the briefing room, eyes slightly misty, and smiled. "So do I," she admitted. "She's old, and they raped her when they gutted her armament, but she's a grand old bitch. She won't let us down in the crunch, and—" she met Honor's eyes again "—neither will Alistair. Whatever his problem is, he won't let you down when it really counts, Skipper. That's—" She paused again, then waved her hand. "That's all I wanted to say."

"I understand, Dominica," Honor said softly.

"Yes, Ma'am." Santos stood and inhaled sharply, then gave Nimitz one last caress and squared her shoulders. "Well, I guess I'd better get back on those taps, Skipper," she said more briskly, and followed McKeon and Cardones out the hatch.

Nimitz settled down in Honor's lap to finish his celery, and she leaned back, running her hand down his flank in long, slow strokes while she considered what Santos had just said. It must have taken guts—and deep concern—for the engineer to risk exposing herself that way. (It never occurred to Honor to wonder if her own actions or example might have had anything to do with Santos's openness.) Most officers, she reflected, would have taken great care to distance themselves from an executive officer they suspected was in bad odor with his CO, lest any of the captain's displeasure splash on them. And *how* Dominica had said it was just as important as what she'd said. Her concern was obvious, and it was for the ship as a whole first and for McKeon as a person second, but the fact that she cared about McKeon was clear.

And important, Honor decided. It spoke well for any officer that one of his juniors would speak up for him, especially when it was the junior who stood to gain the most if he fell short of his commanding officer's standards. More than that, Santos's remarks reinforced her own judgment that

McKeon was grappling with something inside himself, something that even the engineer didn't fully understand.

Dominica Santos would not have spoken for an officer she didn't believe was worth defending, however much she liked him. Honor was certain of that, and as she replayed her own encounters with McKeon, she realized the engineer was right. Whatever his problem was, however hard it seemed for him to meet his captain halfway, he was doing his job. Not as well as he could have, not without a distinctly dangerous disengagement and brittleness, and definitely not the way Honor would have preferred, but he was *doing* it. He was *making* himself do it, even while it was obvious that something was tearing him up inside.

She sighed and rose, transferring Nimitz to her shoulder as the 'cat popped the last half-centimeter of celery into his mouth. He pressed his chin into her short hair, chewing happily, and she folded her hands behind her and started for the hatch herself.

It wasn't fair. She shouldn't have to make allowances for her executive officer, shouldn't have to worry about his support or what inner problems were affecting his duty. But no one had ever said life was fair, and the RMN tradition was that there were no bad crews, only bad captains. That applied to the captain's officers, as well. Much as she might want, even need, for McKeon to drop his barriers, it was her job to work with him—or to replace him. And she couldn't replace him. Not simply because the "chemistry" between them was bad.

And not, she thought as the hatch opened, when Santos was right. Somehow, Honor knew, whatever might be bothering Alistair McKeon, he *wouldn't* let her down in the crunch.

• CHAPTER SEVENTEEN

"Well, now, Mr. Tremaine. Would you look at that?" Sensor Tech 1/c Yammata tapped his display, and Scotty Tremaine leaned close. To the untrained eye, the faint blotch of light in the center of the screen could have been anything; given what they'd been looking for, he knew it could be only one thing.

"How big?" he asked.

"Well," Yammata manipulated controls and frowned thoughtfully, "I figure they're shielded, Sir—I sure can't get a good read on the user end— but the feeder beam seems to be peaking at about two hundred kilowatts." He looked up and met the ensign's eyes expressionlessly. "That's a lot of juice for a bunch of Stilties."

"It is, indeed, Hiro," Tremaine murmured. "It is indeed." He shook himself. "What's the location?"

"Sixty-three klicks west-southwest of the Muddy Wash Valley, Sir," Yammata replied. He tapped another light blotch, smaller but much brighter. "That's their direct feed station, but it must be a relay. It's on the side of a ridge, well below its crest, and I don't see any up-link."

"Um-hum." Tremaine watched the display for a few more seconds while the pinnace's low-orbit sweep took it towards the horizon. Then he nodded and clapped the sensor tech on the shoulder. "Good job, Hiro. I'll make sure the skipper knows who spotted it."

"Thanks, Sir." Yammata grinned, and Tremaine turned to his NPA com officer.

"Punch up the ship, Chris. I think the Old Lady will want to know about this."

* * *

"It looks like you were right, Honor." Dame Estelle Matsuko's face was distinctly unhappy on the com screen. "There's *something* there, anyway, and whatever it is, it certainly isn't legal. The entire Mossyback Range is off limits, and so is the Mossyback Plateau."

"It doesn't necessarily follow that it's a drug lab," Honor pointed out, and Dame Estelle snorted.

"Of course it doesn't—and if you can say that three times in a row with a straight face, I'll buy you a five-course dinner at Cosmo's."

Honor chuckled at the reference to Landing's most expensive, and exclusive, restaurant, but then she sobered.

"You're right, of course," she admitted. "And even if it isn't the lab, it's still illegal. The question, I suppose, is what you want to do about it, Ma'am."

"What do you think I'm going to do about it?" Dame Estelle's expression was grim. "Barney Isvarian is putting together a raiding party right now."

"Do you need any additional manpower? I could land some of Captain Papadapolous's Marines—?"

"I expect we've got all the troops we need, but thanks. I'll check with Barney. If he thinks he needs some help, I'll certainly let you know," Dame Estelle said gratefully.

Major Barney Isvarian, Medusan Native Protection Agency, slithered forward through waist-high knobs of *shemak* moss and tried to ignore the chemical stench of its sap. His mottled fatigues and body armor weren't as good as the Corps' reactive camouflage, but they blended well with the monotonous background. The hugely out-sized insects that served Medusa as "birds" swooped and darted above the moss, and he made himself move even more slowly to avoid startling them. Unlikely though anyone was to be looking this way and notice a sudden eruption of bugs from the moss, it was still possible, and he had no intention of blowing this operation now.

He reached the crest of the rise and paused to catch his breath as Sergeant Danforth eased up beside him. Like Isvarian, Danforth was an ex-Marine, and he unlimbered his massive plasma rifle with reassuring competence. Alloy and plastic clicked as he mounted the one-hundred-fifty-centimeter weapon on its bipod, inserted the heavy power pack, and snapped the electronic sight into place. He hit the self-test switch with his thumb, then nodded and burrowed the stock into his shoulder, peering through the sight at the buildings below.

Isvarian checked his own sidearm, then raised his electronic binoculars to survey the same scene, and his lips pursed in grudging admiration. No wonder the aerial shots hadn't shown anything. The Corps itself couldn't have done a better job of concealing the place.

The structures were clearly off-world in origin—sturdy pre-fabs that might have come from any planet—but they were buried almost to the eaves, and their roofs had been covered in sod. Rolling knobs of *shemak* grew across them, completely breaking up their outlines, and he was willing to bet there was a hefty layer of insulation under each of those roofs to prevent any betraying heat signature. That would only make sense, particularly with the volcanic springs two klicks east of them. Waste heat could be ducted to them and lost forever in their natural cover.

He swallowed a sour curse as he reflected on the fact that the whole damned base had been built right under the NPA's nose. Admittedly, their hands had been full with other matters, but this was more than any single night's work. His people had had every opportunity to spot it going in, and they hadn't.

Well, they were about to make up for that, he reflected with a certain grim satisfaction.

He lowered his glasses and keyed his com twice without speaking, then waited. No one answered with the matching double click that would have indicated a perimeter team not yet in position, and he raised his glasses once more.

Not a sign of life, he mused. Just the silent, moss-covered roofs and walls. That showed more confidence—or stupidity—than *he* would have allowed himself. There should have been at least one lookout, however good they thought their camouflage was. But Isvarian wasn't the sort to look a gift horse in the mouth; if his opponents chose to give him the advantage of complete surprise, he certainly wasn't going to object.

He raised his wrist com to his mouth, never letting his eyes waver from the scene before him.

"Go," he said quietly, and idling turbines screamed to life fifty kilometers to the south. Six armed NPA skimmers rose on their counter-grav, pointed their noses north, and leapt ahead at full power.

Isvarian held his glasses steady as the mounting roar of turbines swept up from behind him. It was faint, at first, little louder than the distant wind, but it grew by leaps and bounds as the skimmers roared forward at over nine hundred kilometers per hour. They exploded over Isvarian's perch in a wave of man-made thunder, battering him with turbine wash, and made one screaming pass above the outlaw base. Two of them killed velocity with savage power, going into a perfect hover directly above the buildings, and the other four peeled out to the sides, spreading to encircle the base before they grounded and popped their hatches.

Armed NPA cops poured out of them, eight from each grounded skimmer, and moved rapidly forward under cover of their transports' dorsal turrets, spreading out as they went. They advanced warily, half-crouched, weapons at the ready, but still there was absolutely no response from the structures, and Isvarian frowned. Half-buried or not, the occupants of those buildings would have to have been stone deaf to miss that thunderous arrival. Surely at least one of them should have poked his head out to see what as going on!

He was raising his com once more to order his strike commander to hold his positions when something cracked viciously from his left. He wheeled towards it as a terrible, gurgling scream sounded over the com, and a second flat, sharp explosion echoed over the rolling terrain. He saw a spurt of smoke this time—gray-white smoke, surging up out of the moss—and then the echoes of the two explosions were drowned in the rippling whine of pulse rifles on full auto.

Bright, spiteful flashes of white fire blossomed as the pulse darts shredded the moss about the burst of smoke like some crazed threshing machine, and Isvarian shook himself out of his momentary paralysis.

"Check fire!" he barked. "*Check fire*, damn it!"

The pulse rifles fell silent in near-instant response, and he darted a glance back at the base. Still no sign of life, and his strike party—frozen as the crackle of combat erupted behind them—began to move forward once more as it ended. They moved more quickly now, rushing to close with the buildings before anyone else got any ideas about opening fire, and he turned back to the flank. The stinking smoke of burning *shemak* floated on the wind, rising from the moss the darts had torn to ruin, and he coughed.

"This is Leader-One," he barked into the com. "What the hell happened over there, Flank-Two?"

"Leader-One, this is Flank-Three," a voice replied. It was flat and tight, over-controlled, and it wasn't Flank-Two. "Matt's dead, Barney. Don't know what it was. Some kind of projectile weapon, but not a pulser. Blew a hole the size of my fist through him, but it didn't explode."

"Oh, shit!" Isvarian groaned. Not Matt Howard. He'd been due to retire in two more years.

"Okay, Flank-Three," he said after a moment. "Make a sweep of the area and find out what the fuck happened. And be careful, we don't want any more sur—"

The terrible, end-of-the-world concussion blew him flat

on his back as the entire base erupted in a red-and-white fireball of chemical explosives.

"Holy Mother of—!"

Ensign Tremaine swallowed the rest of the phrase as a towering plume of smoke and dust spewed up from the base. An entire NPA skimmer cartwheeled away from it almost lazily, bouncing end-over-end across the ground for fifty meters before it disintegrated in a fireball all its own. One of the hovering skimmers vanished, plunging straight down into the inferno as some flying projectile smashed into its counter-grav coils and it lost lift. A fresh explosion roared up out of the chaos, and the last of the six skimmers staggered drunkenly across the sky. It careened downward, barely under control, and its port engine ripped away as it hit. The pilot lost it—dead, unconscious, or simply over-powered by the uneven thrust that spun his crippled mount in a wreckage-shredding ground loop over the rough terrain—but at least it neither exploded nor caught fire.

"There, Skipper!" Hiro Yammata snapped. "Oh-six-five!"

Tremaine ripped his gaze from the deadly chaos below him, and an ugly light blazed in his normally mild eyes as he saw the sleek, high-speed aircar darting out of its camouflage. It rocketed forward, accelerating madly as it streaked away, using a knife-edged ridge of rock for cover against Isvarian's stunned perimeter force.

"Ruth! Get me a pursuit vector on that son-of-a-bitch!" Tremaine snarled, and the heavy pinnace dropped like a homesick rock as Kleinmeuller chopped her counter-grav back to zero. She did more than that; she dropped the nose almost perpendicular to the ground, lined it up on the fleeing aircar, and gave her air-breathing turbines full throttle.

The pinnace shrieked and bellowed down the sky, and Tremaine hit the arming button. He'd never fired a weapon at another human being in his life, but there was no hesitation in him as the targeting screen flashed to life.

Nor did he even consider calling upon the aircar to halt; he was no policeman or court of law, and its sudden flight on the heels of the explosion was all the proof of murder he needed. His lips drew back over his teeth as the target pipper moved steadily towards it, and his finger caressed the trigger grip.

The fleeing aircar's pilot probably never even realized the pinnace was there—not that it mattered one way or the other. His craft had the speed to out-distance anything the NPA had, but no pure air-breather could run away from a Fleet pinnace.

The pipper merged with the aircar, a tone sounded, Tremaine's hand squeezed, and a two-centimeter laser ripped its target into very, very tiny pieces and scattered them across the endless moss like tears of fire.

Dame Estelle was deathly pale on the briefing room com screen, and Honor knew her face showed her own shock. The triumph of finding the lab at last had turned to dust and ashes on her tongue as the commissioner recited the casualty figures. She should have insisted on using Papadapolous's Marines, she thought wretchedly. At least they'd have been in battle armor.

But she hadn't. Fifty-five dead and six wounded. Over ninety percent of the strike team had been killed, and every one of the survivors was injured, two critically. And one of the perimeter team was dead, as well. Sixty-one men and women, wiped away or hospitalized in the space of two minutes. It was a staggering blow to the small, tight-knit NPA, and she felt physically ill over the role she had played, all unknowing, in creating that slaughter.

"Dame Estelle," she said finally. "I'm sorry. It never occurred to me that—"

"It's not your fault, Honor," Matsuko said wearily. "Nor is it Barney Isvarian's, though I think it's going to be a long time before he accepts that. There had to have been a leak at our end. They *must* have known we were coming."

Honor nodded silently. The trap Isvarian's strike team had walked straight into had been deliberately designed to kill as many of them as possible. The druggers had evacuated well before the raiders arrived, but they could have blown their base any time they wanted to. They'd waited until the ground team was right on top of it, and that made it cold-blooded, deliberate murder.

"At least Ensign Tremaine nailed the ones who set it off," Dame Estelle went on. "That's something. I'd have liked to have prisoners, but don't you dare tell him that. He did exactly what I would have done."

"Yes, Ma'am." Honor managed a wan smile. "I'll tell him you said that, not chew him out for a perfectly normal combat response."

"Good." Dame Estelle scrubbed her face with the heels of her hands and straightened her shoulders with a visible effort. "Actually, I'm afraid what happened to Matt Howard worries me even more than what happened to the strike team," she said, and Honor blinked in astonishment.

The commissioner's mouth twisted at her expression, and she rose from behind her desk, turning the com terminal to direct its pickup at her coffee table. A strange weapon lay on it, looking very like some crude version of a pulse rifle, except that it had neither a magazine nor a proper stock. Instead of a vertical butt stock, it ended in a flat, horizontal arc of curved metal, perpendicular to the line of the barrel.

"See this?" Dame Estelle's voice asked from beyond the pickup's range.

"Yes, Ma'am. What is it?"

"This is what killed Matt, Honor. My people tell me it's a single-shot, breech-loading flintlock rifle. One built for a Medusan."

"What?!" Astonishment startled the response out of Honor before she could stop it, and Dame Estelle's hands appeared on her screen as the commissioner lifted the clumsy-looking weapon.

"That was my response," she said grimly. "This—" she touched the curved metal arm "—is the butt plate. It's made of metal because there's no decent wood on the planet, and it's shaped like this because Medusans don't really have shoulders. It's designed to go across the firer's chest to absorb the recoil, but that's not the most interesting part of it. Look."

She turned the weapon on its side and gripped a small knob on the trigger guard, then cranked the entire guard through a half turn. A plug of metal dropped vertically out of the barrel, and the commissioner lifted it to show the opened breech to the pickup.

"It's a very ancient form of breech-closure for nitro-powder weapons, though I understand it usually operates in line with the barrel, not vertically." Dame Estelle's voice was almost distant, a dry, lecturer's voice like a buttress against her own shock. "It's called an 'interrupted screw,' " she went on. "Basically, it's nothing more than a long, coarse-threaded screw with the threads cut away on two sides so it only takes a half-turn to engage or disengage it. One of my com techs is an antique weapons buff, and she tells me it's the only practical way to achieve a gas-proof breech seal on a weapon that uses loose-loaded propellant. They shove a hollow-based projectile of soft lead about eighteen millimeters in diameter in here, put the powder behind it, and close the breech."

Her hands demonstrated on the screen, and she turned the weapon on its side.

"Then they pull back this hammer, which opens this little pan, and they put more loose powder into it. When they pull the trigger—"

The S-shaped hammer snapped forward, striking the lump of flint in its jaws against the roughened inner surface of the pan lid, and a brilliant spark flashed.

Dame Estelle dumped the weapon back onto the table and returned to her desk, swinging her terminal until she looked out of it at Honor once more, and her face was grim.

"A Medusan could reload this a lot more quickly than we could," she went on. "If he puts the butt directly over one of his arms, he could actually reload and re-prime it with that arm without even lowering it from firing position with the other two. And it's a lot longer-ranged and more accurate than you might think. The barrel is rifled, and the explosion of the powder—old-fashioned black powder, not even nitro-cellulose, they tell me—spreads the hollow base of the projectile, forcing it into the rifling and spin-stabilizing it. It's no pulse rifle, Honor, but according to my weapons buff's best guesstimate, this thing is probably accurate to two or even three hundred meters . . . and we have no idea how many of them are out there."

"Dear God," Honor murmured, her mind racing as she envisioned thousands of Medusans armed with those primitive but deadly weapons.

"Exactly," the commissioner said harshly. "It's crude, very crude, but that's because someone took considerable pains to make it *look* that way. The actual manufacture is quite good, and, given the current Medusan level of technology, it's an ideal weapon for them: simple, sturdy, and within their own manufacturing capabilities, even if only barely. But there is no way—*no way*—this many sudden advances could occur naturally in one lump. My com tech tells me it took centuries for Old Earth to advance from crude, fuse-fired smoothbores to anything remotely like this. In fact, she insists no one on Old Earth ever produced one that incorporated all of these features, except for something called a 'Fergusson Rifle,' or something like that. And that one never went into mass production. So—"

"So at least the design had to come from someone off-world." Honor's voice was equally harsh, and Dame Estelle nodded.

"My own opinion, precisely. Some greedy idiot has jumped the Medusans' ability to kill one another—or us—by something like fifteen hundred T-years." The Resident Commissioner looked strained and old, and her hand trembled slightly as she brushed hair back from her forehead. "He's brought this abortion in through my security, and he's turned it over to the nomads in the Outback, not even to the Delta city-states. Even if we nail *him*, there's no way to put this genie back into the bottle if he's taught the Medusans how to build the things. In fact, they're bound to figure out how to make heavier weapons—real, honest-to-God artillery—so unless we want to take over the role of guaranteeing the Delta's security with off-world weaponry, we're going to have to *encourage* the city-states to learn how to make the goddamned things just so they can defend themselves! And worst of all, our forensic people think the Medusans who killed Matt were hopped to the breathing slits on *mekoha*—the same off-world *mekoha* we've been seeing clear on the other side of the Mossybacks."

"But . . . why?" Honor asked slowly.

"I don't know," Dame Estelle sighed. "I just don't know. I can't think of a single commodity on this planet that could possibly be worth this kind of investment, Honor. Not one. And that," she finished softly, "scares me a lot worse than if I could."

The quiet hum of the buzzer turned raucous when no one answered, and Andreas Venizelos jerked up out of his sleep with a muffled curse as it broke into a series of abrupt, jagged bursts of sound, guaranteed to wake the dead. The lieutenant dragged himself to his feet, rubbing sleep from his eyes while he stumbled across his darkened cabin. He hopped on one foot, yelping as a bare toe collided painfully with some invisible obstacle, then half-fell into the chair before the com terminal. The buzzer was still screaming at him, and he glared at the chrono. Oh-two-fifteen. He'd been in bed less than three hours.

This, he told himself savagely, had better be damned important.

He raked a hand through sleep-tousled hair and

punched the audio key with his thumb, refusing visual contact in his disheveled state.

"Yes?" He didn't—quite—snarl the word.

"Andy?" the blank screen said. "This is Mike Reynaud."

"Captain Reynaud?" Venizelos straightened in his chair, rags of drowsiness fleeing, and frowned.

"Sorry to disturb you," Reynaud continued quickly. "I know you just got in a few hours ago. But we've had some traffic up here I think you should know about." The ACS commander sounded anxious, possibly even a little frightened, and Venizelos's frown deepened.

"What sort of traffic, Captain?" he asked.

"A Crown courier boat came in from Manticore about an hour ago and headed in-system," Reynaud replied. "It didn't stop for inspection, of course—" Venizelos nodded; Crown couriers had absolute precedence and complete freedom of passage anywhere in Manticoran space "—but I just got a look at the passenger manifest."

Something about the way he said it touched Venizelos with dread, but he bit his lip and waited in silence.

"It's Klaus Hauptman, Andy," Reynaud said softly. "I don't know what he's doing on a Crown courier, but he's here. And he's headed for Medusa. After what happened with the *Mondragon*, I thought, well . . ."

His voice trailed off, and Venizelos nodded again to the unseeing pickup.

"I understand, Captain Reynaud. And I appreciate it." He rubbed his eyes for a moment, then inhaled deeply. "It'll take me a few minutes to get dressed, Sir. Could you warn the com center I'm on my way up and ask for a scrambled channel to *Fearless*?"

"Of course, Andy." The relief in Reynaud's voice was manifest, and he cut the circuit. Venizelos sat motionless, staring at the silent terminal for long, slow seconds, and his mind raced.

Civilians, no matter how important, had no official business on Crown courier boats. But Klaus Hauptman wasn't just any civilian. It would have been very difficult to refuse him passage. In fact, Venizelos doubted anyone had dared tell Hauptman "no" about anything for decades. Yet how he'd gotten here mattered far less than why, and Venizelos could think of only one possible reason for him to come, especially in secret aboard an official government vessel rather than openly aboard a civilian transport.

He rose and reached for his uniform trousers.

• CHAPTER EIGHTEEN

"Jesus Christ, Westerfeldt! What the *hell* did you think you were *doing*?!"

Wallace Canning crouched forward over his desk, hands braced on its blotter as if he meant to leap over it and physically attack the man standing in front of it. His face was congested with fury and his eyes blazed, but Colonel Bryan Westerfeldt stood his ground.

"I didn't do anything," he replied. He spoke quietly, but there was an edge to his voice—not quite a tremble, but an edge—which suggested he was less calm than he appeared.

"Well *somebody* fucking well did!" Canning spat. "You stu—!"

He shut his mouth with a click, dragging himself back under control, and forced himself back into his chair. Westerfeldt started to speak, but the savage chop of a hand cut him off, and Canning closed his eyes. He inhaled deeply, tension shuddering in his muscles, and made himself think.

Thank God the admiral had departed for the Republic before this fiasco exploded! He swallowed a bitter, half-hysterical giggle at his own choice of verb, and opened his eyes. All their careful work, their cover plan at the lab, the false records—*all* of it—for nothing. For worse than nothing. The NPA would never rest now that the "criminals" had murdered almost sixty of its field agents! And if they didn't find the false trail they were supposed to find, they might—

"All right," he grated more calmly. "I'm waiting. What happened and how?"

"I passed the initial warning to Summervale, exactly as we discussed," Westerfeldt said in a very careful voice. "As you know, we had to warn him, since he already knew we were wired into the NPA. If he hadn't gotten any advance warning at all, Isvarian and Matsuko would have smelled a rat for sure when they interrogated his people after the bust and found out 'the Organization' hadn't even tried to save their operation, and—"

"I know why we decided to warn him," Canning interrupted coldly. "But I also know you weren't supposed to actually tell him the raid was coming. Damn it, Colonel— they were supposed to get caught!"

"That's what I've been trying to tell you, Sir," Westerfeldt said almost desperately. "I *didn't* warn them about the actual raid. I never sent them a word about it!"

"What?" Canning tipped his chair back with an abrupt movement and glared at his subordinate. "Then how did they know?"

"I can only speculate, Sir, but Summervale did think he was in charge of security. If you want it, my best guess is that he had his own spotters out to give him a second information source. *They* must have tipped him Isvarian was coming, because *I* certainly didn't!"

"But why in hell did he blow the lab?" Canning complained in a less angry, almost querulous voice. "We never told him to do that!"

"That . . . may have been my fault, after all, Sir," Westerfeldt admitted unhappily. "He asked me what to do with the hardware, and I didn't give him specific orders." Canning glared at him, and Westerfeldt's own resentment flared. "Damn it, Sir—I thought he'd try to just cut and run! Why shouldn't I have? I didn't know what kind of lunatic he was! Ambassador Gowan's people recruited him on Manticore; if they knew he was that kind of loose warhead, they never should have gone anywhere near him, however good or politically embarrassing his credentials were!"

"All right. All right!" Canning waved a hand in a gesture

midway between anger and placation and bit his lip. "We can't undo it, and at least the fucking Manticorans killed him for us. But you must have known some of the rifles were in the area, Colonel."

"I swear to God I didn't, Sir." Westerfeldt's face was taut. "As far as I know, every one of the rifles we've delivered is still cached in the Shaman's caves. In fact, I ordered a count made at Site One as soon as the shit hit the fan. They haven't completed it yet, but so far the numbers have checked perfectly. I don't think those rifles were ours at all, Sir."

"Oh, crap!" Canning muttered, dragging his hands through his hair and staring at the blotter.

"They must have been Stilty-made, Sir," Westerfeldt said more calmly. "The Shaman's had to hand them out for training sessions. We collect them all afterward, but maybe one of the damned abos took the idea home with him. If we're going to give them weapons that look like they're native-built, then they have to be ones the natives can build, after all. It just never occurred to anyone they might figure out how to make their own gunpowder as well and set up a shop of their own."

"Oh, this is just fucking wonderful." Canning groaned. He closed his eyes in pain, then opened them and impaled Westerfeldt with a glare. "Even if you didn't give the order to blow the lab, Colonel, the field op is *your* responsibility. This is your mess—*you* clean it up!"

"But how?" Westerfeldt took a step closer to the desk, his voice almost pleading.

"I don't know." Canning pounded a fist gently on the blotter for a moment, then sucked in a deep breath. "All right. The NPA knows it was an off-world operation, but they still don't know it was us. And that maniac didn't blow the power relays, so when they track them back at least *that* evidence will still point to a domestic Manticoran operation, right?"

Westerfeldt nodded silently, and Canning's jaw worked in thought. He ought to report this. He knew he should.

But if he did, upstairs would probably cancel the entire op, and if he couldn't hang it all on Westerfeldt, the admiral and ONI would crucify him. On the other hand, as he'd just told the colonel, there was still no direct evidence linking Haven to the massacre.

All right. If Harrington and Matsuko didn't know Haven was behind it, what *did* they know that could hurt him? The rifles. They knew about the fucking rifles, and neither of them were likely to miss the potential danger they represented. So that meant they might try to make some sort of contingency plans, but if they didn't know about the scope of Haven's own plan, then their precautions could hardly be enough to stop it.

He gritted his teeth, knowing full well he was grasping at straws. Yet straws were all he had. If he reported back and the operation was scrubbed, then his career was scrubbed with it. He'd find himself hauled home and buried in one of the Prole housing units on Haven, drawing a Basic Living Stipend right alongside all the other Dolist scum as an example to other fuck-ups, and he came from one of the aristocratic Legislature families. All of his friends, all the other useless drones drawing the BLS with him—*everyone*—would know about his disgrace. They'd laugh at him, mock him, and he couldn't face that. He couldn't.

Yet what option did he have? Unless . . . ?

He forced his jaws to relax and straightened his shoulders. If he warned ONI and the operation was canceled, he was ruined. If he didn't warn them and the operation was launched on schedule but failed, he'd still be ruined for not having warned them. But if the operation *succeeded*, he could survive. His family was owed enough debts by other Legislaturists. They could carry it off, possibly even applaud him for his iron nerve and resolve in driving the op to success despite his handicaps. . . .

It was only one chance in three, but a thirty-three percent chance was infinitely more than zero, and it was the only one that offered him survival.

"All right, Colonel," he said coldly. "Here's what you're going to do. First, get in touch with your NPA contacts. If Harrington doesn't find that tap on Matsuko's power collector on her own, you make damned sure someone points her at it. More than that, I want a watch kept on their deployments. If they start forting up in the enclaves or any of Harrington's Marines get deployed planet-side, I want to know. Then get your ass out to the main site. I don't care how you do it, but you sit on the Shaman for three more weeks. Three weeks, Colonel! If Young isn't back by then, then we'll kick the operation off without him. Understood?"

Westerfeldt cocked his head, his eyes narrow and speculative, and Canning met them with a flat glare. He could almost hear gears turning in the colonel's head, feel the other man following his own chain of logic. And then Westerfeldt gave a slow nod as the totals came together for him, as well. If Canning survived, he survived; if Canning went down, he went down with his superior.

"Yes, Sir," the colonel said flatly. "I understand. I understand entirely, Mr. Canning."

He jerked another, sharper nod at the consul, and vanished through the office door.

"Your ticket, Sir." The Silesian trade factor handed over the small chip with a smile. His freight-line employers offered limited passenger accommodations aboard their bulk carriers, but this was the very first passage the factor had ever booked from Medusa.

"Thank you," the man who didn't look a thing like (and who had the papers to prove he wasn't) Denver Summervale said courteously. He slipped the chip into a pocket, rose with a coolly pleasant nod, and left the office.

He stood outside it for a moment, gazing across at the Haven Consulate, and a smile touched his mouth. The pieces had started coming together for him the moment one of his local contacts arrived at his hiding place to report seeing "the boss" dash out of the Havenite enclave and head for the Outback. That had been all he'd had to know to realize he and the lab personnel had been set up by their real employers—and why.

He'd been tempted to do a little something about that, but cooler counsel had prevailed. After all, he was away free and clear largely because *he*'d set up the aircar pilot to play button man. More than that, it was possible, even probable, that whatever Haven was up to would be even more upsetting to the NPA and the Navy than the drug lab itself had been. If "the boss" pulled it off after all, that would be enough to earn Summervale's grudging forgiveness. If he blew it, then the very people Summervale despised would punish him for his treachery.

He smiled again and turned to walk briskly towards the waiting shuttle.

"I'm sorry, Commander McKeon," Rafael Cardones said, "but we're moving as fast as we can. There's no load on the relay now, and the final stage was an omnidirectional receiver. We're working our way through the possible lines of sight, but with no power flow to track, we're having to do it all by eye. I'm afraid it's going to take time, Sir."

"Understood." Alistair McKeon nodded and patted the younger officer on the shoulder with absent gentleness. "I know you're doing your best, Rafe. Let me know the instant you have something."

"Aye, aye, Sir." Cardones turned back to his station, and McKeon crossed to the command chair. He eased himself down in it and glanced unhappily at the closed hatch to the Captain's briefing room. The catastrophic consequences of the raid on the drug lab had shocked him to the core, and a subdued air of depression hovered over the ship. He knew the Captain blamed herself for it. She was wrong. It wasn't her fault, nor was it the fault of anyone else aboard *Fearless*, but the entire crew seemed to feel a personal sense of guilt over the disaster, one that cut all the deeper because of their earlier sense of achievement.

Yet there was something else under the guilt and depression. Anger. A seething hatred for whoever had set those charges with murder in his heart. He could feel it pulsing about him, bare-fanged and ugly, and it throbbed deep inside him, as well. For the first time since Harrington had taken command, he was truly one with his ship's company, no longer buttressed off by his own resentment and private despair, and the need to rend and destroy simmered in his blood.

He folded his hands in his lap, then looked up as a chime sounded from the com section. He turned his head, and his eyes narrowed as he saw Webster stiffen and begin punching buttons. He was over on the right side of the panel, in the secure channels section, and something about the way his hands moved rang a warning in McKeon's brain.

He slid from the command chair and padded over to the com officer's shoulder just as Webster plugged a message board into his terminal and downloaded the unscrambled message to it. The lieutenant spun his chair and started to spring erect, then stopped as he saw the exec.

"What is it, Webster?" McKeon asked quickly, worried by the lieutenant's pale face and tight expression.

"It's a priority message, Sir. From Lieutenant Venizelos at Basilisk Control. He says—" The lieutenant broke off and extended the board, and McKeon's face clenched as he scanned the brief, terse message. He raised his eyes and locked them with the lieutenant's.

"No one else hears about this until the Captain or I tell you different, Webster," he said very softly. "Clear?"

"Yes, Sir," Webster said, equally quietly.

The exec nodded and turned on his heel, striding briskly across the bridge. "You have the watch, Mr. Webster," he called over his shoulder, and tapped sharply on the briefing room's admittance panel. The hatch hissed open, and he disappeared through it.

* * *

Honor finished the message and laid the board gently on the table. Her face was pale but composed. Only her eyes showed the true depth of her tension as she looked up at McKeon, and the exec shifted his weight uneasily.

"So," she said at last, and glanced at the chronometer. The message had taken ten hours to reach them; Hauptman's courier boat would arrive within another twenty.

"Yes, Ma'am. He has to be coming out to see you personally, Captain," McKeon said softly.

"What makes you so certain, Exec?"

"Ma'am, it *can't* be for any other reason—not on a Crown courier. That's a deliberate statement, a proof of his political clout. If he were just coming out to check on his own factors, he'd've come on one of his own ships. And it can't be to see Dame Estelle, either. He must have already hit every political lever he has at home, and if he couldn't get Countess Marisa to interfere, he knows damned well he won't get Dame Estelle to. That only leaves you, Captain."

Honor nodded slowly. There were gaping holes in McKeon's logic, but he was right. She could feel that he was, and there was genuine concern in his eyes and voice. Concern, she thought, which wasn't for himself. It was for his ship and, perhaps, just possibly, for his captain, as well.

"All right, Exec," she said. "You may be wrong. I don't think you are. But whether you are or not, it doesn't change our duties or our priorities, does it?"

"No, Ma'am," McKeon said quietly.

"Very well, then." She looked sightlessly around the briefing room for a moment, trying to think. "I want you to concentrate on working with Rafe and Ensign Tremaine's ground party. Nail that relay's power source down for me. In the meantime, I'll have a word with Dame Estelle and tell her who's coming to call on us."

"Yes, Ma'am."

"Good." Honor rubbed her temple, feeling Nimitz's tension on the back of her chair. She sounded cool and confident, she thought. The conscientious captain, concerned only with her duty while her stomach knotted with something much too much like fear and her mind filled with uncertainty. But she had no choice. Her duty was all she knew how to do. Yet, for the first time in her career, when she reached out for the steadying weight of responsibility, it wasn't enough. Not enough.

"Good," she repeated, lowering her hand from her temple. She stared at her fingers for a second, then looked back up at McKeon, and the exec thought her face looked even younger—and far more vulnerable—than he had ever seen it. A familiar flicker of resentment stirred within him like an involuntary mental reflex, but with it came another, stronger impulse.

"We'll take care of it, Ma'am," he heard himself say, and saw the surprise in the backs of her eyes. He wanted to say something else, but even now that was more than he could do.

"Thank you, Exec." She inhaled deeply, and he saw her face change. The Captain was back, settling over her bony features like a shield, and she squared her shoulders.

"In the meantime," she said more briskly, "I'll ask Dame Estelle if she can get Barney Isvarian up here. I want him to sit down with Papadapolous and myself to discuss these new Medusan weapons."

"Yes, Ma'am." McKeon stepped back, braced to attention for just an instant, and turned away. The hatch hissed closed behind him.

"There it is, Mr. Tremaine. See?"

The NPA private stepped back from the electronic glasses swivel-mounted atop the power relay on the ridge above the crater which had once housed a drug laboratory. It had taken hours to track the buried cable from the transmitter below to this point, and their real problem had started then, for the receptor wasn't a direct space up-link, and it *was* omnidirectional. They hadn't had a clue where *its* relay was, but now Tremaine peered through the glasses, and his face tightened as he saw the telltale roundness of a parabolic receiving dish. It was on a much higher ridge almost twenty kilometers away, but that smooth arc couldn't possibly be a natural formation, even if it had been painted to look like the rock around it.

"I think you're right, Chris." He looked down at the bearing ring on the glasses' mount, then raised his wrist com to his mouth. "Hiro?"

"Here, Skipper," Yammata's voice came down from the pinnace hovering overhead.

"I think Rodgers has spotted it. Take a look at that ridge to the north, bearing—" he looked back at the ring "—zero-one-eight true from this relay."

"Just a sec, Skipper." The pinnace shifted slightly, and Yammata came back up on the com almost instantly. "Tell Chris he's got good eyes, Skip. That's it, all right."

"Good." Tremaine gave the NPA man a tight nod of approval, then looked back up at the pinnace. "Have Ruth pick us up, and let's get over there."

"Aye, aye, Sir. We're on it."

"Major Papadapolous, Ma'am," McKeon said, and stood aside as Captain Nikos Papadapolous, Royal Manticoran Marines, marched into Honor's briefing room.

There could be only one "captain" aboard a ship of war, where any uncertainty over who someone was referring to in the midst of a critical situation could be fatal, so Papadapolous received the courtesy promotion to avoid that confusion. And he looked every centimeter a major, despite his captain's insignia, like someone who'd just stepped out of a recruiting poster, as he paused inside the hatch. Barney Isvarian was a real major, but far less spruce-looking. In point of fact, he looked like hell. He'd had exactly no sleep in the twenty-nine hours since sixty-one of his best friends were killed or wounded, and Honor was fairly positive he hadn't even changed his clothes.

Papadapolous glanced at the NPA major and clicked to attention, but there was a dubious look in his eyes. The Marine was dark, despite his auburn hair, with quick, alert eyes, and he moved with an assurance just short of cockiness and the limber power of the RMMC's strenuous physical training program. He was probably all spring steel and leather and dangerous as a kodiak max, just like the poster said, Honor thought sardonically, but he looked like an untested recruit beside Isvarian's stained and weary experience.

"You sent for me, Captain?" he said.

"I did. Sit down, Major." Honor pointed to an empty chair, and Papadapolous sat neatly, looking alertly back and forth between his superiors.

"Have you read that report I sent you?" Honor asked, and he nodded. "Good. I've asked Major Isvarian here to give you any additional background you require."

"Require for what, Ma'am?" Papadapolous asked when she paused.

"For the formulation of a response plan, Major, in the event of an attack on the Delta enclaves by Medusans armed with similar weapons."

"Oh?" Papadapolous furrowed his brow for a moment, then shrugged. "I'll get right on it, Ma'am, but I don't see any problems."

He smiled, but his smile faded as the Captain looked back at him expressionlessly. He glanced sideways at Isvarian and stiffened, for the NPA major wasn't expressionless at all. His bloodshot eyes looked right through the Marine with something too close to contempt for Papadapolous's comfort, and he turned defensively back to Honor.

"I'm afraid I can't quite share your confidence, Major," she said calmly. "I think the threat may be somewhat more serious than you believe."

"Ma'am," Papadapolous said crisply, "I still have ninety-three Marines aboard ship. I have battle armor for a full platoon—thirty-five men and women—with pulse rifles and heavy weapons for the remainder of the company. We can handle any bunch of Stilties armed with flintlocks." He stopped, jaw clenched, and added another "Ma'am" almost as an afterthought.

"Bullshit." The single flat, cold word came not from Honor but from Barney Isvarian, and Papadapolous flushed as he glared at the older man.

"I beg your pardon, Sir?" he said in a voice of ice.

"I said 'bullshit,'" Isvarian replied, equally coldly. "You'll go down there, and you'll look pretty, and you'll beat the holy living hell out of any single bunch of Medusans you come across, and that'll be fucking *all* you do while the nomads eat the rest of the off-worlders for breakfast!"

Papadapolous's face went as white as it had been red. To his credit, at least half his anger was at hearing such language in his commanding officer's presence—but only half, and he glared at the haggard, unshaven Isvarian's wrinkled uniform.

"Major, my people are *Marines*. If you know anything about Marines, then you know we do our job."

His clipped voice made no effort to hide his own contempt, and Honor started to raise an intervening hand. But Isvarian lurched to his feet before she got it up, and she let it fall back into her lap as he leaned towards Papadapolous.

"Let me tell you something about Marines, Sonny!" the NPA man spat. "I know *all* about them, believe me. I know you're brave, loyal, trustworthy and honest." The bitter derision in his voice could have stripped paint from the bulkheads. "I know you can knock a kodiak max on his ass at two klicks with a pulse rifle. I know you can pick a single gnat out of a cloud of 'em with a plasma gun and strangle hexapumas with your bare hands. I even know your battle armor gives you the strength of ten because your heart is pure! But this ain't no boarding action,

'Major' Papadapolous, and it's no field exercise, either. This is for real, and your people don't have the least damned idea what they're fucking around with down there!"

Papadapolous sucked in an angry breath, but this time Honor did raise her hand before he could speak.

"Major Papadapolous." Her cool soprano wrenched him around to face her, and she smiled faintly. "Perhaps you aren't aware that before joining the NPA, Major Isvarian was a Marine." Papadapolous twitched in shock, and her smile grew. "In point of fact, he served in the Corps for almost fifteen years, completing his final tour as command sergeant major for the Marine detachment on Saganami Island."

Papadapolous looked back at Isvarian and swallowed his hot retort. The Saganami Marines were chosen from the elite of the corps. They made up the training and security detachments at the Naval Academy, serving as both examples and challenges for the midshipman who might one day aspire to command Marines, and they were there because they were the best. The *very* best.

"Major," he said quietly, "I . . . apologize." He met the older man's red-rimmed eyes unflinchingly, and the NPA man slumped back into his chair.

"Oh, hell." Isvarian waved a hand vaguely and flopped back into his chair. "Not your fault, Major. And I shouldn't have popped off that way." He rubbed his forehead and blinked wearily. "But all the same, you don't have any idea what you're getting into down there."

"Perhaps not, Sir," Papadapolous said, his voice much more level as he recognized the exhaustion and pain behind the NPA major's swaying belligerence. "In fact, you're right. I spoke without thinking. If you have any advice to offer, I would be most grateful to hear it, Major."

"Well, all right, then." Isvarian managed a tired, lopsided grin. "The thing is, we don't have any idea how many of those rifles are out there or what the nomads are planning to do with them. But you might want to bear this in

mind, Major Papadapolous. We've fitted that thing with a
standard butt stock and test-fired it. It's got a kick you
won't believe, but Sharon Koenig was right—it's also got
an effective aimed range of somewhere over two hundred
meters. It could use better sights, but a single hit will kill
an unarmored human being at that range with no trouble
at all."

He leaned back in his chair and inhaled deeply.

"The problem is that your people can undoubtedly trash
any of them you see, but you won't see them unless they
want you to. Not in the bush. A Medusan nomad could
crawl across a pool table without your seeing him if he
didn't want you to. And while your body armor may protect
you, it *won't* protect any unarmored civilians."

"Yes, Sir," Papadapolous said even more quietly. "But is it
really likely that we'll see some sort of mass uprising?"

"We don't know. Frankly, I doubt it, but that doesn't
mean we won't. If it's only a series of small-scale incidents,
then my people can probably handle it, but someone's been
dumping *mekoha* out there by the air lorry load, as well as
teaching them how to make guns. A major incident certainly isn't out of the question. If it comes at one of the
Delta city-states, they should be able to at least hold their
walls until we can get help to them. If it comes at the off-
world enclaves, though—" Isvarian shrugged tiredly. "Most
of 'em are wide open, Major Papadapolous, and they don't
even know it. Their security people haven't even brushed
back the moss on the approaches to establish security or kill
zones, and—" he smiled again, an achingly weary but genuine smile "—ain't none of 'em Grunts like us."

"I understand, Major." Papadapolous smiled back, then
looked at Honor. "Ma'am, I'm sorry I seemed overconfi-
dent. With your permission, I'd like to take Major Isvarian
down to Marine Country and get my platoon commanders
and Sergeant Major Jenkins involved in this. Then I'll try to
give you a response plan that has some thought behind it
for a change."

"I think that sounds like a reasonable idea, Major," Honor said mildly, then glanced at Isvarian. "On the other hand, it might be an even better idea to get some food into Major Isvarian and lock him in a cabin for a few hours' sleep before you confer."

"Now *that's* a real good idea, Captain." Isvarian's voice was slurred, and he listed noticeably as he heaved himself to his feet. "But if Major Papadapolous doesn't mind, I think I'd like a shower first."

"Can do, Major," Papadapolous said promptly, and Honor smiled as she watched him escort a staggering Isvarian from her briefing room.

• CHAPTER NINETEEN

Ensign Tremaine's pinnace drifted in orbit, two hundred meters from the mammoth power collector, while Tremaine, Harkness, and Yammata crossed the vacuum between them. None of them could quite believe where their trace of the power relays had led them.

"You sure you want to do this, Skipper?" Harkness muttered over his suit com. "I mean, this is NPA business, Sir."

"The Captain told *me* to run it down, PO," Tremaine said, much more harshly than usual. "Besides, if we're right, maybe an NPA maintenance crew are the last people we should have checking it out."

"Mr. Tremaine, you don't *really* think—" Yammata began, and the ensign waved a gauntleted hand.

"I don't know what to think. All I know is what we've found so far. Until I do know more—know it for certain— we tell no one. Clear?"

"Yes, Sir," Yammata murmured. Tremaine nodded in satisfaction and freed a powered wrench from his equipment belt. His suit thrusters nudged him a bit closer, and he caught the grab bar above the access panel. He pulled himself down, locking the toes of his boots under the clips provided for that purpose, and attached his suit tether to the bar, then fitted the wrench head over the first bolt.

He squeezed the wrench power stud and listened to its whine, transmitted up his arm to his ears, and tried not to look at the royal Manticoran seal above the panel.

"You're not serious?" Dame Estelle stared at Lieutenant

Stromboli's face in her com screen, and the beefy lieutenant nodded. "*Our* backup power collector?"

"Yes, Ma'am, Dame Estelle. No question about it. Ensign Tremaine and his crew tracked the fix from the primary receiver station and found the feed. It wasn't easy, even after he got to the collector. As a matter of fact, it's built right into the main power ring, not even an add-on. I've got a copy of the altered schematics in my secure data base right now."

"Oh, my God," Matsuko sighed. She settled back in her chair, staring at the com screen, and her brain raced. Was it possible this whole operation was being run by someone *inside* her own staff? The thought was enough to turn her stomach, but she made herself face it.

"Who have you told, Lieutenant?" she asked after a moment, her eyes narrowing.

"You, Ma'am," Stromboli said instantly, and went on to answer the unasked portion of her question. "Mr. Tremaine informed me by tight beam, so my duty com tech knows, I know, his boat crew knows, and you know. That's it."

"Good. Very good, Lieutenant." Dame Estelle tugged at an earlobe, then nodded. "Use your own equipment to inform Commander Harrington, please. And ask her to tell Major Isvarian—he's still aboard *Fearless*, I believe. *Don't* tell anyone else without clearance from me or from your captain."

"Yes, Ma'am. I understand." Stromboli nodded, and the commissioner cut the circuit with a courteous if abstracted nod.

She sat silently for long minutes, trying to grasp the implications. It was insane . . . but it was also the perfect cover. She remembered the holos Isvarian had made of the base before the explosion, seeing once more the meticulous care with which the buildings had been hidden. It was all part of a pattern, a pattern of almost obsessive concealment, yet there was a false note. Concealment, yes, but once that screen of security was breached, the very lengths to which they'd gone to maintain it were guaranteed to touch off a massive hunt for the perpetrators at all levels.

And the way it had been done, the tap off her own power system, the apparent scale of *mekoha* production, the introduction of breech-loading rifles to the natives. . . . All of it spoke of a massive operation, one which went—which must go—far beyond whatever might be earned by selling drugs to a Bronze Age culture!

But why? *Where* did it go . . . and to what end? She was alone in a dark room, groping for shadows, and none of it made any sense. Not any sense at all.

She rose from her chair and walked to her office's huge window, staring unseeingly out over the Government Compound's low wall at the monotonous Medusan countryside. It couldn't be one of her people. It couldn't! Whatever the ultimate objective, whatever the reward, she couldn't—wouldn't—believe that any of her people could feed *mekoha* to the natives and connive at the cold-blooded murder of their own fellows!

But someone had installed a power tap in the one place neither she nor any of Harrington's people had even considered looking. And if it was built in, not added as an afterthought . . .

She closed her eyes, leaning her forehead against the tough, plastic window, and gritted her teeth in pain.

"It's confirmed, Commander."

Rafe Cardones nodded at the data terminal, and McKeon leaned closer to study it. The schematic of the power collector was interesting enough, but that was only part of the data's surprises. The shunt to the drug lab's power system was, indeed, an integral part of the satellite's circuitry, built deep into its core where only a complete maintenance strip-down would have revealed it. More than that, every maintenance seal had been intact, with no sign of tampering, and even with access to government or Fleet equipment, breaking and replacing all those seals would have been a lengthy, time-consuming job. However it got there, the installation of that shunt hadn't been any spur of the moment, rushed bootleg job.

He frowned and punched a key, and the collector's installation and maintenance history scrolled smoothly up the screen before him. He watched the moving lines, tapping gently on his teeth with the end of a stylus as he searched for any suspiciously long blocks of service time, any single name that came up too often among the regular maintenance crews on the normal service visits, but there were none. Either a big enough chunk of NPA maintenance personnel were in on it to rotate their ringers through the regular maintenance schedule and get the job done, or else. . . .

He nodded and tapped another key, killing the scroll command, and looked at Cardones.

"Download all this data to a secure chip, Rafe, and get it to the Captain. And . . . don't discuss it with anyone else, right?"

"Right, Sir." Cardones nodded, and McKeon turned away with a strange light in his eyes. His expression was odd—a combination of frowning unhappiness and something almost like a smile—and his mind was busy.

The Crown courier completed its orbital insertion and almost instantly dispatched a cutter planetward. Honor sat in her command chair, watching the descending landing boat's track on her display, and hoped she looked calmer than she felt.

A shadow fell on the side of her face, and she looked up to see McKeon standing beside her. His face was worried, shorn of its customary armor of formality as he, too, watched the display.

"Any more word from Dame Estelle, Ma'am?" he asked quietly.

"No." Nimitz chittered with soft anxiety in her lap, and she rubbed his round head without looking down. "She's been told to expect a personal dispatch from Countess Marisa; aside from that, they haven't said a word about who else might be on board."

"I see." McKeon's voice was low but strained. He seemed about to say something more, then shrugged, gave her an almost apologetic glance, and moved back to his own station. Honor returned her attention to the display once more, waiting.

A chime sounded behind her.

"Captain?" Lieutenant Webster's voice was tauter than usual. "I have a personal transmission from the courier boat for you, Ma'am." He paused. "Shall I transfer it to your briefing room screen?"

"No, Lieutenant." Honor's voice was as calm and courteous as always, but the com officer's anxiety-sharpened ears detected a flaw of tension at its heart. "Transfer it to my screen here."

"Aye, aye, Ma'am. Transferring now."

Honor's command chair com screen blinked to life, and she found herself looking at perhaps the wealthiest single man in the Star Kingdom of Manticore. She'd never met him, but she would have known that square, bulldog face anywhere.

"Commander Harrington?" The voice was familiar from countless HD interviews: a deep, rolling baritone too velvety to be real. It sounded courteous enough, but the blue eyes were hard in that too-handsome face.

"Yes?" she asked pleasantly, refusing to kow-tow to his reputation or even admit that she knew who he was, and saw his eyes narrow a millimeter.

"I'm Klaus Hauptman," the baritone said after a moment. "Countess Marisa was kind enough to allow me passage aboard her courier when I discovered she was dispatching one."

"I see." Hauptman's face was far too well-trained to reveal anything he chose to conceal, but she thought she sensed a flicker of surprise at her apparent calm. Perhaps he'd never considered that her people at Basilisk Control might be quick enough to realize the significance of his arrival and warn her he was coming. Or perhaps he'd anticipated her foreknowledge and was simply surprised she wasn't already quaking in fear. Well, the fear he couldn't see wouldn't help him any, she told herself firmly.

"The purpose of my visit, Commander," he went on, "was to make a . . . courtesy call on you. Would it be convenient for me to visit your ship during my time here in Basilisk?"

"Of course, Mr. Hauptman. The Navy is always pleased to extend its courtesy to such a prominent individual as yourself. Shall I send my cutter for you?"

"Now?" Hauptman couldn't quite hide his surprise, and she nodded pleasantly.

"If that would be convenient for you, Sir. I happen to be free of any other pressing duties at this moment. Of course, if you'd prefer to delay your visit, I will be happy to see you any time I can work it in. Assuming our mutual schedules permit it."

"No, no. Now will be fine, Commander. Thank you."

"Very well, Mr. Hauptman. My cutter will call for you within the half-hour. Good day."

"Good day, Commander," Hauptman replied, and she cut the circuit and pushed herself back into the cushioned contours of her chair. She'd have to take Nimitz to her quarters and leave him there before Hauptman boarded, she told the icy, singing tension at her core. The 'cat was far too sensitive to her moods for—

"Captain?"

Honor hid a twitch of surprise and looked up as McKeon reappeared beside her.

"Yes, Commander?"

"Captain, I . . . don't think you should see him alone." McKeon spoke with manifest hesitation, but his gray eyes were worried.

"I appreciate your concern, Exec," she said quietly, "but

I am captain of this ship, and Mr. Hauptman will be only a visitor aboard her."

"Understood, but—" McKeon paused and chewed his lip unhappily, then squared his shoulders like a man bracing against a bullet. "Ma'am, I don't believe for a minute that this is a simple courtesy call. And—"

"A moment, Commander." She stood, stopping him with a small gesture, then scooped Nimitz up and and looked at Webster. "Samuel, you have the watch. The exec and I will be in my briefing room if you need us."

"Aye, aye, Ma'am. I have the watch," the com officer said, and Honor beckoned wordlessly to McKeon.

They crossed to the briefing room, and Honor parked Nimitz on a corner of the conference table while the hatch slid shut against her bridge crew's many ears. The 'cat made no protest when she put him down. He merely sat up on his four rearmost limbs and watched McKeon closely.

"Now, Commander," Honor said, turning to him, "you were saying?"

"Captain, Klaus Hauptman is coming aboard this ship to complain about our actions—*your* actions—in this system," McKeon said flatly. "I warned you at the time that he'd be furious. You've embarrassed and humiliated him, at the very least, and I wouldn't be surprised if he or his cartel ends up facing some fairly substantial charges in court."

"I'm aware of that." Honor folded her arms under her breasts, facing the lieutenant commander squarely, and her voice was uninflected.

"I know you are, Ma'am. And I also know you're aware of his reputation." Honor nodded. Klaus Hauptman's ruthless ambition, his fierce pride and bursts of volcanic fury, made good copy for the media.

"I don't think he'd have come this far if all he wanted to do was complain, Ma'am." McKeon met her eyes just as squarely, his expression an alloy of concern and more than a trace of embarrassment. "I think he intends to pressure you to change your operational patterns. At least."

"In which case, he's had a wasted journey," Honor said crisply.

"I know that, Ma'am. In fact—" McKeon stopped himself, unable even now to explain his own complex, ambiguous feelings. He knew Harrington had to be worried sick, but he also knew—had known, from the outset—that she wouldn't let herself be bullied into anything less than she believed her duty required of her. The possible fallout for the ship and for McKeon personally was frightening, but he felt a curious sort of pride in her, despite his resentment. And that only made him more ashamed of his own persistent inability to rise above his feelings and be the sort of executive officer she deserved for him to be.

"Captain, my point is that Klaus Hauptman is known for playing hardball. He's tough, powerful, and arrogant. If you don't agree to change your operations, he's going to try every way he can to . . . talk you into it." He paused again, and Honor raised her eyebrows. "Ma'am, I don't think you should let him do that in private. I think—" he committed himself in a rush "—that you should have a witness to whatever is said."

Honor almost blinked in astonishment. At the moment, McKeon had very little to worry about, personally, even from someone with Klaus Hauptman's reputation for elephantine memory and vindictiveness. He was her exec. He'd obeyed her orders, but the orders had been hers. If he made himself a witness to any discussion with Hauptman, particularly as a witness in her favor, that would change, and he was five years older than she and a full rank junior. If he turned a man like Hauptman into an enemy, the consequences to his career scarcely bore thinking on.

She cocked her head, studying his strained expression, almost able to taste the anxiety behind it. She was tempted to decline his offer, both because this was her fight, not his, and because she couldn't forget in a heartbeat the way he'd steadily avoided exposing himself since she came aboard. But as she looked into his eyes, she knew she couldn't. Whatever his reasons, he'd made his gesture. She couldn't reject it without rejecting *him*, without refusing his offer, however anxious it might be, to become her exec in truth for the very first time.

"Thank you, Mr. McKeon," she said finally. "I appreciate your offer, and I accept."

• CHAPTER TWENTY

Honor stood at the mouth of the boat bay personnel tube, watching through the visual display's bay pickups as her cutter mated with the tube's far end. The small craft moved with deliberate precision in the bay's brightly-lit vacuum, settling its ninety-five-ton mass neatly into the waiting cradle, and the rams moved the tube buffers forward, sealing the tube collar to the hatch. The green pressure light glowed, and she drew an unobtrusive breath as the tube hatch opened.

Klaus Hauptman stepped out of it like a reigning monarch. He was shorter than she'd expected, but solid, with the dramatic white sideburns she'd always suspected were artificial. His square face and powerful jaw had certainly benefited from cosmetic surgery—no one's features could be that regular—but the fundamental architecture had been maintained. There was strength in that face, an uncompromising, self-confident assurance that went beyond mere arrogance and pugnacity, and his eyes were hard.

"Commander Harrington." The deep voice was smooth and cultured, hiding any enmity, and he extended his hand.

She took it, and hid a smile as she felt his fingers work slightly about her own hand, feeling for the crusher grip. She'd never suspected he might be a knuckle-breaker. It seemed a bit petty for such a powerful man, but perhaps he needed to express his domination in all ways. And perhaps he'd forgotten she was a Sphinxian, she thought, and let him squeeze to his heart's content. Her long-fingered hand was large for a woman's, too large for him to secure the purchase points he wanted, and she let him build to maximum pressure, then squeezed back with smooth power. Her smile was pleasant, giving no indication of the silent struggle, but she saw his eyes flicker at the unexpected steeliness of her grip.

"Welcome aboard *Fearless*, Mr. Hauptman," she said, and let her smile grow just a bit broader as he abandoned the struggle and released her. She nodded to McKeon, who stepped forward to her shoulder. "My executive officer, Lieutenant Commander McKeon."

"Commander McKeon." Their visitor nodded, but he didn't offer his hand a second time. Honor watched him flex its fingers at his side and hoped they hurt.

"Would you care for a tour of the ship, Sir?" she asked pleasantly. "Much of it is off-limits to civilians, I'm afraid, but I'm certain Commander McKeon would be delighted to show you the portions of it we can."

"Thank you, but no." Hauptman smiled at McKeon, but his eyes never left Honor. "My time may be limited, Commander. I understand the courier will be heading back to Manticore as soon as he's finished his business with Commissioner Matsuko, and unless I leave with him, I'll have to make special arrangements to return home."

"Then may I offer you the hospitality of the officer's mess?"

"Again, no." Hauptman smiled again, a smile that might have shown just a bit of tension this time. "What I would actually appreciate, Commander Harrington, is a few moments of your time."

"Of course. If you'll accompany me to my briefing room?"

She stepped aside with a courteous gesture for Hauptman to precede her into the lift, and McKeon fell in at her back. The three of them entered the car and rode it in silence to the bridge. It wasn't a restful silence. Honor could feel the bare fangs and flexing claws beneath its surface and told her heart sternly not to race. This was her ship, and the fact that the Hauptman Cartel could undoubtedly have bought *Fearless* out of petty cash didn't change that.

The lift stopped at the bridge. It was Lieutenant Panowski's watch, and the acting astrogator rose from the command chair as his captain stepped onto the command deck.

"Carry on, Lieutenant," she said, and guided her guest toward the briefing room as Panowski sank back into his chair. No one else even looked up from his or her duties. It was a studied refusal to acknowledge Hauptman's presence, and she smothered a wry smile at her bridge crew's unspoken disapproval of the man as the briefing room hatch opened before them. Of course they all knew or suspected why Hauptman was here, and their silent support was even more precious after the listless depression and covert hostility those same people had once shown her.

The hatch closed, and she waved Hauptman to a chair. The business magnate crossed to it, but paused without sitting and glanced at McKeon.

"If you don't mind, Commander Harrington, I would really prefer to speak to you in private," he said.

"Commander McKeon is my executive officer, Sir," she replied with cool courtesy.

"I realize that, but I'd hoped to discuss certain . . . confidential matters with you. With all possible respect to Commander McKeon, I'm afraid I really must insist on discussing them privately."

"I regret that that won't be possible, Mr. Hauptman." Her face was serene, and no one else needed to know how hard it was for her to keep a brittle edge out of her voice. She drew out her own chair and sat in it, beckoning for McKeon to sit at her right hand, and smiled at Hauptman.

The first true expression crossed her visitor's face—a slight flush on the strong cheekbones and a subtle flaring of the nostrils—as she rejected his demand. Clearly, Klaus Hauptman was unused to having his will crossed. That was too bad, but he might as well get used to it now.

"I see." He smiled thinly and sat in his own chair, leaning back and crossing his legs with elegant ease as if to place the seal of his personal possession on the briefing room. Honor simply sat waiting, head slightly cocked, wearing an attentive smile. McKeon's face was less open. He wore the formal, masklike expression she'd come to know and hate, but this time it wasn't directed at her.

She studied Hauptman from behind her smile, waiting for him to begin, and her brain replayed all that she knew and had heard about him.

The Hauptman clan was one of the wealthiest in Manticoran history, but it was completely devoid of any connection to the aristocracy. That was rare in so powerful a family, but by all reports, Klaus Hauptman took a certain reverse snobbish pride in his very lack of blue blood.

Like Honor's own family, the first Hauptman had arrived on Manticore only after the Plague of 22 A.L.—1454 Post Diaspora, by Standard Reckoning. The original Manticore Colony, Ltd., had bid high for the rights to the Manticore System in 774 P.D. precisely because Manticore-A III, the planet now named Manticore, was so very much like Old Earth. Even the most Earthlike world required at least some terraforming to suit it to a human population, but in Manticore's case that had amounted to little more than introducing essential Terrestrial food crops and carefully selected fauna, and despite Manticore's long year and extended seasons, the off-world life-forms had made the transition to their new environment with ease.

Unfortunately, that ease of adaptation had been a two-edged sword, for Manticore had proven one of the very few planets capable of producing an indigenous disease that could prey on humanity. It took forty T-years for a native Manticoran virus to mutate into a variety which could attack human hosts, but once it had, the plague had struck with stunning power.

It had taken more than a standard decade for the medics to defeat the plague, and it had killed over sixty percent of the colonists—almost ninety percent of those born on Old Earth—before they did. The survivors' harrowed ranks had been depleted well below the levels of assured survivability, and far too many of their essential specialists had been among the dead. Yet as if to compensate for the disaster of the plague, fate had given the colony the ability to bring in the new blood it needed.

The original colonists had sailed for Manticore before the invention of the Warshawski sail and gravity detectors had reduced the risks of hyper travel to a level passenger ships could accept. Not even the impeller drive had been available, and their voyage in cryo hibernation aboard the sublight colony ship *Jason* had taken over six hundred and forty T-years, but the mechanics of interstellar travel had been revolutionized during their centuries of sleep.

The new technology had meant new colonists could be recruited from the core worlds themselves in a reasonable time frame, and Roger Winton, president and CEO of the Manticore Colony, Ltd., had anticipated the changes. He had created the Manticore Colony Trust of Zurich before departure, investing every penny left to the shareholders after the expenses of purchasing the colony rights from the original surveyor and equipping their expedition. Few other colonial ventures had even considered such a thing, given the long years of travel which would lie between their new worlds and Sol, but Winton was a farsighted man, and six centuries of compound interest had left the colony with an enviable credit balance on Old Earth.

And so Winton and his surviving fellows had been able not only to recruit the reinforcements they needed but to pay those colonists' passage to their new and distant homes, if necessary. Yet, because they were concerned about retaining political control in the face of such an influx of newcomers, the survivors of the original expedition and their children had adopted a new constitution, converting their colony from one ruled by an elective board of directors into the Star Kingdom of Manticore under Roger I, first monarch of the House of Winton.

The Manticore Colony, Ltd.'s, initial shareholders had received vast tracts of land and/or mineral rights on the system's planets, in direct proportion to their original capital contributions. The new constitution transformed them into an hereditary aristocracy, but it wasn't a closed nobility, for even vaster tracts had remained unclaimed. The new colonists who could pay their own passage received the equivalent of its cost in land credits on their arrival, and those who could contribute more than the cost of passage were guaranteed the right to purchase additional land at just under half its "book" value. The opportunity to become nobles in their own right had drawn the interest of an extraordinarily high percentage of young, skilled, well-paid professionals: physicians, engineers, educators, chemists and physicists, botanists and biologists—exactly the sort of people a faltering colonial population required and all too few out-worlds could attract. They'd arrived to claim and expand their guaranteed credit, and many of those so-called "second shareholders" had become earls and even dukes in their own right.

Of those who hadn't been able to pay their own passage in full, many had been able to pay much of the cost and so had received the difference in land credits on arrival. Small by Manticoran standards, perhaps, but enormous by core-world lights. Those people had become Manticore's freeholding yeomen, like Honor's own ancestors, and their families retained a sturdy sense of independence even today.

Yet for all that, the majority of the new arrivals had been "zero-balancers," individuals unable to pay any of their passage, who, in many cases, arrived on Manticore wearing all they owned upon their backs. Individuals like Heinrich Hauptman.

Today, there was little to differentiate, aside from the antiquity of original homestead land grants and certain purely honorific forms of address which were used with steadily decreasing frequency, between the descendants of yeomen and zero-balancers. But traditional memories of social status remained, and the Hauptman clan had never forgotten its hardscrabble roots. The family's rise to its present greatness had begun two Manticoran centuries before with Heinrich's great-grandson, yet Klaus Hauptman, who could have bought or sold a dozen dukedoms, still chose to regard himself—publicly, at least—as the champion of the "little man." It didn't prevent him from cementing business alliances with the aristocracy, nor from enjoying the power and luxury of his merchant prince status or becoming deeply involved in Manticoran politics, but his "commoner heritage" was fundamental to his fierce, prideful self-image. He regarded himself as a self-made man and the descendant of self-made men, despite the wealth to which he had been born.

And that image of himself was what had brought him here today, Honor told herself, for she'd hurt it. She'd caught him, or his employees, at least, dabbling in illegal trade, and to a man of his pride and self-aware importance that constituted a direct attack upon *him*, no mere business reverse or legal embarrassment. In his own eyes, Klaus Hauptman *was* the Hauptman Cartel, and that made her actions a personal insult he could not tolerate.

"Very well, Commander Harrington," he said at last, "I'll come straight to the point. For reasons of your own, you have seen fit to harass my interests in Basilisk. I want it stopped."

"I'm sorry you see it as 'harassment,' Mr. Hauptman," Honor said calmly. "Unfortunately, my oath to the Crown requires me to execute and enforce the regulations established by Parliament."

"Your oath doesn't require you to single out the Hauptman Cartel for your *enforcement*, Commander." Hauptman didn't raise his voice, but there was a vicious snap under its smooth surface.

"Mr. Hauptman," Honor faced him levelly, folding her hands tightly under the edge of the table, "we have inspected *all* commerce with the surface of Medusa or the Basilisk orbital warehouses, not simply that consigned here by your firm."

"Nonsense!" Hauptman snorted. "No other senior officer on this station has ever interfered so blatantly with Basilisk's legitimate merchant traffic. More to the point, I have numerous reports from my factors here to the effect that your 'customs' parties spend far more time 'examining' *my* shipments than anyone else's. If that's not harassment, I would very much like to know what you feel *does* constitute harassment, Commander!"

"What may or may not have been done by previous senior officers has no bearing on my responsibilities or duties, Mr. Hauptman," Honor said with cool precision. "And if, in fact, my inspection parties have spent more time on Hauptman Cartel shipments, that is entirely because our own experience has indicated that they are more likely than most to contain illegal items."

Hauptman's face darkened dangerously, but she made herself gaze back without any sign of her inner tension.

"Are you accusing me of smuggling, Commander Harrington?" The baritone was deeper and darker, almost silky.

"I am saying, Mr. Hauptman, that the record demonstrates that the incidence of contraband in shipments registered to your firm is thirty-five percent above that of any other firm trading with Medusa. Whether you are personally involved in those illegal activities or not, I cannot, of course say. For myself, I doubt it. Until such time, however, as we have satisfied ourselves that *no* contraband is passing under cover of a Hauptman Cartel manifest, my boarding officers will, at my orders, devote special attention to your shipments." Hauptman's face had grown steadily darker, and Honor paused, regarding him calmly. "If you desire an end to what you regard as 'harassment,' Sir, I would suggest that you insist that your own managers see to their internal housekeeping."

"How *dare* you?!" Hauptman exploded, half-surging to his feet. Honor's hands tightened further under the table, but she sat motionless. "I don't know who you think you are, but I refuse to sit here and be insulted in this fashion! I'd advise you to watch your wild allegations, Commander!"

"I've stated only facts, not 'wild allegations,' Mr. Hauptman," she said unflinchingly. "If you prefer not to hear them, then I suggest you leave."

"Leave? *Leave?!*" Hauptman was fully on his feet now, bracing his weight on the table as his voice filled the briefing room like thunder. "I came here to give you a chance to correct your gross mishandling of the situation! If you prefer, I can take it up with the Admiralty—or the government—instead of dealing with a jumped-up, over-inflated *commander* who insults me to my face by accusing me of illegal activities!"

"That is, of course, your option." Honor felt McKeon's coiled-spring tension beside her, but her own anxiety was fading, licked away by the steadily rising lava of her own anger. "In the meantime, however, you are a guest in my ship, Mr. Hauptman, and you will keep a civil tongue in your head or I will have you ejected from it!"

Hauptman's mouth dropped open in shock at her icy tone, and she leaned into his silence.

"I have not accused you, personally, of any illegalities. I have stated, and the record amply demonstrates, that individuals within your firm *are* engaged in illegal activities. Your threats to resort to higher authority do not alter that fact, nor will they alter my discharge of my responsibilities in light of it."

Hauptman sank back into his chair, jaw muscles bunched. Hushed silence hovered in the briefing room, and then he smiled. It wasn't a pleasant expression.

"Very well, Commander. Since you choose to see the possibility of my seeking redress through the Admiralty as a 'threat,' and since you seem unwilling to see the justice of extending even-handed treatment to my interests here, perhaps I can put this in terms you *can* understand. I am telling you, now, that you will cease harassing my ships and my shipments or that I will hold you personally—not the Navy, not the Government, *you*—responsible for the damage you are inflicting upon my business and personal good name."

"Whom you choose to hold responsible and for what is your affair, not mine." Honor's voice was cold.

"You can't hide behind your uniform from *me*, Commander," Hauptman said unpleasantly. "I am asking only for the courtesy and respect due any law-abiding private citizen. If you choose to use your position as an officer of the Crown to pursue some sort of personal vendetta against me, I will have no option but to use my resources to respond in kind."

"As I've already stated, I have not and do not intend to level any accusation against you personally until and unless clear and incontrovertible evidence that you knowingly permitted your employees to engage in illegal activities is presented. In the meantime, however, threats against me as an individual will have no more effect than threats to pressure me through my superiors." Honor's mind was cold and clear with the ice-hot flicker of her own anger, and her eyes were dark brown steel. "If you wish your shipments to pass with minimal delays for inspection, all you must do is see to it they contain no contraband. That," she added with cool deliberateness, "should not be an insurmountable task for a law-abiding private citizen of your means and authority, Sir."

"Very well, Commander," he grated. "You've chosen to insult me, whatever legalism you care to cloak that in. I'll give you one more opportunity to back off. If you don't, then I'll by God *push* you back."

"No, Sir, you will not," Honor said softly, and Hauptman gave a crack of scornful laughter. His body language radiated fury and contempt as he gave his renowned temper full rein, but his voice was hard and cold when he spoke once more.

"Oh, but I will, Commander. I will. I believe your parents are senior partners in the Duvalier Medical Association?"

Despite herself, Honor twitched in surprise at the complete *non sequitur*. Then her eyes narrowed, and her head tilted dangerously.

"Well, Commander?" Hauptman almost purred. "Am I correct?"

"You are," she said flatly.

"Then if you insist on making this a personal confrontation, you should consider the repercussions it may have on your own family, Madam, because the Hauptman Cartel controls a seventy percent interest in that organization's public stock. Do I make myself clear, *Commander?*"

Honor stiffened in her chair, her face paper-white, and the steel in her eyes was no longer chilled. It blazed, and the corner of her mouth twitched violently. Hauptman's own eyes gleamed as he misinterpreted that involuntary muscle spasm, and he leaned back, smiling and triumphant.

"The decision is yours, Commander. I am merely an honest merchant endeavoring to protect my legitimate interests and those of my shareholders in this system. If you insist on interfering with those legitimate interests, you leave me no choice but to defend myself in any way I can, however distasteful I may personally find the measures to which you compel me . . . or however unfortunate their consequences for your parents."

Honor's muscles quivered with hate, her fingers taloned in her lap, and she felt her lips draw back to spit her defiance in his face, but someone else's flat, cold voice spoke first.

"I suggest you reconsider that threat, Mr. Hauptman," Alistair McKeon said.

The sudden interruption was so utterly unexpected that

Honor turned to him in amazement. Her executive officer's face was no longer masklike. It was tight with anger, the gray eyes snapping, and Hauptman regarded him as if he were an item of furniture whose presence the magnate had forgotten.

"I'm not accustomed to accepting the advice of uniformed flunkies," he sneered.

"Then I suggest you *become* accustomed," McKeon replied in that same, hammered-iron voice. "Ever since your arrival in this briefing room, you have persistently attempted to construe Commander Harrington's actions as a personal attack upon yourself. In the process, you have insulted her, the Royal Navy, and the discharge of our duties to the Crown. You have, in fact, made it abundantly clear that neither the law nor your responsibilities under it are as important to you as your own precious reputation. Despite your calculated insolence, the Captain has maintained an air of courtesy and respect, yet when she refuses to ignore her duty as an officer of the Queen or modify it to suit your demands, you have seen fit to threaten not just her personally, but the livelihood of her parents." Contempt blazed in the lieutenant commander's eyes. "I therefore warn you, Sir, that I will be prepared to so testify in any court of law."

"*Court of law?*" Hauptman reared back in surprise, and Honor felt almost as surprised even through her fury. What was McKeon—?

"Yes, Sir, a court of law, where your persistent attempts to compel the Queen's Navy to abandon its responsibilities will, no doubt, be seen as proof of collusion in treason and murder."

Absolute shock filled the briefing room with silence in the wake of McKeon's cold, hard voice. Hauptman paled in disbelief, but then his face darkened once more.

"You're insane! You're out of your mind! There's no—"

"Mr. Hauptman," McKeon interrupted the sputtering magnate harshly, "forty-seven hours ago, sixty-one Native

Protection Agency police were killed or wounded in the pursuit of their duty. They were murdered, by off-world individuals trading with the Medusan natives in prohibited drugs. The laboratory manufacturing those drugs was powered by way of an unauthorized shunt installed in the backup orbital power collector of Her Majesty's Government's enclave on Medusa. That shunt, Mr. Hauptman, which Navy personnel discovered and positively identified not eight hours ago, was *not* installed after the collector was placed in Medusa orbit; it was installed when the collector was manufactured . . . by the Hauptman Cartel!"

Hauptman stared at him, too shocked to speak, and he continued in the same, grating voice.

"Since that shunt constitutes unimpeachable physical evidence linking your cartel or individuals employed by it with the drug operation, and hence with the murder of those officers, your blatant efforts to divert official attention from your operations here can only be construed as an effort to conceal guilt—either yours, or your employees. In either case, Sir, that would constitute collusion and thus make you, personally, an accomplice after the fact to murder at the very least. And I remind you that the use of Her Majesty's property in a capital crime—particularly one which results in the death of Crown officers—constitutes treason under the law of this kingdom. I respectfully submit—" he didn't sound at *all* respectful, Honor thought in shock "—that it is in your best interest and the interest of your cartel's future business reputation to cooperate fully with Commander Harrington's efforts to discover the true guilty parties rather than place yourself in a position of grave suspicion by obstructing an official investigation of Her Majesty's officers in this system."

"You're insane," Hauptman repeated, this time in a whisper. "Treason? *Murder?* You *know* Hauptman's hasn't—that *I* haven't—"

"Sir, I know only the facts I've just stated. Under the circumstances, and assuming you continue in your vendetta against the Captain—*your* vendetta, Sir, and not hers—I believe it would be my duty as an officer of the Queen to lay those facts before a court."

Alistair McKeon met Klaus Hauptman's disbelieving eyes with a cold, gray glare, and the magnate blanched. Honor made herself sit very still, grinding her heel down on the rage that still roared within her. Not for a moment did she believe Hauptman had been personally involved with the power tap or the drug lab. For that matter, she was almost certain he hadn't been personally involved in *any* of the illegal activities of his cartel in Basilisk. But his overweening pride and arrogance had been able to see the consequences of her actions only as a personal attack, and he had descended to the lowest and most contemptible of tactics simply to divert embarrassment from himself and punish her for daring to do her duty. That casual abuse of his own power and position filled her with as much revulsion as rage, and she had no intention of tempering McKeon's totally unexpected counterattack in any way. Hauptman had set the tone himself; now he could live with it.

"You wouldn't dare," the magnate said softly.

"Sir, I would." McKeon's voice was chipped flint, and Hauptman sat back in his chair, glaring back and forth between him and Honor.

"All right," he grated at last. "I see you've covered yourself after all, Commander Harrington. So go ahead, play tin-god out here. I wash my hands of the entire situation. Examine anything you damned well want, but don't you ever—*ever*—think this is over!"

McKeon gathered himself afresh, but Honor touched his arm and shook her head. She stood in silence, and when the exec made to rise with her, she waved him gently back into his chair. She inclined her head coldly at Hauptman, then gestured at the briefing room hatch, and the seething magnate stalked through it as it opened.

The bridge was still as death when they emerged onto it, but Honor scarcely noticed. She accompanied Hauptman into the lift, and the two of them rode to the boat bay in a silence deeper than the stars. But when they arrived, Honor reached out and pressed the override button, holding the lift door closed, and turned to him.

"Mr. Hauptman," she said in a voice of frozen helium, "you've seen fit to insult me and my officers and to threaten my parents. In fact, you have descended to the tactics of gutter scum, and that, in my opinion, Sir, is precisely what you have proven yourself to be." Hauptman's nostrils flared in a congested face, but she continued in the same ice-cold voice.

"I am fully aware that you have no intention of forgetting this incident. Neither, I assure you, have I. Nor will I forget your threats. I am a Queen's officer. As such, I will react to any personal attack upon me only if and as it arises, and for myself, both personally and as a Queen's officer, I dislike the custom of dueling. But, Mr. Hauptman, should you ever attempt to carry through your threat against my parents—" her eyes were leveled missile batteries and the tic at the corner of her mouth jerked like a living thing "—I will denounce you publicly for your contemptible actions and demand satisfaction. And when you accept my challenge, Mr. Hauptman, I will kill you like the scum you are."

Hauptman stepped back against the wall of the lift, staring at her in shocked disbelief.

"Believe it, Mr. Hauptman," she said very, very softly, and let the lift door open at last.

• CHAPTER TWENTY-ONE

Adrenalin still flared in Honor's blood and nerves as she rode the lift back to the bridge. That had been an ugly side of her, but the petty, repulsive shallowness hiding behind Klaus Hauptman's wealthy front had waked it, and she'd meant every word. More than that, he knew she had. And they both knew that his reputation—his all-important, self-worshipping *reputation*—would never survive should he refuse her challenge if it came.

She drew a deep breath as the lift stopped. The door opened, and she stepped out onto the bridge. Panowski looked up quickly, his face anxious, and she realized some of the vicious confrontation must have leaked past the briefing room hatch. Or perhaps it had simply been the tension between her and Hauptman when they passed back through on their way to the boat bay. It didn't matter. The lieutenant knew. His worried face showed his reaction, and she saw matching expressions on the faces of most of her ratings.

She paused for a moment, forcing herself to smile. Panowski's concern remained, but he relaxed visibly, and she made herself move slowly and calmly as she walked to the center of the bridge and looked around for McKeon. There was no sign of him, but the briefing room door was closed.

She crossed to it, and the executive officer looked up as the hatch slid aside. She didn't like stepping into that compartment just then. Too much cold hatred had washed its bulkheads, and she could feel the prickles of McKeon's residual rage radiating out to mesh and resonate with hers, yet he managed a strained smile and started to rise.

She waved him back and crossed to her own chair. She sank into it and turned it to face him.

"You took a chance, Alistair," she said. It was the first time she'd ever used his given name, but he didn't even seem to notice.

"I—" He wiggled his shoulders. "He just made me so damned *mad*, Ma'am. Coming in here like God descending to smite the sinners. And that last filthy trick of his—" The exec gritted his teeth and shook his head.

"He's not going to forget the way you backed him down." McKeon nodded, and Honor felt a certain bitter irony at the way her words echoed his own warning to her after Tremaine discovered that first illegal Hauptman shipment. "You shouldn't have done it," she went on levelly. "It was my fight and my responsibility, but . . . thank you."

McKeon's head came up, and he flushed.

"It wasn't just your fight, Ma'am. It was the Navy's. Hell, it was *Fearless*'s, and that makes it mine, too." His flush deepened, and he looked back down at the fingers suddenly interlaced in his lap.

"I . . . haven't been much of an exec to you, have I, Ma'am?" he asked quietly.

Honor started a quick reply, then paused, gazing at the crown of his lowered head. This man had just put himself far, far out on a limb for her. He'd antagonized one of the most powerful men in the Kingdom, and she shuddered to think where her confrontation with Hauptman would have ended had she responded without his intervention. The use of the collector tap to turn Hauptman's manipulations back on him had never even occurred to her. She hadn't been thinking clearly enough for that. All she'd felt was hate and disgust and the need to strike back. She knew herself—knew she'd hovered on the brink of physically attacking the man in her fury, and that would have ruined her, whatever the provocation.

McKeon had stopped her before she did that. He'd

seen the opening and taken it, forced Hauptman back onto the defensive, won her time to regain at least some control of herself. She owed him for that—owed him a deep, intensely personal debt she rather doubted she could every repay. And because she did, she wanted to tell him not to worry, to brush over his shortcomings as her first officer.

But she was a warship's captain. Personal feelings and gratitude, however deep or deserved, took second place to that. They must. And so she cleared her throat and spoke in a soft, impersonal tone.

"No, Mr. McKeon," she said. "You haven't." She watched him flinch, saw his shoulders tighten, and wanted to reach out to him. But she didn't. She simply sat there, waiting.

The silence stretched out, tight and painful, and McKeon's hands washed themselves in his lap. She could hear him breathing, listened to the throb of her own pulse, and still she waited. She could feel his need to say something more and knew he needed time to say it in, and that at least she could give him, however long it took.

"I know I haven't, Ma'am," he said finally. "And . . . I'm sorry." He twitched a shrug and looked up at her face. "It's not much, but it's all I can say. I've let you down—let the ship down—and I'm sorry."

"Why, Mr. McKeon?" she asked softly. He winced at the compassion in her voice, but he understood her question. For a moment she thought he might thrust himself up out of the chair and flee, but he didn't.

"Because—" He swallowed and looked around the briefing room without really seeing it. "Because I let my personal feelings get in the way of my duty, Ma'am." He made himself face her as he admitted it, and in that moment their ages were reversed. The tall, powerful executive officer seemed suddenly young and vulnerable, for all his years of experience, while he met her eyes almost desperately, as if begging her to understand.

"You came aboard, and you looked so damned *young*," he went on in a voice of wretched self-loathing. "I knew you deserved the command. God, I only had to check your record to know that! But I wanted it so badly myself. I didn't have the seniority for it—" He broke off and laughed harshly.

"I'll probably *never* have the seniority. I'm a hack, Captain. A plodder. The kind who refuses to stick his neck out. But, God, how I *wanted* this ship. More than I'd ever admitted to myself. And there you were—five years younger than me with one hyper-capable command already under your belt, walking through the hatch straight from ATC and wearing the white beret *I* wanted."

His hands fisted in his lap, and then he did rise. He paced up and down the small briefing room like a caged animal, and Honor felt his anguish and self-condemnation. She could almost see the fog of his misery, wrapped around him like poison, but she sat on her sudden desire to break his monologue, to stop him or defend him from himself. She couldn't. He needed to say it—and *she* needed for him to say it, if there was any hope the barriers between them would truly come down.

"I hated you." His voice was muffled, bouncing back from the bulkhead as he looked away from her. "I told myself I didn't, but I did. And it didn't get better. It got worse every day. It got worse every time I saw you do something right and realized I'd wanted you to do it *wrong* so I could justify the way I felt.

"And then there were the maneuvers." He wheeled to face her once more, his expression twisted. "Damn it, I knew they'd handed you an impossible job after the way they gutted our armament! I *knew* it was impossible—and instead of digging in and helping you do it anyway, I let you carry the whole load because deep down inside I *wanted* you to fail. Captain, I'm a tac officer by training. Every single time something went wrong, every time another one of those goddamned Aggressor crews 'destroyed' us, something inside me kept saying *I* could have done better. I knew I couldn't have, but that didn't matter. It was what I *felt*. I tried to do my duty anyway, but I couldn't. Not the way I should have."

He came closer to the table, leaning forward to brace himself on its top and bend towards her across it.

"And then this." He raised one hand to gesture at the bulkheads. "Basilisk Station." He returned his hand to the table beside its companion and stared down at them both. "I told myself it was your fault, that *you* were the one who'd gotten us sent here, and that was another lie. But every time I told myself one lie, I had to tell another to justify the ones that came before it. So it was your fault, not mine, and all that nonsense about doing our duty, about meeting our responsibilities whether anyone else had ever bothered to meet theirs or not—that was crap, Captain. That was bright-eyed, runny-nosed, idealistic, Academy *crap*, not the real world."

He looked up at her again.

"But it wasn't, was it, Ma'am?" he said softly. "Not to you. I don't know why Young dumped this on you. It doesn't matter why he did. What matters is that you didn't cry and moan. *You* didn't slack off. You just dug in and—" He shook his head and straightened.

"You kicked us in the ass, Captain. You kicked us over and over again, until we got up off our self-pitying backsides and started acting like Queen's officers again. And I knew what you were doing, and why you were doing it, the whole time, and I hated it. *Hated* it. Because every time you did something right, it was one more proof that you deserved the job I wanted."

He dropped into a chair, facing her across the table, and raised one hand almost pleadingly.

"Captain, you were *right*, and I was wrong. What's happening in this system right now proves you were, and if you want me off your ship, I wouldn't blame you at all."

He fell silent at last, hunched in despair, and Honor leaned forward in her chair.

"I don't want you off my ship, Commander," she said softly. His head jerked back up, and she waved a hand in the air between them.

"You're right. You did drop it all on me. I wanted you to meet me halfway—needed you to—and you wouldn't. Everything in the galaxy was coming together and falling on me at the same time, and you just sat there, refusing to open up, and left everything up to me. Oh, yes, Commander. There were days when I would gladly have sent you packing, with an efficiency report that would've put you ground-side forever, if I hadn't been so shorthanded, if I'd had enough experienced officers aboard to replace you with someone I could rely on. But—"

She paused, letting silence linger behind the word, then gave a tiny nod.

"*But*, Mr. McKeon, I would have been wrong to do that." He blinked in astonishment, and she smiled faintly. "Oh, there were times I wanted to kick you, or strangle you, or bite your head off in front of the entire wardroom, but then I realized you *were* trying. I didn't know what the problem was, and you weren't doing things my way, but you were trying. I watched you work with Rafe on that probe reprogramming, and you handled him perfectly. I saw you taking time with Panowski, the way you were never too busy to handle anything that came up—as long as *I* wasn't involved. And I realized something, Mr. McKeon. Whatever else you may be, you're no hack. And you're not a plodder, either."

She leaned back, her eyes level.

"You screwed up. You *did* let me down, and the ship, and it could have been a disaster for all of us. But everyone screws up sometimes, Mr. McKeon. It's not the end of the world."

McKeon stared at her for a long, still moment, then exhaled a wracking breath and shook his head.

"I can't—" He paused and cleared his throat. "One of the things I was always afraid of was that if I told you, if you knew how I felt, you'd react exactly like this," he said huskily. "You wouldn't chew my ass out, wouldn't spit in my face. And that . . . Well, it scared me. It would have been the final proof that you really did deserve the job—and that I didn't. Do you understand what I mean, Ma'am?"

Honor nodded, and he nodded back.

"Stupid, wasn't it? I don't think a kid like Cardones or Tremaine is a worthless fuck-up just because he makes a mistake, admits a problem. But I couldn't admit that *I* had one. Not to you."

"Not stupid, Mr. McKeon. Just very, very human."

"Maybe," McKeon whispered, and stared down at his hands again. Honor let the silence linger for a few heartbeats, then cleared her own throat.

"But whatever the past was like, it's past," she said more briskly. "Isn't it, Mr. McKeon?"

"Yes, Ma'am." The executive officer straightened in his chair and nodded with matching briskness. "Yes, Ma'am, it is."

"Good." Honor stood and smiled at him across the table. "Because since it is, Mr. Exec, be warned! The *next* time I think you're slacking off, I'm going to kick your ass so hard you'll make it all the way to Basilisk Control on pure momentum! Is that clear, Mr. McKeon?"

"Yes, Ma'am." He rose from his own chair with a grin. It looked unnatural and out of place on the face which had been a mask for so long, but it also looked completely right, somehow.

"Good," Honor repeated more softly. She hesitated for just a moment, and then extended her hand across the table. "In that case, Commander McKeon, welcome aboard. It's good to see you back."

"Thank you." He took her hand and clasped it firmly. "It's good to *be* back . . . Skipper."

• CHAPTER TWENTY-TWO

Fat flakes of snow fell like silent, feathery ghosts in the windless sub-arctic night beyond the window. Hamish Alexander stood watching them through the thick, double-paned plastic and felt the welcome heat of the fire against his back. His study was in the oldest part of White Haven, the sprawling Alexander family seat, and the walls of native stone were over two meters thick. Unlike some commodities, rock had been plentiful when White Haven was first built, and enough of it worked just as well as more esoteric off-world insulation would have.

He turned back to the huge fireplace and added another log. He adjusted it with the poker, settling the native hemlock (which, in fact, bore very little resemblance to the Old Earth tree of the same name) into the bed of coals, then straightened and replaced the poker in its stand as he checked the wall clock again. It was twelve past comp, well into the twenty-seven-minute midnight "hour" officially called Compensate that adjusted Manticore's 22.45-hour day to permit use of Standard Reckoning time units, and his eyebrow rose again. Even allowing for the time zone difference, it was unusual for his brother to screen him this late—and even more unusual for him to specify the exact time at which he would call.

The com terminal on his desk beeped as if to punctuate his thoughts, and he walked briskly over to answer it. He sat in the huge, padded chair his great-grandfather had commissioned from the craftsmen of the Sandalwood System over a T-century before and signaled acceptance of the call.

The screen lit with his younger brother's face.

"Hi, Hamish," the Honorable William MacLeish Alexander said.

"Hello, Willie." Alexander tipped the chair back and crossed his legs. "To what do I owe the pleasure?"

"Your Commander Harrington," William replied, coming to the point even more quickly than usual.

"*My* Commander Harrington?" Alexander arched both eyebrows, and William grinned from the screen.

"Don't take that surprised tone with me, Hamish! You've gloated enough over what she's been up to."

" 'Gloat' is such a crude word," Alexander protested. Then he grinned back. "Still, I suppose I have alluded to her achievements a time or two."

"And usually as rudely as possible, when there's a Liberal or Progressive in the vicinity," William agreed.

"A family trait. But just what was it you wanted to say about her?"

"Actually, I'm acting in something of the role of an emissary for my esteemed prime minister." William's words remained light, but there was an undertone of seriousness in his voice. "Were you aware that Klaus Hauptman went out in person to browbeat her into backing off?"

"No, I wasn't." Alexander made no effort to hide his disgust. "I suppose I should have expected it. I doubt he succeeded, though."

"No, he didn't—but I'd like to know why you seem so confident he wouldn't have."

"If Harrington were the sort to back down, she would have done it already. Besides, I've been peeking at Jim Webster's reports on a fairly regular basis. She couldn't be doing the job she is or raising this much general hell if she were stupid or hadn't thought the whole operation through ahead of time. That means she must have known what sort of reaction she was going to face *before* she decided to go ahead and step on the land mine."

"Land mine's a pretty good word," William agreed

with sudden, complete seriousness, "and if she *had* backed down, it might have blown up more than just her career."

Alexander said nothing, but his eyes asked the question, and his brother shrugged.

"Before he went out, Hauptman hit every button he could reach back home in Landing. He didn't make much headway with the Duke, but he certainly bent Janacek's ear. *And* he called in his markers with Countess Marisa and Sheridan Wallace's 'New Men,' too. I think we've underestimated the contributions he's been making to certain parties' coffers, including the New Men, but he definitely has his hooks even deeper into the Liberals than we'd thought. Marisa can't give a centimeter—officially—without breaking with the Government and losing her post as Minister for Medusan Affairs. She's not about to do that, but it's pretty obvious she and Wallace were primed to come down on the Navy's entire handling of Basilisk Station. If Harrington had crumbled at this point, they would've been able to claim the Navy, in her person, had bungled and made the Kingdom a galactic laughing stock by first creating interstellar incidents with our neighbors and then proving its irresolution by backing away from its duties under pressure."

Alexander snorted contemptuously, and his brother gave a grim, wintry smile. "Of course it would all have been gobbledygook. They've never complained about the situation on Basilisk Station before, and jumping on Harrington for going back to the *status quo ante* at the same time they criticize her for changing the *status quo* in the first place would be as stupid as it would be illogical. On the other hand, the Liberals have never been noted for the logic with which they approach Basilisk, have they? And if they talked fast enough and loud enough, they could probably engender enough confusion—especially among the uncommitted peers and MPs who'd probably see any retreat on Harrington's part as a slap in the face to the Kingdom's prestige—to at least get a motion to repeal the annexation onto the table."

"A lot of good *that* would do them," Alexander growled.

"Depends on how they did it, Hamish," William warned soberly. "And on who they got to help them do it. For instance, it looks like High Ridge was ready to support at least their initial moves."

"*High Ridge* was throwing in with Marisa and Wallace? That's a switch," Alexander observed.

"And not one that bodes well for the Conservative Association's continued support for the Duke," William agreed. "I suppose that was Janacek and North Hollow more than anyone else. Harrington's making that ass Young—and, by implication, Janacek himself—look worse every day. But the point is that all the Opposition parties have been riding their rank and file pretty hard to prep them for some big move once Hauptman bullied Harrington into backing down, and Wallace was going to play hatchet man. He even went as far as to put down his name and 'the state of affairs on Basilisk Station' on the list of next month's Official Questions."

"Oh ho!" Alexander shook his head with a small smile. The Official Questions list gave the Opposition a way to force the Government to allow open (and generally partisan) discussion of things it might prefer to avoid. A prime minister could refuse to answer an Official Question only if he certified, with the backing of the Crown and the Chief Justice of the Queen's Bench, that answering it would jeopardize the Kingdom's security. Even then, the Government had no choice but to permit individual members of Parliament to debate the Question in secret session. Potentially, that made the list an extremely effective parliamentary weapon, but it was a double-edged sword, and the timing could go wrong. Like now. Under the unwritten portion of the Manticoran constitutional tradition, a Question could not be withdrawn, even by its author, once it was on the list.

"Clumsy, clumsy," he murmured thoughtfully.

"Absolutely. Since he can't withdraw it now, Harrington's given us the perfect shot to ram through amendments to the original Act of Annexation. But that's only true if she's still senior officer on the station when the Question comes up."

"Well, I know Jim certainly doesn't plan to pull her. And Janacek can't, if Jim and Lucien Cortez stand firm. I think they will."

"And if Young gets himself back on station?"

"Now *that*," Alexander admitted, "is a more ticklish point. Jim and Lucien can't stop him from going back out any more than Janacek can relieve Harrington. Not unless they want to come out into the open and declare war on the Conservatives. And if it comes to an open showdown between them and the First Lord, they'll lose. They have to, or the whole concept of civilian control of the military goes out the airlock."

"That's what I was afraid of." William sighed. "Our spies in the enemy camp suggest that High Ridge is pressuring North Hollow to 'suggest' his son bite the bullet and go back without his ship if he has to."

"Won't work," Alexander said firmly. "In a sense, he was SO in Basilisk only because his ship was assigned there and he went with her."

"What do you mean?" William looked puzzled, and his brother's grin was wicked.

"That's always been one of the problems with the picket there, Willie. You see, officially, there *is* no 'Basilisk Station' to command—not in the sense that there's a Manticore Fleet District or Gryphon Fleet District—thanks to the Act of Annexation and Janacek's own policies. That means the picket's SO isn't in the same position as, say, a squadron commander. In the case of a squadron or an official station or district, a commanding officer is responsible for *all* operations in his designated command area and for every ship assigned to it. But thanks to the mish-mash we've actually got in Basilisk, where there's no formally specified command area at all, Young's primary responsibility was to act as captain of his own heavy cruiser. It was only the fact that he was the senior RMN officer present that made him the picket commander. Or, to put it another way, *Warlock* is his 'designated command area,' and his authority beyond her hull is restricted by her current physical location and functions on a strictly *ad hoc* basis. Oh, if he'd detached himself from *Warlock* to *Fearless* in the first place, the Admiralty wouldn't have objected. In fact, that's what he ought to have done. But when he officially 'delegated' the SO's job to Harrington by removing his ship from the picket, he released himself—unilaterally—from any responsibility for or authority over Basilisk Station until his refit is completed. Technically, he can't go back without *Warlock* without absenting himself from his post unless Lucien cuts him orders to that effect. I can't quite see Lucien doing that, and I *can* see Jim getting awfully stuffy about the letter of the regs all of a sudden if Young tries to reassume command there without *Warlock*."

"But how close is he to getting *Warlock* back from the yard?" William asked anxiously. "Can he get back there *with* his ship before Wallace's Question comes up?"

"He might." Alexander sat back and drummed on the desk blotter with the fingers of both hands. He thought for several seconds, then shook his head. "He just might, at that."

"All right." William drew a deep breath. "You understand, of course, that this has to be completely unofficial, Hamish." Alexander nodded, already guessing what was coming next. "The Duke has asked me to tell you that Her Majesty's Government would find it most convenient if Lord Pavel Young is *not* on Basilisk Station for the next month."

"I understand, Willie." Alexander gazed at his brother for a few more seconds, then shrugged. "I'll see what I can do—unofficially, of course."

"Thanks, Hamish. We appreciate it."

"Anything for a good cause, Willie," Alexander said. "See you later."

His brother nodded, and Alexander cut the circuit. He sat in pensive thought for a moment, and then punched a scramble-coded number into the com. The screen lit with a "WAIT" prompt, then cleared to show a sleep-tousled James Webster.

"Who—? Oh, for God's sake, Hamish! Can't you let a working man sleep?"

" 'Fraid not. I just got off the screen with Willie, and he's got a little job for us." Alexander outlined his conversation with his brother in a few short sentences, and Webster's eyes widened while the last vestiges of sleep faded from them.

"Don't want much, do they?" he asked sardonically when Alexander finished.

"No more than we do. This sounds like the perfect opportunity to catch the Opposition with its shorts around its ankles, Jim. From what Willie's told me in the past, a pretty firm majority in the Lords is impressed enough by Harrington's accomplishments to stand with the Government, and we already had a strong majority in the Commons. If Wallace has to ask his Question while she's still acting SO, the Government can respond using her policies as its basis, not Young's, and make her look like exactly what she is—a decisive officer fully discharging the Navy's responsibilities for the first time in twenty years. And they can argue that what's needed is to see to it that *other* officers are in a position to do the same thing in the future. If that happens, we can actually turn Basilisk Station into something that works instead of a half-assed nightmare. Harrington's done her part for us; all we have to do is keep Young here in Manticore and off her back a little longer."

"Hamish, I'll be the first to admit I dream about a chance like this, but just how do you propose to pull that off? I can guarantee Lucien won't give him permission to quit his ship and that I won't let him go back without her, but *Warlock* can't be all that far from completing her refit."

"I know. But, you know, Jim, even the best refit crews can fall off their stride from time to time."

"I don't think this is something the First Space Lord should know about."

"In that case, don't tell him." Alexander flashed a sudden, boyish grin. "Don't tell me you don't sometimes forget to mention things to your official persona!"

"It's been known to happen from time to time," Webster allowed. "What won't I be telling myself this time?"

"I'm going to go up and have a little talk with Craig, I think. Can I tell him that you've blessed my mission—unofficially, of course?"

"Unofficially, but fervently," Webster agreed.

"Good. Thanks, Jim. Sorry to have dragged you out of bed."

"Don't worry about it. Just go do a good job on Craig."

"Oh, I will," Alexander agreed with a smile. "I will."

Vice Admiral of the Red Sir Craig Warner, Commanding Officer of Her Majesty's Space Station *Hephaestus*, stole the time from his schedule to meet the private yacht personally. Longer ago than he liked to remember, a very young Commander Warner had found himself embroiled in a duel over a drunken insult to the good name of a lady. His captain at the time, a most well-born nobleman, had disapproved rather strongly of the practice of dueling, but when the circumstances and graphic nature of the insult had been explained to him, he had astounded Commander Warner by offering to act as his second. The lady in question was now married to Vice Admiral Warner and the mother of his four children, and his then captain had become a very close friend—and godfather to Warner's oldest son. So when Hamish Alexander asked for a few hours of his time, Warner was only too happy to oblige.

Now the yacht completed its docking maneuver, and

Warner stepped up to the personnel tube to greet his visitor. It was an unofficial visit and Alexander was in civilian dress—he'd been on half-pay since the first week Sir Edward Janacek took over the Admiralty—so no formal courtesies intruded.

"Good to see you again, Craig," Alexander said, shaking his hand firmly. "About ready for a real space-going command again?"

"They also serve who stand and weld," Warner replied solemnly. "On the other hand, I did hear something about a battle squadron that needs a good flag officer."

"Really?" Alexander grinned. "When?"

"I've got another seven months here first, unfortunately. BuShips likes me more than I'd like them to."

"It's because you're so damned efficient," Alexander teased as they headed for the personnel capsules.

"True. Too true. But what can I do for you, Hamish? Want a tour of my little workshop?"

"Maybe later. In fact, I'm sure I would later. But first, I need to bend your ear for a few minutes. In private."

Warner shot his superior a very sharp look indeed, then shrugged and waved him into the capsule.

"In that case, let's take this to my office," he suggested, punching buttons, and Alexander nodded.

The capsule deposited them at a terminal less than fifty meters from Warner's office, and the two admirals walked down the passage side by side, chatting amiably and harmlessly. Warner's aide and personal yeoman were waiting, but their boss shooed them out and closed the hatch firmly behind them. Then he gestured Alexander into a comfortable chair, poured drinks, and sat down behind his desk.

"And now," he said, "what's all this 'unofficial visit' about, Hamish?"

"It's about Basilisk Station," Alexander replied, and Warner blinked in surprise. "More specifically, it's about the possibility of finally getting our hands untied there. Interested?"

"Very. But where do I come in?"

"Well, Craig, it's like this. . . ." Alexander leaned back to cross his legs, and reported his conversation with his brother yet again. Warner listened intently, nodding his understanding of each point, then tipped back his own chair.

"So you and Admiral Webster want me to hang Young out to dry?" he said when Alexander was done.

"More or less—and very unofficially. How about it? Can you swing it for us?"

"I don't know, Hamish." Warner plucked at his lower lip, frowning in thought, then shrugged. "The thing is, I have to admit I've already been dragging my heels ever since word of Harrington's activities started getting around, just to watch the little bastard squirm. He hasn't been getting the work priorities he thinks he should, and he's been in here every other day or so to complain."

"Does that mean you've used up all your tricks?"

"I don't know. . . ." Warner thought some more, then turned to his terminal and punched up the work files on HMS *Warlock*. He frowned at them, whistling tunelessly between his teeth as he paged through the screens of data, and Alexander possessed himself in all the patience he could manage.

"Well, now!" Warner murmured after several minutes. "That's interesting."

"What?"

"When *Warlock* first arrived, Young wanted a complete overhaul of her forward Warshawski tuners. In fact, he was pretty strident about it, but as you know, BuShips—meaning me, in this instance—has to sign off on anything that big." He looked up with a wicked grin, and Alexander smiled back with suddenly dancing eyes.

"And what was your decision, Admiral Warner?"

"I didn't give him one, Admiral Alexander. From what I can see here, he's good for another eight to ten months hyper time on the tuners he's got before he even approaches mandatory replacement wear. I refused to give him an answer mainly just to be a pain in his arrogant ass, but I doubt I'd authorize it, under normal circumstances, with that much time left on the components."

"Ah. But under these circumstances?"

"Why, I think I might just find it my heart to okay the work after all," Warner said generously.

"Good! But will he bite, do you think? I thought you said he's been in here trying to get you to expedite."

"Oh, he has. And I'm almost certain he'll say no thank you if I make him an offer at this point. But there are ways, Hamish. There are ways."

"Such as?"

"Well—" Warner switched off his terminal and turned back to his friend "—I think the first step will be to hold the good news that I've decided to authorize his requested work until the end of this watch. Young's been spending a lot of time dirt-side, hitting the Landing night spots while Commander Tankersley, his exec, does all the work—no love lost there, by the way—and while he's out bar-crawling, he leaves his com link home and lets his message service handle any calls. So if we give him time to clear out, then authorize the work, we'll have a full watch and a half, ten hours minimum, to hit our stride before he gets back. I imagine we'll have his Warshawski sails spread all over the slip before he knows a thing about it."

"Tankersley won't smell a rat and warn him?"

"As I said, there's no love lost between the two of them. Tankersley's a fairly decent sort. I don't think Young's attempt to shaft Harrington sits very well with him, and you can't be exec to a man like Young without getting to know exactly how useless he really is. Under the circumstances, I sort of doubt Young's explained his real motives to him, either, so Tankersley can play the uninformed but earnest exec to the hilt, if he wants to. I imagine he'll screen Young, all right, but probably only to leave a message with his service—and not one with any special priority." Warner tapped lightly on his desk for a moment, then nodded to himself. "Won't hurt to make sure, though. My aide's not just good looking; she's a *very* bright young woman, and she's been spending some off-duty time with Tankersley. That's one reason I figure he must be all right; Cindy wouldn't waste her time on him if he wasn't. Would it be all right if I have her mention to him that I'd appreciate his keeping his next progress report to Young a little vague?"

"We can't involve Jim or the Government, Craig," Alexander warned. "If you're wrong about him, you'll be the one it comes back to haunt."

"I don't think I am wrong, and I'm perfectly willing to run the risk for something like this. Hell, who needs a battle squadron? Carol would rather have me planet-side for good, anyway."

Warner spoke lightly, though both of them knew the loss of his next command or even half-pay was not merely possible but probable if any of this became official knowledge. Their eyes met for a moment, and then Warner smiled.

"Don't sweat it, Hamish. I'll pull it off. And once we get *Warlock's* forward hull opened up, I guarantee she won't leave dock for a good seven weeks. Long enough?"

"Long enough," Alexander agreed. "And thanks."

"Don't mention it. I never liked his father, either. And Carol will be *delighted* when she hears about this. North Hollow was after her before we were married, you know."

"No, I didn't. I wondered why you were so ready to dislike his son, though."

"Hell, that ancient history didn't have anything to do with *that*. Well, not much. This little creep is a disgrace to his uniform all on his own."

Warner sat for a moment longer, running through his plans, then nodded and stood.

"Well, that's that," he said with undisguised satisfaction. "And now, while I wait to put my nefarious plan into effect, why don't I give you that tour? Then we can finish up with supper in the flag officer's mess before you head back home."

"Sounds good to me," Alexander agreed, and the two admirals headed for the office hatch once more. "By the way, how are the kids?" he asked as they stepped through it. "I saw Carol last week, but we didn't have time to talk."

"Oh, they're fine. Sandra just made commander, and it looks like Bob's got a shot at ATC early. Keith and Fred are still in school, of course, and neither of them seems interested in the Navy, but—"

They walked down the passageway, chatting cheerfully.

• CHAPTER TWENTY-THREE

Medusa was still the most boring looking planet she'd ever seen, Honor reflected, brooding over the main visual display once more, but it was beginning to seem appearances could be deceiving. She remembered something she'd read once, some ancient curse from Old Earth about living in "interesting times." It made much more sense now than it had when she first read it.

She hid a sigh, walked across to her chair, and eased herself into it without officially taking over the watch from McKeon. Her brain was busy.

Two days had passed since Hauptman's visit. Two whole days without a single new disaster, which was almost enough to make her skin crawl with anticipation. Not that there hadn't been "interesting" developments. Dame Estelle's sulfurous description of her interview with Countess Marisa's courier had been one. Honor had never imagined the genteel, composed Resident Commissioner could be so elementally enraged. Dame Estelle had looked ready to bite pieces out of the furniture, but as Honor had listened to her account of the meeting, she'd understood perfectly.

It seemed the Countess of New Kiev was feeling the heat from the financial community in general and, apparently, from the Hauptman Cartel in particular. From Dame Estelle's remarks, Honor was beginning to suspect that the big Manticoran merchant cartels had contributed rather more heavily to the Liberal Party's political coffers than she'd ever thought. The notion of an alliance between the parliamentary advocates of increased welfare spending and the captains of industry seemed a bit bizarre to Honor, but something was certainly giving them an awful lot of clout with the Opposition, for Countess Marisa had decided to turn the screws on Dame Estelle to propitiate them.

Honor had been astounded to learn from the commissioner that Countess Marisa had been told in unambiguous terms to keep her hands off the Navy's operations on Basilisk Station. That must have been a rude shock for her, Honor told herself with secret delight, and it reinforced her own suspicion that someone well up the chain of command approved of her actions. It was also, she reflected, the first time since the Basilisk Annexation that the Minister for Medusan Affairs had been told—rather bluntly, she gathered—that her authority ended at the outer edge of the planetary atmosphere. It was a long overdue assertion of the Fleet's authority and responsibility, although, given the officers and ships normally assigned here, she had little faith it would last.

But it was holding for now, and Countess Marisa didn't like it a bit. More, it sounded as if her authority even within her own planetary bailiwick had taken a beating.

Honor hadn't quite understood the gleam in the commissioner's eye once she stopped ranting and started speculating on the political situation back home. Of course, Honor didn't understand most of the machinations that went on inside the Parliament of Manticore. She vastly preferred the Navy, where the chain of command was at least generally clear, whatever infighting went on between factions and power groups. But Dame Estelle *did* seem to grasp the byzantine rules of the game, and she appeared convinced that something deep, complex, and probably drastic was going on beneath the surface . . . and that whatever it was boded ill for Countess Marisa.

Honor could follow some of her reasoning, for as Dame Estelle had pointed out, Countess Marisa, as one of the leaders of the Opposition, held her present post only because the Ministry for Medusan Affairs was traditionally assigned to the Liberal Party as some sort of *quid pro quo* left over from the original, tortuous annexation fight in Parliament. But there were limits to how far from the Government line she could stray without losing her position, and it seemed she'd reached them, for her messenger had arrived in Dame Estelle's office with "suggestions," not directives.

The commissioner hadn't cared for those suggestions at all, and as far as Honor could decipher them, they seemed to have consisted entirely of variations on a single theme. Dame Estelle should remember the commercial importance to the Kingdom of its great trading houses. She should strive to adopt a "more conciliatory tone" when dealing with them and "mediate between the Navy's overly rigorous application" of the commerce regulations and the cartels' "legitimate concerns over sudden and abrupt changes in the regulatory climate." Above all, she should "remember the transitory nature of our custodial presence on Medusa" and avoid any actions which would anger the natives or those who would someday trade with them as equals. And, of course, she should "strive to abate" the possibly over-zealous manner in which the present senior officer on Basilisk Station seemed to be wielding her powers over the remainder of the star system.

It had, Honor reflected, sounded like the most mealy-mouthed, double-tongued case of interstellar arm-twisting she'd ever heard of, and its timing had been unfortunate. Dame Estelle had been back in her office for less than ten minutes after a visit to the Government House hospital, where the worst injured of her wounded NPA troopers had just died, when Countess Marisa's courier caught up with her, and she hadn't been in the mood for it.

She'd snapped the unlucky messenger's head off and sent him home with it under one arm and a detailed account of the nature and severity of recently discovered violations of Her Majesty's Medusan Protectorate's laws under the other. And, she'd told Honor with grim delight, she'd concluded her report with the observation that the discovery of those violations had been made possible solely by the "dedicated, professional, persistent, and outstandingly successful efforts, both in their own right and in association with the NPA" (that was a direct quote) of Commander Honor Harrington and the crew of HMS *Fearless*. Under the circumstances, Dame Estelle had added, she had no intention of striving to abate Commander Harrington's activities and every intention of aiding and abetting them in any way she could. And if Her Majesty's Government disapproved of her intentions, she would, of course, submit her resignation.

The fact that her offer to resign hadn't been taken up seemed, in Dame Estelle's opinion, to validate her conclusion that Countess Marisa was in some sort of trouble back home. Honor wasn't so certain about that, but when she added it to the evidence of unanticipated support from her own superiors, she had to concede that the commissioner might just have a point.

The problem, of course, was that the support might well vanish if she and Dame Estelle couldn't carry through and deliver either the parties behind the drug lab (and, almost certainly, the new weapons, as well), or else demonstrate that those criminals' activities had been stopped once and for all. And the unhappy truth was that they had achieved exactly nothing further since Hauptman and the courier had taken themselves back through the Basilisk terminus to Manticore.

Honor half-reclined in her chair, crossing her legs and steepling her fingers under her chin while Nimitz napped on the chair back, and tried to think of anything else she might have done. Or, for that matter, might still do.

The tap on the power collector was, she was almost positive, a dead end. Oh, she had no doubt it had been installed when the collector was first put in by the Hauptman Cartel, but despite McKeon's savage counterattack on Klaus Hauptman and the investigations no doubt underway back home, it was unlikely anyone would ever be able to prove precisely how. If some highly placed individual within the cartel had ordered it, any records which might once have existed had very certainly been destroyed long since. And if someone had slipped it in when the prefabricated collector components were assembled here in Basilisk, it could have been any one or two of scores of people involved in the project. In either case, the chance of ever figuring out who'd done it was astronomically remote.

But Dame Estelle was right about one thing. Tapping off of the Government's own backup collector had shown a degree of arrogant self-confidence which sat very strangely with how meticulously the lab itself had been hidden. There'd been no *need* to tap that particular collector. Even if they hadn't wanted to use their own collector, a geo-thermal plant, or even a simple hydro generator, installed in the volcanic springs two kilometers from the lab could have provided the needed power. And it could have been run in by wire, without the betraying risk of beamed receptors and relays. It was as if their opponents had a split personality. One side of them hid the presence of their drug-making facilities with obsessive care, but the other ran utterly unnecessary risks that almost seemed to flaunt its nerve by stealing power for those same facilities from its enemies.

And, she thought grimly, there might even be a third personality, given the way the lab had been blown. That had been a terminally stupid thing for any criminal organization to do; the NPA would never give up looking for whoever had ordered it done. It was almost like a deliberate challenge, designed with malice aforethought to goad the authorities into the most violent reaction possible.

The problem was that *none* of it made sense. Not only did the bad guys seem to be going off in half a dozen directions at once in their planning, but the very scale of the operation was absurd. Dame Estelle was right. Whatever these people were after, it wasn't the profits from drug running or selling guns to the natives. It smacked of some organized off-world covert operation, but what was its purpose? Arming the Medusans and feeding them drugs that inspired violence had all the earmarks of an effort to engineer a native insurrection, yet no possible Medusan "uprising" could hope to defeat the forces Manticore could put into Basilisk to stop it. There might be a great deal of bloodshed before it ended, but most of the blood would be Medusan, not Manticoran, and the most likely upshot would be a powerful, permanent military presence on Medusa in place of the lightly-armed NPA troopers now stationed there.

Unless, of course, whoever was behind it (she very conscientiously avoided *assuming* it was the Republic of Haven) might be hoping for another response entirely. It was always possible that a bloodbath on Medusa would be grist for the Liberal/Progressive mill and wake such revulsion in Parliament as to enable the anti-annexationists to finally get Manticore entirely off the planet. It struck Honor as unlikely in the extreme, but it *was* possible. Yet even if that worked, it would never get the Kingdom to renounce its claim on the Basilisk terminus of the Junction, and what good would it do anyone—even Haven—to simply get the NPA off Medusa?

No, there was something else going on here. Something she and Dame Estelle were both missing, but something definitely linked to off-world interests other than a purely domestic Manticoran criminal operation. Honor was certain of that, even if she couldn't quite make the next connection in the chain, and that meant—

"Captain?"

Honor twitched up out of her reverie at the sound of Captain Papadapolous's voice. Her surprise roused Nimitz, and he sat up to yawn at the Marine.

"Yes, Major?" she replied. Then she noticed Barney Isvarian standing by the briefing room hatch, and her eyes narrowed. "You have that deployment plan for me?"

"Yes, Captain. Sorry it took so long, but Major Isvarian—

Well, he was pretty worn out, Ma'am, and then we had to chase around assembling decent maps and some hard figures on what the NPA actually has on-planet."

"No problem, Major," Honor said, and meant it. If there'd been the least trace of defensiveness in Papadapolous's tone she might not have, but he was simply stating facts, not making excuses. She climbed out of her chair and shook herself, then looked over at the officer of the watch.

"Mr. McKeon?"

"Yes, Skipper?" The exec looked up from his displays, and Honor saw one or two heads twitch as if they wanted to turn and look at him. His use of the word "skipper" no longer sounded outright alien, but it didn't sound exactly natural, either. Not yet.

"I'd appreciate it if you could join Major Papadapolous, Major Isvarian, and me in the briefing room. I'd like your input on this."

"Of course, Ma'am." McKeon rose and looked down at Lieutenant Cardones. "You have the watch, Mr. Cardones."

"Aye, aye, Sir. I have the watch," Cardones replied, and McKeon walked briskly into the briefing room with Honor and Papadapolous.

The Marine, who had always seemed detached from Honor's relations with her naval officers anyway, appeared blissfully ignorant of any change in her relationship with McKeon. He crossed to the briefing room table and fed a pair of data chips into one of the terminals, then waited while Honor and McKeon found seats. Isvarian, who looked infinitely better than the last time Honor had seen him in this compartment, also found a seat, and Papadapolous cleared his throat.

"Basically, Captain, Commander McKeon, I'd like to give you a brief overview of our ideas before I show you the actual deployment order. Would that be acceptable?"

"Of course," Honor replied.

"Thank you, Ma'am. Very well, then. First, we had three basic problems to consider. One, we have to respond to a threat whose parameters we cannot establish with any degree of certitude. Two, our resources are limited, and those currently off-planet—*Fearless's* Marine detachment—aren't concentrated in one place at the moment. Three, the ideal solution requires the integration of our Marines and their firepower with the NPA's local expertise and troop strength into a single force operating under a unified field plan.

"After lengthy discussions with Major Isvarian, my platoon commanders and I have come to the conclusion that we won't know how powerful the opposition is until and unless we actually see it coming at us. There's simply no way for us to know at this time, though that may change if new intelligence is developed on Medusa. Anything that gives us some clear picture of potential enemy troop strength would be invaluable, and Major Isvarian has assured us that his people will do everything they can to get that information for us.

"Next, there's the problem of getting our own available strength concentrated. The NPA only has about a five-company field strength, once we allow for essential detachments, and my own company is understrength just now. So, with your permission, Captain, I'd like to recall the Marines currently detached to the customs and inspection parties. I believe the traffic volume has dropped to a level which would permit us to reduce the number of inspection boats and consolidate Navy ratings to crew them, which would release our Marines for possible ground combat. If we can do that, I'd have four full-strength platoons to work with, not three partial ones."

Papadapolous paused and raised an eyebrow at Honor. In turn, she glanced at McKeon and raised an eyebrow of her own.

"I think we could do that, Ma'am," the exec said after a moment. "We can probably get by with two fully-crewed inspection boats, given present traffic levels."

"Very well, Major Papadapolous," Honor said. "You have your Marines back again."

"Thank you, Ma'am. That gives me much greater flexibility." The Marine smiled briefly, and Isvarian nodded his own satisfaction.

"Given that troop strength," Papadapolous resumed, "I'd like to move it down to the surface as soon as possible. Our basic deployment plan is intended to provide maximum coverage for the off-world enclaves with, as Dame Estelle and Major Isvarian have requested, as much capability as possible to go to the aid of any of the native city-states, as well.

"Toward these ends, I intend to reconfigure two squads' worth of our battle armor for the recon role. As you no doubt know, Captain—" the Marine's tone suggested that she might *not* know but chose, diplomatically, to assume that she did "—our powered armor is designed to confer maximum tactical flexibility by allowing us to configure it for specific mission parameters. Normally, we operate with fairly heavy weapon loads, but that limits our endurance in two ways. First, the weaponry itself displaces power cells we might otherwise carry, and second, most of our heavy weapons are energy intensive, which ups the drain on the cells we can carry. It gives us a lot of firepower, but only over relatively short engagement times.

"In the recon role, weaponry is cut back to a bare minimum in favor of additional sensor systems, which simultaneously allows us to add additional cells, reduce overall power requirements, and substantially upgrade sensor capability. A Marine in standard armor configuration has an endurance of less than four hours under sustained combat conditions; in recon configuration, his endurance is over fifty hours, he can sustain speeds of sixty kilometers per hour even through rough terrain, and he can 'see' much better. The trade off is that his offensive power is little greater than that of a Marine in standard battle dress."

He paused and watched his audience's faces as if to be certain they were with him, and Honor nodded.

"All right, what I intend to do is use my two squads of recon-configured armor as scouts. Once we know an incident is under way, the scouts will go out looking for potential hostiles and attempt to identify them so that air strikes can interdict them short of the enclaves if at all possible. They'll have the speed and sensor capability to cover lots of ground, and their armor should protect them from anything the natives have. Major Isvarian assures me that not even a Medusan nomad can hide from full-range battle armor sensors if we know his general area, so even if they're pushed back into the enclaves, I anticipate developing reasonably complete tactical data from them.

"The third squad of battle armor will be configured for maximum combat capability and stationed centrally within the enclaves. As information on enemy movements comes in, it will be shifted in response. Given the firepower each Marine will represent, I can probably deploy them by sections or even in two-man teams to deal with anything short of a massed charge, and they'll represent my primary striking force." He paused and frowned slightly. "I'd really prefer, in some respects, to use them as my reserve, instead, given their mobility and combat power, but I'm afraid they'll prove too valuable in the offensive role to make that practical.

"In the meantime, however, I intend to break up two of my other three platoons and integrate their personnel with Major Isvarian's NPA troopers. Our people have better armor and generally more powerful weapons than the NPA, and they're trained for full-dress combat situations, while the NPA are primarily policemen. I'd like to hand them out on a squad basis, attached to experienced NPA platoon or company-level commanders to supplement their firepower and tactical flexibility. At the same time, I want to cross-attach at least one NPA officer who knows the terrain well to my heavy-armored squad. If possible, I'd like more than one member of the NPA, in case I have to split the squad, since getting maximum utility out of our people will require their knowing exactly where they're going and exactly what the ground will look like once they get there.

"With our Marine elements in support, the NPA will then provide the primary perimeter control force. Its assigned mission will be to cover the enclaves and pin down any attackers until the heavy-armored squad or even scouts in the vicinity can deal with the attack. They will be instructed not to expose themselves to avoidable casualties, since they'll be much less well-protected, but they should be able to take care of themselves if they're forced into sustained action.

"My fourth and final platoon and the heavy weapons section will form our central reserve. The heavy weapons section will be on call for the entire force, and Major Isvarian has assured me of sufficient counter-grav to give us good mobility. I hope to detach the section, or even individual weapon teams, on a purely temporary basis, returning them to the reserve as quickly as possible, but we'll have to play that by ear once something breaks. Fourth Platoon, however, will be maintained intact and concentrated for as long as possible to deal with penetrations. Again, Major Isvarian tells me the NPA can provide us with transport both to reach trouble spots and to return Marines to the reserve as quickly as possible once a problem has been dealt with."

He paused once more, cocking his head as if to consider everything he'd just said, then nodded.

"Under the best possible conditions, Captain, we're going to be spread very thin. On the other hand, our communications should be infinitely superior to the enemy's, as will our sensor capability and individual firepower. Major Isvarian and I have considered the known capabilities of the natives' new rifles, and we believe our people should be able to deal with any single group of enemies relatively quickly, even if outnumbered by a very heavy margin. Our greatest fear is numerous, small, simultaneous incursions which would over-extend our forces and slip at least some attackers past us unengaged. That possibility is especially serious in the relatively built up areas of the Delta. Our sight-lines are going to be a lot shorter than in the open field, and so are our engagement ranges and firing lanes. That's why I want those scouts so badly, and it's also the reason we're deliberately spreading our people out so much—to give us shorter response time to any given threat."

"I understand, Major," Honor said, privately impressed by the difference between what she was hearing now and Papadapolous's original airy, off-handed disparagement of his task's difficulties.

"In that case, Ma'am," the Marine said, punching commands into his terminal, "let me show you the specific initial deployment grid Major Isvarian and I have come up with." A very large-scale holo of the enclaves and the Delta immediately around them glowed to life above the conference table. "As you can see, Captain, we'll place our first scouting element here, along the line of the Sand River tributary channel. Then we'll put another element here, and another here. After that . . ."

Honor sat back and watched the holo blossom with light codes as Papadapolous, with occasional support from Isvarian, detailed their plan. She was a Navy officer, not a Marine, but it looked impressive to her. More importantly, Isvarian seemed completely satisfied with it, and she contented herself with a knowing expression and tried to nod in all the right places. Yet even as she listened something nagged at her. She couldn't quite put her finger on it until Papadapolous finished and turned to her expectantly while the big holo glowed behind him.

"Very impressive, Major," she said then. "It looks to me like you've given careful consideration to maximizing your own capabilities while limiting those of your enemies. Do you mind if I ask a few questions?"

"Of course not, Captain."

"Thank you. First, have you and Major Isvarian discussed this with anyone else ground-side yet?"

Papadapolous glanced at Isvarian, and the NPA major answered for him.

"We've talked to my two senior field men, Dame Estelle, and George Fremont, her deputy. That's all so far, Captain."

"I see. And could you tell me how much advance planning and warning your people would need to make this work, Major Isvarian?"

"At least a week to achieve this kind of integration. In fact, I'd like at least ten days."

"I see," Honor repeated, and hated herself for the question she had to ask next. "And have you determined yet how the operators of that drug lab realized your raid was coming, Major Isvarian?"

The NPA man's face tightened, and she knew he'd suddenly seen where she was headed, but he made himself answer in a level voice.

"No, Ma'am."

"Then I'm very much afraid, gentlemen, that we have a problem," she said quietly.

"Problem, Captain?" Papadapolous looked puzzled, and Honor turned towards him, but Isvarian raised a hand.

"May I, Captain?" he asked heavily, and Papadapolous looked across the table at him as she nodded.

"We screwed up, Nikos," Isvarian sighed. "To be more specific, *I* screwed up. We've got a security problem down there."

"I don't understand, Sir." Papadapolous glanced at Honor. "Captain? How could anything the Medusans know about us materially affect our operations? Surely the technological gap is too extreme for them to realize the sort of threat our weapons represent."

"As far as the natives are concerned, you're probably right, Major," Honor said. "But we have very good reason to believe the weapons we're so worried about were supplied to them by off-worlders, and those same off-worlders would appear to have information sources within the NPA or—more probably, in my opinion—within the NPA's civilian support structure. In either case, any pre-positioning of your people would tip them off as to what we're up to."

"I follow that, Ma'am," Papadapolous said with a frown, "but I'm afraid I'm still not certain exactly what you're getting at. Wouldn't their knowledge serve as a deterrent against any open action?"

"Our problem is that we don't know what they're really after, Nikos," Isvarian said. "I know Dame Estelle thinks it's more than just money, and it looks like Captain Harrington agrees with her." He shrugged. "If both of them think that, I'm certainly not prepared to argue with them. But that means that knowing what we intend to do won't necessarily deter them at all—and it *will* give them the opportunity to adjust their own plans accordingly if they decide to go ahead."

"But to what effect?" Papadapolous asked.

"We can't know that," Honor cut in before Isvarian could reply. She nibbled on her lip for a moment, wondering how much to worry the Marine with. Clearly Papadapolous was concentrating—as he ought to be—on the tactical problem he faced. Equally clearly, he wasn't aware of the behind-the-scenes tension and maneuvering to pull *Fearless*'s (and Honor's) teeth. Or, at least, not of how that might affect his own problems.

"One possibility is that we might scare them back underground," she said finally, choosing her words with care. "Presumably, they're up to something fairly involved, and certainly what we've seen so far suggests some very long-term planning. While our immediate objective has to be to prevent casualties and limit damage, a deterrent that's too effective may handicap our long-term objective of stopping them entirely, since we can't do anything to derail *their* ultimate intentions until they come into the open and try to implement them." She started to add something more about her own possible time constraints, then decided against it.

Papadapolous watched her face with an attentive frown. He seemed quite aware that there was something she hadn't said, but she'd said enough to give him plenty of food for thought.

"I see," he said after a moment. He gazed at his holo, eyes thoughtful, then looked back at Honor. "Would you care to offer any suggestions, Ma'am?"

"Only one," she said, and turned to McKeon. "We've just agreed we can cut down on the inspection flights. Can we restrict them to just the boarding shuttles?"

"I don't see any reason why we couldn't," McKeon said after a moment's consideration. "It's what they were built for, after all."

"In that case, I want all three of those pinnaces reassigned from the Government Compound to *Fearless*," Honor told Isvarian. "With all three of them available, we can land Major Papadapolous's entire force in a single assault drop."

"And retain them all aboard ship without giving away our deployment plans in the meantime," Isvarian said with a nod.

"Precisely. Major?"

"Well . . ." Papadapolous seemed unaware he'd spoken as he peered back down at his display with puckered eyes, and she could almost see the thoughts racing through his brain. He started to speak again, only to pause once more, then nodded slowly.

"It's going to be messier, Ma'am," he warned, "and with all my people up here, there's going to be a lot more room for us to pick up on an incident late or bobble our coordination and let something through into the enclaves. That's what concerns me most, but we're not going to be able to integrate my squads with NPA formations without time for them to train in coordination with their parent units, either, so we're going to lose a lot of flexibility and responsiveness once we're down, too. Still, I think we can probably work something out." He rubbed his jaw, still staring at the holo, then looked up at Isvarian.

"Can you stay aboard another day or so, Major? We're going to have to rethink the entire ops plan, and I'd really value your input."

"I'll be happy to, Nikos." Isvarian rose to join his study of the holo. "And I'm not sure we'll lose quite as much flexibility as you think. We can still plan my people's original positions to tie into your eventual deployments, and maybe we can use First and Second Platoons as squad level reaction forces rather than trying for unit-by-unit integration."

"That's what I was thinking," Papadapolous agreed. "And then—" He broke off and looked at Honor with a hint of apology. "Sorry, Captain. The major and I can get into the nuts and bolts on our own time. I'll try to have a preliminary plan for you by the end of the day."

"That will be fine, Major," Honor told him. She rose and smiled at him and Isvarian. "I'm still impressed, gentlemen, and I have every confidence your final solution will work out equally well."

She gave them another smile and beckoned to McKeon. She and the exec walked out of the briefing room. Behind them, through the closing hatch, she saw the two officers they'd left behind hunched over the holo with their heads close together in earnest conversation.

• CHAPTER TWENTY-FOUR

Lieutenant Samuel Houston Webster hummed to himself as he worked his steady way through the mountain of routine signal traffic. Venerable and sacrosanct tradition required every communications officer to resent the paperwork his position entailed, but Webster was guiltily aware that he failed to measure up in that respect. There were days he resented the *time* it used up, yet the fact that he, alone of his ship's other officers, knew as much about *Fearless*'s information flow as the captain tickled his ego. More than that, it was surprisingly difficult to resent anything he "had" to do for Captain Harrington.

His fingers danced over his console with practiced ease, and a small corner of his mind occupied itself with other matters even as he kept an eagle eye on the secure traffic he was breaking down into clear. The Captain was good people, he told himself. That was about the strongest accolade in his vocabulary, and very few of his superiors ever earned it. Webster wasn't vain or arrogant, but he was entirely aware that the fortunate accident of his birth meant he was almost bound to become a senior officer himself someday. As such, he'd discovered that he had a tendency to look at his superiors of the moment through two sets of eyes. One belonged to the very junior officer he was, eager to learn from their greater experience and example, but the other belonged to the future flag officer he intended someday to be, and that second set of eyes was more critical than his cheerful exterior might suggest.

He'd been very disappointed in Lieutenant Commander McKeon, for example. If anyone on board should have seen what the Captain was up to and helped her achieve it, it was her exec. But McKeon seemed to have come around, and Webster had made a very careful note of the way the Captain had avoided climbing all over him before he did. There'd been times he'd been a little upset with her for not jerking McKeon up short, but the final result she'd achieved with him had been an eye-opener.

It was funny, in a way. Captain Harrington was so quiet. The RMN had its share of characters, and Webster had known captains who could blister battle steel when they were ticked. Captain Harrington never even raised her voice, and he'd never once heard her swear. Not that her calm manner meant anyone but an idiot would ever take liberties with her. In fact, he'd been surprised to realize that her very quietness was even more effective precisely because it was so different from the fire and thunder another captain might have shown.

He admired that, just as he admired the way she maintained her distance from her subordinates, always there, always approachable, but never letting anyone forget that *she* was in charge. Yet at the same time, she could rattle someone's cage any time she chose—like the way she'd forced Rafe Cardones into finding the answer to that problem with the drones—and she seemed to know everything there was to know about all of them. She even knew that while Cardones liked being called "Rafe," Webster passionately hated it when people called him "Sam." He rather doubted that information was listed anywhere in their personnel jackets, and he was at a loss to figure out how she'd acquired it.

Another message flickered on his display, the jumbled symbol groups flowing magically into clear text, and he paused. His eyebrows rose in surprise, and then he began to smile as he read it through. He sat for a moment, tapping on the edge of his console in thought, then nodded to himself. This one would go into the hopper last, he decided. It was only a routine "information" message, but Webster had a keener sense than most of the infinitely polite infighting between the Navy's first families. He rather thought it would make the Captain's day—if not her week—and it would be a nice surprise to finish out the traffic.

He tapped a priority number into the terminal and brought up the next message with a grin.

Honor sat working at her own terminal in the quiet of her cabin. She'd been spending too much time in her bridge briefing room. Knowing the Captain was just on the other side of that hatch, hovering over them, could have an inhibiting effect on junior officers, and with McKeon coming around it was no longer necessary to hover. They'd made great strides over the past week and a half. Not enough to completely compensate for the time they'd lost building their professional relationship, but certainly enough to leave the day-to-day affairs of the ship completely in his hands. So she'd brought her workload "home" to deal with.

She finished Dominica Santos's weekly maintenance report, approved the suggestions the engineer and McKeon had made for dealing with several minor problems, and paused to rub her eyes. The dining cabin hatch slid open, and MacGuiness padded through it with a fresh cup of hot cocoa as if her thoughts had summoned him.

"Thank you, James." She sipped with a smile, and he smiled back.

"You're welcome, Ma'am," he said, and vanished as quietly as he'd appeared. She took another sip and set the mug aside, preparing to jump back into the minutiae of her reports, when the admittance buzzer sounded. She hit the intercom key.

"Yes?"

"Communications Officer, Ma'am," her Marine sentry announced, and she made a face. Not because it was Webster, but because it meant he was bringing her the day's routine message traffic.

"Come in, Samuel," she said, and opened the hatch.

Webster walked in with the message board tucked under his arm, came briefly to attention, and extended it.

"The—"

"—daily traffic," Honor finished for him wryly, and he smiled.

"Yes, Ma'am. No special priorities."

"Well that's a relief."

She took the board and pressed her thumb to the security panel, receipting the traffic, and wondered yet again why the Navy insisted on using up an officer's time hand-delivering a ship's routine mail. Webster could have dumped the whole thing to her terminal direct from the bridge with the press of a key, but that wasn't the way the Navy did things. Perhaps, she thought, hand delivery was supposed to insure captains actually read the stuff.

"Yes, Ma'am." Webster came back to attention, gave her another smile, and disappeared back through the hatch.

Honor sat for a moment, gazing back and forth between the message board and her terminal while she pondered which boring bit of paperwork to turn her attention to next. The message traffic won out—at least it had come from a source outside *Fearless*—and she drew the board towards her and keyed it alive.

The first message appeared on the built-in display, and she scanned it idly, then punched for the next. And the next.

It was remarkable what gems of information the Lords of Admiralty in their wisdom deemed it necessary for their captains to know. She couldn't quite see, for example, why the Acting Senior Officer on Basilisk Station needed to know that BuShips had decreed that henceforth all RMN dreadnoughts should trade in two of their cutters for a sixth pinnace. Perhaps it was simply easier for them to send it to *all* captains than go to the trouble of looking up the ones who really needed it?

Her lips quirked at the thought, and she worked her way more briskly through the traffic. Some of it *was* both pertinent and germane to her duties, like the specific addition of force knives to the contraband list for Medusa, and other bits and pieces were moderately amusing, yet most of it was boring in the extreme.

But then she came to the last message, and her eyes opened very wide indeed. She sat bolt upright in her chair, a corner of her eye noting the way Nimitz had risen on his padded perch to mirror her reaction, and read it a second time.

It wasn't even addressed to her, but her face blossomed into a smile and her eyes began to dance as she read it yet again. It had been copied to her for her "information," not for any required action, and she began to chuckle aloud as she recalled her earlier suspicions that *someone* approved of her actions. Whoever that someone was had apparently decided to give her a very broad hint of his or her approval, for there was no other conceivable reason for this to have been sent to *Fearless*.

It was a routine dispatch from the CO of HMSS *Hephaestus* to Admiral Lady Lucy Danvers, Third Space Lord. Danvers was the head of BuShips, and Vice Admiral Warner's dispatch was a "regret to inform you" response to Captain Lord Young's recent request to BuShips for special refit priority. Admiral Warner's inspection teams had, it seemed, confirmed Captain Lord Young's own initial assessment and determined that heavy wear to the Warshawski sail tuners aboard Her Majesty's heavy cruiser *Warlock* made their replacement a matter of urgent priority. This necessary overhaul meant, unfortunately, that that vessel's refit must be extended for a minimum of eight more weeks in order to carry out the required installation and tests. Vice Admiral Warner would, of course, expedite the work in every possible way and remained Admiral Danvers's obedient servant and etc.

Honor placed the message board carefully on her desk and tried not to giggle. She *hated* the way she sounded when she giggled, but this time she couldn't help it. She rose, still snickering like a naughty schoolgirl with a secret, and reached out to scoop Nimitz off his perch. She held him at arm's length, and the treecat chittered with his own equivalent of a giggle as she whirled him in circles about the cabin.

"Well, that's that, Sir." PO Harkness scrubbed sweat from his forehead with a grubby handkerchief, then returned it to his coveralls' forearm pocket.

"It is, indeed," Ensign Tremaine agreed. He kneaded his stiff back muscles with one hand and wondered if it would be beneath an officer's dignity to do a little brow-mopping of his own.

"Thanks, Mr. Tremaine." Gunny Jenkins—for some reason known only to Marines, the senior Marine noncom on any ship was always called "Gunny," even when, like Jenkins himself, he was a company sergeant-major—wasn't even sweating, Tremaine noticed with some resentment. Jenkins made one last eyeball check of the empty suits of battle armor webbed into the pinnace's cargo bay, made a notation on his memo board, and closed the bay hatch.

"You're welcome, Gunny," Tremaine replied. Harkness was silent, eyeing the Marine with an air of infinite superiority, and Jenkins replied by ignoring the burly petty officer entirely.

"That just leaves the ammo pallets for Pinnace Two," Jenkins went on cheerfully as the three of them headed down the access tube from the pinnace airlock, and Tremaine swallowed a moan. He'd been hoping to leave that till next watch, and the look on Harkness's face said he'd hoped the same thing. The ensign started to object, then bit his lip. No one could have called Jenkins's expression a *smirk*, exactly, but it certainly came close. Perhaps, Tremaine thought, PO Harkness had a point where Marines were concerned. . . not that he intended to give Jenkins the satisfaction of hearing him say so. Instead—

"Of course, Gunny," he said even more cheerfully. "If you'll step right this way? PO?"

"My pleasure, Mr. Tremaine," Harkness said sourly, and Jenkins waved for his work party to fall in astern as they headed across the boat bay towards the stacked pallets.

"—so the pinnaces are combat-loaded if we have to drop them."

McKeon finished his report and switched off his memo pad, and Honor nodded. It was late, by *Fearless*'s clock. The remains of supper lay on the snowy tablecloth between them, and Nimitz was still busy with his own plate at the table's far end. She crossed her legs and watched his needle-sharp teeth remove the flesh from a Sphinxian tree-hopper drumstick with surgical precision as she toyed with a fork. It was remarkable, she thought for the thousandth time, how neat his table manners were where anything but celery was concerned.

"I think we're about as ready as we're going to get, then," she said finally.

"I only wish we knew what we're ready *for*," McKeon agreed a bit sourly, and she gave a faint smile.

"We've had the better part of two whole weeks since Hauptman's visit with no alarms and excursions at all," she pointed out.

"Which only makes me think something extra nasty is sneaking up on us." McKeon sighed, then produced a wry smile of his own and stood. "Well, whatever happens will happen, I suppose, Ma'am. Good night."

"Good night, Mr. McKeon."

He gave her a small nod, and she watched him leave. Quite a change there, she told herself with undeniable satisfaction. Quite a change.

She stood herself and reached for the sadly depleted bowl of salad. Nimitz's head came up instantly, his green eyes bright, and she smiled.

"Here, Greedy Guts," she told him. She handed over the

celery stalk and turned towards her private head. She could already feel the luxury of a long, hot shower.

The raucous sound of a buzzer woke her.

Honor's eyes popped open as the buzzer snarled a second time. She was a heavy sleeper by nature, but her first tenure in command of a Queen's ship had changed that, and Nimitz complained sleepily as she sat up quickly. The 'cat half-slid and half-rolled down into her lap from his favorite sleeping perch on her chest, and she set him gently aside with one hand as she turned and punched the com key with the other.

The buzzer stopped snarling at her acknowledgment, and she ran her hands quickly through her short hair. That was one advantage of wearing it like a man. There was no point pretending she was a beauty, anyway, and at least this way she didn't have to waste time making it look pretty when someone woke her in the middle of the night. She snatched the kimono her mother had given her for her last birthday from the bedside chair and slipped into it, then hit the com key a second time, accepting the call with full vision.

The screen was painfully bright in the dark cabin. It was also a split-image conference call, and Dame Estelle looked out of one side of it. *Fearless* had adjusted her shipboard day to match that of the Government Compound, and like Honor, Matsuko wore a robe over her nightclothes, but Barney Isvarian was in uniform in the other half of the image. Honor saw Surgeon Lieutenant Montoya, her own assistant physician, behind him and recognized the antiseptic cleanliness of one of the NPA's native clinics in the background.

"Sorry to wake you, Honor, but it's important." The commissioner sounded almost frightened, and Honor sat straighter as she finished belting her kimono.

"What is it, Dame Estelle?"

"Two pieces of information. One came in two days ago, but it was so vague I decided to sit on it a while before I passed it on to you. Barney just screened me with the second, and it changes the one I already had."

Honor nodded and cocked her head, inviting the commissioner to continue.

"I had a visit from Gheerinatu, one of the Medusan nomad clan chiefs, Wednesday," Matsuko said. "He doesn't like the Delta city-states any better than any other nomad, but we helped his clan out two years back. Given the weather here, the nomads tend to migrate from hemisphere to hemisphere—or at least to the equatorial zone and back—with the seasons, but Gheerinatu's clan got caught in an early storm while it was crossing the Delta. We pulled most of his clansmen and about half their herds out of a flash flood with NPA counter-grav just before they all drowned, and that makes us friends of his."

She paused, eyebrow quirked as if to ask if Honor was with her, and Honor nodded.

"All right. Gheerinatu's from the north—his clan's part of the Hyniarch . . . well, I guess we'd call it a clan federation. Anyway, he's heading south for the winter, but he's got relatives all over the northern hemisphere, and he dropped by to tell me that one of those relatives from up near the Mossybacks sent him a message. It wasn't a very specific message, but Gheerinatu thought we should hear about it. Roughly translated, it was a warning that the Delta would be an unwise place for Gheerinatu and his herds to pass the winter."

Honor's face tightened, and Dame Estelle nodded.

"Exactly what I was thinking, but it's the first whisper we've heard from the native side, and, as I say, it was pretty darn unspecific. That's why I didn't pass it on to you—until this other thing came up." The commissioner nodded at her own pickup, her eyes turning to the side of her screen which held Isvarian's image. "You want to take it from here, Barney?"

"Yes, Ma'am." Isvarian shifted in his chair and looked straight at Honor. "I'm over in the clinic we run up by

Dauguaar on the Three Forks, Captain," he said. Honor thought for a moment, summoning up a mental map of the Delta, then nodded. The Three Forks River was well up to the north, and Dauguaar was about the farthest north of all the city-states. Which meant it was also closest to the Mossybacks.

"We got a call late this morning," Isvarian went on, once she had the geography in mind. "A nomad had staggered up to the city gates and collapsed, and the city guard had dragged him to the clinic and turned him over to us. The duty medic recognized the symptoms immediately—*mekoha* poisoning, and a pretty advanced case, at that—but he also noticed that the nomad had an unusual-looking belt pouch. He opened it up while his native orderlies carted the nomad off." Isvarian reached for something beyond the field of the pickup, then showed Honor a leathery-looking pouch. He opened it, and her mouth tightened as she saw the dull gleam of bullet-shaped lead projectiles.

"He had a powder horn, too," Isvarian resumed grimly. "No one saw any sign of a rifle, but that was enough to sound all the alarms and get me out here as fast as I could move an aircar. Fritz here—" he gestured at Montoya, who gave his captain a tired smile "—wanted to come with me to see *mekoha* poisoning first-hand, so I brought him along. The two of us spent most of the time since sitting by his bedside, listening to him babble till he died about ten minutes ago."

The NPA man shrugged, and his eyes were unhappy.

"He was pretty far gone. *Mekoha* doesn't leave a lot of IQ when you get to such an advanced stage, and his motor control was shot, which made him even harder to understand, but I got enough to scare the hell out of me, Captain. He kept going on about new weapons—the rifles—and some nomad shaman whose 'hands overflow with holy *mekoha*.' That's pretty near a direct translation."

"Oh, crap," Honor whispered before she could stop herself, and Isvarian nodded.

"It gets worse, Ma'am," he warned. "That was enough to confirm this shaman—whoever the hell he is—has some direct link both to the people who built the lab *and* whoever introduced the rifles, assuming they're not the same people. I think we can abandon any hope that they aren't, though. According to our dying nomad, the shaman's had a direct vision from the gods. It's time for the natives to drive the accursed off-worlders from the sacred soil of Medusa, and the gods have given him these magical weapons to do the job with. Worse, the gods have told him that not *all* off-worlders are evil. Some are servants of the gods and revere them with proper awe, and these godly off-worlders are the source of his 'holy *mekoha*.' It sounds like he's been putting together some kind of nomad army, and he's been promising them that when the evil off-worlders have been driven away or given to the gods as proper sacrifices, these good off-worlders will come to the nomads and give them even more wonderful weapons and all the *mekoha* they can ever want."

The major fell silent, his face tight with strain and worry, and Honor bit her lip hard. Silence dragged out, broken at last by the Resident Commissioner.

"So there it is, Honor. It's *not* some kind of criminal operation. It's a deliberate attempt by someone to engineer a major native uprising and push the Kingdom right off the planet."

"Haven," Honor and Isvarian said simultaneously, and blinked at one another.

"That was my first thought, too," Matsuko said quietly. "But because it's the first possibility to occur to all of us, I think we'd better work on keeping an open mind about it. On the other hand, I can't think of anyone else it might be, and Haven has certainly been the most persistent in insisting that we don't have real sovereignty down here."

"True," Honor said. She rubbed the tip of her nose and frowned at the com screen. "I suppose it *might* be the Andermani," she said at last. "Gustav XI wouldn't mind getting a firm toehold in Basilisk, and he could figure we'd automatically jump to the conclusion that it was the Peeps. I can't quite see it, though, however hard I try. His attention is focused on Silesia right now, and he'd be worrying more about the Midgard Federation than us. Any jump this way could only antagonize us, and he doesn't need that if he's thinking about taking on the Silesians and their allies."

"What about somebody else? One of the single-system nations in the area?"

"I doubt it, Dame Estelle. Everybody out here is too busy keeping her head down and trying not to attract Haven's attention. Besides, what good would Medusa do any of them?"

"But what good would Medusa do *Haven?*" Isvarian asked doubtfully.

"I'm not sure." Honor rubbed her nose harder. "Haven's ultimate objective would have to be the terminus, and I can't quite see how getting us off Medusa would help them there, even if it got them onto the planet in our place. But just because you and I can't see how it would help them doesn't mean *they* can't."

"I'm afraid I'll have to go along with that." Matsuko sighed. "But the fact that we can't see any logical reason for them to be doing this means that I've got to have absolute proof that they are before I start leveling any sort of official complaints or charges."

"Agreed." Honor leaned back and crossed her arms under her breasts. "We need more information." She looked at Isvarian. "Do we know where this dying nomad came from, Barney?"

"Not specifically. Judging by the style of his personal gear and his dialect, he was a long way from home for someone traveling on foot or *jehrn* back. I'd guess he's probably from somewhere in the Mossyback Plateau area, maybe a little south of there. Call it seven or eight hundred klicks north of the Delta."

"Could he have made it that far in his condition?"

Isvarian glanced at Montoya, and the lieutenant shook his head. "I don't believe so, Ma'am. I'm no expert on Medusans, but I spoke with the clinic doctor, and given the patient's condition and how quickly he faded after we got here, I'd be surprised if he stayed on his feet more than twenty to thirty hours after his last pipe."

"How far could he have come in thirty hours, Barney?"

"Not seven hundred kilometers, Captain, that's for sure. Medusans move faster on foot than we do, but even with a _jehrn_, he couldn't have made more than two, three hundred klicks, max, in his condition."

"All right. That gives us a rough idea of where to start looking for anyone he might have been with."

"Right." Matsuko nodded firmly. "Barney, I want a patrol sent up that way soonest."

"Yes, Ma'am."

"Better send them in some force," Honor warned. "Just to be on the safe side."

"And with somebody who keeps his head in command," Matsuko agreed, and Isvarian nodded again.

"I can have an armed ten-man skimmer on its way just after local first light," he said. "Call it eight hours from now."

"Good. In the meantime," Honor said with a wry, taut grin, "since you two have ruined my night's sleep, I might as well ruin a few people's nights up here. I don't know if we'll come up with any bright new insights, but it can't hurt to ask. And I'll pass the word to Papadapolous, too. He'll probably want to talk directly with you, Barney."

"No problem. Dame Estelle has my personal com code. Government House can relay to me over a secure channel wherever I am."

"Fine. In that case, Dame Estelle, if you and Barney will excuse me, I think I'd better get dressed. I'll screen you back in a couple of hours to let you know what we come up with—or let you know if we don't come up with anything at all."

"Thank you, Honor." The relief in Dame Estelle's voice was unmistakable, and Honor smiled at her as she cut the connection.

It was a smile that died instantly into a worried frown when the screen went blank. She stood abruptly and started looking for her uniform.

• CHAPTER TWENTY-FIVE

Honor looked around the briefing room table at her officers. Aside from Cardones, who had the watch, every department head and acting department head was present. Ensign Tremaine sat in, as well, for Honor had wanted his input from his own experiences planet-side. Each face was tight and worried as she finished briefing them on Dame Estelle's call.

"So that's the situation," she said quietly. "For the first time, we have a clear indication that what we're up against is an off-world government's covert operation of some sort, not a domestic criminal enterprise. We don't know its ultimate objectives, nor do we know when or how it's supposed to kick off, but we know that much."

McKeon nodded, pushing a stylus around in aimless circles on the table before him while he thought. Then he raised his head.

"One thing I think we ought to consider, Ma'am, is just how reliable this dying nomad's information is. Could this *mekoha* have made him see and hear things that weren't there? Or misunderstand things that were?"

"A point," Honor agreed. She looked down the table at Lois Suchon. "Doctor? What's your opinion?"

"*My* opinion, Captain?" Suchon's voice held a note almost of petulance, and her shoulders twitched a quick, sulky shrug. "I'm a Navy doctor. I don't know anything about abo physiology."

Honor pressed her lips firmly together and gave the physician a long, level glance. Suchon's dark face flushed, but she looked back with stubborn, petty defiance. She knew she was covered, Honor thought in disgust. She'd been kept abreast of the situation and knew how important information on *mekoha's* effects on Medusans might become, but no one had specifically asked her to check the literature available from the NPA. Someone, Honor thought, should have. Someone like Commander Honor Harrington, who knew perfectly well that nothing short of a direct order could have gotten Suchon out of her comfortable chair to do so.

"Very well. I'll raise that point with Dame Estelle—and Lieutenant Montoya—after our conference, Mr. McKeon." Honor tapped a note into her own memo board and smiled faintly as Suchon's mouth twisted at the offhand reference to her absent junior. She met the doctor's burning gaze, and her own eyes were cool and brown, holding Suchon's until the surgeon commander looked away angrily.

"I think it's a good question," Honor went on after a moment, "but for the present, let's proceed on the assumption that the information is accurate."

McKeon nodded, and Papadapolous raised his hand.

"Yes, Major?"

"There may be some good news mixed in with the bad, Ma'am," the Marine offered. "Major Isvarian's people should be able to develop at least a little new intelligence on the Stilties' capabilities out of this. At best, they may be able to pinpoint a target outside the Delta for us. If the major can find this shaman, we might be able to stage a quick raid in battle armor and snap up his weapons— maybe even grab him—before he ever gets close enough to the enclaves to be a threat."

"Agreed," Honor said. "On the other hand, we're going to have to be very careful about any moves we make in that direction. Dame Estelle is specifically barred from using the NPA to interfere with native religious matters, and I can't act unilaterally on the planet without her approval. If we can't demonstrate direct off-world interference, her hands—which means *our* hands, as well—are tied unless and until the shaman's followers actually start using their weapons."

"Understood, Captain. But just knowing where to look and what to look for makes me feel a lot better. I'd much rather catch them in open terrain that lets us use our air support, mobility, and greater weapons ranges than tangle with them inside the enclaves at pointblank."

Honor nodded to the Marine, and he sat back. He'd contributed his bit. Anything else was a matter for the Navy to deal with, and some of the interest in his eyes faded as he waited for them to get on with it.

"You know, Skipper," Dominica Santos said slowly, "I've been thinking about what you said. About all this being just a part of some overall off-world scheme." Honor cocked her head, and the engineer waved a hand.

"It seems to me the only logical suspect is Haven, Ma'am. I know we can't prove that, but I can't see anyone else who'd do something like this. And even if it isn't them, shouldn't we proceed on the assumption that it is? I mean, no one else could hurt us as badly as the Peeps, so if we assume it's them and we're wrong, we'll leave ourselves a lot less exposed. But if it *is* Haven and we bend over backward to keep from assuming that it is, we're likely to miss something important, aren't we?"

"A point, Skipper," McKeon agreed. "Definitely a point."

"Agreed." Honor drummed gently on the table, then looked back at her exec. "Let's assume for a moment that this is a Havenite covert op, Mr. McKeon. Do you think they'd kick off something like this and then just sit back to let it develop in isolation?"

"I don't think there's any way to know," McKeon said after a moment's thought. "My gut reaction is that they wouldn't, but without knowing their ultimate objective I just can't say."

"Captain?" The voice was hesitant and very young, and Honor gave the speaker a reassuring smile as she turned to him.

"Yes, Mr. Tremaine?"

"Uh, I just wanted to mention something, Ma'am. I noticed it a couple of days ago, but it didn't seem very important then. Now, though—" The ensign shrugged uncomfortably.

"Mention what, Mr. Tremaine?"

"Well, it's just that I've been sort of keeping an eye on the space-to-surface traffic patterns since you called me back aboard, Ma'am. Habit, I guess. And I noticed there doesn't seem to be any Havenite traffic at all, anymore."

"Ah?" Honor looked at McKeon and twitched an eyebrow. The exec looked startled for a second, then grinned wryly.

"Out of the mouths of ensigns," he said, and Tremaine blushed at the chuckle that ran around the table. Then he grinned back at the exec.

"I don't know what it means, Ma'am," McKeon went on more in a more serious tone, "but he's right. There's no Havenite traffic to the surface at all. Hasn't been in almost a week."

"Now, that's interesting," Honor murmured, tapping another note into her memo board. "Have they pulled anyone out of their enclave? Any sign of a cautionary evacuation?"

"You'd have to ask Major Isvarian or the commissioner about that, Ma'am, but I certainly haven't noticed anything to suggest it."

"They might not have to, Captain." It was Tremaine again. "Their consulate's more like a fort than most of the enclaves, and they've got an awful big security force." The ensign paused with a frown and rubbed his chin. "Still, Ma'am, they *do* have a couple of other enclaves—trade stations with the natives right on the edge of the Delta. They're pretty far to the north, too, now that I think of it. Wouldn't that mean they'd get hit first if this shaman really does attack the Delta?"

"How big are they?" McKeon asked, and his gray eyes were intent.

"Well, I've only overflown them, Sir," Tremaine said uncomfortably, "but they're not very big. Maybe a dozen off-worlders and a native staff in each, I'd say, but it's only a guess."

"You think their size is significant?" Honor asked Mckeon, and the exec shrugged.

"I don't know, Ma'am. But it occurs to me that if their objective is to chase us out and move in themselves, it might just suit their purposes to have a few casualties of their own. Another thing," he added in an even more thoughtful voice. "If we end up with some sort of bloodbath down there and they *don't* take any casualties, isn't it possible some of the other off-worlders, not just us, might wonder exactly why they were so lucky?"

"You may have a point." Honor made another note and tried to hide an inner shiver at the cold-blooded calculation McKeon's hypothesis suggested. The exec nodded very slowly, then frowned and sat straighter in his chair.

"Wait a second, Skipper. I just thought of something." He tapped on his terminal for a moment, then nodded to himself. "I thought I remembered that." He turned back to his captain. "You remember when we were talking about the decline in Havenite traffic to Medusa?" Honor nodded. "Well, the fact is that their *Junction* traffic is still running at normal levels, but there are only two Peep ships in Medusa orbit right now. That courier boat of the consulate's and the freighter *Sirius.*"

Honor frowned as something about the name *Sirius* jogged her memory. Then her eyes widened.

"Exactly," McKeon said. "That ship's been sitting in a parking orbit for over three months. I may be getting paranoid, but that strikes me as a mighty interesting coincidence in light of what the NPA's reporting."

"Excuse me, Skipper, but what do we know about this *Sirius?*" Santos asked. "Do we have any idea why she's here?"

Honor gestured at McKeon. He glanced back at his screen, then looked at Santos.

"She's big—a seven-point-six m-ton *Astra*-class," he said. "Captain Johan Coglin, People's Merchant Service, commanding. According to our files, she suffered an engineering casualty—or, more precisely, she's afraid she will if she moves on. Coglin reported his engineers spotted a fluctuation in his Warshawski tuners when he left hyper and declared an emergency. She's waiting for replacement tuners from home."

"She's *what*?" Santos twitched upright in her chair and frowned.

"A problem, Commander?" Honor asked.

"Well, it just seems awfully odd, Skipper. Of course, I don't know a lot about Havenite maintenance patterns, and a Warshawski flutter isn't anything to monkey around with. If she's really got one, Captain Coglin was probably right to declare an emergency. The only thing is that a fluctuation isn't something that usually creeps up on you. The tuners take more strain than any other sail component, so unless you're terminally dumb, you watch for the tiniest frequency kicks like a hawk. By the time you start showing actual flutter, you're normally well past the point at which they should've been pulled for routine refit, and the Haven government owns all Haven-flagged freighters. They're self-insured, too, so if they take a loss, they can't recover from anyone else on it. It doesn't sound to me like they'd be cutting maintenance corners the way some private owners do."

"Another thing." McKeon's eyes were very bright. "A flutter is something you're more likely to notice going *into* hyper than coming out. The power bleed when you transit downward tends to hide it."

"But what good would it do them to cook up a reason to keep a freighter in orbit?" Lieutenant Panowski asked a bit plaintively. Honor looked at him, and he squirmed a little. "I mean, they've already got a courier boat in permanent orbit, Ma'am. What would a freighter do for them that a courier boat wouldn't?"

"I don't know about that," Santos said, "but I just thought of something else odd about *Sirius*'s story. They've got tuner flutter, right? Well, why sit here and wait for spares from home? They've already been here for three months, but unless they're way up into critical failure levels, they could pop through the terminus to Manticore. That's a short hop, with minimal tuner stress and demand, and one of the big yards there could put in a whole new sail, much less tuners, in less than two months. But even if they were afraid to transit the Junction, why not order the replacements from Manticore? It'd be a hell of a lot cheaper and faster than shipping them out from home, and we've got scads of privately-owned repair ships. If they send new tuners from Haven, they're either going to have to send their own repair ship to install them or else charter one of ours, anyway, and the time they're spending in orbit has to be costing them a lot more in lost profit than paying us for the parts would." She shook her head. "No. They've got to be up to something, Skipper. There's just no logical economic or engineering reason for the way they're going about this."

"What do we know about the ship's cargo, Captain?" Lieutenant Brigham asked. "Do we know what she's carrying or where she was supposed to be bound from here, for instance?"

"Commander McKeon just told you everything we know," Honor said wryly. "She's been on station since before we arrived. That means Captain Young cleared her."

People sat back around the table with careful non-expressions of disgust, and despite her worries, Honor had to raise a hand to hide a smile.

"In that case, Ma'am," Ensign Tremaine said, "maybe we should make a customs check on her? I could take PO Harkness and a cutter, and—"

"No, Scotty." Honor spoke almost absently and missed his flush of pleasure as she used his nickname. "We can't do that. *Sirius* has already been checked by *Warlock*—" Someone snorted, and Honor paused to bite her tongue.

Then she gave them all the closest she could come to a severe look and turned back to Tremaine.

"The point is, she's been officially cleared. We can't go back to re-inspect without some sort of hard evidence that her master lied to Lord Young. And while I think Commander Santos is right and their excuse for being here probably is bogus, we really don't have any evidence, do we?"

Tremaine shook his head unhappily, and she gave a slight shrug.

"More importantly, perhaps, if we did go back to give her a second look, we'd tip our hand. They'd know we figured something was fishy about their ship. If we *are* being 'paranoid'—" she flashed McKeon a tight smile "—over an innocent coincidence, that might not hurt anything. But if they're really up to something, we could scare them into backing off or finding another way to do whatever they're trying to do. A way we don't know anything about."

"There's another point, too, Skipper." McKeon sighed. "As you say, she's been cleared once. Her skipper might just refuse to let us back aboard, and without evidence that they're involved in what's happening dirt-side or that they lied to Lord Young, we wouldn't have any probable cause to justify forcing him to. We'd kick off all kinds of interstellar protests."

"That I could live with." Honor's voice was cold. "I just don't see any way to do it without giving too much away."

"You know, Skipper," Santos mused, "we might not be able to get aboard her, but it's possible a good, close external scan could tell us something." Honor looked at her, and the engineer shrugged. "I don't know what, but there could be something." She paused for a moment, and then her eyes narrowed. "For one thing, I'd really like to see how their drive compares to the specs they gave *Warlock*. If this Coglin cobbled up a report on a phony engineering casualty, it's possible he slipped up and built in an inconsistency."

"Such as?"

"Depends." Santos scooted down to sit on the end of her spine and plucked at her lower lip. "There might not be anything—in fact, if they're smart, there probably won't be—but if they have a genuine flutter problem, then there damned well ought to be a lot of wear on their alpha nodes. We should see at least some pitting, maybe a little outright scoring, and the main coil should certainly have a fairly old replacement stamp."

Honor nodded thoughtfully. The main gravity coils in a starship's alpha nodes were always replaced whenever the tuners were. In a sense, the coils were part of the tuner, sharing in its wear, and each of them carried a date stamp when it was installed. More to the point, the grav coil was open to space. There was an excellent chance the date stamp would be visible to a close external examination.

"If we get close enough for that, Ma'am," Webster offered, "I should be able to get a good read on her com activity, too. Maybe even tap into it." He blushed as Honor looked at him, for what he suggested was illegal under half a dozen solemn interstellar conventions. He could be severely disciplined just for making the offer.

"I like it," McKeon said suddenly. "If we turn up a discrepancy like Dominica's talking about, it might just constitute the sort of evidence you need, Skipper."

"It's not impossible for a tuner to go bad early," Santos agreed, "but it's certainly unusual. If we've got a discrepancy between observable wear on the alpha nodes and normal tuner wear, I can give you a written declaration of my own suspicions, Skipper. That's expert testimony, and expert testimony constitutes probable cause for any admiralty court."

"Any *Manticoran* admiralty court," Honor corrected gently, trying to hide the lump in her throat. The officers who had once been so hostile were now sticking their professional necks far out for her, and she looked down at her hands for a moment.

"Very well, ladies and gentlemen. I'll screen Dame Estelle with your comments and suggestions. In the meantime, I want our orbit shifted." She looked at Panowski. "I want us placed within two hundred kilometers of *Sirius*. Once we get there—" she turned her eyes to Tremaine "—I want you to take a cutter to the closest Manticoran ship. I'll give you a hardcopy dispatch for her master."

"A dispatch, Ma'am? What sort of dispatch?"

"I won't know that until we know which ship it is," she said dryly. "But I'll come up with something once we do. The point is, your trip will be our pretext for changing orbit—that's why I want you in a cutter instead of a pinnace—and also why I want you to be obvious about your trip."

"Oh." Tremaine sat back for a moment, then nodded. "Yes, Ma'am. I see."

"I'm sure you do." She turned back to McKeon. "While Lieutenant Panowski and Lieutenant Brigham plot our move, Mr. McKeon, I want you to sit down with Lieutenant Cardones. I want this all done with passive sensors. I know we won't get as much, but an active probe would be as big a tip-off as actually boarding her. We're going to need the most intensive passive scan we can come up with, though, and I want you to help Rafe set it up in advance."

"Yes, Ma'am." McKeon met her eye confidently. "We'll take care of it."

"Very good." Honor drew a breath and rose, sweeping her officers with her eyes once more. "Then we know what we're going to do, people, so let's be about it." They rose in turn, only to stop as she raised a hand.

"Before you go," she said quietly, "I just want to say thank you."

She didn't specify for what. And as she looked into their faces, she knew she would never have to.

• **CHAPTER TWENTY-SIX**

HMS *Fearless* spiraled gently outward and settled into
her new orbit without fuss or bother, and a cutter departed
her boat bay and scudded away towards a mammoth
Manticoran-registry freighter with a formal, written invitation for the ship's master to join Commander Harrington
for supper. The merchant skipper would no doubt be
astonished by—and possibly a little apprehensive over—
that invitation, but none of the people on *Fearless's* bridge
gave him a thought or paid the cutter much heed. Their
attention was bent upon their readouts as passive instrumentation probed cautiously at PMSS *Sirius*.

She was a big ship, Honor mused, watching her own
visual display from her command chair. *Fearless* herself
could have been stowed comfortably in one of the
freighter's main holds, and that sort of carrying capacity
lent weight to Santos's observation. Letting that much ship
sit idle any longer than you had to was like pouring money
straight out the airlock. No owner—not even a government
bureaucracy like Haven's Ministry of Trade—would do
that without a very good reason.

She leaned back and glanced across at the tactical station. Cardones and McKeon had their heads together over
the main sensor console, and Webster was equally intent on
his communications panels. If any message traffic was
going out from that ship, it was on a tight beam, and tight
beams were hellishly hard to detect, but the com officer's
fingers moved like a surgeon's as he gentled his computers
through the search. If there was even a whisker beam out
there, Webster would find it. Honor was certain of that.

An intercom signal beeped from her panel, and she depressed the stud on her chair arm.

"Bridge. Captain speaking," she said.

"Skipper, we got a good relay from Tactical's visual search down here—" Dominica Santos's answering voice sounded excited "—and I'm replaying the scan of *Sirius's* after nodes on my screen. I don't see any pitting or scoring, and the date stamp isn't visible, but I can tell you there's something really strange about them."

Nimitz bleeked softly in Honor's ear, but she shushed him with a gentle stroke of her fingers.

"Can you relay your imagery to my display, Dominica?"

"Sure thing, Ma'am. Just a sec." Honor's display blanked as *Sirius* vanished from it, then relit almost at once with a frozen, hugely magnified view of the freighter's after hull. One of her drive nodes, smaller than a pinhead against the ship's stupendous size in the main visual display, filled the center of the screen, and Honor frowned. Something about that image looked subtly *wrong*, somehow, but she couldn't quite put her mental finger on the discrepancy.

"What is it, Dominica?" she asked after a moment.

"It's a lot bigger than it ought to be, that's what it is, Ma'am, and the whole thing's shaped wrong," Santos replied. "Look." A cursor blipped onto the display, indicating the point at which the node passed through *Sirius's* outer plating, and Honor cocked her head as she noted the wide, soot-black band of shadow. "See that gap around the base of the node head? That shouldn't be there. And look here." The cursor vanished, and a bright green line arced up the side of the exposed node. It started out flush with the node's base, but then it curved much more sharply inward. By the time it reached the node's rounded apex, over a third of the node's total mass lay beyond the line.

"That's a normal node profile, Skipper," Santos said, manipulating the green line to make it flash. "This thing's way too broad for its length, and it's not just a design peculiarity. You can't build one with this profile—the physics won't let you. Besides, look here." The cursor reappeared, pointing to a thick, blunt cylinder protruding a slight distance from the end of the node. "That's the main grav coil, and that thing is almost twice as big in diameter as it ought to be for a node this size. That cross section's better suited to a superdreadnought than any freighter drive I've ever seen, and if they powered it up with no more governor housing than we see, it'd slag the entire after hull."

"I see." Honor stared down at the display, rubbing her nose. "On the other hand, they've obviously built what we're looking at, and they got here under their own power."

"I know," Santos replied, "but I think that's where the gap around the node base comes in. I think the damned thing's on some kind of ram. When they power up, they run the rest of the node—the part we can't see because of the plating—out to clear the hull. That's why the opening's so large; the node head's greatest width is still inside the outer skin, and they have to get it outboard for safe operation. Skipper, that's a pretty well camouflaged military-grade impeller node, or I'll eat my main engineering console."

"*Very* good, Dominica," Honor murmured. She gazed at the imagery for a moment longer, then nodded. "Make me the best estimate you can of their actual acceleration capability—impeller and Warshawski mode—and write it up. Make sure you save all your data, too. We'll want to pass it on to BuShips for evaluation."

"Aye, aye, Ma'am." Santos cut the circuit, and Honor looked up to find McKeon standing beside her chair, his eyebrows raised.

"Commander Santos says we have a definite discrepancy here, Mr. McKeon," she said, and the exec nodded.

"Yes, Ma'am. I caught the last little bit of your conversation. And I've got something to add, too. Lieutenant Cardones and I have determined that *Sirius*'s nodes are hot."

It was Honor's turn to feel her eyebrows rise. "Could it be a systems test?"

"I don't think so, Ma'am. We're reading a full standby load on all the alpha and beta nodes on this side of her hull, fore and aft both. A systems test would probably run up just the alphas or the betas, not both. And why should they test both the forward and after nodes simultaneously? Besides, the power level's held steady for over ten minutes now."

Honor leaned back to regard him pensively and saw her own thoughts flicker behind his gray eyes. There was no regulation against a ship's holding her impeller drive at standby in parking orbit, but it was almost unheard of. Power was relatively cheap aboard a starship, but even the best fusion plant needed reactor mass, and impeller energy demands were high, even at standby. Maintaining that sort of load when you didn't need to was a good way to run up your overhead. Nor was it good for the equipment. Your engineers couldn't carry out routine maintenance while the drive was hot, and the components themselves had limited design lives. Holding them at standby when you didn't need to would certainly reduce their life spans, and that, again, ran up overhead.

All of which meant no freighter captain would hold his drive at standby without a very compelling reason. But a warship's captain might. It took almost forty minutes to bring your impeller wedge up from a cold start; by starting with hot nodes, you could reduce that to little more than fifteen minutes.

"That's very interesting, Mr. McKeon," Honor murmured.

"Curiouser and curiouser, Ma'am," McKeon agreed. "Oversized impeller nodes and a full standby load. Sounds to me like you've got your discrepancy if you want to go aboard, Captain."

"Maybe, and maybe not." Honor nibbled her lower lip and felt Nimitz nip her earlobe as he detected her worry. She grinned and hoisted him down into her lap to protect her ears, then sobered once more as she looked back up at McKeon.

"The problem is that nothing requires them to give us the real specs on their drive," she pointed out, "and no law says they have to build a freighter whose drive makes economic sense. The fact that their nodes are live and don't show the sort of wear we ought to see if they've got tuner failure would certainly seem to argue that they lied to *Warlock* about the nature of their engineering problems, but that's all we've got. A good lawyer could probably argue that away, and we'd have to admit that they haven't even sent a shuttle down to the planet—or anywhere else, for that matter—in over two and a half months. Without their making physical contact with anyone else, we can hardly accuse them of smuggling. They've just sat here in orbit, minding their own business like good little law-abiding merchant spacers. That means our probable cause is still awfully weak, and I still have reservations about tipping our hand, as well."

She rubbed Nimitz's ears, wrestling with an unaccustomed indecisiveness. On the one hand, she could probably justify, however thinly, sending an examining party on the basis of her observational data. But if she did, and if the Havenites truly were up to something, they'd know she suspected that they were. And they'd be certain to lodge all sorts of diplomatic protests. What bothered her most was her inability to decide whether it was fear of revealing her suspicions or fear of the protests which most daunted her. She thought it was the former, but a nagging little voice wondered if it weren't the latter.

She closed her eyes, making herself stand back and consider the options with all the detachment she could muster. The real problem was that, under interstellar law, the freighter's master could still refuse her inspectors entry, whatever she cited as probable cause, unless she had evidence that they'd violated Manticoran law or posed a direct threat to Manticoran security, and nothing she had constituted an actual criminal violation. If Captain Coglin refused her the right to board his ship, her only options would be to accept the slap in the face or expel *Sirius* from Manticoran space. She had the authority to do that to any ship which refused to allow her examination, with or without probable cause, should she so choose, but it was an action she would have to justify to the Admiralty, and she could just see the headlines it would provoke. "RMN EXPELS MERCHANT SHIP WITH DEFECTIVE DRIVE." "FREIGHTER SENT TO DIE IN HYPER BY HEARTLESS MANTICORAN OFFICER." "HAVEN PROTESTS HARRINGTON'S INHUMAN EXPULSION OF DAMAGED FREIGHTER."

She shuddered at the thought, but she rather thought she could face the fallout if it came to that. Lord knew some of the news services back home had already had some fairly terrible things to say about her—especially the ones Hauptman and his cronies controlled! Yet the real cruncher was that while she might put a crimp into Haven's plans if she *did* expel *Sirius*, she would neither learn what those plans might have been nor insure that they couldn't be reactivated some other way. And it seemed likely that anything as involved as this appeared to be—whatever it was!—would have built-in backups, and that meant—

"Captain?"

She opened her eyes to find Webster standing beside McKeon.

"Yes, Mr. Webster?"

"Excuse me, Ma'am, but I thought you'd want to know this. There's a three-cornered secure com net between *Sirius*, the Haven consulate, and the consulate's courier boat, Ma'am." Honor cocked her head, and Webster gave a small shrug. "I can't tell you much more than that, Skipper. They're using mighty tight-focused lasers, not regular com beams, and there's not much traffic. I've deployed a couple of passive remotes, but they're just catching the edge of the carriers. I can't tap into them without getting a receptor into one of the lasers itself, and they'd be sure to notice that."

"Can you tell if it's scrambled?"

"No, Ma'am. But given how tight their beams are, I'd be surprised if it wasn't. They don't need whiskers this tight for any technical reasons at this piddling little range. It has to be a security measure."

"I see." Honor nodded, and her indecision vanished into tranquillity. "Mr. McKeon, as soon as Mr. Tremaine returns aboard, I want us returned to our original orbit, but put us back into it astern of the Havenite courier boat."

"Aye, aye, Ma'am." McKeon responded automatically, but Honor saw the puzzlement in his eyes.

"Keep a close eye on *Sirius*, but see if you can determine whether or not the courier's nodes are hot, too," she went on. "I think we've pretty definitely established that something strange is going on out here, and that Haven is at the bottom of it, but we still don't know what. I want to know that, Exec. I want to catch them with their hands dirty and nail them in front of God and everybody."

"Yes, Ma'am." McKeon's puzzlement had turned to understanding, and Honor nodded.

"In the meantime, I want *Fearless* held on standby for impeller, as well. If either of those two start going anywhere, I want to be able to go in pursuit. Clear?"

"Clear, Ma'am."

"Good." She turned back to her com officer. "Mr. Webster, I need a secure link to Dame Estelle."

"Aye, aye, Ma'am. I'll get right on it."

Honor watched her two subordinates return to their stations and leaned back, rubbing Nimitz and looking back down at the frozen imagery of *Sirius*'s impeller node with distant eyes.

"You're right, Honor. They're definitely up to something." Dame Estelle looked tired on the com screen, and Honor wondered if she'd gotten back to sleep at all after their midnight conversation.

"I don't think there's any doubt," Honor agreed.

"Especially not now that we've confirmed the courier boat's drive is hot, too. I hate to say it, Dame Estelle, but I *really* don't like that."

"Don't blame you." Matsuko rubbed her eyes, then lowered her hands to her desk with a sigh. "They wouldn't be on standby if they didn't figure there was a pretty good reason to be going somewhere, and that damned courier boat has diplomatic immunity. We can't touch it if it starts to leave."

"I'm less worried about whether or not I can touch it legally than I am about the fact that there are two of them, Ma'am," Honor said bleakly. Dame Estelle looked at her sharply, and she shrugged. "I'm not looking forward to any diplomatic incidents, but my big problem is that I only have one ship. If I've got two targets headed in different directions, I can only chase one of them."

"But what's the *point?*" the commissioner almost groaned. "I've got drug-crazed natives armed with blackpowder rifles and primed to slaughter off-worlders in job lots, and you've got two starships with drives on standby! Where's the connection?"

"I don't know—yet. But I *am* certain there is one, and all this com traffic seems significant to me, too."

"I have to agree with that." Dame Estelle sounded glum. "I'll see what I can find out for you."

"Find out?" Honor raised her eyebrows in surprise, and Dame Estelle produced a tired smile.

"I'm afraid I'm not quite as trusting as my exalted superiors in the Ministry for Medusan Affairs would like. My people and I have, ah, *acquired* a few communications devices not on the official equipment list for my compound down here. We keep a pretty close watch on the message traffic from the off-world enclaves."

"You do?" Honor blinked in astonishment, and Dame Estelle chuckled.

"You don't have to mention that to anyone, Honor. There'd be all kinds of repercussions if you did."

"I imagine there would," Honor agreed with a slow smile of her own.

"You imagine correctly. But as far as the Havenites are concerned, we can keep an eye on their traffic volume, but we can't do much with specific transmissions. They not only scramble their signals but routinely encrypt them, as well. We've managed to break their latest scramble codes—unless they've shifted them again in the last day or so, and I just haven't heard yet—but we can't do much with their encryption."

"Do you think they know you're doing it?"

"Hard to say. They may, though, particularly if there's direct traffic between their courier boat and this freighter of theirs," Dame Estelle said thoughtfully. "We can't touch their ship-to-ship traffic from down here, so that would give them at least one secure com channel."

"But that would assume their mastermind is up here," Honor pointed out. "Otherwise, they'd still have to pass all their command signals through the consulate."

"True." Matsuko's fingers tapped a nervous syncopation on the edge of her desk, and she made a face. "I *hate* all this guesswork," she sighed.

"Me, too," Honor agreed. She rubbed the tip of her nose. "Well, whatever they're up to, they've obviously been working on it for a long time, and your clan chieftain said his relative warned him the Delta would be a bad place to spend the *winter*. That's—what? Another two months from now?"

"About that. So you think we've got that long to get on top of this?"

"I don't know. But I do know that we're just beginning to put the pieces together, and that's bound to give us a sense of urgency whether they're really on the edge of activating their operation or not. On the other hand, we've already turned up enough for me to go official with it."

"Go official? How?"

"I'm putting together a dispatch, complete with all of my facts, suspicions, and conclusions, for the personal attention of the First Space Lord," Honor said grimly. "He may think I'm crazy—but he may also just get some help out here."

"How long would that take?"

"At absolute best, given the tenuousness of our information, it would probably take something like fifty hours, and that's assuming he doesn't just decide I'm crazy and he has someone he can divert straight out here. Frankly, I'd be surprised if we saw any useful reaction in less than three or four days, but at least it'd be a step in the right direction."

"And until then, we're on our own," Dame Estelle observed.

"Yes, Ma'am." Honor rubbed her nose again. "What's the status on Barney's patrol?"

"They should be pulling out in about—" Dame Estelle glanced at her chrono "—twenty minutes, now. Barney's down at the hangar for their final brief; then he'll come back here. They're under express order not to land anywhere without checking back in, but he's going to have them keep a close eye on everything they overfly en route to the target area. At least we should be able to determine where this shaman and his parishioners *aren't*, anyway."

"Good. I'd like to add his findings, good or bad, to my dispatch to Admiral Webster. And I'll feel a lot more comfortable personally once we have some sort of accurate idea of just how bad the situation ground-side really is."

"So will I." Dame Estelle shook herself. "All right, Honor. Thanks. I'll get on my end of things. Keep me posted if anything breaks up there."

"I will, Ma'am."

Honor killed the com link and crossed her legs. She steepled her fingers under her jaw in her favorite thinking posture, and the occasional soft murmur of command and response flowed over her as her bridge crew went about its duties. She never knew exactly how long she sat there, but finally she snorted softly and lowered her hands.

"Mr. McKeon."

"Yes, Ma'am?" The exec looked up. She beckoned to him, and he crossed to her chair as she stood.

"I think we're moving into the end-game phase," she said quietly, pitching her voice for his ears alone. "I'm trying to keep an open mind about that, but too many things seem to be coming together here." She paused, and McKeon nodded in agreement.

"I've been over Papadapolous's deployment plan, and it looks good," she went on, "but I want two changes made in it."

"Yes, Ma'am?"

"First, I want the Marines moved aboard the pinnaces now. There's room for them to bunk aboard—they'll have to hot-bunk, but they can squeeze in—and I want them ready to drop on zero notice. They can armor up on the way down or even after they hit dirt."

"Yes, Ma'am." McKeon pulled out his memo pad and keyed notes into it. "And the second change?"

"I want Lieutenant Montoya and our other medical people back up here. Get them aboard by mid-watch, if you can."

"Excuse me, Ma'am?" McKeon blinked, and Honor hid a sour smile.

"Officially, I've decided that it would be unfair to ask Dame Estelle and the NPA to make do with the services of our *junior* physician in the event of an incident on Medusa. In light of Commander Suchon's many more years of service, I feel it would be much more reasonable for us to put her experience to good use down there."

"I see, Ma'am." There was a faint gleam in McKeon's eyes. "And the, um, *un*official reason?"

"Unofficially, Mr. McKeon," Honor's voice was much grimmer, "Dame Estelle and Barney Isvarian have quite good medical staffs of their own, and there are a good many other civilian doctors in the enclaves down there. Between them, they should be able to carry Suchon's dead weight." McKeon winced at the acid bite in his captain's voice, but he nodded.

"Besides," Honor went on after a moment, "Lieutenant Montoya may be ten years younger than Suchon, but he's a better physician than she'll ever be. If we need a doctor up here, we're going to need him in a hurry, and I want the best one I can get."

"Do you really think we're going to need one?" McKeon couldn't quite hide his surprise, and Honor shrugged uncomfortably.

"I don't know. Call it a feeling. Or maybe it's just nerves. But I'll feel much more comfortable with Suchon dirt-side and Montoya in *Fearless*."

"Understood, Skipper." McKeon put away his memo pad and nodded. "I'll take care of it."

"Good. In the meantime, I'll be in my quarters. I've got a dispatch to write." She produced a smile—a strange smile, compounded of fatigue, worry, awareness of her own ignorance, and an odd undercurrent that might almost be excitement—and McKeon felt a tingle sweep over him as he saw it.

"Who knows?" she finished softly, still with that same, strange smile. "I may even have something interesting to put in it in a few more hours."

She walked into the lift with her treecat, and McKeon stood for several seconds, looking at the door which had closed behind her and wondering why her smile had frightened him so.

• CHAPTER TWENTY-SEVEN

Lieutenant Frances Malcolm, Medusan Native Protection Agency, stretched and yawned in her bucket seat. The skimmer swept onward above the rugged foothills, humming across the endless kilometers of moss on the quiet whisper of its turbines, and something thumped behind her. She turned in her chair and looked back just as Corporal Truman, the skimmer's gunner, dropped down out of his dorsal turret.

"Sorry, Franny." Malcolm hid a reflexive wince. Like Barney Isvarian, she was an ex-Marine, but the NPA wasn't real big on punctilious formality, and Truman was a career cop who'd transferred in from the San Giorgio City Police on Manticore. She'd given up on trying to turn him into anything resembling a soldier. There was no point in it. For that matter, she told herself firmly, there was probably no reason. The NPA wasn't the Corps, but while its members might seem casual to an outsider, they kept their heads when someone dropped them in the pot.

"I forgot my thermos," Truman went on. He scooped up the insulated container and hopped back up onto the raised firing step. Malcolm heard the thermos open and the gurgle as he poured coffee at his station and shook her head with a slight grin. No, this *definitely* wasn't the Corps.

"Coming up on the three hundred-klick mark, Franny," her pilot murmured, and Malcolm nodded. They'd flown a standard sweep pattern since leaving the Delta, and that had slowed their rate of advance to little more than seventy-five kilometers per hour. It made her feel as if they were barely poking along, especially in light of the urgency Isvarian had stressed in his briefing, but at least they were nearing the limit of their best estimate of how far the dead nomad could have come. And, she thought, she could say with certainty that there hadn't been any large numbers of rifle-armed Medusans in the area they'd swept. No one could hide that many iron rifle barrels or warm bodies from her sensors, and—

"What's that?" Sergeant Hayabashi's voice broke into her thoughts, and Malcolm raised her head. The sergeant was frowning down at his own instrumentation, and Malcolm felt her lips purse as she saw the bright blip shining from Hayabashi's screen.

"It's a power source," she said unnecessarily. "Could be an aircar's electrical system, or it might be a small generator."

"Well whichever it is, it shouldn't be here, should it?" Hayabashi asked, and Malcolm shook her head.

"Nope. But let's not jump to any conclusions, Sergeant," she said in her most judicious voice. "We're supposed to be looking for hopped-up natives. This could be someone grounded with a mechanical failure."

"Yeah, and I could be my own maiden aunt, Ma'am," Hayabashi replied, and Malcolm grinned at the sergeant's sour tone. "Anyway, it—"

The sergeant broke off as the blip vanished. He tapped keys, then frowned at the lieutenant. "Something cut off the scan, Ma'am," he reported.

"I saw." Malcolm adjusted her own systems. "We've lost the LOS. Maybe a ridge line cut it off—or it could be hidden behind something and we just happened to get a peek."

"Hidden?" Hayabashi gave her a sharp glance, and she shrugged.

"I didn't say I thought it was innocent, Sergeant. I only said it *could* be." Malcolm turned to her pilot. "Bring us back in a circle, Jeff. And drop us to a hundred meters or so. I want a visual on this thing if we can spot it."

"Coming back around now," the pilot replied. The

skimmer swept around in a sharp turn, and Hayabashi grunted as he switched to visual.

"Well, shit," he muttered a moment later, then grimaced. "Sorry, Ma'am, but you were right. See there?"

The sergeant's finger tapped his display, and Malcolm craned her neck to look. Her eyes narrowed as she saw the camouflage-netted aircar nose parked just inside what looked like a natural cave opening. She shook her head, and glanced at her thermal and magnetic sensors. There was nothing on them, and she looked up at the pilot.

"Hold us in hover, Jeff. And you get sharp, Truman," she added, glancing back over her shoulder as she activated her com link to NPA Control. "I don't really expect any trouble, but remember the lab raid. This looks awfully sus—"

An alarm shrilled on her own console, and she whipped back to it in shock. Magnetic signatures glared suddenly, and with them came heat sources, as well. They blossomed all over her display like heat lightning, almost as if they were springing out of the ground itself—and that, she realized an instant later, was precisely what they *were* doing. The aircar's cave was only one entry to what must be an enormous cave system almost directly under her skimmer, and the natives were boiling out of it as if her return to check the aircar had been some sort of signal!

And they were firing. Puffs of smoke sprouted from the moss like toadstools, merging into an incredible carpet of gray-white fog. The skimmer bucked as hundreds of eighteen-millimeter projectiles slammed into its belly, and someone screamed behind Malcolm.

The skimmer wasn't armored. Its composites were tough and elastic, but they weren't armor, and more bullets punched through its thin skin. She heard Truman cursing in a high, incredulous falsetto, but his pulser turret was already in action, each barrel spitting fifteen-millimeter explosive darts cased in ceramic frag jackets at a cyclical rate of over a thousand rounds per minute. His fire cut across the ground like a lash of flame, shredding moss and

Medusan with equal abandon, yet he could fire in only one direction at a time, and still more armed natives were erupting out of other holes in the ground.

The turbines shrieked as the pilot gave them full throttle, but he was too late. Sergeant Hayabashi jerked in his chair with a hoarse, wracking grunt of explosive agony as a massive slug ripped vertically through his body. It emerged between his shoulders, spraying blood and tissue across the cabin roof, and the sergeant toppled wearily forward over his displays. Malcolm smelled blood and the stench of ruptured organs, and then ragged holes punched themselves through the starboard turbine casing and the engine began to stream the bright, hot flame of burning hydrogen.

None of it was real. Shock and horror yammered at the core of her brain, but her hands moved with a life of their own. Her fingers didn't even tremble, and her voice was very calm as she pressed her boom mike closer to her lips.

"NPA Center, this is Sierra-One-One. My position three-zero-zero kilometers north Three Forks River." The damaged turbine exploded, wrapping one whole side of the fuselage in flame until the frantic pilot cut the hydrogen feed, and Malcolm felt the skimmer start to vibrate with a strange, wild harmonic as the incredible hail of crude bullets battered its grav-coils. "I am under fire by armed natives. We have taken casualties. We are going down." Truman shrieked and fell out of his turret, clutching at a blood-spouting belly wound, and the heavy pulsers fell silent.

"*Ditching stations!*" the pilot screamed, but he went on fighting his dying controls. Every second he kept his plunging craft aloft put a tiny bit more distance between him and the Medusans trying to kill him.

"Repeat, Sierra-One-One is going down, NPA Control," Malcolm said in that same flat, unnaturally calm voice. "Require assistance. Repeat, require assistance!"

She jerked off the com headset and lunged across the shrieking, writhing Truman for the dorsal turret. She dragged herself up into it, fighting the dying skimmer's shuddering heaves as she slammed her shoulders into the shock frame harness Truman should have donned. The straps dropped and locked, her hands found the firing grips, and she poured a tornado of fire into the howling mob of Medusans charging towards the only smooth place the pilot could hope to set them down.

They hit with a bone-breaking shock, and Malcolm clung to her weapons, grunting in anguish as the harness straps bit into her. She heard someone else scream, but the pilot had known what he was doing. The skimmer porpoised across the ground in a bow wave of shredded moss, shedding bits and pieces through a billowing cloud of dust, yet they were down and intact.

And thousands of screaming Medusan nomads were charging straight after them.

Malcolm heard sobs and moans and bubbling screams from her wounded and dying crew, but she also heard firing ports slamming open and the high, shrill whine of the first pulse rifle. She'd struck her head on something during that wild, careening slide, despite the shock frame, and flowing blood blinded her left eye, but her right was clear. The power light still blazed on the turret's twin weapons, and the training gear hummed smoothly when she hit the pedal.

She traversed her fire, sweeping it back and forth across that incredible tidal wave of bodies. She killed them in scores, in hundreds, and still they came. The turret starred as more bullets slammed into the skimmer. Some of them came from behind her, and flying plastic chips cut her face, spalled from the thick canopy's inner surface, but Malcolm clung to the grips, pouring her fire into the shrieking mob.

She was still firing when clubs and rifle butts smashed the turret and dozens of Medusan hands dragged her out of it.

The knives were waiting.

* * *

The com terminal buzzed quietly on Honor's desk.

She stepped out of the shower, toweling her short fuzz of hair vigorously, then dragged her kimono over her wet skin and punched acceptance.

"Captain?" It was Webster, and her nerves tightened as she heard the anxiety in his voice. "Priority signal from Lieutenant Stromboli, Ma'am."

"Put him through."

"Aye, Ma'am." Webster vanished from the screen, replaced by Max Stromboli's worried face.

"What is it, Lieutenant?" Honor deliberately pitched her voice lower than usual and spoke slowly, and the lieutenant swallowed.

"Ma'am, I thought you should know—we copied some message traffic from an NPA skimmer about fifteen minutes ago. They said they were under fire from Stilties and going down. Then they went off the air. Air Control is still trying to raise them, but we're not getting anything back."

"Was it Major Isvarian's patrol?" Honor's voice was suddenly sharper, despite her self-control.

"Yes, Ma'am, I believe it was. And—" Stromboli broke off and looked away for a few seconds as someone said something from off-screen, then he turned back to Honor. "Ma'am, I don't know if it's connected—I don't see how it could be—but that Havenite freighter, the *Sirius*, just started to move out of orbit, and she sure didn't clear it with us."

Stromboli looked more puzzled than concerned by his latest datum as he gazed into his own com screen at his captain, but Honor felt her skin twitch. The same humming certainty that filled her as she grappled with a complex tactical maneuver filled her now as all the pieces snapped instantly and intuitively into place. It couldn't be. The whole idea was preposterous! Yet it was also the only answer that even began to fit the known data.

Stromboli flinched back from his com as her eyes hardened in sudden understanding. She noted his reaction and made herself smile at him.

"Thank you, Lieutenant. You did well. I'll take it from here."

She cut the circuit and flipped up a clear plastic shield on the side of her terminal. Only the captain's cabin terminal had that shield, and she jammed her thumb down on the big, red button it had covered.

The ululating scream of *Fearless*'s battle stations alarm wailed through the light cruiser's hull. Crewmen rolled out of their bunks, dropped cups of coffee, jumped up from mess tables, threw down playing cards and book readers, and bolted for their stations. That shrill, electric sound was brutal, designed to get inside a person's bones and snarl there, and only a dead man could have ignored it.

Honor let the alarm shriek and punched the intercom for the bridge. Panowski was officer of the watch, and his eyes were wide and stunned as he recognized her.

"Bring the drive up—*now*, Lieutenant!" she snapped.

"Aye, aye, Ma'am!" Panowski actually saluted his pickup, then licked his lips. "What are we doing, Captain?" he blurted, and she chopped her hand at him.

"I'll explain later. Have communications raise Dame Estelle. I'll speak to her when I reach the bridge. Now move on that drive, Lieutenant!"

She cut the circuit and whirled to her own locker. She jerked it open and yanked out her vac suit and shed her kimono in one flowing movement, then sat on the edge of the bed and shoved her feet into the suit. The Navy's skin suits were little more cumbersome than pre-space scuba suits, unlike the hard suits of meteor miners and construction workers, and Honor was glad of it as she made the plumbing connections with painful haste and hauled the suit up over skin still wet from the shower. She thrust her arms into the sleeves, then sealed it and grabbed her helmet and gauntlets from the locker even as her eyes checked the suit telltales and found them all green.

Nimitz had hurtled from his perch at the first shrill of the alarm. He'd been through this same drill as often as she, and he scurried across the cabin to the boxlike affair she'd had clamped to the bulkhead below her sailplane plaque immediately after coming aboard. That box wasn't Fleet issue, and it had cost Honor a small fortune, for it was a custom-built life support module, sized to Nimitz's stature and fitted with the same search and rescue beacon as a Fleet vac suit. It was good for a hundred hours on its internal life support, and the door slammed automatically behind him as he fled into it. He couldn't open it from the inside, but unless something scored a direct hit on it, he could survive even if battle damage opened the cabin to space.

She paused to give the module door lock a single double-checking slap, and then she vanished through the cabin hatch and headed for the lift at a run.

The alarm stopped screaming while she was in the lift, and she made herself move briskly but confidently when the door opened onto the bridge. All stations were manned, and she heard the background mutter of voices reporting readiness states while the battle board moved from amber to the steady, scarlet glow of readiness with gratifying speed.

McKeon had beaten her there. He stood beside her command chair, hands clasped behind him, his face calm, but there were beads of sweat along his hairline. She nodded acknowledgment of his presence and slipped past him into her chair. Its displays and monitors began deploying about her as she sat, surrounding her with a flow of information that awaited her slightest glance, but she kept her eyes on McKeon.

"Status?"

"All stations manned, Captain," the exec said crisply. "Impeller wedge coming up—we should have movement capability in another ten minutes. *Sirius* has been underway for six-point-eight minutes ... at four hundred and ten gees."

He paused, and Honor's jaw clenched. That was low for most warships, but impossibly fast for a freighter, and it confirmed Santos's deduction. Only military impellers could have produced that kind of acceleration for a ship *Sirius's* size ... and only a military grade inertial compensator could allow her crew to survive it.

"The courier boat?" Her voice was sharp, and McKeon frowned.

"She started powering her wedge just after we did, Ma'am."

"Understood." Honor looked over her shoulder. "Do we have a link to the Resident Commissioner, Mr. Webster?"

"Yes, Ma'am."

"Put it on my screen." Honor looked back down just as a pale-faced Dame Estelle appeared. The commissioner opened her mouth, but Honor raised a hand and spoke first. "Excuse me, Dame Estelle, but time is short. I think I know what's going on now. Have you heard anything more from your patrol?" Matsuko shook her head mutely, and Honor's face went more masklike still.

"Very well. I am dropping my Marines now." She shot a sideways glance at McKeon, and he nodded and hit an intercom key to give the order. "Aside from that, there's very little we can do for you, I'm afraid. And unless I miss my guess, we're going to have problems of our own soon enough."

"I understand," Dame Estelle broke in, "but there's something you should know before you do anything else, Captain." Honor cocked her head and gestured for the commissioner to continue. "We picked up a transmission from the general area where our patrol went down just after we lost contact with Lieutenant Malcolm," Matsuko said quickly. "It was scrambled but not encrypted, and we just broke the scramble. The transmitter didn't identify himself, and he used a code name for his recipient, but we detected a transmission to the freighter from the Haven Consulate immediately afterward, so I think we know who it was intended for."

"What did it say?" Honor demanded. Dame Estelle didn't answer in words; she simply played the message off, and Honor's eyes went cold and flat as a male voice gasped over her com.

"*Odysseus!* It's Odysseus *now*, damn it! The frigging Shaman's lost his goddamned mind! They're boiling up out of the caves, and I can't hold them! The hopped-up bastards are kicking off right fucking now!"

A surflike roar of Medusan voices and the whiplash cracks of countless rifles echoed behind the words, and then the sounds cut off as Dame Estelle stopped the playback.

"Thank you, Dame Estelle," Honor said flatly. "I understand what's happening now. Good luck."

She killed the circuit and bent over her maneuvering display, ignoring McKeon as she punched in the parking orbit pattern and laid vectors across it. It was going to be close, but there was far less orbital traffic than there had been, and if she could pull it off . . .

"How long for impeller now?" she asked without looking up.

"Four minutes, twenty seconds," McKeon said tightly, and Honor nodded to herself. She could do it. Probably. She fed McKeon's readiness numbers into her display, and a time-to-execution readout began to blink its way steadily downward.

"Thank you. Are the Marines away?"

"Yes, Ma'am. And Commander Suchon. Lieutenant Montoya came aboard an hour ago."

She did look up at that, and her stony face flared with a brief but real smile as she saw the amusement in McKeon's eyes. Then the smile faded, and she bent back to her maneuvering display.

"We'll be going in pursuit of *Sirius*, Mr. McKeon. It's

imperative that we stop her from leaving the system. What's her current heading?"

"She's steadied down on two-seven-four by zero-niner-three true from the primary, Captain," Lieutenant Brigham's crisp voice replied for the exec.

"What's out there, Mercedes?"

"At her current heading and acceleration she'll hit the hyper wall about one light-minute this side of the Tellerman wave, Captain," Brigham said after a moment, and Honor swallowed a silent curse. She'd been afraid of something like that.

"Impellers in three minutes, Ma'am," McKeon reported.

"Mr. Webster!"

"Yes, Ma'am?"

"Stand by to record a signal to Lieutenant Venizelos at Basilisk Control for immediate relay to Fleet HQ. Fleet scramble, no encryption. Priority One."

Heads turned, and Webster's swallow was clearly audible.

"Aye, aye, Ma'am. Standing by to record."

"'Mr. Venizelos, you will commandeer the first available Junction carrier to relay the following message to Fleet HQ. Message begins: Authentication code Lima-Mike-Echo-Niner-Seven-One. Case Zulu. I say again, Zulu, Zulu, Zulu. Message ends.'" She heard McKeon suck air between his teeth at her shoulder. "That is all, Mr. Webster," she said softly. "You may transmit at will." Webster said absolutely nothing for an instant, but when he replied, his voice was unnaturally steady.

"Aye, aye, Captain. Transmitting Case Zulu." There was another brief pause, then, "Case Zulu transmitted, Ma'am."

"Thank you." Honor wanted to lean back and draw a deep breath, but there was no time. The message she'd just ordered Webster to send and Venizelos to relay to Manticore was never sent in drills, not even in the most intense or realistic Fleet maneuvers. Case Zulu had one meaning, and one only: "Invasion Imminent."

"Captain, are you sure—?" McKeon began, but her raised hand stopped him.

"Time to impellers, Exec?"

"Forty-three seconds."

"Thank you." She punched in the new estimate, a corner of her mind noting that Dominica Santos was shaving whole seconds off her original numbers. The time-to-execution display flickered to a new value, then resumed its steady downward march. "Chief Killian?"

"Aye, Captain?" The coxswain's shoulders were tight, but his voice was calm.

"Come to three-five-seven by one-seven-one, Chief Killian. On my command, I want three hundred gravities acceleration on that heading for ten seconds. Then come directly to two-seven-four by zero-niner-three true and go to maximum military power."

Stunned silence gripped the entire bridge, deeper even than that provoked by her Code Zulu, and then Chief Killian looked over his shoulder at her.

"Captain, that course—"

"I know precisely where that course will take us, Chief Killian," Honor said crisply.

"Captain—" it was Brigham this time, her voice very formal "—regulations require me to point out that you will be violating planetary traffic patterns on that course."

"Noted. Chief Braun—" Honor didn't even look up at the quartermaster, and her voice was almost absent "—please log the Sailing Master's warning and note that I assume full responsibility."

"Aye, aye, Ma'am." Braun's voice was absolutely toneless, but his expression was wary, as if he expected her to begin gibbering at any moment.

"Impeller wedge up and nominal, Ma'am," McKeon rasped, and Honor kept her eyes glued to her maneuvering display, watching the time display tick downward.

"Is that course laid in, Chief?"

"Ah, yes, Ma'am. Three-five-seven one-seven-one.

Acceleration three-zero-zero gravities for one-zero seconds. Course change to two-seven-four zero-niner-three true also laid in, Captain."

"Thank you." Honor felt McKeon's tension at her shoulder, but there was no time to deal with that. "Courier boat time to impeller readiness?" she snapped.

"Thirty-six seconds, Ma'am," Lieutenant Cardones said in a small voice.

"Very well." She paused for just a beat, and then the timer hit zero. "Execute, Chief Killian!"

"Executing," the coxswain said in an almost prayerful voice, and HMS *Fearless* leapt instantly forward and "down" at an acceleration of just over twenty-nine hundred MPS^2.

Honor's hands tightened on her chair's arms, but she didn't even blink as her eighty-eight-thousand-ton command screamed down into the very heart of Medusa's orbital traffic. She'd laid in that vector by eye, without the careful calculations and double-checking The Book required, but there was no time for that, and her mind was still in that odd overdrive. She *knew* it was correct, with an absolute certainty that admitted no doubt, and *Fearless* rode the invisible rail she'd nailed down in space as her speed mounted by almost three kilometers per second with every second that passed.

The Havenite courier boat loomed directly ahead of her on Honor's visual display, impeller nodes beginning to glow as they started to come up, but they weren't on line yet. Vapor spewed from the boat's emergency maneuvering thrusters as her skipper tried frantically to avoid *Fearless's* mad charge, yet those thrusters were far too weak to move the boat more than a few meters in the time they had, and the light cruiser stooped upon the eggshell courier like a vengeful falcon.

Breath hissed as her officers tensed for the inevitable, suicidal impact, but Honor's face was carved stone as the edge of *Fearless's* drive field slashed past the courier at less than two kilometers, far inside its drive safety perimeter.

Vaporized alloy burst from the smaller vessel's stern as the cruiser's vastly more powerful impeller wedge blew her after nodes to incandescent gas; then *Fearless* was past, and the starscape slewed crazily in the visual display as she shot up and away from the planet in a mad skew turn and went instantly to full emergency power, accelerating at five hundred and twenty gravities.

"My God!" someone gasped as *Fearless* streaked past an orbiting four-million-ton freighter at a bare ten kilometers' separation. Honor didn't even turn her head. Her eyes were already reaching out for the scarlet light dot of the fleeing *Sirius*.

"Captain?" Webster sounded as shaken as anyone.

"Yes, Samuel?" Honor asked absently.

"Captain, I have an incoming message from that courier boat. They sound pretty upset, Ma'am."

"I imagine they do." Honor surprised herself with a grin and sensed the sudden release of her bridge crew's tension. "Put them on my screen."

"Yes, Ma'am."

Her screen lit with the image of a very young officer in the green and gray of the People's Navy. He wore a lieutenant's insignia, and his face was a curious, mottled blend of furious red and terrified white.

"Captain Harrington, I protest your reckless, illegal ship-handling!" the youngster shouted. "You almost destroyed my ship! Our entire after—"

"I'm very sorry, Captain," Honor interrupted in her most soothing tone. "I'm afraid I wasn't watching where I was going."

"*Weren't watching wh—?!*" The Havenite lieutenant strangled his exclamation and gritted his teeth. "I demand you heave to and assist my command in dealing with the damage you've inflicted!" he snarled instead.

"I regret that that's impossible, Captain," Honor said.

"Under the interstellar convention of—" the lieutenant began again, but she cut him off with a pleasant smile.

"I realize I'm technically in the wrong about this, Captain," she said in that same, soothing tone, "but I'm sure Her Majesty's Resident Commissioner will be able to provide any assistance you require. In the meantime, we're a little too busy to stop. Good-bye, Captain."

She switched off the com, killing the lieutenant's protest in mid splutter, and leaned back in her chair.

"My, that *was* a little sloppy of me, wasn't it?" she murmured.

Her crew gawked at her for just a second, and then a chorus of relieved laughter ran around the bridge. She smiled, but when she looked up at McKeon, his face was grim, and there was no humor in his eyes.

"You stopped the courier, Skipper," he said quietly, under cover of the others' laughter, "but what about the freighter?"

"I'll stop her, too," Honor said. "Any way I have to."

"But *why*, Ma'am? You said you understood what's going on, but I'll be damned if *I* do!"

"*Sirius*'s departure was the last piece I needed." Honor spoke so softly he had to lean forward to hear her. "I know where she's going, you see."

"What?!" McKeon started, then grabbed for his self-control and looked around the bridge. A dozen pairs of eyes were locked on him and his captain, but they whipped back to their own instruments under the impact of his fiery gray glare. Then he returned his own questioning gaze to Honor.

"Somewhere out here, Alistair, probably within only a few hours' hyper flight, there's a Havenite battle squadron. Maybe even a full task force. *Sirius* is headed for a rendezvous with them."

McKeon's face went white, and his eyes widened.

"It's the only answer that makes sense," she said. "The drugs and guns on the planet were intended to produce a native attack on the enclaves. It was supposed to come as a complete surprise and produce a bloodbath as the

Medusans slaughtered off-worlders right and left—including, as you yourself pointed out, their own merchant factors in those northern trade enclaves. In fact," she spoke more slowly, lips tightening and eyes hardening in sudden surmise, "I'll lay odds *Sirius* is officially assigned to one of those enclaves by the Havenite government." She nodded to herself. "That would make this just about perfect, wouldn't it?"

"How, Ma'am?" McKeon was out of his depth, and he knew it.

"They're trying a *coup de main* to seize the planet," Honor said flatly. "*Sirius*'s master is 'fleeing in panic' from the native insurrection. In the course of his flight, he'll 'just happen' to encounter a Peep squadron or task force in the area on 'routine maneuvers.' Naturally, he'll spill out his story to the Havenite commander, who, horrified and overcome with a sense of urgency and the need to save off-worlder lives, will immediately proceed to Medusa with his entire force to put down the native uprising." She stared into McKeon's eyes and saw the dawning understanding.

"And once he's done that," she finished very softly, "he'll proclaim *Haven's* possession of the entire system on the grounds that Manticore has demonstrated its total inability to maintain order and public safety on the planet's surface."

"That's insane," McKeon whispered, but his tone was that of a man trying to convince himself, not truly a protest. "They know we'd never stand for it!"

"Do they?"

"They must! And the entire Home Fleet's only a single wormhole transit away, Skipper!"

"They may believe they *can* get away with it." Honor's voice was cool and dispassionate; her thoughts were neither. "There's always been a certain anti-annexation movement in Parliament. Maybe they think enough bloodshed on Medusa, coupled with their presence here, will finally give that movement the strength to succeed."

"Not in a million years," McKeon growled.

"Probably not, no. But they're looking in from the outside. They may not realize how little chance of it there is, and maybe they figure they can pull it off however Parliament's xenophobes react. If this had worked the way they planned—assuming I'm right about their intentions—we'd have had no prior reason to suspect their involvement. Under the circumstances, any ship on the picket here probably would have been too busy reacting to the dirt-side situation from a cold start to worry about *Sirius*'s departure. We might not even have noticed it, in which case she'd have slipped away to alert their task force, or whatever, and bring it back in without anyone on our side even suspecting they were coming until they actually arrived. If that had happened, their forces would have been in Basilisk before Home Fleet could even start to react."

She paused and began punching numbers into her maneuvering systems with an unaccustomed speed and accuracy that amazed McKeon. The results flashed on her screen, and she pointed at them.

"Look. If they pop out of hyper right at the hyper limit on a reciprocal of *Sirius*'s present course, they'll be barely twelve light-minutes out from Medusa. If they translate downward at the maximum safe velocity, they can be into planetary orbit in under three and a half hours, even at superdreadnought acceleration rates. They'll also be just over eleven-point-three light-hours from the terminus, so they can reach *it* in twenty-eight hours and forty-five minutes. If we didn't know they were coming until they dropped out of hyper, they'd have plenty of time to be set up right on the terminus when Home Fleet tried to make transit through it."

McKeon paled. "That would be an act of war," he protested.

"So is that." Honor jabbed a thumb in the general direction of Medusa. "But what's happening dirt-side would only be an act of war if we knew who'd done it, and they've done their level best to convince us it was Manticoran criminals who supplied the guns and drugs. By the same token, their interdiction of the terminus would only turn into an act of war if we tried to transit *and they fired on us*. If I'm right about their plan, they can't have their entire fleet waiting around out here. For that matter, if they *did* have their entire fleet out here and they were really ready to fight, they wouldn't need any pretexts. They'd just come crashing in and sit on the terminus, and that would be that. But if they've only got a battle squadron or two, then, yes, we could kick them out of the system even if they were waiting for us. Our losses would be brutal, but theirs would be virtually one hundred percent, and they have to know that."

"Then what in God's name do they think they're *doing?*"

"I think they're running a bluff," Honor said quietly. "They hope we won't push it and risk engaging them if they're in a position to hurt us badly enough—that we'll stop to negotiate and discover public opinion back home won't stand for heavy casualties to take back a system the anti-annexationists don't want anyway. But if it *is* a bluff, that's another reason to use a relatively small force. They can always disavow the actions of their commander on the spot, claim he was carried away by understandable concern for off-worlders in the wake of the Medusa Massacre but that he exceeded his authority. That leaves them a way to back out and save face, especially if no one knows they *caused* the massacres. But think about it, Alistair. Events on Medusa are really just a side show. A pretext. They're not after the planet; they're after control of a second Junction terminus. Even if there's only one chance in fifty that they could pull it off, wouldn't the potential prize be worth the risk from their viewpoint?"

"Yes." There was no more doubt in McKeon's voice, and his nod was grim.

"But I may be wrong about the size of their force or how willing they'll be to fight," Honor said. "After all, their fleet's bigger than ours. They can stand the loss of a couple of battle squadrons as the opening round in a war, especially if they can inflict a favorable rate of exchange in return. And it's going to be a horse race to get anything here from Manticore in time to stop them, even with our Code Zulu. Our message will take thirteen and a half hours to reach Fleet HQ, but *Sirius* can be into hyper in two hours and fifty minutes—call it three. Let's say they reach their rendezvous three hours after that. Assuming a Fleet acceleration of four-twenty gees, that means their units could be back here in as little as twelve hours and on the warp point in forty-one, which leaves HQ just twenty-seven and a half hours from receipt of our Code Zulu to cover the terminus. Assuming Admiral Webster reacts instantly and dispatches Home Fleet from Manticore orbit with no delay at all, that'll take them—" She punched more numbers into her maneuvering plot, but McKeon was already ahead of her.

"Call it thirty-four hours for superdreadnoughts, or thirty-point-five if they don't send anything heavier than a battlecruiser," he muttered, jaws clenched, and Honor nodded.

"So if they *are* prepared to fight, they'd have over three hours to deploy energy mines on the terminus and take up the most advantageous positions before Home Fleet can possibly arrive. Which means the only way to be sure we don't wind up with a major fleet engagement is to stop *Sirius* from reaching her rendezvous."

"How do you plan to stop her, Ma'am?"

"We're still in Manticoran space, and what's happening on Medusa certainly constitutes an 'emergency situation.' Under the circumstances, I have the authority to order *any* ship to heave to for examination."

"You know Haven doesn't accept that interpretation of interstellar law, Ma'am." McKeon's voice was low, and Honor nodded. For centuries, Haven had championed the legal claim that the right of examination meant no more than the right to interrogate a ship by signal unless it intended to touch or had, since its last inspection, in fact touched the territory of the star system in which the examination was demanded. Since turning expansionist, the Republic had changed its position (within its own sphere) to the one most of the rest of the galaxy accepted: that the right of examination meant the right to physically stop and search a suspect ship within the examiner's territorial space regardless of its past or intended movements. But Haven had *not* accepted that interpretation in *other* star nations' territory. In time, they would have no choice but to do so, since the double standard they claimed was so irritating to the rest of the galaxy (including the Solarian League, which had all sorts of ways to retaliate short of war), but they hadn't yet, and that meant *Sirius's* master might very well assert Haven's old, traditional interpretation and refuse to stop when called upon to do so.

"If he won't stop willingly, then I'll stop him by force," she said. McKeon looked at her in silence, and she returned his gaze levelly. "If Haven can disavow the actions of an admiral or vice admiral, Her Majesty can disavow those of a commander," she pointed out in that same quiet voice.

McKeon stood looking at her a moment longer, then nodded. She didn't have to mention the next logical step in the process, for he knew it as well as she did. A flag officer could survive being officially disavowed; a commander could not. If Honor fired into *Sirius* and provoked an interstellar incident which left Queen Elizabeth no choice but to disavow her actions, then Honor's career was over.

He started to say so, but a tiny shake of her head stopped him. He turned away and walked towards the tactical station, then stopped. He stood for a second, and then he retraced his steps to the command chair.

"Captain Harrington," he said very formally, "I concur completely in your conclusions. I'd like to log my agreement with you, if I may."

Honor looked up at him, stunned by his offer, and her brown eyes softened. He could hardly believe what he'd just said himself, for by logging his agreement he would log his official support for any actions she took in response to her conclusions. He would share her responsibility for them—and any disgrace that came of them. But that seemed strangely unimportant as he looked into her eyes, because for the first time since she'd come aboard *Fearless*, Alistair McKeon saw total, unqualified approval of himself in those dark depths.

But then she shook her head gently.

"No, Mr. McKeon. *Fearless* is my responsibility—and so are my actions. But thank you. Thank you very much for the offer."

She held out her hand, and he took it.

his official support for any reason — he had, in response to her complaints. He would share her responsibility for them — and any disgrace that came of their — but that seemed strangely unimportant as he looked into her eyes...

Maltin MacZen...

...those dark eyes...

...If they she shook her head again.

• CHAPTER TWENTY-EIGHT

"NPA Control, this is Falcon. Inbound. ETA the source of Sierra-One-One's last signal three minutes. Have you any more information for us?"

Captain Nikos Papadapolous glanced back over his shoulder while he waited for a response. Despite the cramped confines of the pinnace, Sergeant Major Jenkins and Lieutenant Kilgore had most of Third Platoon's three squads into their battle armor already. Other Marines, bulky in unpowered body armor, were paired off with each battle-armored trooper, running check lists on external monitors, and a background chatter of crisp commands and metallic equipment sounds filled the big troop compartment.

Surgeon Commander Suchon sat just behind the captain, hunched forward in her seat. Her dark face was sickly pale, and she clutched her emergency medical kit to her armored breastplate with clawlike hands.

"Falcon, NPA Control," a voice said suddenly, and Papadapolous turned back to his own panel. "Negative information."

"NPA Control, Falcon copies. No additional information. We'll keep you advised."

"Thank you, Falcon. And good hunting. NPA Control clear."

"Falcon clear," Papadapolous responded, and turned his attention to the map display at his elbow. They couldn't know precisely where Sierra-One-One had gone down, but they had a pretty fair idea. Unfortunately, the terrain looked uninviting, to say the least. Someone paused beside him, and he looked up to see Ensign Tremaine.

"Our scanner people are picking up a couple of energy sources down there, Sir," the ensign said. "We've already relayed the data to NPA Control."

His face was taut, but he leaned forward almost diffidently to press buttons on Papadapolous's map display. Two light dots appeared on it, separated by just over five kilometers. Both were faint, but one flickered much more weakly than the other. The captain studied them for a moment, brow furrowed, then tapped the flickering one.

"That's Sierra-One-One," he said positively.

"How can you be certain, Sir?"

"Look at the terrain, Mr. Tremaine. This one—" Papadapolous tapped the display again "—isn't just weaker, it's in the middle of a valley that offers the only flat ground within klicks, but *this* one—" he tapped the other dot "—is right on top of a hill. Or under it," he added in a thoughtful tone.

"Under it?"

"It's only a trace source, Mr. Tremaine, and solid ground makes a pretty good shield against sensors. Burying it would make sense, but if that's what they did, they didn't do a very good job. We see it, and *something* brought Sierra-One-One down where the Stilties could get at her. They may have picked up this other source and come in for a closer look."

"I see." Tremaine stared at the suspect light, young face hard as he remembered another raid on a power source in the Outback. He rubbed his chin, then looked back at the Marine. "You think it was a decoy? That they sucked the NPA in on purpose?"

"It's possible," Papadapolous agreed, "but I'm inclined to think it was just sloppiness. I can't see any reason they'd want to start their 'insurrection' way out here in the boonies. Can you?"

"No, Sir. But with your permission, I'll detail one of the pinnaces to keep an eye on that source. That'll still leave two of us to support your people, but if someone down there did attract the NPA's attention on purpose and tries to bug out, we'll nail him."

"I think that's an excellent idea, Mr. Tremaine," Papadapolous said. "In fact—"

"Falcon, this is NPA-Two." Barney Isvarian's voice drew the captain's attention back to his com link.

"NPA-Two, this is Falcon. Go ahead." He said crisply.

"Nikos, we're still fifteen minutes out, but I'm looking at the Navy's sensor data. I think the source to the west has to be our people. Do you concur?"

"Affirmative, Major."

"What are your intentions?"

"I'll be dropping my first squad of scouts in—" Papadapolous glanced at his chronometer and checked it against the status board on Third Platoon's first squad "—ninety-five seconds. They'll secure the area around the suspected crash site and check for survivors as their first objective. The remainder of my people will be going in twenty klicks south-south-east along Ridge One-Three-Five. We've got a nice, long valley running north-south to that point, and it's got steep sides. We'll try to form a stopper to hold the enemy in it, then turn it into our killing ground."

"Understood. I've got two companies with me. I'll drop one of them with your main force, then use the counter-grav to swing the other north. Maybe we can come in behind them and pin them between us if they try to run." There was a pause, and Papadapolous braced himself for the question he knew was coming. It came very softly. "Is there any sign Lieutenant Malcolm's people are still alive down there, Nikos?"

"Negative, Major." Papadapolous's voice was flat, and Isvarian sighed over the com.

"Do your best, Nikos," he said.

"We will, Sir." A harsh buzzer snarled, and a bright light flashed over the pinnace's troop hatch. "We're dropping the first squad now, Major. We'll keep you advised. Falcon clear."

* * *

Sergeant Tadeuz O'Brian stepped through the yawning hatch into a thousand meters of air as the pinnace flashed on past him. He plummeted downward, the rest of his squad close behind him, and popped his grav canopy. It wasn't a regular counter-grav unit—there wasn't room for that. Instead, it generated a negative-gee force at the far end of its attachment harness, and he grunted involuntarily as an enraged mule kicked with vicious power. But O'Brian was used to that. He didn't even blink. Instead, he hit his armor thrusters and turned in midair, the movement almost instinctive after endless hours of armor drill, to align his sensors and built-in electronic binoculars on the smashed NPA skimmer. Even a scout suit's systems weren't good enough to get a reading through the shattered hull, but the sergeant's face tightened as the bodies sprawled all about it registered.

There must have been three or four hundred dead Stilties strewn across the mossy ground, most of them mangled and torn by the heavy pulser darts of the skimmer's dorsal guns. They weren't alone, and O'Brian controlled an urge to retch as he saw the first human body. It looked as if at least one of the NPA troopers had tried to make a run for it and been caught in the open; his weapons lay near the grisly ruin which had once been a man. O'Brian prayed that he'd already been dead when the Stilties reached him, but the knives driven through his limbs to pin his eviscerated body to the moss suggested that he hadn't been.

His armor's exoskeleton took the shock as the sergeant grounded and checked his display. It looked good—like a textbook drop. The squad's beacons glowed in precise alignment, encircling the skimmer, and he brought his own pulse rifle into ready position.

"Sharon, you're on perimeter security. I'll take Bill's people to check the skimmer."

"Aye, Sarge," Corporal Sharon Hillyard's voice said in his earphone. Hillyard was tough as nails, young but with seven years' service already behind her, yet he heard her relief. "Stimson, Hadley," she called her section's two plasma gunners, "take that ridge to the north and set up to cover us. Ellen, I want you and—"

O'Brian tuned her out and waved to his other corporal, and the five members of the squad's second section fell in on his flanks as he advanced on the wreck.

It was bad. In fact, it was even worse than O'Brian had feared. The skimmer's gunner had been dragged out of her smashed turret, and it was hard to tell that shattered, flayed body had been a woman's. Hell, it was hard to tell she'd even been *human*, and he swallowed his gorge as he made his way across the blood-soaked ground. It was going to take the forensic people to identify the bodies, he thought. After they gathered up all the pieces.

He made his way to a gaping hole in the skimmer's side, his armor's audio sensors picking up the sputter and pop of arcing circuits but not a single sound of life from the interior, and drew a deep breath. Then he thrust his armored torso through and looked upon obscenity.

He jerked back and swallowed hard, and his white face was suddenly streaked with sweat. Nothing this side of Hell itself should look like that, a small voice said through the horror in his mind. He closed his eyes, then made himself look again, trying to pretend it was a scene from HD, not reality.

It didn't help. The skimmer's interior was splashed and daubed with crimson, as if lunatics with buckets of blood had run amok within it. Consoles were shattered and smashed, and everywhere he looked were bits and pieces of people. The hacked, mutilated jumble of limbs and torsos and eyeless, severed heads filled him with something worse than horror, but he made himself step fully through the hole. He ground his emotions down, refusing to think, relying on instinct and training, as he walked through the entire skimmer.

There were no survivors, and as he fought to keep the hideous nightmare about him from registering, he was glad. Glad that no one had lived through the Stilties' butchery. He completed his iron-faced sweep and turned to make his way stiffly from the wreck, and a single, horrified thought quivered though his frozen mind. Dear God. Dear God in Heaven, what could make *anyone* do what had been done to these people?

He paused outside the broken hull and locked his armor. He leaned back limply against its supporting strength and closed his eyes while he fought back tears. He sucked in deep breaths, grateful for the sealed environment that isolated him from the stench of blood and death he knew surrounded him, until he could open his eyes again at last. Then he cleared his throat.

"No survivors," he told his squad. Even to himself his voice sounded rusty and old, and he was grateful no one asked any questions. He switched to the command channel

"Falcon-Five, Falcon-Three-Three," he said, and waited.

"Falcon-Three-Three, Falcon-Five," Sergeant Major Jenkins replied. "Go."

"Falcon-Five, there are no survivors. Repeat, no survivors."

"Falcon-Five copies, Falcon-Three-Three. Wait one."

O'Brian stood with his back resolutely to the skimmer, eyes focused on nothing, while Jenkins conferred with Captain Papadapolous. Then the captain himself came on the line.

"Falcon-Three-Three, Falcon Leader. Understand no survivors. Are there any signs of hostile natives still in your area?"

"Negative, Falcon Leader. We've got several hundred dead, but no sign of live hostiles." He started to say something else, then paused as Hillyard's beacon flashed an attention pattern on his display. "Wait one, Falcon Leader." He changed channels again. "Yes, Sharon?"

"I've been listening in, Sarge. You might want to tell the skipper I don't see any rifles lying around out here. Looks like they stripped their own dead before they moved on."

"Copy, Sharon." He punched back into the company command net. "Falcon Leader, Falcon-Three-Three. Be advised we see no Stilty rifles on site. It appears they stripped their dead before leaving."

"Understand no rifles on site, Falcon-Three-Three. Maybe they've got more bodies than guns. Any sign they took the NPA's weapons, as well?"

"Negative, Falcon Leader. They . . . spent enough time here to do it, but I've seen several pulse rifles and sidearms. Looks like they might not have understood how to use them."

"We can hope, Falcon-Three-Three. All right. I've got a new mission for you."

The first flight of NPA skimmers swept overhead, curving back into the south to move their troops in behind the wave of Medusans flowing towards the Three Forks River and the enclaves. O'Brian watched them, noting the way they banked sharply to eyeball the ground as they crossed Sierra-One-One's desecrated wreckage, while he listened to Papadapolous's voice.

"The Navy tells me there's another energy source five-point-three klicks from you at zero-three-niner true. That may be what sucked the NPA in close enough to get hit, so investigating it could be just as important as stopping the Stilties. Ensign Tremaine has a pinnace parked on top of it, but you're the closest ground troops. The Navy is on channel four, call sign Hawk-Three, standing by for ground support if you need it. Check it out and report back. Anybody you find there, we want them. Copy?"

"Aye, aye, Falcon Leader. Falcon-Three-Three copies. Check out the power source at zero-three-niner, secure the site, and report back. Navy call sign Hawk-Three. We're on it, Sir."

"Good, Three-Three. Keep me informed. Falcon Leader clear."

"Falcon-Three-Three clear."

O'Brian switched back to the squad net while he brought up his map. If there was a power source up there, it had to be underground, but he and his people had the sensors to find it.

"Sharon, Bill. You copied that?"

"Aye, Sarge," Hillyard responded, and Corporal Levine seconded her.

"Okay. Bill, I want your section on point. Stay sharp and watch yourself. If we've got off-worlders in this, we may be looking at off-world weapons, as well, so remember what happened when the NPA hit that lab."

"You got that right, Sarge."

"Sharon, put Stimson and Hadley on the flanks to cover Bill, but I want the rest of your section watching our six. Got that?"

"Check, Sarge," Hillyard replied, then paused a moment. "Sarge, did the skipper say he wanted those people *alive*?"

"He didn't say, and I didn't ask," O'Brian said flatly. The silence which answered him was eloquent. "All right, people, let's move our asses."

The squad of armored Marines turned their backs on that place of horror and headed east.

"Falcon Leader, Falcon-Three. Falcon-Three-Two reports movement coming at him from zero-three-seven."

Lieutenant Kilgore's voice was low, as if pitched to avoid the Medusans' ears. Papadapolous glanced at his display in his hastily selected command post and nodded to himself. It seemed Major Isvarian had been right about the effect *mekoha* had on the Stilties. The bastards were making a beeline straight toward the enclaves from the site of the ambush, and that didn't seem to indicate very much in the way of caution or forethought. Which was just fine with Captain Nikos Papadapolous.

"Falcon Leader copies, Falcon-Three. Keep your people falling back and stay clear of our fire lanes."

"Aye, Falcon Leader."

"Falcon Leader to all Falcons. Hostiles approaching from zero-three-seven. Prepare to engage on my command."

He looked up as metal and plastic clicked behind him. A half-dozen of Isvarian's NPA medics labored furiously, setting up an emergency aid station, and Papadapolous frowned. He gestured to the Fourth Platoon's platoon sergeant, standing beside him.

"Yes, Sir?"

"Where's Dr. Suchon, Regiano?"

Sergeant Regiano glanced away for a moment, then met her commander's eyes levelly.

"She's back where the shuttle dropped us, Sir." Papadapolous's head tilted dangerously, and the sergeant answered his silent question. "She refuses to move any closer to the front, Skipper."

"I see." Papadapolous drew a deep breath, and his eyes were hard. "Sergeant Regiano, you will return to the LZ. You will inform Commander Suchon, with my compliments, that her presence is required here. Should she refuse to accompany you back to the aid station, you will use whatever means are required—up to and including the threat and application of force—to bring her. Is that understood, Sergeant?"

"Aye, aye, Sir!" There was undisguised satisfaction in Regiano's eyes as she saluted sharply and marched off to the rear. Papadapolous swallowed a venomous curse, then shook himself and forced his mind away from its fury at Suchon and back to the task at hand.

He turned to the visual display at Sergeant Major Jenkins's right knee. It showed a birds-eye view of the valley, relayed from one of the two pinnaces invisible on station high above him, and his skin crawled as the ground itself seemed to flow towards his positions. The Stilties were coming at him in a mob more than two kilometers wide and three deep, flowing through the moss like a vast, ragged tide. There must be at least ten thousand of them out there, and that was far more than he'd allowed even his worst-case estimates to assume. Even with the NPA reinforcements, his people were outnumbered thirty or forty to one, and thank *God* they'd caught them in the open instead of in among the enclaves!

He'd chosen his kill zone because the valley was the broadest opening through a tortuous east-west ridge line, the most logical avenue for the natives' advance southward, and the wave of Medusans flowed towards it, exactly as he'd hoped. They began to funnel together as they entered its northern end, and he checked his deployments one last time.

An awful lot of his plan was built around Third Platoon's battle armor, and he wished he'd been able to bring O'Brian's squad back to thicken his lines. But he couldn't. He needed that power source checked before anyone there could bug out. That was all there was to it, yet it left Kilgore's platoon spread mighty thin. His squad of heavy armor formed the stopper at the southern end of the valley, as well as Papadapolous's heaviest single fire unit. They should be well able to take care of themselves, particularly with the support of Sergeant Howell's heavy weapons section and the turret mounts of Isvarian's grounded skimmers, but that left Kilgore only one squad of scouts to watch over the Stilties' advance and cover both flanks, and that was nowhere near enough for the captain's peace of mind.

He heard angry voices behind him, one of them the shrill whine of *Fearless*'s senior physician, and then what might have been the sound of a blow, but he tuned them out to concentrate on more important things. The scouts were withdrawing up the sides of the valley now, bouncing from cover to cover in their jump gear, and he gnawed his lower lip as he watched them.

He wasn't worried about his battle-armored people, but the rest of his troops were in standard body armor, and the NPA company Major Isvarian had brought in to flesh out his people were even more lightly protected. He had no doubt his weapons could turn that valley into a slaughterhouse, yet even with air support that many enemies might manage to break at least some of their number out of the zone. It seemed preposterous in the face of modern weaponry. Every manual he'd ever read, every lecture he'd ever heard, said ill-armed aborigines could never break through that much state-of-the-art firepower. But the manuals and lectures had never contemplated facing a horde like this precisely because modern killing power made such a concentrated body of troops suicidal. That meant he didn't have any real way to estimate how much fire the Medusans—especially if they were all on *mekoha*—could absorb without breaking, and he'd have only a single section of armored scouts on each flank to intercept them. If they were hopped up enough to keep coming, if they got in among his lightly armored people in any numbers . . .

"Keep a close eye on the flanks, Gunny," he told Jenkins softly, and turned to his Navy channel. "Hawk-One, Falcon Leader. Watch the slopes. If we get a breakout, I want you on it in a hurry."

"Hawk-One copies, Falcon Leader," Ensign Tremaine replied. "We'll watch your flanks."

"Thanks, Hawk-One." He returned his attention to his map display as the light codes of hostiles began to flow into the valley. Another fifteen minutes, he thought.

Lieutenant Liam Kilgore watched his armor display with one eye while he checked his pulse rifle with the other. His scouts had done their first job by spotting the Stilties, then fallen back before them without being spotted in return. Now it was time for them to get the hell out of the way and get ready to kick some ass, and he grunted approval as they filtered neatly back into the positions he'd selected in such haste. His armored people were supposed to intercept any Stilty breakouts and stop them short of the less well-protected types behind them, but there were an awful lot of hostiles out there. He wished O'Brian's squad was with him to help thicken the flanks, but even if O'Brian had been there, it wouldn't have thickened them enough. Still, if there were a lot of Stilties, there was also a lot of firepower on the ridges above his people. Maybe even enough.

Jesus, there were a lot of the bastards! More and more of them flowed forward, and he no longer needed his armor sensors to see them. The mark-one eyeball worked just fine, for the nomads weren't even trying to hide. Their vaunted skill in concealed movement seemed to have deserted them, and his audio sensors picked up the high, shrill sounds of some barbaric chant as they forged ahead with their weird, swinging gait. Perhaps half of them were cavalry, mounted on *jehrns*, the odd, upright riding beasts of the northern hemisphere nomads; the rest were on foot, and all of them advanced waving rifles, swords, and spears—even clubs—and screaming encouragement to one another. There were actually bayonets on most of those rifles, and there was something peculiarly bloodcurdling about the Medusans' frenzied sounds and obvious unconcern for anything they might run into. Kilgore almost imagined he could smell the acrid stench of *mekoha* wafting from them, and the thought of fighting someone who couldn't even feel pain, much less fear, wasn't one Marines were accustomed to.

On the other hand, he told himself grimly, the Stilties weren't accustomed to facing modern firepower, either. They were in for a shock, and—

"Falcon Leader to all Falcons. *Engage!*" a voice snapped, and Kilgore's pulse rifle swung up into position without conscious thought. His thumb snapped the selector to full-auto, not the normal semi-automatic, and his little finger pressed the stud that selected the explosive magazine. He paused for one bare heartbeat, seeing the mob of Medusans through cold, suddenly distant eyes, and then he squeezed the trigger.

It wasn't a slaughter. It was worse than that. The Medusans had never heard of dispersion; they were packed shoulder-to-shoulder, crowded into a single, huge target. Anything that missed one of them was bound to hit another.

Kilgore's pulse rifle surged back, its recoil almost imperceptible through his armor as its small, powerful grav coil spat a stream of four-millimeter darts downrange. The explosions of the darts weren't the clean, white flashes of practice on the range; they were red and steaming as Medusan bodies blew apart in geysers of blood. He swept his fire across the shrieking natives, emptying a full hundred-round extended magazine into them in less than twenty seconds, and his was only one of almost three hundred modern rifles flaying that screaming thong.

Darts screamed down over his head from the crest of the valley's sides, and the shattering thunder of his third squad's heavy, multi-barreled pulsers ripped into the Medusans from the south. Searing flares of plasma incinerated Stilties by the score as the heavy weapons section opened up, and some of Isvarian's NPA troopers were armed with rocket and grenade launchers that blasted severed limbs and gobs of Medusan flesh across moss and boulders. The rocky valley was a pocket of Hell, and not even *mekoha* could fully barricade the natives against the horror. They howled in shock and agony, writhing like ants in a flame, yet even as they screamed and died, others lunged outward, running up the slopes with the impossible agility of their three-legged gait, charging straight into the fire tearing them apart.

It was incredible. Kilgore slapped a fresh magazine into his rifle and emptied it. Slammed in a third and opened up again, ears cringing from the savage discord of shrieks and explosions bellowing over his audio pickups, and he couldn't believe it. The Stilties were charging so fast, their mob formation so thick, that he couldn't kill them fast enough to stop them! Any sane opponent would have broken and run from that murderous fire; the Stilties didn't. They were a living wave, willing to take any losses to reach their foes. They surged over their own dead and dying, frothing ever higher up the sides of the valley, and his scouts were spread far too thin to contain them.

"Falcon-Three, Falcon Leader! Get back, Falcon-Three! Clear the slopes for the Navy!"

"Aye, Falcon Leader." Kilgore's voice sounded strange in his own ears through the thunder and slaughter. It was flat and level, leached of all expression by the horror before his eyes, and he heard it passing orders to his scouts. He abandoned his cover, feeling crude bullets skip and whine off his armor like hail as the Medusans saw him at last, and his people hit their jump gear, vaulting higher up the steep slopes. Marines and NPA troopers above them checked their fire as the armored scouts suddenly went bobbing and weaving through their fire lanes, and the Stilties screamed in triumph as the avalanche of death slackened. They charged after their fleeing enemies even while those on the valley floor continued to wither and die in the hurricane of destruction sweeping up from its southern end, and Kilgore's ears rang as a rifle bullet spanged off his armorplast helmet in a smear of lead.

But then the scouts were clear, and the pinnaces screamed down, lasers and autopulsers raving. They swept along the sides of the valley, cluster bombs and napalm erupting beneath them, lasers and guns plowing a ten-meter wide swath of absolute destruction through the howling Medusans, and then they swept back to do it all over again. And again.

And again and again and again . . . until the dead lay five and six deep and there was no living thing in all the blasted nightmare of that valley of death.

Sergeant O'Brian heard the sudden explosion of combat far behind him, but his attention was on other things. His squad squatted and crouched in firing positions along the shallow, razor-backed ridge, and he peered through his binoculars at the cave mouth across the ravine below him.

The nose of an aircar protruded from it, and his jaw tightened as he saw the pulser muzzles like tusks on either side of the front gear well. The sleek vehicle bore no markings that he could see, and the presence of those heavy weapons made it illegal even if it had once been properly registered. The problem was what he did about it. He was no cop, and with the horror of the NPA skimmer fresh in his mind, he was in no mood to act like one.

He grunted decisively and hit the button that flipped the binoculars up out of his way.

"Hawk-Three, Falcon-Three-Three," he said into his com. "Are you ready to nail them if they bug out?"

"Affirmative, Falcon-Three-Three," the pinnace's commander replied. "But we're not going to leave much in the way of evidence if we do."

"Understood, Hawk-Three. We'll try to keep them on the ground, but stay on your toes."

"Will do, Falcon-Three-Three. Luck."

"Thanks." O'Brian shifted back to the squad net. "You see that overhang above the aircar, Stimson?"

"Yo, Sarge," the plasma rifleman's reply was laconic, almost bored-sounding, but O'Brian wasn't fooled.

"I want that cave plugged with the aircar inside it. It may be evidence, so I don't want it destroyed, either. Think you can drop the overhang on its nose?"

"Might be able to," Stimson said thoughtfully, "but that's mighty thick rock, an' I wouldn't care to bet money on doin' it from up here. This baby of mine don't have all that much penetration, and the angle's bad from here. I prob'ly can if I get a little lower, though, Sarge."

"Can you do that without being spotted?"

"He can work around the north end of the ridge, Sarge," Hillyard suggested. "It tails off in some broken ground and boulders down that way."

"Sounds good to me, Sarge," Stimson agreed.

"Do it, Stimson."

"On my way."

O'Brian grunted in satisfaction, but his armor sensors were already picking up revving turbines, and there were other machinery noises, coming both from that cave and an equally large cave mouth just below it. There might be more aircars in there, or even ground vehicles.

"Hadley, you watch that lower cave," he said. "If anything starts to move out of it, nail it, and the hell with evidence."

"My pleasure, Sarge."

"Sharon, when Stimson takes out the aircar, I want you to take the rest of your people in to cover that smaller cave to the left. Bill, you take Parker and Lovejoy to that one on the extreme right. Turner and Frankowski, you're with me on the one in the middle. Hadley and Stimson will lie back to cover us. Everyone copy?"

A chorus of assents came back, and he made himself wait in patience while Stimson slithered cautiously into position. It seemed to be taking forever, though he knew the delay felt far longer than it was. The thunder of weapons from the south grew even louder, and he bit his lip as its intensity registered. There must be even more of the bastards than they'd thought. He tried not to remember what the Stilties had done to those poor damned NPA types, tried not to think about them doing it to his own people, and concentrated on the task in hand.

"In position, Sarge," Stimson's voice said.

"Then take 'em out," O'Brian grated, and an eye-aching gout of incandescence flashed below him.

The plasma bolt liberated its energy almost instantaneously against the lower edge of the stony outcrop. Vaporized soil and glowing quartz gravel erupted away from the searing impact, but the outcrop held . . . for a second. And then another bolt smashed into the glowing hole. A second scoop of rock and earth vanished, and the massive stone ledge broke loose and crashed downward across the cave mouth. It crunched into the aircar, blocking the cave and smashing through the fuselage just behind the nose like a blunt guillotine, and O'Brian was on his feet.

"Move in!" he shouted, and his armored squad hurled itself forward in instant response.

O'Brian covered the distance to the central cave mouth in less than thirty seconds, diving aside to cover himself against any waiting weapons behind a shoulder of solid rock and dirt. He stabbed a quick look at his display and grunted in satisfaction. They were all closed up against their objectives. Now someone had to poke his head inside and hope to hell no one blew it off.

"Watch my ass, Turner," he growled, and thrust himself cautiously around the edge of the opening.

A narrow, rough-walled gut, more like a tunnel than a cave, opened before him. He moved down it slowly, rifle ready, sensors probing, and grunted again as he picked up additional power sources ahead of him. So. This *was* the base they'd been looking for . . . and somewhere up there were the bastards who'd given the Stilties their fucking guns. His lips drew up in a hungry smile at the thought, but he made himself maintain his slow, cautious pace.

The cave swung to the left and opened out, and light glowed around the bend. He sidled up to it cautiously, and his eyes narrowed as he saw a dozen coughing humans crouched behind out-thrust swells of rock and piles of off-world freight canisters and cargo-handling equipment amid the fog of dust and smoke Stimson's shot had blown back into the cave. It looked as if they'd been loading the aircar for a frantic evacuation, but there'd been a change in plans, O'Brian thought coldly. They weren't going anywhere now.

Most of them wore unpowered body armor, and he saw some fairly heavy weapons down there, as well as sidearms and half a dozen pulse rifles. On the other hand, *his* people were in full battle armor, and none of those bastards knew he was here above them yet, now did they?

He started to squeeze his trigger, then stopped. He was no cop, but he supposed the brass would like prisoners. And physical evidence.

"Solid shot only," he murmured over his com. "Try not to tear things up too badly if you have to shoot—they're gonna want evidence—but don't take any stupid chances."

Acknowledgments came back to him, and his own little finger squeezed, switching over to the non-explosive rounds in the secondary magazine. He drew a deep breath and eased further forward, keeping as low as he could while Turner slid up to his right. She moved as carefully and quietly as he and settled down in position to watch his back. He and the private looked at one another, and O'Brian nodded.

"Throw down your weapons!" he barked suddenly. His voice boomed and roared through the cavern, hugely amplified by his armor's external speaker, and the people before him jerked in surprise. Faces swung towards him, and two or three of them dropped their weapons, raising their hands in sheer reflex.

"No, Goddamnit!" someone screamed. Heads whipped around, and blinding light and searing heat flashed from the cave wall three meters to O'Brian's right as the man who'd screamed fired a plasma carbine desperately in his direction. The sergeant didn't even blink, but his eyes glowed with a hard, vicious light. He didn't repeat his surrender demand. His rifle muzzle angled slightly to the right, and he bared his teeth as he squeezed the trigger twice with cold deliberation.

The non-explosive darts screamed across the cavern at two thousand meters per second, and Tadeuz O'Brian was qualified Expert Marksman with the pulse rifle. Body armor slowed them, but it couldn't possibly stop them at such a short range, and they struck precisely where he'd intended—a centimeter below Colonel Bryan Westerfeldt's navel.

The sergeant stood fully upright, listening to the clatter of weapons on stone. He started down into the cave, and the cold, bitter hate at the core of him hoped the ghosts of the NPA's slaughtered patrol could hear the high, tearing screams of the gutshot bastard dying on the floor before him.

• CHAPTER TWENTY-NINE

Commander Honor Harrington sat in her command chair and watched her displays as HMS *Fearless* tore through space under maximum emergency power. The cruiser accelerated at a steady five hundred and twenty gravities—more than five kilometers per second per second—in pursuit of the freighter *Sirius*; Honor's face was still and cold, a mask against her own anxiety, while her mind churned behind her eyes.

She was almost certain she had it right . . . but only almost. And if she was wrong, if she hadn't guessed correctly after all, if—

She chopped off that train of thought and made herself lean back. The timing of *Sirius*'s departure could mean only one thing, she told herself, and Brigham's projection of her course confirmed it. *Sirius* was, indeed, headed for the Tellerman wave, and the Tellerman was one of the "Roaring Deeps," the most powerful grav waves ever charted. More than that, it headed almost directly towards the People's Republic of Haven. If there truly was a Peep battle squadron out here, the Tellerman would take *Sirius* to meet it at two and a half or three thousand times the speed of light.

Back in the early days of hyper flight, spacers would have avoided something like the Tellerman like death itself, for death was precisely what it would have meant for any starship that encountered it.

The original hyper drive had been a mankiller, yet it had taken people a while to realize precisely why that was. Some of the dangers had been easy enough to recognize and avoid, but others had been far more difficult to identify and account for—mainly because people who encountered them never came back to describe their experience.

It had been discovered early on that translating into or out of the alpha band, the lowest of the hyper bands, at a velocity greater than thirty percent that of light was suicide, yet people had continued to kill themselves for centuries in efforts to translate at speeds higher than that. Not because they were suicidal, but because such a low velocity had severely limited the usefulness of hyper travel.

The translation into or out of any given band of hyper space was a complex energy transfer that cost the translating vessel most of its original velocity—as much as ninety-two percent of it, in the case of the alpha band. The energy loss dropped slightly with each "higher" hyper band, but its presence remained a constant, and for over five standard centuries, all hyper ships had relied on reaction drives.

There were limits to the amount of reaction mass a ship could carry, and hydrogen catcher fields didn't work in the extreme conditions of hyper space. That had effectively limited ships to the very lowest (and "slowest") hyper bands, since no one could carry enough reaction mass to recover velocity after multiple translations. It also explained why more stubborn inventors had persisted in their costly efforts to translate at higher velocities in order to maintain as much starting velocity in hyper space as possible. It had taken over two hundred years for the .3 c limitation to be fully accepted, and even today, some hyper physicists continued to search for a way around it.

Even after one had resolved the problems of safe translation speeds, however, there was the question of navigation. Hyper space wasn't like normal space. The laws of relativistic physics applied at any given point in hyper, but as a hypothetical observer looked outward, his instruments showed a rapidly increasing distortion. Maximum observation range was barely twenty light-minutes; beyond that, the gravity-warped chaos of hyper and its highly charged particles and extreme background radiation made instruments utterly unreliable. Which, of course, meant that astrogation fixes were impossible, and a ship that couldn't see where it was going seldom came home again.

The answer to that one had been the hyper log, the interstellar equivalent of the ancient inertial guidance systems developed on Old Earth long before the Diaspora. Early-generation hyper logs hadn't been all that accurate, but they'd at least given astrogators a rough notion of where they were. That had been far better than anything that had come before, yet even with the hyper log, so many ships never returned that only survey vessels used hyper space. Survey crews had been small, fantastically well-paid, and probably just a bit crazy, but they'd kept hyper travel in use until, eventually, one or two of them encountered what had killed so many other starships and survived to tell about it.

Hyper space itself was best considered as a compressed dimension which corresponded on a point-by-point basis to normal space but placed those points in much closer congruity and so "shortened" the distance between them. In fact, there were multiple "bands," or associated but discrete dimensions, of hyper space. The "higher" the band, the shorter the distance between points in normal space, the greater the apparent velocity of ships traveling through it . . . and the higher the cumulative energy cost to enter it.

That much had been understood by the earliest theorists. What they hadn't quite grasped was that hyper space, formed by the combined gravitational distortion of an entire universe's mass, was itself crossed and crisscrossed by permanent waves or currents of focused gravity. They were widely separated, of course, but they also might be dozens of light-years wide and deep, and they were deadly to any ship which collided with one. The gravitational shear they exerted on a starship's hull would rip the hapless vessel apart long before any evasive action could even be contemplated, unless the ship happened to impact at precisely the right angle on exactly the right vector, and its bridge crew had both the reflexes and the reaction mass to wrench clear in time.

As time passed, the survey ships that survived had mapped out reasonably safe routes through the more heavily traveled regions of hyper space. They couldn't be entirely relied upon, for the grav waves shifted position from time to time, and sticking to the safe lanes between waves often required vector changes reaction-drive ships simply could not make. That meant hyper voyages had tended to be both indirect and lengthy, but the survival rate had gone up. And as it climbed, and as physicists went out to probe the grav waves they now knew existed with ever more sophisticated instruments, observational data increased and ever more refined theories of gravity were proposed.

It had taken just over five hundred years, but finally, in 1246 P.D., the scientists had learned enough for the planet Beowulf to perfect the impeller drive, which used what were for all intents and purposes "tame" grav waves in normal space. Yet useful as the impeller was in normal space, it was extraordinarily dangerous in hyper. If it encountered one of the enormously more powerful naturally occurring grav waves, it could vaporize an entire starship, much as Honor herself had blown the Havenite courier boat's impeller nodes with *Fearless*'s impeller wedge.

More than thirty years had passed before Dr. Adrienne Warshawski of Old Earth found a way around that danger. It was Warshawski who finally perfected a gravity detector which could give as much as five light-seconds' warning before a grav wave was encountered. That had been a priceless boon, permitting impeller drive to be used with far greater safety between grav waves, and even today all grav detectors were called "Warshawskis" in her honor, yet she hadn't stopped there. In the course of her research, she had penetrated far deeper into the entire grav wave phenomenon than anyone before her, and she had suddenly realized that there was a way to use the grav wave itself. An impeller drive modified so that it projected not an inclined stress band above and below a ship but two slightly curved plates at *right angles* to its hull could use those plates as giant, immaterial "sails" to trap the focused radiation hurtling along a grav wave. More than that, the interface between a Warshawski sail and a grav wave produced an eddy of preposterously high energy levels which could be siphoned off to power a starship. Once a ship had "set sail" down a grav wave, it could actually shut down its onboard power plants entirely.

And so the grav wave, once the promise of near certain death, had become the secret to faster, cheaper, and safer hyper voyages. Captains who had avoided them like the plague now actively sought them out, cruising between them on impeller drive where necessary, and the network of surveyed grav waves had grown apace.

There had still been a few problems. The most bothersome was that grav waves were *layers* of focused gravity, subject to areas of reverse flow and unpredictable bouts of "turbulence" along the interfaces of opposed flows or where one wave impinged upon another. Such turbulence could destroy a ship, but it was almost more frustrating that no one could take full advantage of the potential of the Warshawski sail (or, for that matter, the impeller drive) because no human could survive the accelerations which were theoretically possible.

Improved Warshawskis had tended to offset the first difficulty by extending their detection range and warning ships of turbulence. With enough warning time, a ship could usually trim its sails to ride through turbulence by adjusting their density and "grab factor," though failure to trim in time remained deadly, which was why *Sirius*'s claim of tuner flutter had been so serious. A captain still had to see it coming, but the latest generation detectors could detect a grav wave at as much as eight light-minutes and spot turbulence within a wave at up to half that range. The problem of acceleration tolerance, on the other hand, had remained insoluble for over a standard century, until Dr. Shigematsu Radhakrishnan, probably the greatest hyper physicist after Warshawski herself, devised the inertial compensator.

Radhakrishnan had also been the first to hypothesize the existence of wormhole junctions, but the compensator had been his greatest gift to mankind's diaspora. The compensator turned the grav wave (natural or artificial) associated with a vessel into a sump into which it could dump its inertia. Within the safety limits of its compensator, any accelerating or decelerating starship was in a condition of internal free-fall unless it generated its own gravity, but the compensator's efficiency depended on two factors: the area enclosed in its field and the strength of the grav wave serving as its sump. Thus a smaller ship, with a smaller compensator field area, could sustain a higher acceleration from a given wave strength, and the naturally-occurring and vastly more powerful grav waves of hyper space allowed for far higher accelerations under Warshawski sail than could possibly be achieved under impeller drive in normal space.

Even with the acceleration rates the compensator permitted, no manned vessel could maintain a normal space velocity above eighty percent of light-speed, for the particle and radiation shielding to survive such velocities simply did not exist. The highest safe speed in hyper was still lower, little more than .6 c due to the higher particle charges and densities encountered there, but the closer congruity of points in normal space meant a ship's *apparent* velocity could be many times light-speed. Equipped with Warshawski sails, gravity detectors, and the inertial compensator, a modern warship could attain hyper accelerations of up to 5,500 g and sustain apparent velocities of as much as 3,000 c. Merchantmen, on the other hand, unable to sacrifice as much onboard mass to the most powerful possible sails and compensators the designer could squeeze in, remained barred from the highest hyper bands and most powerful grav waves and were lucky to make more than 1,200 *c*, though some passenger liners might go as high as 1,500.

And that brought Honor right back to *Sirius*, for the ship in front of her obviously *had* a military-grade drive and compensator. Her sheer mass meant her compensator field was larger and thus less efficient than *Fearless*'s, but no freighter should have been able to pull her acceleration. Even a superdreadnought, the only warship class which approached her mass, could only manage about four hundred and twenty gees, and *Sirius* was burning along at four hundred and ten. That left *Fearless* an advantage of barely a hundred and ten gees, little more than a kilometer per second squared—and *Sirius* had a head start of just under fifteen minutes.

It would have been worse if *Fearless* hadn't been at standby or Dominica Santos hadn't cut corners and chopped almost a full minute off the time it took to put her drive fully on line. As it was, Honor could still overhaul before *Sirius* reached the hyper limit, but not with as much margin as she might have wished. *Sirius* would hit the hyper limit in just under a hundred and seventy-three minutes from the time she left orbit. Honor had been in pursuit now for almost ten minutes. By cutting the safety margin on her own compensator to zero, she could match velocities with the freighter in another forty-six minutes, but it would take her over an hour just to reach effective missile range. Completely overtaking the freighter would require just over another hundred and seven minutes, leaving her less than twenty minutes before *Sirius* reached the hyper limit. And even if she did overtake completely, forcing the freighter to heave-to would be far from easy. Worse, momentum alone would carry *Sirius* beyond the hyper limit, even if she braked at max in response to Honor's demand, unless she began her deceleration within the next hour and a half, and Honor had no way of knowing just how far beyond the hyper limit a Havenite battle squadron might be lurking. No normal space sensor could see across the hyper wall. The entire Havenite Navy might lie less than a light-second beyond the limit, and no one in Basilisk would know a thing about it, so it was entirely possible *Sirius* needed only to break into hyper at all to accomplish her mission.

Which meant that, somehow, Honor had to stop her within the next ninety-seven minutes. If she didn't, then the only way to prevent her from translating into hyper would be to destroy her.

Captain Johan Coglin sat on his bridge. He'd run out of curses ten minutes before; now he simply sat and glared at his display while anger flowed through his mind like slow lava.

Operation Odysseus had seemed like a reasonable plan when he was first briefed for it. A few too many ruffles and flourishes, perhaps, but reasonable. There'd been no special reason why they had to use *his* ship for it, yet no one had listened when he suggested they use a genuine freighter. They'd wanted *Sirius's* higher acceleration levels and hyper speed "just in case," and he'd been far too junior to argue the point. And, he supposed, if things had gone as planned, it wouldn't really have mattered in the long run. Only the idiots who'd orchestrated the operation should have realized it would never work from the moment *Fearless* replaced *Warlock* on Basilisk Station. They should have scrubbed it weeks ago, and he'd told Canning that.

From the beginning, Odysseus had relied on deception, diversion, and the half-assed way the Royal Manticoran Navy policed Basilisk. Now it was all blowing up in their faces. What should have been a neat, clean sucker punch had turned into a fiasco which might yet become outright disaster, in large part *because* his ship had been used, and Coglin knew NavInt, the General Staff, and the War Cabinet were all going to fight like hell to pin it on someone else.

There was no doubt in his mind that *Fearless*'s captain had grasped the essentials of Odysseus, and even in his anger, his own professionalism had to admire Harrington's instant, iron-nerved response. Blowing the consulate courier boat's drive that way had been incredibly risky but brilliant, reducing the players to *Sirius* and *Fearless* instead of leaving her two potential targets to pursue, and his sensors had detected the separation of three pinnaces from *Fearless*. That had to be the cruiser's entire Marine detachment, and the speed with which Harrington had dispatched them was clear proof Canning and Westerfeldt had grossly underestimated the contingency planning that must have gone on between her and the NPA. Given the numbers of rifles Westerfeldt had handed the Shaman, that planning might not have helped that much if the Stilties had surprised the enclaves, but a full company of Marines with Navy air support would slaughter the natives in an open field engagement.

Which meant that Coglin's part of Odysseus was probably already pointless. With no massacre in the enclaves, Haven could hardly claim that their naval forces had responded only to save off-worlder lives.

Coglin ground his teeth together. That asshole idiot Canning was as stupid as he was blind. He'd jumped the gun by ordering *Sirius* out of orbit before the Stilties actually hit the enclaves. If he'd waited just twenty minutes—just twenty *minutes!*—they'd have known about the Marines and could still have aborted the entire space-borne portion of the operation. But Canning had panicked, and Coglin hadn't known enough about the situation dirtside to argue, even if he'd had the authority to refuse the consul's orders.

So here he was, running from *Fearless*, his very flight confirming Harrington's every suspicion, while every hope for Odysseus went down the crapper behind him.

Yet he had no choice now. Canning had alerted the task force for an execution date only six days away. If the courier

boat had still been hyper-capable, she could have been sent
to quietly stand the task force down, but the courier
couldn't be sent now. Which meant that unless Coglin
reached the rendezvous with *Sirius*, the entire force might
well move in anyway. That had to be prevented, and even if
it hadn't, he couldn't possibly permit Harrington to board
Sirius, for that was the one thing which would absolutely
prove that Haven had been behind the Stilty uprising.
There was no way to hide what his ship truly was from a
naval boarding party.

He queried NavInt's files for the readout on *Fearless*'s
armament. She was one of the last of the old *Courageous*-
class ships, almost eighty T-years old and small for her rate,
by modern standards. But that didn't mean she was senile.
The surviving units of her class had been thoroughly over-
hauled over the years, and they packed a nasty weight of
metal for their age and size. They were light on defense, virtually unarmored and with relatively weak radiation
shielding (for warships), but they mounted a pair of grasers,
two thirty-centimeter lasers, and seven missile tubes in
each broadside. They lacked the magazine capacity for a
sustained missile engagement, but they could throw surprisingly heavy salvos for their size while their ammo
lasted—more than enough to reduce any freighter to glowing vapor. Or it should have been, anyway.

He looked away from the readout and returned his eyes
to the maneuvering display. *Fearless*'s light dot swept after
him, still losing ground but accelerating steadily, and he
glared at it and clenched his fists. *Damn* Canning—and
damn Harrington, as well! Yet even as he cursed her per-
sistence, he felt a certain sorrow deep inside for his
pursuer. That was a remarkable officer back there, one
sharp and quick enough to reduce Haven's carefully laid
plans to humiliating wreckage in less than two Manticoran
months.

And now her very success was going to cost her her life.

* * *

"Coming up on fifty-six minutes, Captain. Velocities will match at one-seven-one-zero-six KPS in thirty-two seconds."

"Thank you, Mr. McKeon." Honor rubbed her fingers over her thigh, wishing her suit gloves let her actually feel the contact. She glanced over at Webster.

"Lieutenant, prepare to record a transmission to *Sirius*."

"Recording, Ma'am," Webster replied.

"Captain Coglin," Honor said slowly and clearly, "this is Commander Honor Harrington of Her Manticoran Majesty's Starship *Fearless*. I request and command you to heave to for examination. Please cut your drive and stand by to receive my boarding party. Harrington out."

"On the chip, Ma'am," Webster said. "Prepared to transmit on your command."

"Thank you." She leaned back in her chair and glanced at the maneuvering display, waiting until the velocity of her ship exactly matched that of *Sirius*, then nodded. "Send it now."

"Transmitting, aye, Ma'am."

Almost seven-point-seven million kilometers separated the two ships as Honor's message raced after *Sirius*. It took the transmission over twenty-five seconds to cross that gulf of space—twenty-five seconds in which *Sirius* moved another four hundred and forty-one thousand kilometers. The total transmission time was over twenty-seven seconds, and Johan Coglin's face went hard as stone as his com officer played it for him. His eyes dropped to the light dot astern of him—the light dot which had stopped losing ground and started, oh so slowly, to overhaul—and he said nothing.

"No response, Ma'am," Webster reported.
Honor bit her lip but made herself nod calmly, as if

she'd expected it. And perhaps she had. Perhaps she simply hadn't wanted to admit to herself that she'd known all along *Sirius* would refuse to stop. She was virtually certain Johan Coglin was no merchant service officer. Or, if he was, he held a reserve naval commission, as well. Haven wouldn't have trusted this operation to a merchant skipper, and a Navy officer would have his orders. He would no more stop than Honor herself would have. Not unless he was made to.

Her mind shied away from the thought of firing into an unarmed freighter, but if Coglin refused to heave to, she would have no choice, and she castigated herself for using all three pinnaces for the Marines' combat drop. She could have held one of the boarding shuttles for that, fleshed it out with her cutters, if she'd had to, and retained at least one pinnace aboard *Fearless*. She had the acceleration and the time to overhaul *Sirius*, and pinnaces were expressly designed, among other things, to put boarding parties aboard ships under way. Her velocity when she overtook the freighter would be barely four thousand KPS greater than her quarry's. Pinnace impeller drives were far weaker than a regular starship's, but if she'd dropped a boatload of Marines or even armed Navy ratings as she overran *Sirius*, its drive would have sufficed to decelerate for a boarding rendezvous.

She hadn't thought clearly enough when she realized what was going on, she told herself. Not that there'd been time to change her plans once *Sirius* began to move even if she had thought it through. Depriving Dame Estelle and Barney Isvarian of a third of Papadapolous's Marines with a full-fledged native war under way would have been criminal. But she should have considered the possibility in advance.

"Mr. Webster," she said.

"Yes, Captain?"

"Record this. 'Captain Coglin, if you refuse to heave to, I will have no option but to fire into your ship. I repeat.

You are requested and required to cut your drive immediately.'"

"Recorded, Captain." Webster's voice was soft with suppressed tension.

"Transmit immediately."

"Transmitting now, Captain."

"Mr. Cardones."

"Yes, Ma'am?"

"Prepare to fire a warning shot. Set it for detonation at least five thousand kilometers clear of *Sirius*."

"Aye, aye, Ma'am. Setting for detonation five-zero-zero-zero kilometers clear of target."

"Thank you."

Honor leaned back in her chair and prayed Coglin would listen to sanity.

". . . fire into your ship. I repeat. You are requested and required to cut your drive immediately."

Coglin grunted as he listened to the message, and his first officer looked up from his own instruments.

"Any reply, Captain?"

"No." Coglin frowned. "She'll fire at least one warning shot first, and the further out we are when she decides to do something more drastic, the better."

"Should we prepare to turn back towards her, Sir?"

"No." Coglin considered for a moment, then nodded to himself. "We'll keep running, but blow the after panels," he ordered.

"Aye, Sir. Blowing after panels now."

"No response, Captain," Webster said very quietly.

"Thank you, Lieutenant. Mr. Cardones, I—" Honor broke off, frowning at her own tactical display as something tumbled away from *Sirius*.

"Captain, I'm picking up—"

"I see it, Mr. Cardones." Honor forced her frown away and looked at McKeon. "Comments, Exec?"

"I don't know, Ma'am." McKeon replayed the tactical readouts and shook his head. "Looks like some kind of debris. I can't think of what it might be, though."

Honor nodded. Whatever it was, it was unpowered and far too small to be any sort of weapon. Could *Sirius* be jettisoning some sort of incriminating cargo?

"Run a plot on it, Mr. Panowski," she said. "We may need to run it down for examination afterwards."

"Aye, aye, Captain." Panowski tapped commands into his panel, feeding the debris' trajectory into his computers.

"Mr. Cardones. Range and time to target?"

"Two-five-point-six-two light-seconds, Ma'am. Flight time one-niner-two-point-eight seconds."

"Very well, Mr. Cardones. Fire warning shot."

"Aye, aye, Ma'am. Missile away."

The missile belched from *Fearless*'s number two missile tube and sped ahead at an acceleration of 417 KPS^2, building on *Fearless*'s own velocity of just over eighteen thousand kilometers per second. It could have accelerated twice as fast, but reducing its acceleration to 42,500 g raised its small impeller's burnout time from one minute to three, which not only gave it three times the maneuvering time but increased its terminal velocity from rest by almost fifty percent.

It raced after *Sirius*, seeming to crawl, even at its speed, as the freighter continued to accelerate. At three minutes, more than ten million kilometers from launch and with a terminal velocity of just over ninety-three thousand KPS, its impeller drive burned out and it went ballistic, overhauling its target on momentum alone.

Captain Coglin watched it come. He'd been certain it would be no more than a warning shot, and its vector quickly proved it was. Even if it hadn't been, he would have had almost thirteen seconds after burnout to take evasive action, during which his ship would move almost two hundred and forty thousand kilometers. His maximum possible vector change was barely over four KPS^2, but the missile was no longer able to follow his maneuvers, and the cumulative effect would have made *Sirius* an impossible target at such a range.

Yet there was no need. He watched the missile race up alongside, five thousand kilometers clear of his ship. It detonated in a savage pinprick of thermonuclear fire, and he grunted.

"Jamming ready, Jamal?"

"Aye, Sir," his tactical officer replied.

"Stand by. I doubt she'll waste another warning shot, but we've got twenty minutes yet before she can reach effective firing range."

"Aye, Sir. Standing by."

Coglin nodded and turned his eyes to the chronometer.

"Nothing, Captain," McKeon said quietly, and Honor nodded. She hadn't really expected there to be any change in *Sirius*'s course. She checked her maneuvering display. Another nineteen minutes before even the longest range shot could reasonably hope to hit the freighter. Tension wrapped itself around her nerves as she realized she was committed, but something else poked at the back of her brain. Something about that debris *Sirius* had jettisoned. If her captain had no intention of halting anyway, why jettison cargo so soon? He had almost a full hour before *Fearless* could physically overhaul him and board. It just didn't make—

She stiffened in her chair, eyes wide. Dear God, perhaps it *did* make sense!

"Mr. McKeon." The exec looked up, and Honor beckoned him over to her chair.

"Yes, Ma'am?"

"That debris from *Sirius*. Could it have been hull plating?"

"*Hull* plating?" McKeon blinked in surprise. "Well, yes, I suppose it could have been, Skipper. But why?"

"We know that ship has a military grade drive and compensator," Honor said very softly. "Suppose it has something *else* military grade aboard? Something that was hidden behind false plating?"

McKeon stared at her, and then his face slowly paled.

"A Q-ship?" he half-whispered.

"ONI says they've got some heavily armed fleet colliers," Honor said in that same, soft voice. "She might be one of them, but we know they used disguised merchant raiders when they went after Trevor's Star and Sheldon." Her eyes held his levelly. "And if that *is* a Q-ship, she could be armed more heavily than we were *before* they modified our armament."

"And she's a lot bigger than we are," McKeon agreed grimly. "That could mean she's got one hell of a lot more magazine space than we do."

"Exactly." Honor drew a deep breath, her thoughts racing like honed shards of ice. "Warn Rafe, then punch up our data base and see what if anything we have on file about the Q-ships we know Haven's used in the past."

"Yes, Ma'am."

"And warn Dominica, too." Honor smiled a cold, bitter smile. "Our damage control officer may have her hands full shortly."

• CHAPTER THIRTY

"I'm afraid we don't have much on their merchant raiders, Skipper." The air-conditioned bridge was cool, but Alistair McKeon scrubbed irritably at a drop of sweat on his forehead as he downloaded what he did have to Honor's secondary tactical display.

"We don't have anything at all to indicate they've modified *Astra*-class ships like *Sirius*, so there's no telling what they did to her, but some of the refugees from Trevor's Star gave ONI pretty good stats on a Q-ship built on a *Trumball*-class hull. She was over a million and a half tons smaller than *Sirius*, but it's all we've got."

Honor nodded, studying the readout and trying not to show her dismay. Smaller than *Sirius* or not, the *Trumball*-class Q-ship had been more powerfully armed than most modern heavy cruisers, and she scrolled through the data till she found the notes on its chase armament. Three missile tubes and a pair of spinal mount lasers fore and aft. If *Sirius*'s chasers had simply been scaled up proportionally, her fire would be twice as heavy as anything with which *Fearless* could reply.

She leaned back in her chair and felt her bridge crew's tension. This was no Fleet maneuver, and even if it had been, there was no brilliant ploy to let them ambush *Sirius*. A stern chase sliced away the options, and *Fearless*'s sole, tiny advantage was that she was a smaller target. Even that was offset by the fact that the open front of her impeller wedge was twice the size of the after edge of *Sirius*'s wedge, and despite her lower acceleration, the "freighter's" greater mass gave her wedge more powerful stress bands and, probably, sidewalls, as well.

She bit her lip while her mind raced, searching for an answer, but her thoughts slithered like a groundcar on ice. Once her overtake velocity was high enough, she could try turning from side to side. At anything above two or three million kilometers, she couldn't turn far enough to completely interpose her sidewalls—not without giving up too much of her acceleration advantage, if she meant to stop the other ship short of the hyper limit—but at least she might deny *Sirius* straight down-the-throat shots by zigzagging across her wake. It wasn't much, but it was absolutely all she could do, and her mouth tried to twist bitterly. All those clever maneuvers at ATC, all that sneaky forethought she'd put into ambushing Admiral D'Orville's flagship, and all she could think of to do now was writhe like a worm in hot ashes to avoid destruction.

She glanced back at McKeon, trying to get behind his eyes and read his thoughts. He was a tac officer by training, too; what did *he* think she should do? Had it occurred to him that all she had to do was break off the pursuit? *Fearless* was the pursuer, not the pursued. If Honor let Coglin go, *Sirius* would simply vanish into hyper space, and *Fearless* would survive.

But it wasn't an option. She might well be wrong about *Sirius*'s mission. She was preparing to throw away her ship and her crew's lives in pursuit of a foe at least five times as powerful as they were when it was entirely possible that foe posed no threat to the Kingdom at all. Yet she couldn't know that, and she *did* know that if Haven was prepared to risk open war to secure Basilisk, Coglin's freighter *might* bring overwhelming firepower into the system before Home Fleet could respond.

Which meant she had no choice at all.

She checked the chronometer again. Sixty-three minutes into the pursuit. She'd come thirty-six and a half million kilometers, and the range was down to seven-point-six million kilometers. Another thirteen-plus minutes until her missiles could reach *Sirius* before burnout. She looked down at the Havenite's light dot and wondered what he was thinking.

"What's the range, Jamal?"

"Two-five-point-three-five light-seconds, Captain."

"Time to hyper limit?"

"Ninety-four-point-six minutes."

"Their overtake speed?"

"Four-five-eight KPS, Sir."

"Missile flight time?"

"Approximately one-eight-nine seconds, Sir."

Coglin nodded and rubbed his lower lip. His missiles would still burn out nine seconds before they reached *Fearless*, and part of him wanted to wait. To conceal the fact that *Sirius* was armed until *Fearless* was close enough that his birds' drives would last all the way to their target. The chance of a hit would be marginally greater if they retained their power to maneuver and follow *Fearless*'s evasion, but only marginally at such a range. And, truth to tell, it probably wouldn't really make a good goddamn's difference. Under power or ballistic, the flight time would be long enough to give the cruiser's point defense plenty of time to engage them.

Then again, he thought sourly, it was possible Harrington already suspected *Sirius* was armed. She certainly seemed to have figured everything *else* out! If she did suspect, holding his fire to try to surprise her would be pointless, yet even if she did suspect the truth, it was unlikely she realized quite how heavily armed the big Q-ship actually was. Coglin had come to possess a lively respect for the Manticoran officer's sheer guts as he watched her actions in Basilisk, but this was entirely too much like a mouse chasing a cat.

He considered his options carefully. The smartest thing to have done, he acknowledged grudgingly, would have been to obey Harrington's order to heave to. If he'd stopped, let the cruiser come into energy range, and *then* blown his panels, he could have wiped her out before she even realized what was happening. But he hadn't, and that mistake left him with a much less attractive range of choices.

Fearless was out-gunned by a factor of ten, whether Harrington knew it or not, but RMN cruisers were tougher than the numbers might suggest. If he turned on her, she would not only have the higher base velocity as they closed, but her higher acceleration and lower mass would make her far more maneuverable than *Sirius* in close combat. The way she'd taken out the courier boat's drive told him Harrington was no shiphandler to take lightly, and if his sidewalls were tougher than hers, her main impeller bands were just as impenetrable as his own. If he got drawn into a close-range dogfight against a more agile opponent, she might just get lucky and score a hit or two in the right place before she died. If she crippled his Warshawski sails, for example, it wouldn't even matter whether or not he could get into hyper. He'd get home eventually, no doubt, but he could never reach the rendezvous in time to stop the task force. Not under impeller drive alone, and especially not when he'd have to detour *around* the Tellerman rather than using it.

On the other hand, holding to his present course pointed his vulnerable stern straight at her, and it was always possible she might pop a missile past his point defense and through the rear of his wedge to score that same lucky hit. The odds were against it, given the angle at which any missile would have to come in, but it was possible. Yet his after firepower was three times as great as *Fearless*'s forward armament, and her hull form meant her forward drive nodes were more exposed than his after ones. Besides, he had missiles to burn, many times the number that could possibly be crammed into a *Courageous*-class cruiser's magazines. That meant he could start firing early and hope he got lucky, whereas Harrington's limited ammunition supply would force her to hold her fire until she could reasonably hope for a hit. And her ship's greater theoretical maneuverability wouldn't help her as long as he held the range open while he smashed at her.

The only drawback was that she might break off once she realized what she was up against, and if she did, he would have to let her go. He hated that. The instant he opened fire, she'd have proof he was armed. That would be bad. Not only would it give away the fact that Haven had armed some of its *Astra*-class ships as commerce raiders, but the fact that a Q-ship had been in the system would certainly be persuasive evidence that Haven had played a major role in fomenting the native unrest on Medusa. And if he opened fire before she did, then *Haven* would be guilty of committing the first overt act of war, as well. On the other hand, her only proof would be her instrument readings, and everyone knew data could be faked up. In effect, it would be Manticore's word against Haven's, and while that might be embarrassing to certain high-ranking jackasses who had planned this entire abortion, it wouldn't necessarily be disastrous to the Republic. More importantly, it wouldn't be disastrous to PMSS *Sirius*, the waiting task force, or Captain Johan Coglin.

No. Obliterating *Fearless* before she could tell Manticore—and the galaxy at large—that *Sirius* had been armed would be the best possible outcome, and if Harrington didn't break off or if an opportunity to destroy her without jeopardizing his primary mission presented itself, that was precisely what he would do. In the meantime, he'd concentrate on discouraging her and keeping her from reporting back in case he *did* get a chance to kill her, but he'd do it while he kept right on running away . . . even if he did have the more powerful ship.

"Inform me when missile flight time drops to one-eight-eight seconds, Jamal," he said. "And stand by to jam on my firing command."

"Yes, Sir."

* * *

The range continued to fall as *Fearless*'s greater acceleration boosted her speed relative to *Sirius*. It wasn't a tremendous advantage at first, not when viewed against their absolute velocities, but it grew steadily, and a strange sort of tranquillity settled over Honor as it climbed.

She was committed. The first shot had yet to be fired—indeed, she didn't yet have any real proof *Sirius* was even armed—but she knew what was going to happen. Not how it was going to come out, perhaps, but how it was going to begin . . . and what she would do about it.

"Mr. Cardones," she said quietly.

"Yes, Ma'am?" Cardones sounded tense, perhaps a bit breathless, and very young, and she smiled at him.

"I imagine we're going to be under fire for some time before we can reply, Guns," she said, and saw his quick flush of pleasure, the slight relaxation of his shoulders, at her choice of title. "I don't want to do anything to suggest we suspect *Sirius* is armed until and unless she actually opens fire—she may let us in closer if she thinks we're unaware of the danger—but be ready to bring up the ECM and point defense the instant something comes our way. Don't wait for my order."

"Aye, aye, Captain."

"Mr. Panowski."

"Yes, Captain?" The navigator sounded much more anxious than Cardones, perhaps because he was a bit older, a bit more aware of his mortality.

"We're committed to a stern chase. Once we close to two million kilometers, however, I will want to zig-zag randomly either side of his base course to interpose our sidewalls as far as possible. Set up your plot accordingly and maintain a running update for Chief Killian."

"Aye, aye, Ma'am." Panowski turned to his console with renewed energy, as if relieved to have something to do. Or, Honor thought, perhaps it was her suggestion that they would *survive* to within two million kilometers. She felt herself smile once more, and to her amazement, it felt completely genuine. She looked up to see McKeon smiling back at her and shook her head at him. He shrugged, his smile suspiciously like a grin for just a moment, and she returned her attention to the chronometer. Sixty-six minutes into the pursuit.

"Missile flight time now one-eight-eight seconds, Sir."

"Very well." Coglin settled himself in his chair and crossed his legs. "Commence jamming and open fire with tubes twenty and twenty-one."

Buzzers snarled aboard *Fearless*.

Honor opened her mouth to snap orders, but Rafael Cardones had the reflexes of the very young. He had already reacted. The tactical board flashed as his ECM sprang from standby to active, and two fifty-ton decoys snapped out of their broadside bays, popping through specially opened portals in *Fearless*'s sidewalls. Tractors moored them to the cruiser, holding the driveless lures on station to cover her flanks, as passive sensors listened to the incoming missiles, seeking the frequencies of their active homing systems, and jammers responded with white noise in an effort to blind them while fire control systems locked on the small, weaving targets.

Cardones started to reach for his counter-missile firing key, then paused and glanced over his shoulder at her.

"Not yet, Mr. Cardones," she said quietly. "Let the plot settle. Fire at a half-million kilometers to catch them as their drives go down."

"Yes, Ma'am."

The youthful tactical officer tapped the command into his computers, then sat tense and still, waiting, and Honor looked at Webster just as the com officer sat back from his own console in disgust. She raised an eyebrow in question, and he nodded.

"We're jammed, Ma'am. We're too far out on the wrong vector for me to hit any of the buckets in Medusa orbit with a laser, and they're blanketing everything else."

"Understood, Mr. Webster." She returned her attention to the tactical display, watching the missiles race towards her, and counted down the range. There! Cardones's counter-missiles streaked away at over ninety thousand gravities, charging to meet them, and she watched the incoming weapons' drives burn out. They coasted onward, suddenly sitting targets, unable to maneuver, and the counter-missiles adjusted their own vectors with finicky precision. They carried no warheads; their small but powerful impeller wedges were their weapons, sweeping the space before them, and she watched *Sirius's* missiles vanish from the display.

But there were two more behind them, and another pair launched as she watched. Cardones tapped keys, bringing his point defense laser clusters on line, and she made herself look calmly and deliberately at her own tactical readouts.

Ten more minutes before she could return fire with any realistic hope of a hit, and her forward magazines held less than sixty missiles. She couldn't waste them hoping for a lucky hit as *Sirius* was doing, and she cursed Lady Sonja Hemphill with cold and silent venom. If Hemphill hadn't butchered her armament, she might have turned long enough to open her broadside and pump a full seven-missile salvo back at *Sirius*, just to test the limits of her point defense. But she no longer had a seven-tube broadside, and even if she'd had one, she didn't have the missiles to support that kind of fire.

She looked back up as Cardones picked off two more missiles and suckered the third pair with his decoys.

Johan Coglin snorted through his nose as his light-speed sensors reported what had happened twenty-five light-seconds behind him. The speed with which *Fearless's* decoys and ECM had sprung into action certainly answered the question of whether or not Harrington had suspected *Sirius* was armed! And they were better than NavInt had projected, he noted. Fleet HQ had been unable to provide him with solid data on Manticoran system capabilities, and it seemed their estimates had been low.

He watched his display, noting the cool professionalism with which *Fearless* had held her counter-fire until she had perfect targets, and filed that away with all his other data on Commander Harrington's capabilities. A dangerous, dangerous woman, he told himself as two of his missiles were decoyed off course and exploded harmlessly outside *Fearless*'s sidewalls. But not dangerous enough to make up for the difference in firepower.

"Go to rapid fire on twenty and twenty-one, Jamal," he said.

Honor winced inwardly as the Q-ship ahead of her began to spit paired missiles at fifteen-second intervals. They came racing astern from the big freighter, and the sheer prodigality of that stream of deadly projectiles was frightening. At that rate of fire, *Sirius* would fire off more missiles than her own forward magazines held in barely seven minutes, and she doubted it was a panic reaction. Coglin had been too cool and deliberate throughout. He knew precisely what he was doing, and that meant he had the magazine capacity to burn through ammo this way.

"Evasion pattern Echo-Seven-One, Chief Killian," she said.

"Aye, aye, Ma'am. Commencing Echo-Seven-One."

Echo-Seven-One was just about the simplest evasion pattern Honor had practiced with Killian, little more than an erratically timed barrel roll along the same vector. It only moved them a few dozen kilometers either side of their base course each time they rolled, but there wasn't a lot else *Fearless* could do to evade *Sirius*'s fire. Not unless Honor wanted to angle far enough off the base track to interpose a sidewall, and that would give away too much of her acceleration advantage over the Q-ship. Yet it wasn't quite as useless as one might have thought, for she'd included Cardones and McKeon in the same drills. Now Cardones retained control of his active defenses, but McKeon took over the passive systems and began a deliberate jingle-jangle between the flanking decoys. *Fearless's* rolling progress swept them in a complete circuit about the cruiser, and the exec shifted their power levels in a carefully timed pattern which gave the impression that the ship's heading was veering from side to side, as well. It wasn't, of course, but, hopefully, *Sirius's* tactical officer would be forced to use up missiles covering the course changes the cruiser *might* be making because he couldn't be certain she wasn't.

Honor certainly hoped he would. The Q-ship's missiles were still burning out before they came in, but the engagement time between salvos was too short for Cardones to wait them out. He had to launch sooner, with poorer solutions and lower counter-missile accelerations to give him more time—and range—on their impeller wedges. The laser clusters began to fire as a handful of *Sirius's* shots got past his counter-missiles, and she looked up at the main visual display as incandescent bursts of brilliance pitted the starfield ahead of her. Unless she missed her guess about the warheads those missiles carried, she had to stop them at least twenty thousand kilometers short of her ship, and they looked frighteningly close.

But none of them were getting closer than a hundred thousand . . . yet.

"Coming up on twenty-four light-seconds' range, Captain," Lieutenant Commander Jamal reported. "We're getting them in closer, but those decoys of theirs are better than anything I've ever seen before."

Coglin grunted acknowledgment without even looking up from his tactical display. Jamal was right. Oh, there was more than a bit of ass-covering in his remark, but *Fearless's*

ECM *was* a hell of a lot better than NavInt had believed possible, and it was making Jamal's job a pain in the ass. It was also using up a lot of ammunition, and he hated to think about how much money each of those missiles cost. He knew damned well some braided idiot was going to climb all over him for the expense, but they cost a lot less than *Sirius* did.

Honor flinched as Cardones finally missed an incoming missile. It darted in to twenty-two thousand kilometers; then it vanished in a brilliant eyeblink, and she bit her lip as her worst fears were confirmed. *Sirius* was using laser warheads, turning each missile into a remotely targeted cluster of bomb-pumped x-ray lasers.

The rate of closure was over seventy-seven thousand KPS, which didn't allow for a lot of accuracy from the fire control that could be squeezed into a warhead, especially not fire control dazzled by McKeon's ECM, but one of the beams picked off her port decoy. McKeon deployed another without orders or comment, but there was no need for comments. *Fearless* carried only three more decoys; when they were gone, her ECM's effectiveness would be more than halved, and she hadn't even gotten into range of her opponent yet.

Captain Coglin's smile was thin as his first warhead got close enough to detonate. There was no sign it had inflicted any damage, but that would come in time.

"Range coming down to twenty-three-point-four light-seconds." Cardones's harsh voice showed the strain of thirteen minutes under fire to which he could not reply, but there was exultation in it, as well.

"Very good, Guns." Honor heard a shadow of matching hunger in her own voice. They'd lost another decoy, but they'd been incredibly lucky so far. *Fearless* was undamaged—and she had the range at last.

"Fire plan Tango on my command," she said.

"Aye, aye, Ma'am. Setting up fire plan Tango." The lieutenant punched commands into his systems. "Fire plan Tango locked."

"Then you may engage, Guns."

"Engaging."

"Incoming fire!" Jamal snapped, and Coglin smothered a curse. Damn it, what did it take to *hit* that frigging ship?! He'd fired over ninety missiles so far; six of them had gotten through *Fearless*'s counter-fire, but the cruiser's ECM was hellishly effective, and not *one* of them had scored a hit! Now Harrington was shooting back, and despite his firepower advantage, he felt a shiver of anxiety. But if the range was low enough to let her fire full-power shots, the same was true for him, he told himself firmly.

"Jesus!"

Coglin's head jerked up as Jamal spat out the incredulous curse. A damage alarm screamed, the bridge twitched, and he whipped around to his display in panic, then relaxed convulsively. The laser warhead had savaged *Sirius*'s flank, ripping number four cargo hold open to space like a huge talon, but number four was empty, and *Sirius* had suffered no casualties. Her capabilities were unimpaired, and he swiveled his cold eyes to the tactical officer.

"Well, Jamal?" he snapped.

"They suckered me, Sir," Jamal admitted. Sweat beaded his forehead, but his fingers were already racing across his panel. "They fired a pair of laser warheads and staggered their launch." He pressed the commit key, locking his new firing orders into the point defense computers, and twisted around to return his captain's look. "The interval was less than half a second, but the lead missile mounted some kind of ECM emitter, Captain. I'm not sure what it was, but it covered the gap between their launch times. The computers thought they were coming in simultaneously, and our fire solution missed the separation, so we nailed the lead bird, but the second one got through. It won't happen again, Sir."

"It better not," Coglin growled. "It's a hell of a long walk home." He glared at his display and bared his teeth. So Commander Harrington wanted to show him a few surprises, did she? Well, he had one for her, as well.

"Go to rapid fire on all after tubes," he said coldly.

"A hit, Ma'am!" Cardones crowed. The gush of escaping air was clear to his sensors, like blood on a wounded animal's flank, and a soft sound of approval rippled across the bridge.

Honor didn't share it. She was watching her other sensors, and there was no change in *Sirius*'s energy profile. She understood Cardones's jubilation perfectly—a similar hit on *Fearless* would have inflicted serious damage—but he'd forgotten how big *Sirius* was. She could suck up far more destruction than *Fearless* could, and—

The tactical display blinked, and Honor inhaled sharply. *Sirius* was no longer firing salvos of two missiles each; she was firing six at a time.

The two ships charged onward, and *Fearless* writhed from side to side under her opponent's steady pounding. Honor felt sweat trickle down her temple and wiped it irritably away, hoping no one had noticed it. She was losing a tiny fraction of her effective acceleration advantage, yet she had no choice; the shallow S-turns she'd added to Killian's wild, erratic rolls weren't much, but she'd lost another decoy. She had only one spare left, now, and the hail of missiles sleeting at her from *Sirius* was inconceivable. A regular capital ship might have fired more in a single salvo, but no warship—not even a superdreadnought—boasted the magazine capacity to keep up such density for so long! She herself was able to fire little more than one salvo a minute; for every missile she sent after *Sirius*, the Q-ship sent *twelve* back into her teeth.

Sweat plastered Cardones's hair to his scalp, and McKeon's face was etched with strain as the two of them battled against that incredible weight of fire and tried to strike back. They were outclassed. She knew it, and every one of her officers knew it as well, but she no longer even thought of breaking off. She *had* to stop that ship, and somehow—

Fearless lurched. The entire ship bucked like a terrified thing, alarms howled, and Killian's head jerked up.

"Forward impellers down!" he barked.

Dominica Santos's face went white in Central Damage Control as the focused blast of X rays slashed into *Fearless*'s bows. Alarms shrieked at her, screaming like damned souls until Lieutenant Manning stabbed the button that killed them.

"Forward hold open to space. Mooring Tractor One's gone. Heavy casualties in Fusion One," Manning snapped. "Oh, Jesus! We've lost Alpha Two, Ma'am!"

"Shit!" Santos pounded on her keyboard, querying the central computers, and swore again as a scarlet-daubed schematic of the forward impeller nodes flashed before her. She studied the damage for just a moment, dark eyes bitter, then hit her intercom key.

"Bridge. Captain," a cool soprano, barely frayed about the edges, said in her ear.

"Skipper, this is Santos. The whole forward drive segment's gone into automatic shutdown. We've lost Number Two Alpha node, and it looks like Beta Three went with it."

"Can you restore them?" There was urgency in the captain's voice, and Santos closed her eyes in furious thought.

"No way, Ma'am," she said through gritted teeth. Her eyes popped back open, and she traced the blinking schematic with a fingertip while her mind raced. Then she nodded to herself. "The main ring's broken at Alpha Two and Beta Three. I think we've got some more damage at Beta Four, but the rest of the ring looks okay," she said. "I can probably route around the wrecked nodes, then run up Beta Two and Four—assuming Four's still with us—to compensate in the impeller wedge, but it's going to take time."

"How long?"

"Ten, maybe fifteen minutes, Ma'am. At best."

"Very well, Dominica. Get on it as quickly as you can."

"I'm on it, Skipper!" Santos unlocked her shock frame and jerked up out of her chair. "Allen, I'm going forward. You're damage control officer till I get back."

"But what about Fusion One?" Manning demanded. "It's open to space and we've lost two-thirds of the forward power watch!"

"Oh, *shit!*" Santos bent over his panel, studying the readouts, and her face tightened. Not only were most of her people dead, but there was already an imbalance in the fusion bottle temperature. She stabbed keys and grunted in relief as the data readouts changed.

"The bottle's holding steady," she said quickly. "Cut the reactor out of the circuit to be safe—Fusion Two can handle the load—and keep an eye on that temperature. If it starts climbing any faster than it is, let me know."

"Yes, Ma'am." Manning bent back over his console, and Santos headed for the hatch at a run.

"Direct hit, Sir!" Lieutenant Commander Jamal announced, and Coglin nodded in sharp approval. At last! And about damned time, too; they'd been firing at *Fearless* for over seventeen minutes.

"Her acceleration's falling, Sir." Jamal's voice was sharp with excitement, and he grinned hugely. "We must have taken out her forward impellers!"

"Good, Jamal. Very good! Now do it again," Coglin growled.

"Aye, aye, Sir!"

* * *

Honor bit her lip so hard she tasted blood, but somehow she kept the sickness from her face. *Fearless* had just dropped to half power, which was bad enough, but the loss of the alpha node could be disaster. Despite the loss in acceleration, she was continuing to close the range on *Sirius*, if more slowly, for her velocity was almost fifteen hundred KPS higher than the Q-ship's. But *Sirius* was now out-accelerating her by almost 1.5 KPS^2. Unless Santos could restore the forward nodes, the range *would* begin to open again in less than seventeen minutes.

Yet that was the least of Honor's worries. She stared into the visual display, watching it sparkle and flash as *Fearless*'s over-strained point defense beat aside the missiles coming in at shorter and shorter intervals, and fought her despair.

Without the alpha node, *Fearless* couldn't reconfigure her forward impellers for Warshawski sail. If *Sirius* broke through into hyper space and reached the Tellerman, she would run away from *Fearless* at over ten times the cruiser's maximum acceleration . . . and Honor couldn't follow her into the wave on impellers alone, anyway.

She had forty-three minutes to destroy the Q-ship; otherwise, it had all been for nothing.

• CHAPTER THIRTY-ONE

Surgeon Lieutenant Montoya didn't even look up as the
sickbay hatch hissed open yet again. Three crewmen stumbled through it, white-faced and pale and carrying another
survivor from Fusion One. They fought to protect their
moaning burden from bumps or jars, but the sudden,
wrenching impact of a second hit threw them off balance
just as they entered sick bay. They staggered against a bulkhead, and the woman they carried shrieked in agony as her
shattered legs took the shock.

Montoya looked up at that. His face was blank of all
expression, driven into non-feeling by the horror about
him, and his eyes were flat as they darted to the injured
woman. Her scream died into a sobbing gasp of hurt, and
he grunted as he identified her condition as one which was
not immediately life-threatening. He lowered his head
once more, flipping it to drop his magnifiers back down off
his forehead as his wet, scarlet-gloved hands moved in the
shattered wreckage which had once been a power room
tech's torso.

A harried sick berth attendant—the only one he could
spare from emergency surgery to triage the wounded—
hurried over to the newcomers, and Montoya's hands flew
as he fought to save the fading life before him.

He failed.

The flat, harsh buzz of the monitors told its tale, and he
stepped back from the corpse, already stripping off his
gloves to re-glove for the next. A fresh, limp body was lifted
into position, a woman who'd lost one arm already and was
about to lose another, and Montoya moved like a machine

as he jammed his hands into the fresh gloves and bent over the table once more. He leaned forward into its sterile field with a face of stone . . . and the hatch hissed open behind him yet again.

"Not there—*here!*" Dominica Santos snapped. "Get your ass over here and *heave*, goddamn it!"

Huge, blue-white sparks spat and glared about her, silent in the vacuum of the shattered drive compartment, and Boatswain MacBride grabbed one of her suited repair party and literally dragged the man into position.

"Get your back into it, Porter!" the bosun snarled at the electronicist, and stepped up close beside him.

There was neither time nor space for them to reach into the conduit with tools, and the two of them wrapped their gauntleted hands about the half-molten, fire-fountaining cable run. Bright, savage discharges rippled up their arms and haloed their shoulders, and the harsh, straining grunt of their effort echoed over Santos's suit com. One end of the cable harness ripped loose, the sparks died, and Santos stepped in with a laser cutter. She stood ankle-deep in burned out circuit boards and bits of bulkhead blown away by battle damage or chopped frantically aside by her damage control party. Wreckage slid and shifted about her feet, and she gasped in triumph as she got the cutter in and slashed away the end of the damaged cable.

MacBride and Porter staggered backward, crashing into the compartment's rear bulkhead, and the engineer waved savagely at the work party behind her.

"Get that replacement cable in here now. *Move*, damn you!"

Johan Coglin flinched involuntarily as yet another of *Fearless's* missiles punched through Jamal's defenses. It detonated, and the deadly rapiers of its clustered lasers clawed at his ship. One of them hit, punching through the radiation shielding inside the wedge as if it were tissue paper, and a fresh boil of atmosphere gushed from *Sirius's* side.

"Heavy casualties in after control!" a voice shouted. "We've lost Damage Control Three, Sir!"

Coglin spat a curse and glared at his tactical display. Damn it, what was keeping that fucking ship *alive*?! He'd hit her at least twice, possibly three times, and she was still back there—lamed, perhaps, out-gunned and out-massed and bleeding air, but there, and she was still hitting *him*. Her salvos were far smaller than his, yet she was getting almost as many hits in as he was, for her missiles were incredibly hard targets for point defense. The Manticoran Navy's electronic missile penetration-aids were at least as much better than estimated as their defensive ECM was. He knew that, and it made him feel absolutely no better about his damage and casualties. He jerked around toward Jamal with fiery eyes and opened his mouth—then froze as one of the tactical officer's warheads detonated less than a thousand kilometers from *Fearless's* prow.

The universe went mad. Stilettos of X-ray radiation stabbed deep into *Fearless's* lightly-armored hull, breaching compartments, killing her people, clawing and rending at her bulkheads and frame members. And then, a sliver of a second later, the light cruiser smashed into the blast front of the warhead itself.

It was below her as she drove forward, not the direct frontal collision from which nothing could have saved her, but a savage eruption of plasma spumed up beneath her belly through the vacuum of space. Generators howled in protest as the massive shock front of radiation and particles smashed at her shielding like a flail, but they held— barely—and *Fearless* heaved like a goaded horse as she shot the rapids of destruction.

Dominica Santos screamed as she was hurled from her feet. She wasn't alone, and her com was a cacophony of other screams and cries as her work party was hurled about the compartment like so many discarded dolls. The concussion slammed her into and through a half-fused bank of circuit-breakers, scattering it in an explosion of debris. She bounced back, arms windmilling in a wild clutch for any anchorage, and a terrible, bubbling shriek filled her ears. She caught the heat-slagged edge where cutters had slashed away a buckled access panel, jerking her body to a brutal halt, and swallowed vomit as she saw electronicist 2/c Porter clawing at the spearlike hull fragment projecting from the belly of his suit. The wreckage thrust out from the bulkhead behind him, impaling him, and he writhed upon that dreadful spike like a soul in hell while his scream went on and on and on, even as blood and internal organs began to bubble and boil from the wound. Globules of blood and more horrible things sprayed out into the vacuum, and then, mercifully, the 'tronicist's ghastly sounds sobbed into silence and his arms went slack. He hung on the wreckage, the inside of his helmet opaque with the blood that had sprayed from his mouth and nostrils, and Santos stared at him, petrified by shock and nausea, unable to make herself look away.

"Come on, you people!" Sally MacBride's voice cracked like a whip. "Move your asses—*now!*"

Dominica Santos dragged herself up out of her pit of horror and stumbled back towards the gutted drive circuits.

Honor clutched at her command chair, head snapping savagely back despite her shock frame as *Fearless* leapt about her. Fresh damage signals shrilled, and she shook her head, fighting off the blurred vision and confusion of concussion.

She made herself look at her battle board. At least a dozen compartments were open to space now, and Lieutenant Webster smashed both fists against his own console.

"Direct hit on the com section, Ma'am," he reported in a voice of raw, dull anguish. He turned to look at her, his face shocked and white, and tears gleamed in his eyes. "It's gone. Dear God, half my people went with it, too."

"Understood, Lieutenant." The sound of her own voice startled her. It was too calm, too detached. She was murdering her own ship by matching it against *Sirius*. She knew she was . . . just as she knew she wouldn't—couldn't—break off. She wanted to say something else, to share Webster's pain and loss, but the words wouldn't come, and she turned back towards Cardones just as he punched his firing key again.

A missile spat from *Fearless*, but only one, and a warning buzzer snarled. Cardones jerked at the sound and hit a system-test button. Then his shoulders clenched, and he turned towards his captain.

"Missile One is down, Ma'am. We're down to one tube."

Honor stabbed her intercom key. "Damage Control, this is the captain. What's the status of Missile One?" she snapped.

"Sorry, Ma'am." Lieutenant Manning's voice was slurred and indistinct. "Two of my people are dead down here. We've got damage reports from all over the ship, and—" The acting damage control officer paused, and his voice strengthened as he dragged himself back together. "Sorry. What did you say, Ma'am?"

"Missile One. What's the status of Missile One?"

"Gone, Ma'am. We've got a four-meter hole in the starboard bow. The whole compartment's gone—and its crew."

"Understood." Honor released her key and looked back at Cardones. "Continue the engagement with Missile Two, Guns," she said.

"That last one must have hurt her bad, Sir," Lieutenant Commander Jamal said, and Coglin grinned back at him in triumph. The range was down to under six million kilometers, and the vaporized alloy and atmosphere streaming back from *Fearless*'s bow was plain on their sensors. More than that, the cruiser was firing only single-missile salvos. Now if only—

Sirius shuddered as another Manticoran missile detonated just astern of her, and crimson damage signals flashed on Coglin's panel.

"Spinal Four gone, Sir!" someone reported. "We've lost the secondary fire control sensors, too. Primaries unaffected."

Coglin spat out a savage curse. "Hit that fucker again, Jamal!" he snarled.

Dominica Santos waved MacBride aside and slammed the last replacement box into place. The green ready light glowed, and she switched back to Central Damage Control's net.

"We're back up, Al!" she snapped.

"Understood, Ma'am. I'm initiating circuit tes—"

"Fuck that!" Santos barked. "There's no time for tests. Just tell the Captain we're in and give these impellers juice *now!*"

Honor's eyes blazed like hot, brown steel as *Fearless's* acceleration surged suddenly back up. The maimed cruiser gathered herself, driving forward, and she sensed her ship's determination like her own. Numbers flickered upward on her maneuvering plot, and her lips drew back in a hungry snarl as Killian read them off.

"Five hundred . . . five-zero-three . . . five-zero-six . . . five-zero-eight gravities, Captain!" the helmsman announced. "Steady at five-zero-eight."

"Excellent, Chief Killian! Go to Delta-Niner-Six."

"Aye, aye, Ma'am. Going to Delta-Niner-Six."

"Their acceleration's coming back up, Captain," Jamal reported tensely. "It doesn't seem— No, Sir, it's definitely not going all the way back up. It's leveling off."

"What is it?" Coglin snapped.

"I make it approximately five-oh-eight gees, Sir. Call it five KPS squared. And she's starting to make some real evasion maneuvers."

"Shit!" Coglin caught himself before he punched the arm of his chair again, then glared at the weaving, dodging dot on his display. Goddamn it to hell, what did it take to *stop* that ship?!

Lieutenant Commander Santos headed aft, running back towards Central Damage Control. She didn't know what else had happened while she was up forward, but she knew it had been bad, and—

A fresh, brutal blow threw her from her feet, and she skidded down the passageway on her belly.

The warhead detonated at fifteen hundred kilometers, and twenty-five separate beams of energy stabbed out from its heart.

Two of them hit *Fearless*.

One struck almost amidships, ripping inward through half a dozen compartments. Nineteen men and women in its path died instantly as it gutted forward life support, slashed through the forward crew mess, and reduced two of the cruiser's port energy torpedo launchers to wreckage, but it didn't stop there. It sliced deep, just missing the combat information center, and ripped its ghastly way clear to the bridge itself.

Plating shattered, and Honor slammed her helmet shut as air screamed out through the gaping hole. Her suit whuffed tight, protecting her against vacuum, but some of her people were less lucky. Lieutenant Panowski never even had time to scream; the hit blasted huge chunks of bulkhead into splinters, and a flying axe of steel decapitated him in a fountain of gore, then carried on to smash his entire panel to spark-spewing ruin. Two of his yeomen died almost as quickly, and Chief Braun had been out of his chair, unprotected by his shock frame. He flew through the thinning air and slammed into a bulkhead, stunned and unable to move. He died in a flood of aspirated blood before anyone could reach him to close his helmet for him.

Mercedes Brigham's suit was daubed and streaked with scarlet where Panowski's blood had sprayed across her. She'd been looking at the astrogator when he died, and more of his blood dripped down her face where it had splashed before she closed her own helmet. She couldn't even wipe it, and she spat to clear it from her mouth as she brought her own computers on line to replace Panowski's.

Honor swept her gaze about the bridge. Sparks and smoke streamed up into the near vacuum as Panowski's splintered command station consumed itself, and her mouth tightened as she saw the way Webster clutched at his chest through his suit. The com officer hunched forward in his chair, his face gray, and blood bubbled at his nostrils.

"Damage control to the bridge! Corpsman to the bridge!" she barked, and made herself look away from her injured officer.

The second beam hit further forward, and Lieutenant Allen Manning stared at his console in horror as a lurid light began to flash. He unlocked his shock frame and shoved a corpse which once had been a friend from the chair beside him to clear an emergency panel, and his hands darted across it.

Nothing happened. The light continued to flash, and a harsh, ominous audio signal joined it. He hammered an alternate command sequence into the console, then tried still a third, and the light only flashed brighter still.

"Commander Santos!" he gasped into his intercom. There was no answer. "Commander Santos, this is Manning! Please respond!"

"W-what is it, Allen?" The senior engineer sounded shaken and woozy, but Manning almost wept when he heard her voice.

"Fusion One, Ma'am! The mag bottle's fluctuating and I can't shut down from here—something's cut the circuits!"

"Oh, Jesus!" Santos's voice was no longer blurred. It was sharp and frightened. "I'm on my way. Get forward and join me!"

"But, Commander, I can't leave Cen—"

"Goddamn it, Allen, move! Put Stevens on it!"

"I *can't*, Ma'am," Manning said wildly, then clutched at his self-control. "Stevens is dead, and Rierson can't leave Fusion Two. I'm all alone—there's no one *left* to take over down here!"

"Then tell the Skipper to fucking well *get* you someone," Santos snarled. "I need you up there right goddamned now!"

"Yes, Ma'am!"

Honor paled as Manning's frantic message registered. *Fearless* could move and fight on a single reactor. She only had two for the security of redundancy, and that was also why they were at opposite ends of the hull, but if that mag bottle went down—

"Understood, Manning. Go. I'll get somebody down there to replace you."

Manning didn't waste time replying, and she raised her head to scan her bridge, trying to think who she could send. There was only one choice, she realized with a sudden, icy calm.

"Mr. McKeon!"

"Yes, Skipper?" He made it a question, but she saw in his eyes that he already knew.

"You're the only one I've got with the experience for it. Slave your ECM panel to my remotes and get down there."

He wanted to argue, to protest. She read it in his face, but he didn't.

"Aye, aye, Ma'am." He unlocked his shock frame and dashed for the lift, and Honor ran a quick check of the ECM. She was down to her last two decoys, but the programs McKeon had set up seemed to be working well. She started to key in a modification, then stopped as Cardones spoke without looking away from his console.

"Skipper, we're down to twelve birds for Missile Two, and I'm out of laser heads."

"What about Missile One's magazine?"

"Twenty-three rounds left, including eleven laser heads, but the transfer tube's been breached."

"Engage with standard nukes," she told him, and plugged her suit com into the damage control net.

"Bosun, this is the Captain. Where are you?"

"Just finishing a bulkhead patch at frame forty, Ma'am," MacBride replied instantly.

"Take a work party and get forward. I need you to shift missiles from Missile One to Missile Two and the transfer tube is down. Move the laser heads first."

"Aye, aye, Ma'am. I'm on it," MacBride said flatly.

"Thank you, Bosun," Honor said, and MacBride's eyebrows rose. She hadn't even protested the impossibility of the assignment, for she was beyond protest. She was a professional, and she knew survival was no longer a realistic option. Yet the Captain's voice had been almost absently courteous despite the the stress she had to be feeling.

The bosun drew a deep breath and glared at the people around her. "You heard the Old Lady!" she barked. "Harkness, Lowell—get me a dozen Mark Nine counter-grav collars. Yountz, I need drag lines. Find me a spool of number two wire and a cutter. Jeffries, you and Mathison get forward and check the tractor grab in Passage Nineteen. I want to know if—"

She went on spitting orders, goading her subordinates into action, and far behind her on *Fearless*'s bridge, Honor Harrington returned her attention to her ECM just as a fresh salvo of missiles came streaking in.

Johan Coglin peered at his display in disbelief. He'd pounded *Fearless* for almost thirty minutes, hit her at least half a dozen times, and she was *still* after him. Not only after him, but already making up the velocity advantage she'd lost while her forward impellers were down! Goddamn it, why couldn't Harrington just leave him the hell alone? All he wanted was to get out of here and tell the task force *not* to come!

Another missile exploded just short of the ship, and he winced as the huge fireball blossomed astern. They must be out of laser heads. That had been a standard megaton-range warhead, and that could be very, very bad news. The standard nukes weren't stand-off weapons; they had to get in much closer to inflict damage, which gave the laser clusters more time to kill them, but a near-miss from one of those monsters could wreak untold havoc.

Sweat beaded his forehead, and he wiped at it irritably. His ship was far more powerful than Harrington's. He'd reduced her cruiser to a wreck—she had to be some kind of wizard just to hold it together, much less go on shooting at him! He longed to turn on her, finish her off, and get the hell away to safety, but all the old arguments against a close-range action remained.

Or did they?

He cocked his head, eyes narrowed as he rubbed his chin in speculation. She was still on his tail, yes, but she was firing only single missiles at a time, even if she was firing at shorter intervals, and the fact that she was using standard nukes was a clear sign her forward magazines were running low. Which didn't make any sense at all. A *Courageous*-class ship had a seven-tube broadside, for God's sake, and her overtake velocity was over eleven hundred KPS. Why wasn't she veering to bring those tubes to bear? She could zig-zag back and forth across his stern pouring in broadsides as she crossed, and hit him with *more* missiles than he was firing at her, damn it!

Unless . . . Unless he'd hurt her even worse than he knew? Maybe *that* was why she was still charging straight up his wake. Could his hits have gone in further aft than he'd thought? Been spread over a wider area and wrecked her broadside armament or fire control? It was a possibility. Perhaps even a probability, given the way her forward fire had dropped. If she *hadn't* lost most of her broadside firepower, then she damned well ought to be using it instead of lunging doggedly forward through his missiles like a punch-drunk fighter while he pounded her!

And if that was true, then he might—

Sirius heaved like a shipwrecked galleon.

"*Yes!*" Rafael Cardones screamed, and Honor felt her own heart leap as the savage boil of light erupted just off the Q-ship's starboard quarter.

"Heavy damage aft. Fourteen dead in Missile Two-Five. No contact at all with Two-Four or Two-Six. Sir, we've lost a beta node; our acceleration is dropping."

Lieutenant Commander Jamal was white-faced, his voice flat with a strained, unnatural calm, and Coglin stared at him in disbelief. *Half* their after launchers gone to a single hit? Harrington wasn't a wizard—she was a goddamned *demon!*

He cocked his head, overcome by an absurd desire to giggle—

The two ships raced onward, ripping at one another with thermonuclear fire, shedding debris, streaming atmosphere like trails of blood. The big freighter began to twist and writhe in ever more violent evasion as her tiny, battered foe clung stubbornly to her heels. *Sirius* was reduced to three-missile salvos, and *Fearless* was overhauling more and more quickly.

Lieutenant Montoya made himself stand back, shutting his ears to the groans and sobs about him while his sick berth attendants cut Lieutenant Webster out of his suit. He couldn't look at the mass of wounded. The hatch was locked open, and burned and broken bodies spilled out of his cramped sickbay's bunks. They were lying in the passages now, covering the decks, and more and more of them were unprotected even by the transparent tents of emergency environmental slips. His mind shuddered away from the thought of what would happen if sickbay lost pressure now, and he stepped closer to the table as Webster's suit was stripped away. One of his assistants ran a sterilizer/depilator over the lieutenant's chest while the other looked up from her monitors to meet Montoya's eyes.

"Not good, Sir. We've got at least two ribs in his left lung. It's completely collapsed, and it looks like we may have splinter damage to his heart, too."

Montoya nodded grimly and reached for a scalpel.

"All right—*heave!*"

Sally MacBride bent her own back to the struggle, and the seventy-ton missile floated across the passage. The overhead tractor rails were out, and the passage was open to space. Her vac-suited people grunted and strained, man-handling the ten-meter-long projectile, leaning their weight desperately against it to point it down the shaft to Missile Two's magazine. The counter-grav collars reduced its *weight* to zero, but they couldn't do anything about momentum and inertia.

MacBride's own feet scrabbled against the deck as she leaned back against the drag wire, hauling the nose around by pure, brute force while Horace Harkness threw himself against it from the other side, and the long, lethal shape began to pivot toward her.

Another savage concussion shook the ship, smashing the boat bay to wreckage, and the missile twisted like a malevolent beast. It broke away from its handlers, swinging like a huge, enraged tusk, and MacBride hurled herself desperately to one side.

She almost got clear. Almost. Seventy tons of mass slammed into her, crushing her right thigh and pelvis against the bulkhead like a sledgehammer on an anvil, and she shrieked her agony into her com as the missile rolled and ground against her.

Then Harkness was there. He stood on the missile, shoulders braced against the bulkhead, heels jammed hard into a recessed service panel, and his explosive grunt of strain could be heard even through MacBride's screams. Veins stood out like cables on his temples as his back straightened with a lunging, convulsive snap, forcing the floating missile off her, and the bosun fell to the deck in a broken, moaning heap.

Her work party rushed forward, bending over her, and Harkness punched and slapped them away.

"Get back on those frigging drag lines!" the petty officer snarled. "We need this bird moved!"

The ratings staggered back, clutched numbly at wires, and heaved, and Harkness himself crouched over the bosun. Her face was white, her cheekbones standing out like knobs of ivory, but her eyes were open and her teeth were locked in a rictus of agony against her screams. He pressed her med panel, flooding her system with pain-killers, and she shuddered in relief while blood ran down her chin where her teeth had bitten through her lip. He patted her shoulder awkwardly.

"Corpsman to Missile Two!" he grated, and blinked away furious tears even as he hurled himself back into the battle with the missile.

Dominica Santos skidded to a halt just inside the forward reactor compartment, and her eyes widened. The damage that had cut Damage Central's links to Fusion One was appallingly evident. A jagged, meter-wide rent had been slashed through the primary control systems from a hit on the far side of the hull, ripping the compartment's inboard bulkhead like a saw-toothed knife. Only one of her power gang was still alive, and she was trapped. The woman's hands thrust weakly at the buckled frame member pinning her to the deck, and her helmeted head rolled towards Santos.

"How bad are you hurt, Earnhardt?" Santos was already reaching for the backup computers as she spoke.

"I'm not hurt at all, damn it!" Earnhardt snapped. She sounded far more angry than afraid. "I just can't get out from under this thing!"

"Well, sit tight, and I'll do what I can in a minute," Santos said absently, her gloved fingers already feeding commands into the computers. "I've got other things on my mind right now."

"Fucking A," Earnhardt agreed hoarsely, and Santos managed a strained grin.

It vanished an instant later as scarlet damage codes flashed before her. Her face tightened. Whatever had ripped through the primary systems must have sent a power surge through the backups. Half her command files were scrambled or completely wiped.

Someone stepped up beside her, and she turned her head. It was Manning. Her assistant stared at her display and pursed his lips in silent dismay.

"Jesus, Commander! What do we do now?"

Santos grunted a smothered curse and slapped another switch. Nothing happened, and she darted a frightened glance at the reactor itself. She knew it had to be her imagination, but she almost believed she could *feel* the containment field pulsing.

"We've lost most of the bottle software—I don't know how it's holding together now," she said rapidly, already ripping off access panels. "And we've lost *all* the hydrogen feed files. The bastard's running away on us."

Manning nodded silently, jerking off other panels at her side.

"If the plasma hits overload levels with an unstable bottle—" Santos broke off and flung herself on her belly, peering into the guts of the console, and grunted.

"We've got maybe five minutes before this thing blows, and I don't dare screw around with the mag governors."

"Cut the feed?" Manning said tautly.

"All we can do, but I'm going to have to cross-wire the damned thing by hand. I lost my cutter when we took this hit. Get me another, and hunt up four—no, five—alpha-seven jump harnesses. Fast!"

"Yes, Ma'am." Manning leapt away, and Santos turned her head without rising. Her eyes rested for just a moment on a big, red switch on the bulkhead beside her, and then she jerked them away.

"Bridge, Missile Two." The voice on the intercom was harsh with exhaustion. "We've got two laser heads shifted. They're numbers five and six on your feed queue. I'm working on shifting number three now."

"Missile Two, this is the Captain. Where's the bosun?" Honor asked quickly.

"On her way to sickbay, Skipper. This is Harkness. I guess I'm in charge now."

"Understood. Get that third missile shifted as quickly as possible, PO."

"We're on it, Ma'am."

Even as Honor spoke, Cardones's hands flashed across his console, reprioritizing his loading schedule. Fifteen seconds later, a fresh laser warhead went scorching out of his single remaining tube.

Sirius's bridge was a tiny pocket of hell. Smoke billowed, circuit boards popped and sizzled and spat actinic fury, and Johan Coglin retched as the smoke from burning insulation filled his lungs. He heard Jamal's agonized, hacking coughs as he fought to retain tactical control, and someone was screaming in pain.

"We've lost—lost—" Jamal broke off in another tortured spasm of coughing, then slammed his helmet. Coglin followed his example, rasping for breath as his suit scrubbers attacked the sinus-tearing smoke, and Jamal's voice came over his com.

"We've lost another beta node, Sir. And—" Coglin

peered through the smoke, watching the tactical officer work on his console. Then Jamal cursed. "Point defense is hurt bad, Captain. I've lost four laser clusters and half my phased radar array."

Coglin swore viciously. With two beta nodes gone, his maximum acceleration was going to be reduced by over nine percent—he'd be lucky to pull three hundred and eighty gees. He still had his alpha nodes, which meant he still had Warshawski capability, but how long was that going to last? Especially with half his last-ditch laser clusters gone?

"Missile fire control?" he demanded harshly.

"Still functional. And my ECM suite's still up—for what it's worth," Jamal added bitterly.

"Range?"

"Coming up on one-point-five million kilometers, Sir."

Coglin nodded to himself, his eyes bitter. With the open front of *Fearless*'s wedge toward him and no sidewalls to interdict, effective laser range was right on a million kilometers, but he'd lost one of his own spinal lasers, and the back of his wedge was as open as the front of the cruiser's. If *Fearless* got into energy range. . . .

Energy range, hell! His point defense was down to less than half efficiency! If Harrington realized it, turned and hit him with a multiple-missile salvo—

He bit off another curse. This couldn't be happening to him! It wasn't possible for a single, over-aged, under-sized light cruiser to *do* this to him!

"I think he's in trouble, Guns," Honor said, staring at the readouts from her ECM suite's passive sensors. "I think you just took out most of his missile tracking capability."

"I hope so, Skipper," Cardones said hoarsely, "because I'm down to just three more birds, and—"

"Got it!" Santos shouted as she bridged the last circuit and started to slide out from under the console. Now all she had to do was cut the fuel feed and—

Fearless twisted and leapt. The savage motion picked the engineer up and smashed her down. The side of her helmet crashed against the deck, and she grunted in shock, stunned for just an instant.

It was an instant she didn't have. She blinked back into focus, and her mouth went desert dry. She couldn't hear the alarm in Fusion One's vacuum, but she could see the numbers flashing blood-red on the panel. The mag bottle was going, counting down with lightning speed, and there was no longer time to kill the plasma flow.

She rolled across the deck, trying not to think, knowing what she had to do, and drove her hand toward the scarlet bulkhead switch.

"Jesus Christ, we *got* her!" Jamal screamed. "We *nailed* the bitch!"

The emergency jettisoning charges hurled the entire side of Fusion One out into space a microsecond before the ejection charges blew the reactor after it. There had to be a delay, be it ever so tiny, lest a faltering mag bottle be smashed against an intact bulkhead and liberate its plasma inside the ship. But small as that delay was, it was almost too long.

Dominica Santos, Allen Manning, and Angela Earnhardt died instantly. The dying containment field failed completely just as the reactor housing blew through the opening, and the terrible fury of a star's heart erupted back into the compartment as well as out. Fusion One vanished, along with seven hundred square meters of *Fearless*'s outer hull, Missile Two, Laser Three, Point Defense One, Rad Shield One, all of her forward fire control sensors, and her forward port sidewall generators, and forty-two of *Fearless*'s surviving crewmen died with them. A streamer of pure energy gushed out of the dreadful wound, and the light cruiser heaved bodily up to starboard in maddened response.

* * *

Honor clung to her command chair, and her ship's agony whiplashed through her own flesh. Her ECM panel went down. The main tactical display locked as the forward sensors died. Chief Killian's shock frame broke, and the coxswain flew forward over his console. He thudded into a bulkhead and slid limply down it, and every damage sensor in the ship seemed to blaze in scarlet fury before her eyes.

She slammed the release on her own shock frame and lunged towards the helm.

"Look at that, Sir!" Jamal exulted.

"I see it." Coglin fought his own exultation, but it was hard. *Fearless* staggered sideways and her fire died suddenly. He didn't know exactly what Jamal had hit, but whatever it was had gutted the cruiser at last.

Yet she wasn't dead. Her wedge was weakened and fluttering, but it was still up, and even as he watched someone was bringing her back under command. He stared at the crippled cruiser, and something hot and primitive boiled deep within him. He could run now. But *Fearless* was still alive. Not only alive, but battered into a bloody, broken wreck. If he left her behind, the Royal Manticoran Navy would have far more than instrument data to prove *Sirius* had been armed.

He sensed the danger of his own emotions and tried to fight his way through them. What had happened out here was an act of war—there were no two ways to look at that—and Haven had fired the first shot. But no one knew that except *Sirius* and *Fearless*, and *Fearless* was helpless behind him.

And dead men, he thought, told no tales.

He told himself he had to consider all the options, had to evaluate and decide coldly and calmly, and he knew it was a lie. He'd suffered too much at that ship's hands to think calmly.

"Bring us about, Mr. Jamal," he said harshly.

". . . nothing left at all in the port broadside," Alistair McKeon's hoarse voice reported from Central Damage Control, "and the port sidewall's down clear back to Frame Two Hundred. We've lost an energy torpedo and Number Two Laser out of the starboard broadside, but at least the starboard sidewall is still up."

"And the drive?" Honor demanded.

"Still up, but not for long, Ma'am. The entire port impeller ring's unbalanced forward. I don't think I can hold it another fifteen minutes."

Honor stared around her bridge, seeing the exhaustion, tasting the fear. Her ship was dying about her, and it was her fault. She'd brought them all to this by refusing to break off, by not being smarter and quicker.

"*Sirius* is turning, Skipper." Rafael Cardones sat awkwardly hunched to one side, favoring obviously broken ribs, but he was still watching what was left of his sensor readouts. "She's coming back at us!"

Honor's eyes whipped down to the helmsman's maneuvering display in front of her. It wasn't as detailed as a proper tactical display, but it was still live, and she saw the angry red dot of the Q-ship swinging to decelerate savagely towards her. Coglin was coming back to make certain.

"Skipper, if you bring us hard to port, I can get off a few shots from our starboard missile tube," Cardones said urgently, but Honor shook her head.

"No."

"But, Skipper—!"

"We're not going to do a thing, Rafe," she said flatly. Cardones whipped around to stare at her in disbelief, and she smiled at him, her eyes like brown flint. "Not a thing except let her close . . . and bring up the grav lance," she said very, very softly.

Johan Coglin listened to the thunder of his pulse as his

ship braked with all her power. *Fearless* limped slowly and painfully to port, turning her starboard side toward him, but her acceleration was a crawl. Even with *Sirius*'s node damage, it would take her less than five minutes to reach pointblank range.

Jamal sat stiff and silent at Tactical, poised over his missile defense panel. A small sigh of relief had escaped him as *Sirius*'s turn brought his undamaged forward sensors to bear, but he obviously dreaded what *Fearless*'s broadside might do to him.

Only it wasn't doing a thing, and Coglin felt a bubble of vengeful laughter tearing at the back of his throat. He'd been right! The cruiser's armament must have been gutted—no captain would pass up the opportunity to fire his full broadside down the throat of a wide open impeller wedge!

He completed his turn, swinging the vulnerable front of his wedge away from *Fearless*, closing at an oblique angle and presenting his port broadside to her. The range fell with flashing speed, and his smile was ugly.

"Range five hundred thousand," Cardones said tautly. "Closing at three-three-nine-two KPS."

Honor nodded and eased the helm another degree to port. Her crippled ship turned like a dying shark, and *Sirius* plunged towards her.

"Four-eight-five thousand." Cardones's voice was harsh. "Four-seven-five. Four-six-zero. Four-four-five. Rate of closure now four-zero-two-one KPS. Time to energy range one-one-point-nine seconds. Time to grav lance eight-two-point-six-five seconds."

"Stand by grav lance." Honor's voice was quiet, and her mind raced. Would he come all the way in? Or would he stand off? He had less than a minute and a half to make his mind up, and if no fire came at him. . . .

She sat very still at the helm, gloved right hand poised lightly on the stick, and watched the range fall.

* * *

"Give her a broadside at four hundred thousand," Coglin said softly. "Let's see how she likes that."

"Four-zero-zero thous—"
Even as Cardones spoke, Honor whipped *Fearless* up on her side.

"Shit!"
Coglin slammed a fist into his chair arm as the limping cruiser spun suddenly. Damn it, didn't Harrington know when it was over?! She was done. All she could do was stretch out the agony, but she didn't seem to know it, and her turn presented her impenetrable belly stress band even as he fired, as if she'd read his mind. He'd more than half expected it, but that didn't make him any happier to see it.

Sirius's side flashed with the fury of a Fleet battlecruiser, and Honor had cut her maneuver just a fraction of a second too late. *Fearless*'s belly bands came up in time to intercept the missiles, but two of the lasers got through. The sidewall bent and attenuated them, but not enough, and the cruiser lurched as they ripped deep into her hull and smashed her single, unfired missile tube and two of her energy torpedoes.

Yet she survived . . . and so did her grav lance.

"All right, goddamn it," Coglin snarled. "Take us in, Jamal!"
"Aye, aye, Sir."

Honor watched the chronometer tick down, and her mind was cold and clear, accepting no possibility of failure. The sensors she had left couldn't track *Sirius* clearly through her belly stress band, and her current vector gave the Q-ship four options: retreat and break off the engagement, roll up on her own side relative to *Fearless* and shoot "down" through the starboard sidewall as she overflew the cruiser, cross her bow, or cross her stern. She might do any of them, but Honor was betting her ship—and her life—that Coglin would cross her bows. It was the classic maneuver, the one any naval officer instinctively sought—and he knew her forward armament had been destroyed.

But if he was going to do that, then he ought to be coming into position . . . just . . . about . . . *now!*

She slammed the helm over, wrenching her ship still further round to port and rolling to swing the broadside she'd denied *Sirius* back towards her with blinding speed.

Lieutenant Commander Jamal blinked. It was only for an instant, only the briefest hesitation. There was no logical reason for *Fearless* to suddenly swing back, and for no more than a heartbeat, he couldn't quite believe she had.

And in that heartbeat, Rafael Cardones targeted his grav lance and fired.

Sirius staggered. Captain Coglin jerked upright in his chair, his eyes wide, face shocked in disbelief as his sidewall went down, and then *Fearless*'s four surviving energy torpedo launchers went to rapid, continuous fire.

The armed merchant raider *Sirius* disappeared forever in a devastating boil of light and fury.

• CHAPTER THIRTY-TWO

Captain Honor Harrington, Royal Manticoran Navy, stood once more in a spacedock gallery aboard HMSS *Hephaestus*. Her hands were clasped behind her, and Nimitz sat very tall and straight on her shoulder. One hand-paw rested lightly atop her beret—the plain, back beret of the RMN undress uniform—and his green eyes were dark mirrors of her emotions as she stared through the thick, armored plastic.

HMS *Fearless* floated beyond the window, her hull broken and shattered, like a toy stepped on by some careless child. The gaping hole where Dominica Santos had died faced the window, stretched back along the cruiser's flank in a long, ink-black wound of broken bulkheads and melted frames. Other wounds marred that once sleek and immaculate hull. Small, some of them looked, hiding the reality of the ruin within them, and Honor felt her eyes sting as she recalled once more the people who had died under her command.

She blinked angrily, drew a deep breath, and straightened her spine, and her mind went back—back to the numbed moment when she and her surviving crew had realized they'd won while the terrible fury of *Sirius*'s destruction lingered in the visual display like a curse. Judging by the Q-ship's performance and the weaponry she'd revealed, *Sirius* must have had a crew of at least fifteen hundred, and there had been no survivors. Even now, Honor could close her eyes and resummon that cauldron of light and energy in every hideous detail and feel the same sick revulsion at the work of her own hands and mind . . . and the vaulting exultation and triumph.

But triumph at such cost. She bit her lip again, feeling the pain. One hundred and seven of her crew, more than a third of those aboard at the start of that terrible pursuit and slaughter, had died. Another fifty-eight were wounded, though the medics and base hospital teams would probably return most of them to duty in the next few months.

The cost in blood and pain had been terrible enough, but that had been fifty-nine percent of her total crew, even before detachments, including Dominica Santos and two of her three commissioned assistant engineers. She'd had barely a hundred and twenty uninjured people left for her repair parties, and *Fearless* had been a shambles. Her forward impeller nodes had failed completely within seconds of *Sirius's* destruction, and this time there had been no way to repair them. Worse, her *after* impeller ring had gone for over forty-five minutes, as well—three-quarters of an hour in which she had coasted another ninety-four million kilometers outward while damage reports flooded in to her airless bridge.

For a time, Honor had believed her crew would follow *Sirius's* into death. Most of *Fearless's* life support was down, three-quarters of her computer support was inoperable, the grav lance had shorted out three of her after beta nodes, the inertial compensator was off line, and seventy percent of her normal engineering and damage control personnel were casualties. Crewmen, many of them wounded, had been trapped in airless compartments all over the ship. Her own quarters had taken a direct hit that left them without pressure for over six hours. Only Nimitz's shielded life-support module had saved him, and her sailplane plaque was heat-warped and twisted, one corner blown completely away. It had been that close for Nimitz, and she reached up to touch the treecat yet again, reassuring herself of his survival.

But Alistair McKeon and Ilona Rierson, Dominica

Santos's sole surviving lieutenant, had labored like Trojans amid the wreckage, and Petty Officer Harkness and his missile-loading party had been in Missile One's magazine when Missile Two was wiped away. They'd survived, and Harkness had needed no orders to begin working his way aft to meet McKeon and Rierson. Between them, they'd not only gotten the compensator back up but even managed to get two of the damaged after nodes back on line, giving her a deceleration capability of over two and a half KPS^2.

Honor's wounded ship had taken four more hours just to decelerate to rest relative to Basilisk, but her people had used the time well. McKeon and Rierson had continued their repair activities, bringing more and more of the internal control systems back on line, and Lieutenant Montoya (and thank *God* she'd gotten rid of Suchon!) and his medical parties had labored beyond collapse, dragging the wounded out and laboring over their broken bodies in sickbay. Too many of Montoya's patients had slipped away from him, far more than he would ever find it easy to live with, but it was thanks to him that people like Samuel Webster and Sally MacBride had lived.

And then there had been the long voyage home. The long, slow voyage that had seemed to crawl, for *Fearless's* communications had been out. There was no way to tell Dame Estelle or the Admiralty what had happened, who had won, or the price her people had paid. Not until *Fearless* limped brokenly back into Medusa orbit thirteen hours after she'd left it and a white-faced Scotty Tremaine brought his pinnace alongside her air-bleeding wreck.

It had taken two months for the Fleet maintenance ships to make enough repairs for Honor even to bring her ship home through the Junction to *Hephaestus* at last. Two months during which the entire Home Fleet, summoned by her desperate Case Zulu, had conducted "unscheduled war games" in Basilisk—and greeted the three Havenite battle squadrons who'd arrived on a "routine visit" six days after Captain Papadapolous's Marines and Barney Isvarian's NPA had annihilated the rifle-armed Medusan nomads.

Honor's grief for her own dead would never fade entirely, yet it had been worth every moment of heartbreaking labor, every instant of self-doubt and determination, to witness that. To hear the hidden consternation in the Havenite admiral's voice as he acknowledged Admiral D'Orville's courteous welcome. To watch the faces of the Havenite officers as they endured the remorseless barrage of courtesy visits D'Orville had arranged to make them comfortable—and to drive home the warning that Basilisk was Manticoran territory and would remain so—before they were finally allowed to depart once more with their tails figuratively between their legs.

And then, at last, there had been the voyage home, accompanied by an honor guard of an entire superdreadnought battle squadron while the Manticoran anthem played over every Navy transmitter in the system. Honor had thought her heart would burst when D'Orville's stupendous *King Roger* flashed her running lights in the formal salute to a fleet flagship as *Fearless* entered the terminus to transit home, yet under her pride and bittersweet joy had been a fear she dared not admit. All the time the repair ships had labored upon her battered command, Honor had made herself believe *Fearless* might be returned to service, but the yard techs' survey had killed that hope.

Fearless was too old. She was too small, and she'd taken too much. Given too much. Repair would require virtual rebuilding and cost as much as a newer, bigger ship, and so the decision had been made. Within the week, she would be towed out of her slip once more and delivered to the breakers at one of the orbital recovery stations, where she would be stripped, cut into jagged chunks of alloy by workers who could never truly understand all she had been and meant and done, and melted down for reclamation.

She deserved better, Honor thought, blinking on her tears once more, but at least she'd ended as a warrior. Ended in combat and then brought her surviving people home, not died in her sleep after decades in mothballs. And even when she was gone, something of her would remain, for HMS *Fearless* had been added to the RMN's List of Honor, the list of names kept perpetually in commission by new construction to preserve the battle honors they had earned.

She drew another deep breath and turned from the window, and her melancholy eased as she looked at the three men who stood with her. Alistair McKeon looked very different and yet utterly right, somehow, with the three gold cuff bands of a full commander and the white beret of a starship's captain, and the destroyer *Troubadour* lay waiting for him, already under orders for the new, heavily reinforced Basilisk Station picket. Not a single over-aged light cruiser, but a task force, covering the terminus while construction of its own network of forts got under way.

She smiled at him, and he smiled back. Then she turned her gaze to the other two officers standing with her. Lieutenant Commander Andreas Venizelos looked as dapper and darkly handsome as ever beside a Lieutenant (Senior Grade) Rafael Cardones, who no longer seemed quite so young. They wouldn't be leaving with McKeon. They had a new assignment to a new ship, just as Honor did. It would be another few months before she exchanged her black beret for a white one once more, but when she did, Venizelos would be with her as her executive officer, with Cardones at Tactical. Honor had insisted on that, despite Cardones's lack of seniority, and no one at BuPers had dared argue with her.

"Well, Alistair," she held out her hand, "I'll miss you. But *Troubadour* is lucky to have you—and the Fleet will need an old Basilisk hand to keep them straight. Make sure Admiral Stag stays on his toes."

"I will, Ma'am." McKeon's smile became a grin, and he squeezed her hand, then frowned quickly as his wrist com beeped. "That's my boarding shuttle, Ma'am. I've got to run."

"I know. Good luck, Captain McKeon."

"The same to you, Captain Harrington." McKeon stepped back, saluted sharply, and vanished down the passage, and Honor smiled after him. Then she turned back to Venizelos.

"Did you get that crew list glitch straightened out, Andreas?"

"Yes, Skipper. You were right—it was a snafu at BuPers. They promised to have it corrected by tomorrow morning."

"Good." She cocked her head in thought for a moment, then shrugged. "I suppose you'd better get back to the slip, then. These yard dogs need a real officer keeping an eye on them."

"Yes, Ma'am." Venizelos grinned and beckoned to Cardones, and the two of them trotted off towards the building slip at the far end of *Hephaestus* where Honor's new command, the *Star Knight*-class heavy cruiser HMS *Fearless*, was nearing completion. She watched them go, then turned back to the old *Fearless* with another sigh.

Taken all in all, it had ended well, she thought a bit sadly. Too many good people had died to undo the mistakes and greed and stupidity of others, but they'd done it. The Hauptman Cartel had been cleared of knowing collusion in Basilisk, but the Queen's Bench had decided they *ought* to have known what their employees were doing and slapped them rather firmly on the wrist with several million dollars worth of fines. And the Court of Admiralty had condemned *Mondragon* as a legitimate prize for smuggling—a decision which had, just incidentally, made Captain Honor Harrington a millionaire. Most importantly of all, Haven's attempt to grab off Medusa and the Junction terminus had galvanized the political situation. Fear that Haven might try again had turned the Conservative rank and file against Janacek's long fight to downgrade Basilisk Station, and the

Liberals and Progressives had been driven into full retreat. In fact, the Act of Annexation had been amended in ways that neither Countess Marisa nor Baron High Ridge had ever imagined in their worst nightmares.

And then there was Pavel Young.

Honor allowed herself a rare, gloating smile as she considered Young, and Nimitz echoed it with a purr. His family and political connections had saved him from a court martial or even a court of inquiry, but nothing could save him from the judgment of his peers. There wasn't an officer in uniform who didn't realize exactly what he'd tried to do to Honor, and surprisingly few of them, given his family's power, bothered to hide their opinion of him. Bad enough that he'd used his rank to knife a junior in the back, but it was also Lord Pavel Young who had completely ignored the situation on Medusa itself. It was Lord Pavel Young who had never bothered to board *Sirius*, never even suspected she was armed, and personally certified the Q-ship's false engineering report and cleared her to remain indefinitely in Medusa orbit. And no one seemed to have the least doubt what the outcome of Haven's plans would have been had Lord Pavel Young remained the senior officer on Basilisk Station.

He and *Warlock* had been banished to escort duty, poking along through hyper to guard tramp freighters plying back and forth to the Silesian Confederacy. Not even First Lord Janacek or his father had been able to save him from that. He was lucky they'd been able to keep him on active duty at all.

As for the People's Republic of Haven, Queen Elizabeth's Government and Navy weren't yet strong enough to embrace open war, especially not when the battered Opposition could still point out—accurately—that all evidence linking Haven to the *mekoha* and rifles on Medusa was circumstantial. It was highly suspicious to find a member of the Havenite Consulate's staff (and a full colonel in the Republic's army, no less), supplying the shaman's army, but he was dead, and the Republic had insisted—and produced the splendidly official documentation to "prove"—that Colonel Westerfeldt had been discharged from his consular position for peculation weeks before the unfortunate incident. No doubt he had been involved even then with the Manticoran criminals who had really supplied the natives. The criminals in question, captured by Papadapolous's Marines, hadn't been able to prove Haven had been their paymaster, nor would they ever be able to prove anything again. The last of them had faced the firing squad over a month ago.

Not that anyone who mattered doubted Haven's involvement. The Opposition parties might claim that they did in their determination to avoid the war they dreaded, but they knew the truth as well as Honor did. Nor would anyone who had been on Medusa—who had seen what the Medusans had done to Lieutenant Malcolm's patrol, who remembered the drug lab explosion or the slaughter to which Haven had delivered the Medusan nomads—forget or forgive, and in the meantime, the Queen had taken steps to express her displeasure.

By Crown Proclamation, *any* Haven-registered ship passing through the Junction, regardless of destination or normal diplomatic immunity, must submit to boarding and search before she would be allowed passage. Moreover, no Havenite warship would be permitted transit under any circumstances. There had been no negotiation on those points; Haven could take it or leave it . . . and add months to every cruise their freighters made.

The Republic had accepted the deliberate, calculated humiliation, for refusal would have driven even their own cargoes into freighters which *could* use the Junction, with disastrous effects upon their carrying trade. But because there was no proof, Haven had still been able to protest its innocence and scream to galactic public opinion over the Kingdom's "highhanded discrimination" and the lengths to which Manticore had gone to smear its good name.

No Manticoran believed them, of course, just as no one in the Kingdom believed their violent protests about one Commander Harrington's unprovoked attack upon an unarmed merchantman and her callous murder of its entire crew. It wasn't as if they'd had much choice about protesting, unless they wanted to admit what they'd actually been up to, but they'd gone so far as to demand Honor's extradition to stand trial for murder in a Havenite court. She'd been amused by that, until one of the government's foreign affairs experts explained the propaganda theory of the "big lie" to her.

She found it difficult to credit, even now, that *anyone*, anywhere, could possibly believe the nonsense being spouted by the Haven Information Ministry, but the expert had only shaken his head and sighed. The bigger the lie, apparently, the more likely the uninformed were to accept it, simply because they couldn't believe any government would tell such an absurd story unless it were true. And, she supposed, the fact that Haven had tried her *in absentia* (legal under what passed for Havenite law when Manticore refused to extradite her), found her guilty, and condemned her to death, had been the frosting on the cake.

But the Kingdom had responded to Haven's claims in unambiguous fashion. Honor smiled and straightened her cuffs, brown eyes glinting as she savored the four gold rings of a Captain of the List. They'd jumped her two full grades, clear past captain (junior grade), and Admiral Cortez had been almost apologetic about the fact that she hadn't been knighted. He'd talked his way around the point for several minutes, concentrating rather unconvincingly on the diplomatic repercussions and the effect on "neutral opinion" should the Crown knight someone Haven's courts had sentenced to death as a mass murderer, but the way he'd said it had carried quite another message. It wasn't Haven or the Solarian League which concerned the Government; it was the Liberals and Conservative Association. They'd taken a beating over Basilisk, but their power hadn't been broken, and in typical politico fashion, they blamed all their trials on Captain Harrington and not their own stupidity and short-sightedness.

Honor didn't mind. She looked down at the ribbon of the Manticore Cross, the Kingdom's second highest award for valor, gleaming blood-red against her space-black tunic. She had that to signify the Navy's and her Queen's opinion of her, just as she had her new ship, and she'd made list at last. Her feet were firmly on the ladder to flag rank, and no one—not Pavel Young, not the Republic of Haven, and not Countess Marisa or Sir Edward Janacek—could ever knock her off it again.

She sighed and raised a hand, pressing it to the plastic as if to bid *Fearless* farewell, then turned to leave, only to pause as someone called her name.

"Captain Harrington?"

She turned back to see a portly commodore puffing his way along the gallery towards her. She'd never seen him before, but he came to a halt before her and beamed, almost as if he intended to throw his arms about her.

"Yes, Sir?" she replied in a puzzled voice.

"Oh, excuse me. You wouldn't know. I'm Andrew Yerensky." He held out his hand, and Honor took it.

"Commodore Yerensky," she said, still wondering why he'd obviously sought her out.

"I wanted to talk to you about your action in Basilisk, Captain," Yerensky explained. "You see, I'm on the Weapons Development Board down at BuShips."

"Oh." Honor nodded. *Now* she understood; it was about time somebody finally took official notice of the stupidity of *Fearless*'s armament alterations.

"Yes, indeed," Yerensky beamed. "I've read your combat report. Brilliant, Captain! Simply brilliant the way you sucked *Sirius* in and took her out! In fact, I'm hoping that you'd be willing to address a formal meeting of the board about your action and tactics next week. Admiral Hemphill's our chairman, you know, and she's placed consideration of the demonstrated effectiveness of the grav lance/energy torpedo weapons mix on the agenda."

Honor blinked. *Admiral Hemphill?* He couldn't possibly mean—!

"We were delighted by the outcome of your action, Captain," Yerensky burbled on. "It was a brilliant vindication of the new armament concept! Just think—your old, undersized little cruiser took on and defeated an eight-million-ton Q-ship with the armament of a battlecruiser! Why, when I think how impossible that would have been with one of the old, traditionally-armed cruisers, I can hardly—"

Honor stared at him in disbelief as he babbled on and on about "new thinking" and "proper weapon systems for modern warships" and "gave you the edge you really needed, didn't they?"—and something hot and primitive boiled deep within her. Her eyes hardened, and Nimitz hunkered down on her shoulder and bared his fangs while her fingers twitched with the physical urge to throttle the pompous twit. His "new thinking" had gotten over half her crew killed or wounded by forcing her to close straight up *Sirius*'s wake, and it wasn't "proper weapons" which had saved what was left of *Fearless*—it had been Honor's people, their guts and blood and pain, and the definite partiality of Almighty God!

Her nostrils flared, but the commodore didn't even notice. He just went on and on, patting himself on the back so hard she expected him to sprain his shoulder, and the corner of her mouth began to twitch.

Talk to his board members? He wanted her to *talk* to his board members and tell them what a stroke of genius *Fearless*'s refit had been?! She glared at him, sucking in breath to tell him exactly where he could put his invitation, but then a new thought struck her. She reared back to consider it, and the tick died. Her eyes began to twinkle instead of glare, and she fought back a sudden urge to giggle in his face as he slithered to a halt at last.

"Excuse me, Commodore," she heard herself say, "but let me be sure I've got this straight. You want me to address an official panel of the Weapons Development Board and give them my combat evaluation of *Fearless*'s weapon systems?"

"Precisely, Captain!" Yerensky enthused. "Our more progressive members—the whole Navy, in fact—would be eternally in your debt. The personal testimony of an officer who's proven their efficacy in actual combat would have tremendous weight with the more reactionary, stick-in-the-mud board members, I'm sure, and God knows we need all the help we can get. Why, some of those die-hards actually refuse to admit it was your weapons—and skill, of course—which made your victory possible!"

"Shocking," Honor murmured. She cocked her head, and her glowing brown eyes danced while her firm lips blossomed into an immense smile. "Well, Commodore Yerensky, I don't see how I could possibly turn your request down. It happens that I *do* have very strong feelings about the new armament—" her smile grew even broader "—and I'd be *delighted* to share them with Admiral Hemphill and her colleagues."

• Appendix

A Note on Time

Like all extra-Solar colonies, the Manticore Colony, Ltd.'s original investors found it necessary to create a new calendar to reflect the axial and orbital rotations of their new home. In their case, however, the situation was complicated by the fact that whereas most star systems are fortunate to have a single habitable world, Manticore, a GO/G5 distant binary system, possessed *three* of them, each with its own day and year.

As the rest of humanity, Manticorans use standard seconds, minutes, and hours, and Old Earth's 365.26-day year serves as the "Standard Reckoning Year," or "T-year," the common base to which local dates throughout known space are converted for convenience in interstellar trade and communication. Like most extra-Solar polities, the Star Kingdom of Manticore's history texts follow the convention of counting years "Post Diaspora" (i.e., in T-years from the year in which the first interstellar colony ship departed Old Earth) as well as in terms of the local calendar.

The Kingdom's official reckoning of dates is based on the rotational and orbital periods of Manticore-A III, the planet Manticore. This calendar is used for all official records, the calculation of individuals' ages, etc., but doesn't really work very well for the seasons of any planet other than Manticore itself. Accordingly, both Sphinx (Manticore-A IV) and Gryphon (Manticore-B IV) have their own, purely local calendars, which means that a single star system routinely uses no less than *four* calendars (including standard reckoning). Needless to say, date-conversion software is incorporated into virtually every Manticoran computer.

The Kingdom's planetary days and years are:

Planet Name	Day in T-Hours	Year in Local Days	Year in T-Days	Year in T-Years
Manticore	22.45	673.31	629.83	1.73
Sphinx	25.62	1,783.28	1,903.65	5.22
Gryphon	22.71	650.46	615.51	1.69

The clocks of each planet count time in full 60-minute standard hours with an additional, shorter "hour" called "compensate" (or, more commonly, simply "comp") to make up the difference. Thus, the planet Manticore's day consists of 22 standard hours hours plus a 27-minute-long comp, while Sphinx's day consists of 25 hours plus a 37-minute comp. Gryphon's day, like Manticore's, is 22 T-hours long, but with a comp of approximately 41.5 minutes.

The planetary week is seven planetary days long in each case, and Manticore's day is used aboard all Royal Navy vessels.

The official year of the Kingdom is 673 days long, with a leap year every third year. It is divided into 18 months, 11 of 37 days and 7 of 38, alternating for the first 6 and last 8 months, named (simply, if rather unimaginatively) First Month, Second Month, Third Month, etc. The Gryphon local year is also divided into 18 months (16 of 36 days and 2 of 37 days) with the extra days in Ninth and Tenth and one extra day in Eleventh Month every other local year. The Sphinxian year, however, is divided into 46 months, 35 of 39 days and 11 of 38 days (the shorter months fall in even-numbered months from Twelfth to Thirty-Second), with a leap year every 7 years. All of these calendars are reckoned in "Years After Landing" (abbreviated A.L.), dating from the day (March 21, 1416 P.D.) the first shuttle from the colony ship *Jason* touched down on the present-day site of the city of Landing. Obviously, this means that each planet's local year is a *different* "Year After Landing" from any of the others. Thus, Honor Harrington's orders to *Fearless*, dated Fourth 25, 280 A.L. (using Official Manticoran Reckoning, or the Manticore planetary calendar), were also written on March 3, 1900 P.D. (Standard Reckoning), and on Second 26, 93 A.L. (using the local Sphinxian calendar). This plethora of dates is a major reason Manticorans tend to convert time spans into T-years for comparison purposes.

TURN
PAGE